Praise for *Cruel Summer*

'With a lively cast of characters, each with their own unexpected secrets to hide, plenty of twists and turns and a glamorous Mediterranean setting, this is an entertaining and accessible mystery that will keep readers guessing as they try to work out 'whodunnit'. A perfect poolside summer read'
Booktrust

'a book that needs to be made into a teen horror film pronto'
Kirsty, Overflowing Library

'*Cruel Summer* is a brilliant mix of the adolescent drama in *Pretty Little Liars* and the ridiculous humour combined with crazy violence of *Scream* . . . a seriously fun, beach thriller (who knew they existed?), with a motivation for murder that you'll never guess'
The Pretty Books

'It's a book that I'm going to be recommending non-stop and I just want to gush about it . . . Everybody must read this book!'
Queen of Contemporary

'This book blew me away . . . if you grew up reading the Point Horror books then you will love this'
Serendipity Reviews

Also by James Dawson

Hollow Pike

CRUEL SUMMER

James Dawson

Indigo

First published in Great Britain in 2013
by Indigo
This paperback edition first published in Great Britain in 2014
by Indigo
a division of the Orion Publishing Group Ltd
Orion House
5 Upper St Martin's Lane
London WC2H 9EA

An Hachette UK company

1 3 5 7 9 10 8 6 4 2

A catalogue record for this book is
available from the British Library.

ISBN 978 1 78062 175 3

Typeset by Input Data Services Ltd,
Bridgwater, Somerset

Printed in Great Britain by
CPI Group (UK) Ltd, Croydon, CR0 4YY

www.orionbooks.co.uk

In loving memory of Amy Breen
1921–2008

All the world's a stage,
And all the men and women merely players:
They have their exits and their entrances;
And one man in his time plays many parts . . .

From AS YOU LIKE IT by William Shakespeare

FADE IN: ONE YEAR AGO

Against the white cliffs, the girl in the red dress was as vivid as a drop of blood. Even by moonlight, the rugged shoreline was visible for miles at sea: two vast cave mouths yawned, black stains scarring the chalk. The tide was coming in, advancing on a dark, rocky beach; the surf sighed over the shingle as the waves crept closer.

The girl knew the cliffs like old friends. She'd lived in Telscombe Cliffs her whole life. This was backwards though; usually she looked up at the cliffs from the beach, not down on them from the top. They seemed bigger from up here; the pebble beach was a long way below. It was dizzying. Vertigo played tricks with her eyes, so that they focused then unfocused like a wild camera lens. The tips of her shoes were level with the edge of the cliff. All it would take was one step forwards. One step and it'd be over.

The shoes were brand new, never worn before tonight. They pinched her toes and heels. She'd bought them especially for the ball. Red satin to match her equally new dress. Fresh tears rolled down her face.

How could he do this to me?

What a state she must look, the folds of her dress flapping in the wind. The sheer fabric clung to her legs. Streaks of eye-liner stained her cheeks. Angry gusts of wind whipped around her, blowing ribbons of her thick chestnut hair across her face so that it caught in her lip-gloss. Only hours earlier she'd had it curled at the salon, excited to the point of giddiness about the night ahead. Her leavers' ball. It should have been the night of her life. Now it would be her last.

They humiliated you. You are a laughing stock.

She looked again at the beach. A mosaic of sand, shingle and seaweed. Salt air filled her nostrils – a promise of what was to come. The tide would roll in to collect her body, to swallow her. She would become part of something bigger, joining all those souls lost at sea. The thought spurred her on. It was dangerous, romantic and dramatic. Another inch. If the soil crumbled, she would go over. How long would it take to die? Would it hurt? She edged her toes another centimetre over the edge.

Just do it, you coward. Show him what he made you do. They'll never forget you after this.

But what about Mum and Dad? What about Harry? Covering her face with her hands, she sobbed. She couldn't do it. Another gust and she staggered away from the cliff edge and fell to her knees, her dress fanning out across the grass. The sobs came heavily now, wracking her body.

You are so weak! You're pathetic. You can't even do this right.

She wiped away the trails of make-up that ran down her cheeks, her breath shaking. What was she meant to do now? She was shamed. Everyone had seen. Everyone knew. It felt red and sore and fresh. In the course of a single evening, her perfect world had been broken into pieces and stamped on for good measure.

Footsteps. Even over the wind ringing in her ears, she heard footsteps. She turned away from the sea and looked towards the path. She pulled a damp tendril of hair out of her eyes. There was no one there. The pub had long since closed and only a few windows of the hotel cast light over the grassy clifftop. A cloud drifted across the moon and suddenly it was too dark. In the dim light of the coast lamps, the grass seemed to ripple silver as the breeze rolled over.

The town was dead at this time of night and she felt like the only person awake in the world. More footsteps, though: the telltale crunch of gravel. She wasn't alone. In the other direction there was a car park, but that only held the ice-cream van, which, all closed up, was a sad-looking shell.

So why did it feel like there were eyes on her skin, watching her every move? She still couldn't see anyone. It must have been someone arriving at the hotel. No one was coming to save her. No one cared enough.

They didn't even chase after you.

The cloud rolled off the moon. When she was younger she had often sat on the beach and asked the moon questions. Her father had been away so often, but it had brought her comfort to know that, wherever he was, they both looked up at the same moon. 'What am I meant to do now?' she said aloud, her voice trembling.

The moon, as ever, didn't answer, but gazed down at her sympathetically.

More footsteps, someone running, coming closer. She whirled around. There *was* someone there.

A figure watched from the shadows, almost blending into the night. Whoever it was now stood motionless, arms hanging at their sides. Her heart fluttered, her chest suddenly tight. If it was a dog-walker, they wouldn't just stand. Also, no dog.

The figure started towards her, but walked clear of the coastal footpath and its lanterns.

'Who's there?' She wiped her nose on the back of her hand. Fumbling with her gown and unsteady on her heels, she rose to her feet and scanned the plateau, worry furrowing her brow.

The silhouette came closer. She squinted at the shape.

'I said, who's there?' Moonlight revealed who approached. 'Oh, it's you. Don't come anywhere near me! I mean it. I don't wanna talk to you.' She took a step backwards, her heel only inches from the very edge of the cliff.

The figure came closer. Arms reached out towards her.

'Stay away!' she snapped.

As she fell, she didn't even scream. The red dress. The white chalk. She really did look like a drop of blood.

SCENE 1 – RYAN

'Katie? What do you think really happened to Janey?'

The first line is a voice-over. Opening shot: Pan from endless, star-spattered sky to a linear and deserted stretch of road in the middle of the Spanish countryside. You can tell it's Spain because of the arid landscape, chatter of crickets and accompanying overture of flamenco guitars. The vista is barren; almost alien. It's late at night. Slivers of wispy cloud trail over a jaundiced, sickly moon. Zoom in on a lonely silver rental car. It's caked in thick orange dust as it pelts along the asphalt.

The headlights, even on high beam, only managed to cast a feeble pool of light along the abandoned highway. The road was rod straight – to Ryan, this really was the road to nowhere. He suddenly felt a long way from home.

RYAN HAYWARD RETURNS FOR A FEATURE-LENGTH HOLIDAY SPECIAL. Ryan often imagined his life as a long-running TV show in which he was the star. The high-school series had come to an end with Janey's death and the last year had been his solo spin-off: *Ryan: The Drama School Years* or possibly *Ryan: Acting Up*. This holiday was supposed to be a 'summer special' – a ratings-winning reunion of the original cast: *Ryan: One Year On*. It was pretty sick, but what had happened to Janey had made quite the series finale. He knew it was wrong, but thinking of it all as a TV show, with himself and his friends as famous actors, made it somehow easier.

Janey wasn't dead, she was just some actress whose contract was up.

'What do you mean?' His companion, Katie, was a pretty redhead with alabaster skin, almost luminous in the dark.

'Oh, come off it! You know what I mean.'

'I don't understand . . .' Katie wrinkled her nose. 'She . . .' a difficult pause, 'killed herself.'

Ryan put his feet on the dashboard. The night was sauna-dry, like that wave of hot Spanish air that greets you as soon as the plane doors open. His bare legs stuck to the leatherette seats. He popped a duty-free sweet in his mouth. 'And you believe that?'

Katie grabbed a sweet too. 'Must we talk about Janey? Maybe we could pick a more cheerful subject, like vivisection or famine or something?' she quipped. She focused on the road ahead, gripping the wheel a little tighter.

When someone young and beautiful dies, a shroud falls over a community. The sun stopped shining on Telscombe Cliffs when Janey Bradshaw vanished. It felt as though there were a blanket ban on laughter and no one was allowed to say her name except in reverence. You certainly weren't allowed to ask questions. Ryan had questions.

'Yeah, but don't you think—'

'Ryan, knock it off!' Katie interrupted. Her almond-shaped eyes were wide, blue and sweet. She'd grown up this year – like all of them. She looked tired and thin, even a little gaunt. That was the 'story arc' this year – *the aftermath*. Katie Grant was Ryan's high-school best friend and, quite literally, the 'girl-next-door'. She was the first person he'd told that he was gay. She was pretty, but relatable; she was clever, but never aloof; she was deep, but not tortured. Or perhaps he was overthinking it slightly. In Ryan's head, she was second in the credits after himself.

'Talking about Janey was not the purpose of this holiday,' Katie continued. 'I think . . . I think we need to jolly well move on. It's been a whole year. A monumentally hard year. You've been in Manchester. I've been up to my eyeballs in books. What we need now is R and R. I have had my fill of teen angst. I was starting to feel like the protagonist in a vampire novel.'

Ryan laughed. '*So* not a good look. Maybe you're right.' He wanted the reunion to be a touching, heartfelt comedy, but since they'd left the hypermarket at the airport he'd had an odd *displaced* feeling – a sense of being lost. The bright lights of Madrid were far, far behind and Katie seemed to be driving them into oblivion.

He tried to shake it off. Unsolved mysteries had always bothered Ryan. That feeling of something you've forgotten to do – the weird panic in the night that you've left the oven on, or neglected to pay a bill. That was how he felt constantly about their dead friend. Things just didn't add up. 'You know, I miss her, though.'

'Oh, God, I do too!' Katie conceded. She tucked an escaped auburn curl behind her ear.

Ryan smiled. 'Do you remember those plays we used to put on?'

'For your poor mum? Gosh they were terrible!' The car passed through what looked like orange groves. The crickets were out in full force – a cacophony. It took Ryan a moment to realise the shadowy triangles darting among the trees were bats, not birds.

'Do you remember how I was always called David? I always wanted to be called David. What a lame-arse character name! You'd think I'd have been more creative. Something like Javier or Storm would have been better.'

Katie laughed, cloudy eyed on memory lane. 'Janey and I were always twins. We were obsessed with *Sweet Valley High*. I was the good girl and she was the evil twin . . . what did we call ourselves?'

'Shana and Lana!' Ryan cackled. 'Do you want to know a secret? I always longed to be Dana!'

Katie laughed so hard, she almost hit a stray dog in the middle of the road. She stood on the brakes and swerved around it. 'Oh, my God! He came out of nowhere!'

Ryan took his feet down and steadied himself on the dashboard.

Katie gave his thigh a pat. 'I missed *you* this year, Ry.'

'I know. That old-school, romantic letter-writing thing never really worked, did it? But, after what happened . . . some serious drifting was probably inevitable.'

Katie adopted the ropey Californian accent she'd used in their old plays. 'Dana, promise me we'll never drift apart again.'

'I promise, Lana.' He leaned over and gave her a peck on the cheek. He'd missed her too, but things were different now. There was a question mark looming large over last summer. Loose plot ends that needed tying up. Viewers had been waiting on tenterhooks for a whole year. In TV you can't leave loose ends; everything has to be resolved or you end up with a mess like *Lost*.

What really happened to Janey Bradshaw? Ryan had to confess that, although he'd been dying to catch up with the gang, part of the reason he'd agreed to the holiday had been to try to clear up the niggles he felt over Janey's death. He just wanted some answers. Ryan didn't believe for a second that Janey Bradshaw had killed herself.

SCENE 2 – RYAN

Ryan's favourite time of day was about nine in the morning. He'd woken ahead of Katie and was glad of the time to himself. He was *vile* before a cup of coffee and a shower – as Katie was already well aware from years of witnessing his early-morning post-sleepover hissy fits. A cool, wake-up breeze rolled in off the sea and he pulled the blanket around his shoulders but, without a cloud in the sky, it was going to be a scorcher. That was what he liked best of all – the promise of the day ahead; anything could happen. Anything except rain, by the looks of it.

He took in a deep breath of holiday: sun cream, ocean breeze and a trace of seaweed. Ryan loved it. One whiff and a million childhood memories came flooding back. If only you could stay young forever, Ryan thought, pulling his knees up to his chest. If only last year hadn't happened.

Ryan ran a hand through his off-blond curls, longer than they'd ever been before. His hairdresser – some tattooed bear in a Manchester salon with a ring through his nose – had convinced him to grow it out a little: 'Michelangelo style, like David' apparently. He messed it up further. Might as well go for beachy – they were on the beach, after all.

It was quite the setting, Ryan had to admit. Katie's dad had great taste. Everything as far as the eye could see was turquoise and white like a photo in some high-end holiday brochure. White walls, white sand, white tiles. Blue sea, blue sky, blue infinity pool seeping over the horizon. Everything was stacked in perfect horizontal stripes: white, blue, white, blue. The only splash of orange was the traditional terracotta roof.

The villa was built into the slope of a bleached rocky hillside, the levels of the house like a flight of stairs. Bedrooms at street level, living room underneath (very Mediterranean) and then the terrace level and the pool below that.

Ryan closed his eyes, angling his face to the sun. He felt the heat on his skin, imagining how the light must bounce off his cheekbones and full lips. Where was a photographer when you needed one? In photoshoots, Ryan had learned, you must always work your angles and find your light.

Eyes closed, he listened. Gulls squawked as they picked for worms in the wet sand near the surf, and the boat clinked against its mooring on the jetty. This was paradise.

A certified caffeine-addict, and miles from the nearest Starbucks, Ryan gulped down the remains of his first cup of coffee and was making a second when he heard bare feet slapping across the floor tiles. A creased and bleary-eyed Katie padded into the kitchen. She wore a pretty kimono over her polka-dot bikini. As ever, her red hair tumbled over her shoulders.

'OMG, I had the most bonkers dream!' she said, rubbing her eyes. 'I had to marry your dad and you were demanding a dowry!'

Ryan laughed. 'I wonder if it's a portent.'

'Ooh, maybe!' Katie chuckled. 'You're dad's such a silver fox – I could do worse.'

He mimed puking all over the tiles. 'Gross. You'll put me

off my cornflakes! You want a tea?' Katie always drank tea, never coffee – she was so, so English.

'Yes, please. My head feels positively crusty.' She came over and gave his abs a prod. 'Check out the six pack!'

He tensed and breathed in for maximum effect. 'Thanks. I got a trainer. He's called Fabrizio, and he's straight – although you'd never think it to look at him. It's such a waste.'

'Well, it's paid off! Ryan, you have never looked better.'

He felt himself blush and busied himself at the kettle. It was true, he'd worked really hard to bulk up; never again did he want to be the skinny dweeb he'd been at thirteen. '*Gracias*,' he grinned. He pronounced it grass-ee-ass.

Katie laughed. 'It's pronounced gra-*thee*-ass. You're not in South America! Apparently, hundreds of years ago, the king of Spain had a lisp so the commoners adopted it and it stuck that way.'

'Really? Oh, well, points for trying.' He smiled.

Katie slid the patio doors all the way open and wandered out onto the terrace. She sank down into one of the dainty wrought-iron chairs. 'Did you sleep OK?' she asked. By the time they'd finally found the villa, they'd been so tired they'd almost collapsed into bed.

'Yeah, not too bad,' Ryan replied, stirring her tea before hurling the teaspoon into the sink. Joining her at the terrace table, he put her tea down and took a sip of his own much-too-hot coffee before slipping his shades on. 'When do the others arrive?'

'Not until about two.'

'OK. This morning I'm all about the pool and reading scripts, then. Did I tell you about the play last night?'

'You might have mentioned it once or twice, yes,' Katie told him with a grin. Much of the journey from the airport had involved Ryan firing off a year's worth of improv' workshops, auditions and at least one salacious encounter with a well-known movie-star-turned-theatre-director.

'This play is *soooo* good though, Katie. Imagine *Inception* but on a much smaller scale and with aliens. I can't wait.'

'Sounds marvellous,' Katie said, perhaps too quickly.

The sun was getting higher in the sky with every minute. Hotter and hotter too. From this part of the world, it was so much easier to think of the sun as something that truly *burned*: a white ball of flame. Katie stuck to the shade of the terrace – with her milky complexion she'd be crispy baked lobster within minutes.

'How's it going in Norwich?' Ryan asked – aware he'd neglected to ask his friend how she'd been getting on this last year. He nipped back inside and grabbed some Lays crisps from the kitchen counter. At the hypermarket near the airport last night, he'd found it hysterical that Walkers crisps were called 'Lays' in Spain and bought about ten bags. 'Yes, I'm having Lays for breakfast, shut up.' He winked. 'You should get Lays more often, too.'

Katie laughed. 'Pervert! Norwich is good. And you know what studying English is like – pretty booky during the week. Then on a Saturday I work in a bookshop. It's a book-a-rama.'

'Boring!' he yelled. 'I meant have you got a new PLI?'

'A what?'

'A Potential Love Interest! Who's the "New Ben"?'

Katie blushed and chewed on a fingernail. 'There is no "New Ben".'

'Really?'

'I swear. I've been too busy. I wanted the full fresher experience, so I joined pretty much every society and club on campus. I actually played lacrosse! Can you believe it?'

Ryan smiled – wholesome fun sounded about right for Katie. 'Not a single drunken traffic-light party?'

'If I *had* gone to a traffic-light party, I'd have been wearing red.'

'With your complexion? Girl, no!' Ryan laughed. 'But why not? Isn't that what being a fresher's all about?'

Katie shrugged, hiding behind her tea. 'Little bit of Ben. Little bit of Janey. I suppose I needed some time.'

Ryan didn't push her any further. He knew that, even now, she still wasn't over Ben. In his TV drama, Ryan figured, this was the point where you inserted a flashback for the benefit of new or casual viewers. An overview of the story so far . . .

Series One. Katie and Ben had first met at Longview High. Although Ryan hadn't actually been present at their first fateful meeting he imagined it had gone something like this. They would have bumped into each other by a locker (although their school didn't have lockers) and the plinky-plonky piano backing music would have made it clear that they were *meant* to be together. They had probably done that thing of being so in-love-at-first-sight that they could only mumble half sentences as the LOVE overrode basic speech, but, however it had happened, everyone except them had instantly known that they were made for each other.

They didn't kiss until the end of the first series. Ryan had been there for that. It was on a starlit garden swing at Liv Hewitt's fifteenth birthday party. Katie had been upset because there was a misunderstanding about something (Ryan couldn't remember what, but, needless to say, at the time it had seemed HUGE) and Ben had been comforting her.

Series Two. In the second series, fate had intervened to keep the young lovers apart. As every TV scriptwriter knows, if you get the romantic leads together too soon all the sexual frisson dies and there's nowhere for the characters to go. In this case 'fate' had been two sets of well-meaning but meddling parents. Obviously, in the grand tradition of young love, the obstacles had been overcome and by the time they sat their finals, Katie and Ben were officially together.

Series Three. But plain sailing doesn't make for very good TV. There have to be bumps in the road. For some reason, Katie and Ben had decided to call time on their relationship the Christmas of Year Twelve. Ryan vividly remembered Katie's red, puffy eyes that night as Ben held her under the mistletoe – no kisses for them, only tears. Ryan had never understood why they'd broken up when they were so perfect together.

Series Four. In order to move the plot forward, Ben had been paired with Janey – an odd couple at best – and they had been together until the night of the ball . . . the night when she . . .

Well, we all know how that went, Ryan mused.

Now, here they were for the summer special reunion, and Ryan couldn't *wait* to see what twists were in store for Katie, the beautiful redhead, and her handsome ex. Whatever happened, it was destined to be must-see TV.

The others arrived just as Katie and Ryan were finishing lunch. It was so weird; the second Ryan went somewhere sunny, his body started demanding tuna toasties and chocolate milk – so that was just what they'd had. Then, Katie washed the dishes while he leafed through the *Mindprobe* script. He was staring at the page, but failing to see the words; Janey was on his mind again.

Perhaps, on the verge of their reunion, this was the first time he'd properly confronted the lingering sadness, unresolved questions and general *weirdness* of the whole affair. Last summer had been so awful, he hadn't been able to get out of Telscombe Cliffs fast enough. He'd thrown himself into his reinvention spin-off series. After all, it was his story, not Janey's.

But now, even with the hot kiss of the sun on his skin, he couldn't get Janey out of his head. He thought back to the funeral. God, that had been a miserable day. Granted, funerals aren't meant to be a LOL-fest, but he hadn't been at all steeled for the wave of grief that had greeted him like a black tide at that chapel. The memories were black and white, because the day had been black and white. Black clothes in the white chapel. A black coffin covered with white flowers.

The friends had gone as a group. In fact, it was the last time – save for his reunion with Katie last night – that he'd seen any of them. They'd sat at the back of the church to allow Janey's family the best seats. Edgar Allan Poe once described the death of a beautiful woman as 'the most poetical topic in the world' and Janey's death had certainly fit the bill: an event so startling, so scandalous, almost all of Year Thirteen had attended. It had been a full house, standing room only. Janey's funeral – the hottest ticket in Telscombe Cliffs.

Ryan had sat with Katie, holding her hand throughout. That day had been especially awful for her. After what had gone down at the prom, the judgement had been almost palpable. The whispering from their classmates hadn't helped. *'She's got some nerve. How can she show her face?'* No matter how many times Ryan had told Katie it wasn't her fault, he had still been able to feel her guilt. That was Katie all over – she did the time even if she hadn't committed the crime.

The grief hadn't hit Ryan until he'd seen Janey's mum. Up until that point the funeral had been a spectacle – easily the most dramatic episode they'd ever dared screen, probably the highest ratings their little soap had ever won. When he saw Mrs Bradshaw, however, her perfect-hostess exterior betrayed by the watery eyes and wavering breaths, it all became real. Janey wasn't an actress who'd left the series to film some straight-to-DVD movie; she was *gone*.

The crunch of gravel under tyres snapped Ryan back into the moment. This was it. The others had arrived.

Katie left the dishes and turned to the patio doors. 'Ryan! They're here!' She chewed her bottom lip. 'I'm really nervous.'

He took her hand. 'Don't be – it'll be fine,' he said, although he couldn't deny a couple of butterflies of his own. 'We're all friends, remember.'

The pair headed through the lounge and upstairs to the bedroom floor, which was also the entrance level. From the hallway, Ryan could hear the voices on the driveway. The butterflies in his stomach turned into fireflies and his initial nervousness became excitement. He threw the door open and galloped onto the drive.

A glossy orange jeep, looking like it had come straight from a pop video safari, was parked next to Katie's rental halfway down the drive. Definitely Greg's choice, Ryan guessed. Typical of him to go for the flashiest thing available.

Greg was already unloading suitcases from the boot. His sister, Alisha, struggled out of the back seat, a huge box of rattling bottles on her lap.

She took one look at Ryan and screamed. 'There he is!'

'Oh, my God!' Ryan burst into a run while Katie hung

back, seemingly unsure of herself. Alisha placed the box on the drive and threw her arms around him.

'You look so good!' Ryan told her. 'Really, really well.' Normally, this was something you'd say to an octogenarian recovering from a hip transplant, but in this case Ryan meant it; Alisha *for once* looked really healthy – i.e. neither wasted nor hungover, which, for her, was quite something. Her tight black curls had been coloured a warm caramel shade which made her blue eyes sparkle even more than usual next to her light-brown skin.

'Thank you!' Alisha grinned. She still had that gorgeous husky voice. 'As do you, baby boy. Have you been working out?'

Ryan blushed. 'Yeah. A little.' Every day, in fact, but he thought it best to play it down.

Alisha moved on to Katie with more screaming. Alisha's volume button started at about eleven and didn't turn down.

Greg rolled Alisha's suitcase towards her before wrapping Katie up in a hug. 'All right, Katie?' Greg kissed the top of her head. 'How's it going?'

'I'm good, thanks,' Katie said, smiling. 'How are you? Beyond looking insanely buff!'

Greg flexed his biceps for her. 'Shucks, thanks.' He winked. Ryan burned with envy. Even a visit to the gym *twice* a day wouldn't earn him a body like Greg Cole's. He had to admire it. Through the cotton of his T-shirt, Ryan could see Greg's arms, chest, stomach – everything was taut, lean and defined. As a superstar pro footballer, his body was his career.

There was no mistaking the fact that Greg and Alisha were twins. Equally irresistible, they were poster twins for physical perfection but, if that wasn't enough, those incredible blue eyes were *identical*.

Greg left Katie and turned to Ryan, who held out his hand. Greg shook it, perhaps a little awkwardly. Ryan didn't know quite what to say to Greg – he'd not had so much as a text from him all year. Theatre and football make for odd bedfellows, he figured.

A beautiful girl walked around the bonnet of the jeep. The brunette had a cute crop with a sweeping fringe and long, tanned legs in wedge heels. She was every inch a footballer's wife in training. She came to Greg's side so he could introduce her.

'Katie, Ryan, this is my girlfriend, Erin. Erin, this is Katie, whose dad owns the villa, and my mate Ryan from school.'

Erin smiled an impossibly white smile. She was incredibly cute, like the queen pixie of Elftown or something. 'Hi, lovely to meet you both. I've heard so much about you.'

Ryan kissed her on both cheeks. 'Oh, I dread to think!'

'All the gossip, I'm afraid!'

Ryan grinned. 'Well, did he tell you about the time he pissed himself in class at primary school because he thought there were ghosts in the boys' toilets?'

Alisha cackled and Erin snorted. 'Ha! No, he didn't,' she laughed.

While Katie hugged Erin, Greg struck back. 'Thanks mate! Wait until I get started on how you wrote Miss Forrest a love letter . . .'

'Dude, the piss story's worse,' said the final member of the party as he emerged from behind the jeep, carrying two cases.

Ryan stood back to gain the best and most cinematic view of the Katie and Ben reunion. Time seemed to slow and Ryan swore he saw Katie gulp like she was dry-swallowing a huge pill.

Ben. Somehow he'd grown even more handsome. Ryan and Ben had attended nursery school together – hell, their mums had been pregnant at the same time – so it was impossible for Ryan to see Ben as anything other than a brother figure. That said, there was *something* about Ben Murdoch. Girls *loved* him. It might be the dimples or the perpetually messy hair. It could be the lopsided smile or warm chocolate eyes that melted under heavy brows. There was a lot to be said for his broad shoulders, which he always hunched a little, as though he were self-conscious about how tall he was. He'd used his first year of university to cultivate some stubble and it totally worked. The best thing about Ben, though, was that he genuinely had no idea how cute he was. Ryan had missed him.

It was as if someone had pressed Pause. An eternity passed while Katie and Ben mirrored each other, standing awkwardly on the drive, hands hanging heavily at their sides.

'Ben,' Katie said finally, as though it encapsulated everything she had to say.

That was the permission he needed to approach and give her a hug. He stooped down and folded his arms across her back. It lasted no longer than three seconds and he even gave her a pat on the shoulder as if to signal how platonic the embrace had been. 'How've you been?'

That's it? Ryan thought, irrationally angry. *The young lovers reunite after a year apart and all I get is 'How've you been?'?* Time to sack the scriptwriters.

'I'm marvellous,' Ben said, his voice weird and nervous. 'How are you?'

'Not too bad, thanks. Nice beard.' Katie softened, a smile playing across her lips. It reminded Ryan of how they used to be and he felt a little envious of their sweetness.

'Thanks. I sit in the library and stroke it sometimes,' Ben mused.

'How Cambridge of you.'

'I know, right? You look awesome. I like your hair.'

Katie's fingers flew to her newly cut fringe. 'Thanks.' Her eyes fell and the awkwardness was back. 'OK,' she said. 'Let me show you where your rooms are.'

'Sounds good,' Greg agreed, gallantly taking not only his but the girls' cases in hand, 'but I need a beer in under two minutes.'

'Done,' Katie replied with a smile.

Greg deposited the cases in the bedrooms and then Katie gave them a tour of the villa. Ryan was happy to stand back and let her show everyone around while he soaked up the chatter. The first stop was the kitchen, to unpack the boxes of groceries they'd brought from the hypermarket.

Greg brought in two boxes of booze before helping himself to a beer.

Ryan surveyed the alcohol stash. 'OK, so this is Alisha's supply,' he said with a smile. 'What about the rest of us?'

Alisha punched him on the arm. 'Oh, very funny,' she laughed. 'Note – I'm drinking mineral water!'

'Makes a change,' Greg muttered, only half under his breath. Alisha chose to ignore him.

Erin left Greg's side and looked out of the sliding doors. She turned to Katie. 'Is your dad, like, a sultan or something?' she asked. The tour group followed her from the air-conditioned dining area onto the baking terrace.

Katie laughed, putting her sunglasses back on. She now wore a loose-fitting shirt over her bikini to protect her shoulders. 'Ha, no! Not at all.' Katie *hated* people thinking she was posh. Ryan recalled once trying to teach her how to sound less plummy at school – a venture that had failed entirely. 'He's just a property developer.'

'Ah, makes sense.'

'My stepmum openly hates me, so my dad overcompensates by letting me use the villa whenever I like.'

'Seriously,' Ryan chipped in. 'Actual wicked stepmother.'

The tour continued down the stone steps to the pool level. 'Well, I think it's gorgeous,' Erin concluded.

'Thank you. I'm glad you found it OK.'

Greg polished off his first bottle of beer in record time. 'Ah! That hit the spot. I know what you mean. This place is literally in the middle of nowhere. El Benjamino has many talents, but map reading is not one of them.'

'Thanks, mate.'

'Had you listened to me, we'd have been here in half the time,' Alisha said, pouting. 'But, no, girls can't read maps, apparently.'

Greg smiled broadly and wrapped an impressive arm around his sister's shoulder. 'I never said that. I said *you* can't read maps properly. Big difference.' He kissed her hair.

'Children,' Katie giggled, 'simmer down. It's not *that* remote. We're about thirty minutes from town. You can follow the coast on foot in about an hour, an hour and a half, perhaps.'

'I thought there'd be some tavernas and restaurants and stuff,' Ryan put in.

'Nope,' Katie replied cheerily. 'The nearest resort is Zahara de los Atunes, which is why I told you to get everything you needed at the hypermarket. But we should do some trips. We could drive out to Cádiz for a big night, and perhaps visit Gibraltar one day, too.'

'We've got everything we need,' Ben said. 'Loads of booze.

Enough burgers for about fifty barbecues. What more could you want?'

'Oh, I don't know . . . Ryan Gosling and some massage oil?' Alisha suggested.

'Get in line,' Ryan laughed.

Katie swept her arm across the horizon like a game-show hostess. 'Pool and beach,' she said. 'This concludes our tour.'

'You *know* what we have to do now . . .' Greg grinned and took hold of Erin's hand.

'No! Don't!' his girlfriend squeaked.

'We have to – it's the rules! Come on. Phones and wallets out of pockets.' There was a flurry of activity as phones, shoes and sunglasses were deposited onto loungers. 'Ready? One . . . two . . .'

They formed a human chain, hand in hand. Ryan found himself in between Ben and Katie and had never felt more like a third wheel in his life.

'Three!' Greg yelled.

With a scream, they leapt into the bracing blue water.

SCENE 3 – ALISHA

Alisha Cole had been crossing off the days on her calendar, counting down to the holiday. During the miserable, drizzly weeks in Telscombe Cliffs, the promise of a fortnight in Spain with her old friends had been all that kept her spirit alive.

The holiday was off to a fine start, too. After their impromptu dip, they had remained around the pool to dry off and catch up; they could worry about unpacking later.

Alisha let her legs dangle in the infinity pool, the icy water cooling her off. It might not be enough though; a further cold shower might be necessary. Alisha needed nun-like self-discipline to resist staring at Ben's wet form; his damp white T-shirt clung in all the right places and was pretty much see-through.

Man, he was looking super-duper fine these days. When he'd met them at the departure lounge she'd hardly recognised him. She'd clocked some Dolce-and-Gabbana-type model, and was about to point the hottie out to Erin, when she'd realised it was the new and improved Ben Murdoch. He'd put on weight, but in a totally good way – he wasn't the geeky beanpole any more. The light stubble around his jaw said that he'd left for university a boy and returned a year later as a man. She wondered if she'd changed as much as he had.

Probably not – it felt as though her friends had all grown up while she'd been stuck at school for another year, retaking her flunked A-levels.

Ogling Ben Murdoch was seriously bad behaviour. He was off limits. He and Katie had so much history and Alisha knew only too well what it felt like to have your boyfriend taken by a skeezy magpie.

'You OK, Lish?' Damn. He'd caught her staring. That was embarrassing.

'I'm fine. Just drying off.' She teased out her wet-noodle hair. Thanks to the low-cost airline's 'no reserved seating' policy, they'd all had to sit separately on the flight – although, if she was honest, she'd hardly been able to keep her eyes off Ben, anyway. He'd been reading a course textbook while she'd leafed through photography magazines, trying to find inspiration for her portfolio. 'Are *you* OK?' she asked him. 'You were pretty quiet in the car on the way here.'

Ben smiled, or smouldered – Alisha wasn't sure what the right descriptive word was. 'Yeah, I'm all right. Adjusting to holiday mode. Got a lot on my mind.' This new Ben was somehow more closed than the one she'd been to school with – his eyes seemed darker, cloudier.

'Right.' She knew just what he meant. *Nobody mention the dead girl.* She swung her legs out of the pool and crossed to the lounger opposite Ben, leaving wet footprints on the tiles as she went. Katie was up in the kitchen making drinks while Greg applied sun lotion to Erin's shoulders. Ryan was currently drifting on a hot pink inflatable in the pool; with his shades on, it was impossible to tell if he was even awake.

'You know what, though?' Alisha said to Ben. 'This holiday is the best idea Katie's ever had. I don't know about you, but I've really missed you guys this year.'

Ben thought about this. He didn't seem nearly as certain. She realised she could see the dark circles of his nipples through the T-shirt. *Maintain eye-contact, Alisha.*

'Yeah,' he said finally. 'I missed you too.'

Alisha looked out at the horizon and saw a whole lot of nothing. The beach seemed to cook, the air shimmering up off the sand and distorting the view of the sea. There wasn't a soul in sight. She figured that holidaymakers didn't need to come this far down the coast because the big resort beaches had all the tourist essentials – cafes, bars and tacky shops with bunches of inflatables hanging above the doors. You'd only come this far down the beach if you were in need of some serious Buddhist-level tranquillity.

Katie's flip-flops clattered down the stone steps from the top terrace. Ice cubes jangled in the jug she balanced on a tray. 'OK, who wants Katie's Special Sangria?' she asked in a sing-song Spanish accent.

Erin's hand shot up first. 'Oh, I do! I love sangria!'

'If you're forcing us,' Ryan agreed, peeking out over his sunglasses.

'I'm quite proud of my sangria, actually,' Katie said as she reached the poolside. 'The housekeeper taught me her old recipe. It's a special blend of red wine, sparkling apple juice instead of orange, cinnamon, mint and fruit. It's summer in a glass! There's a little secret ingredient too that I promised to take to the grave.'

'What is it?' Ryan asked.

'Some of us, Ry, can keep secrets,' Katie told him.

Ryan raised a perfect eyebrow. 'Oh, I don't know. I'm better at secrets than you might think.'

Alisha scoffed at that. Ryan had a notoriously big mouth. It was hard to imagine him keeping anything to himself.

'I'll have a taste,' Greg said. Katie gave him a beaker and, in typical team-sports fashion, he downed it in one mouthful. 'Hot damn, Kate, that stuff is lethal.'

'They make it strong out here. Like it?'

'Yeah! It's freaking awesome. Give us a refill.'

'Hang on a sec,' Katie said. 'Lish? You want some?'

Alisha thought about it for a moment. She was aware her reputation as a hot mess preceded her. 'No, I'm OK for now. I'll have some later . . . I'm feeling too dehydrated.' She waggled her bottle of water at Katie and took a sip of that instead. Then she fanned the back of her neck with her magazine. She loved her Beyoncé 'fro, but it was a blessing and curse in equal measure. 'Greg can have mine.'

'Good lord, that's an actual first.' Ryan grinned from his lilo in the centre of the pool. 'Alisha Cole refusing alcohol. Hold the front page! Hell has officially frozen over!'

'You little bitch!' Alisha laughed.

He blew her a kiss.

Ben changed the song on the iPod and light, summery R 'n' B floated over the pool. Alisha recognised the songs. These were the tunes that reminded her of the summer before Janey. Before everything had gone wrong.

'Can you do my shoulders again?' Katie asked as she returned to her spot in the shade.

'Sure thing.' Alisha put down her magazine and grabbed the bottle of sun cream. As she massaged the lotion into her friend's shoulders, Katie picked up the camera resting by Alisha's feet. She took it with her wherever she went. Who knew when inspiration might strike? Frankly, if inspiration didn't strike soon, she faced the very real prospect of not having a portfolio ready for September: a prospect that kept her awake at night.

'Is this for school?' Katie asked, reminding her that, in theory, this was a working holiday.

'Afraid so. It's that time again.'

'Portfolio?'

'Yep. Assuming I get the grades—'

'This time!' Greg hollered from the other side of the pool. Erin sat between his open legs as he gave her a shoulder rub.

'Oh, shut up, Greg. I'm not talking to you.'

'You know I'm only messing. Don't be hating.' He smiled broadly and she smiled back, unable to stay mad at her twin for long. That's the thing with twins. You're always connected, whether you want to be or not. He could be such a tool, but she actually cherished the weird psychic bond they shared.

She turned back to Katie. 'Assuming I get the grades this time, I'll be starting the art foundation course in September, so I need some stuff in place before I start.'

'How's it been this year?'

'Repeating Year Thirteen? How do you think? It blew. All those little bitches in Year Twelve . . . well, guess who had to have classes with them.' It had been a *tough* year. One by one the gang had left her behind to fester in Telscombe Cliffs while they went on to bigger, better things. The abandonment, however, had brought out the fighter in her. She was getting *out*.

'I'm sorry.' Katie rolled onto her side to face Alisha properly.

'It's not your fault I messed up first time round, is it? Man, I better get the grades this time. I'm properly freaking out.' She attached a lens to her camera and pointed the thing in Katie's face to take a test shot.

'Don't! I look like a hag!' Katie held a hand over the device like a papped celebrity. 'You'll be fine. How did the exams go? Better this time?'

Alisha exhaled, expelling the toxic nerves in her belly. 'I think so, but I don't wanna jinx results day.'

'At least she turned up to sit them this year.' Greg threw a grape at her head. Cackling, she picked up the grape and hurled it back.

'True. I think that was the key to success. Sitting the exams . . .'

Ben raised his drink from where he sat, his legs dangling in the pool. 'I propose a toast to Alisha finally getting the hell out of Longview High School!'

'I'll drink to that.' Alisha raised her water. 'To graduating! A year after everyone else!'

They chatted around the pool for what felt like hours, Greg and Ryan name-dropping from the worlds of professional football and theatre school. Ryan told them all how he'd come out to his mum and dad after being busted for some questionable online material. Love lives were discussed but, it seemed that aside from Greg and Erin, romance hadn't been a priority. After what had happened at the ball, that kinda made sense.

A nasty twinge of envy nipped at Alisha's insides. Greg and Erin, Katie and Ben. When was it her turn? She wanted the cuddles and secret glances, the little phrases whispered in *her* ear. It had been a long time, too long, since Callum. As she thought of her ex, a familiar bilious sensation burned the back of her throat. However much time passed, however 'over it' she was, that episode still left a bad taste. A bad taste called 'Roxanne Dent'. Boyfriend-stealing, manipulative, two-hundred-faced witch.

Alisha made a conscious effort to shake it off, refocusing on the merriment around the pool. She intended to spend the rest of the afternoon taking candid black-and-white shots of her old friends as they laughed and joked. If they didn't make her portfolio they'd do for her Tumblr.

Erin settled herself on a lounger. 'It's so weird. Don't you lot ever chat on Facebook? It's like you haven't seen each other all year.'

That was awkward. There was a reason they hadn't spoken all year. Alisha pretended to fiddle with her camera. Ryan held his nose and jumped back into the pool.

Ben spoke first. 'I guess we've all just been doing our own thing.'

Katie stood, acting like she'd failed to hear the question. 'I'm going to make more sangria. Does anyone want some?'

There were a few nods. Erin looked puzzled, aware of the ripples her harmless comment had made. Alisha caught Ryan's eye and knew they were sharing the same thought: *When are we gonna tell her about the whole dead girl thing?*

The track on Ben's playlist changed, creating a perfect diversion from *that* conversation. Alisha sprang off her lounger. 'Oh, my God! TUNE! Can you remember this? Can you remember the routine?'

Ryan clambered out of the pool and ran to Alisha's side. 'The routine! Amazing! Katie, quick!'

Katie panicked but ran to join them. 'I can't remember that – it was years ago.' It was some now-defunct girl band, and it had been *the* summer tune three years ago. It was time travel – Alisha swore she could actually taste the Cherry Coke and Monster Munch.

'What *are* you doing?' Greg smiled.

'Wait, wait, wait!' Alisha said as Katie took up position to her left and a touch behind so she could follow her lead. 'Here comes the chorus.'

'Left, right, arm, arm,' Ryan called as he performed the

moves. It came back to Alisha like it was programmed into her. She wasn't as slick as Ryan, but their amateur dance routine had muscle memory. She howled with laughter.

'And dutty wine!' Alisha sang, winding her rear end down like a corkscrew. It at once hurt her thighs; she was so out of shape.

'And again,' Ryan laughed.

Alisha could hardly breathe. She saw Ben laughing and Greg clapping along. It had been a long, troubled year, but she finally had all her friends back in one place. She vowed to find a way to keep them together this time. Looking up, she saw only endless blue – the bluest baby-blue she'd ever seen. There wasn't a cloud in the sky.

SCENE 4 – RYAN

Menace builds drop by drop. You don't know when it will strike, but you know 'the conflict' is coming. The audience knows *something* is about to happen – *something* lurking just out of sight. Here they all were dancing around in the glorious sunshine; it must look like some sort of skincare commercial with loads of hot, skinny people partying around the pool. But the audience has the upper hand. They *know* that while the beautiful people frolic, they're ignorant to the alien invasion or impending train wreck or, in this case, the shadow of . . . murder?

Ryan didn't like being ignorant.

Maybe he was being dramatic. OK, he was *definitely* being dramatic, but it just didn't make sense. Some major drama had gone down at the leavers' ball last year, but he just didn't accept that Janey had killed herself. He couldn't get Janey out of his head.

The media loves a missing white girl, so Janey Bradshaw's death had been the biggest thing ever to happen to the sleepy seaside town in which they'd all grown up. Her only press competition had been Tilda Honey's prize-winning marrows – it was no contest. The suicide of a promising, beautiful teenage cellist had 'stunned the community' as the papers were so fond of saying.

According to the coroner, Janey had jumped from Telscombe Cliffs and was carried out on the tide. Her body had been found by fishermen almost four weeks later. Those weeks had been torture for everyone. God, what her poor family went through: the TV appeal for witnesses, camera crews cluttering their front drive.

Because of what had happened at the ball, people had jumped (no pun intended) to suicide conclusions, but Ryan knew Janey pretty well. If she'd killed herself she'd have left a note – hell, she'd have left an essay! Janey loved the drama almost as much as he did. She'd have wanted the final word on the matter, he knew it.

So while everyone else had been sobbing, he'd been suspicious. He figured there were only so many possible explanations for Janey's death . . .

1. Suicide. He wasn't buying it.
2. Random murderer. Ryan had researched this. People are very rarely killed or attacked by strangers, which brought him to . . .
3. Family. Everyone always assumes it's the dad, and Janey's death was no different. The ghoulish townsfolk had seemed almost disappointed when it had turned out that Mr Bradshaw hadn't molested his daughter; he had an ironclad alibi, as did her mother. That just left . . .
4. Friends. Someone from school. One of them.

Ryan squirmed on his lounger. It was such an awful idea, he almost felt bad for thinking it. And what was the motive? Why would any of them have wanted to kill Janey? It made little sense, but then neither did the official version of events. Janey had *seemed* like a normal eighteen-year-old girl from a

33

nice town with a *nice* family in a *nice* house with a *nice* dog. But Ryan knew it was never that simple; there's always something going on backstage. Behind every smiling mantelpiece photo, there are secrets. Ryan wondered what secrets Janey had had, and whether Greg, Alisha, Katie or Ben had known them too. Ryan hoped his Ray-Bans hid his suspicions.

Greg sat on the other side of the pool, fiddling with his mobile phone. 'Can anyone else get, like, *any* bars?'

Katie replied, 'Good luck with that. Reception out here is atrocious. Sometimes you can get a bar or two in the bedrooms. You're more than welcome to use the landline, though.'

'We're meant to be on holiday,' Erin moaned, going over to the pool. Even in bare feet she walked on tiptoes like she was wearing invisible stilettos. 'Not constantly bloody texting.'

'I wanna check my Twitter.'

Katie gestured towards the villa. 'There's wi-fi in the house, just no phone signal.'

A thought occurred to Ryan and he sat upright on his lounger. 'You know what?' he said, snapping out of his Janey funk.

'What?' Alisha replied. She took a picture of him and he poked his tongue out.

'This is so the beginning of a horror film!' Right on cue a door slammed inside the house. They all jumped; sangria sloshed over the side of Erin's glass.

'Christ! What was that?' she asked.

'The doors slam if you leave windows open, that's all,' Katie reassured her with a smile.

'It so is!' Ryan went on. 'Think about it. We're in this remote villa, with no one else for miles and miles around. Our mobiles can't get a signal. We're all young and beautiful, especially me. We're dead meat! We should run a sweepstake

– what's it gonna be? Axe-murderers? Zombies? Matadors? Spanish fishermen ghosts?'

'As long as they're *cute* fishermen ghosts I'm down with that,' Alisha said, to much approval from Katie and Erin.

'Witches are on trend right now. I'm putting my money on witches.' Katie poured more sangria for herself and Ryan.

'Dude, there is no way I'm getting killed by witches.' Greg turned his nose up. 'That's chick-flick territory right there.'

Ryan almost spat his sangria out. 'Please! Greggle, you are so dying first.'

'How the bloody hell do you figure that out?' Greg demanded.

'Well, actually a girl normally dies first – we did this in film studies last year. The theory goes that a largely male horror audience doesn't believe male characters can experience abject terror, so the girl death scenes are always much scarier.'

'So how am I gonna die first?'

'Well, maybe not *first*, but you're a jock and you're half black, so you're a goner.'

'Dude! That's well racist!'

'Don't hate the player, hate the game,' Ryan told him, peeping over the rim of his sunglasses and fixing the football star with his most flirtatious gaze. It was useless fighting it; Greg hadn't become any *less* hot over the last year.

Alisha raised a finger. 'Actually, it became so predictable that the black guy would always die, that now he sometimes makes it.'

'Only if he's funny,' Ryan replied. 'The comic relief survives.'

Katie laughed. 'Let me guess, Ryan – you're the comic relief?'

Ryan feigned surprise. 'Well, look at that! I guess I'm gonna be OK! Although I am gay. Gay characters are untested

35

ground in modern horror. It could go either way – which is ironic, because I don't!'

More laughter.

'Well what about the rest of us?' Erin asked.

Ryan buzzed. He couldn't help it. He loved being the centre of attention – always had, ever since the reaction he'd got when he'd pulled his pants down in a Reception nativity play. 'Let's see.' He pointed at Ben. 'Geek.' He moved onto Erin. 'New girl.' Katie. 'Good girl.' And last of all Alisha. 'Bad girl.'

'How am I the bad girl?' Alisha exploded.

'None of the rest of us had to repeat Year Thirteen.'

She hid behind her camera and grinned. 'Can't argue with that.'

'So which stereotype survives this low budget Spanish bloodbath?' Katie smiled.

'Duh! The virgin,' Ryan told her.

Wild hoots of derision flew around the pool. 'Oh, so we're *all* dead then?' Ben laughed.

Ryan held his hands up. 'Just saying, the Final Girl is always the "good girl".'

'What's a Final Girl?' Greg asked, munching on a handful of Lays.

'In every horror film one girl has to survive. The audience goes in knowing that however horrific it gets, however much blood is shed, the good girl will always defeat the killer and live to face the sequel. Otherwise, it's just too bleak.'

Ben raised his glass. 'Well, here's to Katie, then. You're the only one who's getting out of this alive!'

Katie obliged and raised her glass. 'Well, obviously! But you still didn't tell us, Ryan . . . who's going to be the first to die?'

Ryan smiled. 'Wait and see.'

SCENE 5 – ALISHA

Later, as the sun melted into the sea, Alisha and Ryan went for a walk in the sand dunes, looking for photo opportunities. The scene was sweeping and remote, almost like an alien planet, the white sand turning Martian orange as the sun set. For a while Ryan rolled around in the sand while Alisha fulfilled his *Next Top Model* fantasies, clicking away on her camera. She couldn't remember the last time she'd laughed so hard and felt so much like her old self. In fact, this was even *better* than her old self, because she wasn't too drunk to walk in a straight line.

When they returned to the villa, Ben had long since fallen asleep on his lounger and the happy couple were also napping, so while Katie read her book on the top terrace, Alisha decided to beat the rush for the bathroom and get ready for the evening. She and Ryan had (perhaps foolishly) offered to cook paella, so there was no time to waste.

As far as she could tell, there were three bedrooms in the villa. There was the master bedroom with an en suite bathroom, which Katie had let Greg and Erin take, since they were a couple. Alisha and Katie were sharing the second bedroom, while Ryan was in the smallest of the three, thrilled to get a double bed all to himself. Ben didn't seem too put out at sleeping on the sofa-bed in the lounge.

Alisha examined her face in the mirror. A cluster of freckles had emerged over the bridge of her nose and shoulders, and her skin was browner than ever. With a tan she looked so much more like her mum, and a glimmer of pride at her Bajan heritage blossomed within.

She twisted the shower on and pulled the curtain along before peeling off her damp, chlorine-scented bikini, noting some already impressive tan lines. Steam billowed over the top of the curtain rail and she stepped in. The water stung her back at once. Maybe she'd had too much sun. She made a mental note to get Katie to bathe her in cocoa butter as soon as she got out. The water jet pummelled her head and gold grains of sand started to wash down the plughole. That was the only downside to being near the beach – the sand. She'd be emptying the stuff out of her shoes long after she got back to Telscombe Cliffs.

She shampooed her hair and scrubbed her skin, glad to be rid of the greasy suncream feeling. Alisha breathed a sigh of relief as the hot water streamed over her face. All things considered, today could have been worse. A lot worse, in fact. Maybe this week was a sign that her life was turning a corner. She'd pass her sodding exams, complete the art foundation course, and then go live out the rest of her life somewhere achingly cool – she could be a photographer in Hoxton or something. Then she'd be free to meet someone and fall in love, the way that everyone else seemed to every day.

That was when she heard the voices. Her hands flew to her collar bone (God only knew why she thought *that* was the part to cover), thinking that someone had entered the bathroom. She was about to scream, 'I'M NAKED!' when she realised the voices were drifting in through a small, brown plastic air vent above the shower head. It dawned on her that the villa's ventilation system must carry sound.

She listened closer, trying to pick up the conversation. The main bathroom was connected to the master bedroom. The voices she could hear belonged to Erin and Greg. The clarity with which the sound travelled was uncanny. The couple could almost be in the shower with her, a most disturbing thought.

Alisha stopped listening and hummed one of the tunes from Ben's playlist, but she couldn't block out the voices.

'Oh, come on,' Erin laughed.

'Not with my sister here . . .' Greg muttered through what sounded like kisses.

'She's in the shower, I think. Come on . . . we can be quick.'

'It's weird!'

'Charming!' Erin giggled.

'You know what I mean.'

'Nobody can hear us. I'll be quiet.'

'Oh, HELL NO!' Alisha promptly switched the shower off and grabbed a towel. Conditioning her hair could wait until later. She had no desire to experience an audio-only version of her brother in full swing – she'd never be able to afford the therapy. Making a loud 'lalalalala' noise, Alisha scurried into the corridor where she collided head on with Ben.

'Oh, there you are,' he said. 'I was looking for you.'

Alisha was suddenly very aware that she was wearing only a towel, and that even that was being held up by her armpits and willpower. Ben had seen her in a bikini all afternoon, but this seemed much worse even if she was actually more covered up. 'You were?'

'Yeah. I got you something.' Ben handed her a stripy pink

and white paper bag, like the kind you got penny sweets in when you were little.

Tucking her towel a little tighter, Alisha slipped her hand inside and felt that tell-tale cuboid shape. She pulled it out and couldn't stifle a gleeful gasp. 'Oh, my God! Ben! Do you know what this is?'

He raised an eyebrow. 'Well, I'm not an expert, but – is it a camera?'

She punched his arm, almost losing the towel and her dignity in the process. 'This is not just a camera, Ben Murdoch, this is an original Diana F+ circa 1960. Where on earth did you get this?'

He shrugged as if it were nothing, but he seemed pleased with her reaction. 'It was my mum's. She was having a clear-out and it was going in the bin, but I thought you might like it.'

'Ben, I *love* it. That is so sweet of you . . . but you know these are worth, like, a hundred quid, right?'

He laughed. 'Really? I didn't, no . . .' He grinned. 'Can I . . . erm . . . have it back then?'

She hugged it to her chest, laughing. 'No you bloody can't, sucker!'

He'd changed into some slouchy khaki shorts and a polo shirt. He stuffed his hands in his pockets, looking just like a bigger version of the boy she'd grown up with. 'Hopefully you can get some cool shots for your portfolio with it.'

'Thanks. This is ... . great. Seriously, thanks.'

'No worries.' He smiled. 'You're dripping, so I better . . .'

'What? Oh, yeah. I need to dry off.' Suddenly feeling extra-exposed, Alisha skirted Ben and slipped into her room. Shutting the door behind her, she examined the retro equipment in her hands, delicately turning the little baby-blue case over in her palm as if it were a priceless Fabergé egg.

The fact that Ben had thought of her at all, the kindness of his act . . . for some reason her skin felt red hot – and it was nothing to do with sunburn.

SCENE 6 – RYAN

R yan had to confess, this wasn't going as badly as he'd thought it might – not just the vast pan of paella he was currently stirring, but the whole holiday thing. When he'd turned his back on Telscombe Cliffs, he'd assumed he'd kissed goodbye to his school friends forever, but this was like slipping back into a familiar pair of comfy socks.

He was torn. Despite his lingering suspicions about Janey, he'd had fun today. Genuine, *real* fun. His cheeks ached from laughing. Since he'd been at drama school, he'd met *fabulous* people and done some *amazing* 'networking'. Most of the people he'd met called him 'darling' or 'babe' because, in the theatre, no one knows your real name. He was just as bad as the rest of his classmates – all air kisses and schmoozing.

Ryan had drunk a lot of champagne over the last year, but now he wanted a cup of tea. These were his 'cup of tea' friends, and they knew his name. Perhaps Katie was right. Perhaps he should let Janey go – accept there was something very odd about her death and just gloss over the myriad plot holes surrounding it

While Ryan and Alisha were preparing dinner, Greg was attempting to teach everyone how to play poker in the lounge – with limited success by the sound of it. Ben was never going to master a poker face and Katie couldn't get her head around which hands were better than which. *The young lovers finally reunited:* Katie and Ben. Ben and Katie. Bentie. Ken. They were meant to be together. If they hadn't had a snog by the end of the week, Ryan would eat his limited-edition Fred Perry military cap.

Ryan had changed into a sharp shirt for dinner, and he noticed that the others had gone to a similar effort. Perhaps it was because everyone had been expecting at least some nightlife near the villa, or maybe it was just because it was the first time they'd seen each other in ages; either way, everyone looked great.

'I think,' he said, 'that this is about done. What do you think?' Alisha left her salad and came to the stove. He held out a wooden spoon with a sample.

'Yum, it's good,' she decided. 'Where did you learn to cook?'

'*Masterchef* obviously!'

Alisha laughed and took another mouthful. Ryan was pleased to see Alisha looking so healthy – hopefully her boozalicious phase was over. It had been a hugely entertaining car-crash to watch, but he could only imagine the toll it had taken on his friend's body.

Alisha took over the paella, adding some seasoning and attempting to tip the contents of the pan into a family-sized serving dish. Her arms wobbled. 'Jesus Christ, this pan is heavy. What's it made of?'

Ryan smiled. 'I know, right? It's like lead. Hey, you lot, it's about done.' He walked through into the lounge.

The card game had finished and Greg was fiddling with some artefacts on the living-room mantelpiece that looked like they'd come from a pirate ship. 'What's all this stuff?' Greg asked Katie. He struck a pose with a battered goblet. 'Do I look like Captain Jack?'

Katie plucked it from his hands. 'Careful, these are my dad's prized possessions. Some old galleon went down off the coast about two hundred years ago. This stuff literally washes up on the beach. My dad had it assessed – some of it's quite valuable; most of it's junk, though.'

'It's cool.' Ben picked a sturdy-looking dagger off the wall. It was in a decaying leather sheath with a matching grip. He slipped the dagger out. Years at sea hadn't dulled the glint of steel; the blade gleamed, deadly as a shark's smile.

'That *is* cool!' Greg agreed. 'Give it here. Watch this.' He took the knife and crouched in front of the coffee table. He made a pile of Erin's fashion magazines.

'Greg, baby, what are you doing?' his girlfriend asked.

'Have you ever seen that thing?' he replied.

Ryan grinned. 'Honey, remember the changing rooms after PE? We've all seen your thing!'

Greg shot him a deathly look. '*This* thing.' He splayed his fingers, laying his palm flat on the magazines. Then he held the blade over the gap between his thumb and forefinger and brought the dagger down with a flash of light. In an instant, he pulled it back up and stabbed the space between his forefinger and index finger. Then onto the next gap. As he repeated this, he moved faster and faster. Ryan screwed his eyes shut; Greg was going to lose a finger.

Luckily, Erin felt the same. 'Don't you bloody dare!' She barged into Greg, halting him.

'Watch it, you'll have my finger off!' he snapped.

'Yeah, that's what'll go wrong, numb-nuts. Give me that.' Erin snatched the knife from him and handed it back to Katie.

'Spoil sport,' grumbled Greg, and Erin kissed the top of his shorn head.

Ryan let out a long breath. He wasn't great with blood. Disaster averted. 'Come on you lot, food's getting cold.'

The waves breathed in and out in the distance while crickets and cicadas chirruped in the hills. A hideous windchime that Katie's stepmum had strung up clanged as the breeze whispered across the terrace, where they had chosen to eat their Spanish feast. Tea lights sputtered on the table and there was laughter. Lots of laughter. Somehow, even though everyone had mostly avoided the past as a topic of conversation, there was still plenty to talk about. The annoying thing was that, after Erin's shrewd observation at the poolside, Ryan was dying to talk about Janey. He knew Katie accepted the suicide theory, but what about the others? Did Ben really believe his girlfriend had killed herself over some stupid fight at a prom?

Although questions perched on the tip of his tongue, Ryan sensed this wasn't the time to raise them. It was all going so well and he didn't want to be the bad fairy who turns up and ruins the party.

After they'd eaten, although their stomachs were bloated, Ben talked them into doing something he'd always wanted to do: build a bonfire on the beach.

The fire was impressive: angry flames roared as kindling cracked within. Even sitting at a safe distance on the sand, Ryan could feel the heat on his face. 'What is it with men and open fires?' he mused.

Ben threw another twig on the fire. 'It's in our caveman DNA.'

'Man make fire,' Greg agreed, sipping a beer. Erin was nestled in the crook of his arm.

'Plus it's pretty and romantic,' Ben said absent-mindedly. As soon as he'd said it, his face flushed and he looked into the

45

flames. Ryan could tease, but he chose not to. It *was* romantic. The woody smoke was intoxicating, making his eyelids heavy. If only he had someone to cuddle up to.

The white moon rippled on the ocean and the lights of the villa still glowed but, other than that, there was only darkness. The nearest town twinkled miles down the coast. The firelight was almost a bubble – they were in their own little cosmos. Ryan felt warm and wine-sleepy.

Towards the surf, Alisha and Katie were practising handstands and cartwheels with glee. If Alisha was drunk, she was in happy-drunk mode and not evil, vindictive-drunk mode, which suited Ryan fine. The pair eventually ran back to the fire, giddy and out of breath, their amateur gymnastics apparently over.

Erin sipped her wine. 'So you were all at school together?'

'Yep,' Ben replied, giving the fire a prod. 'I went to a different primary school, but I already knew Ry because our mums are mates.'

Erin nodded. 'I was worried it'd be like you were all speaking a foreign language or something and I wouldn't be able to keep up, but you haven't talked about school all day.'

Ryan eyed Erin suspiciously. He hadn't figured her out yet. In a lot of films, she'd be the main character. The new girl, the one who has everything to learn, who is the eyes and ears of the audience because they start on a blank slate together. Erin *seemed* nice enough – smiley and full of thoughtful questions – but he couldn't find anything more to latch on to. Then he noticed that she seemed to be waiting for a response.

'Ah well, that's because Greggle actually enjoyed school,' Ryan told her. 'As you can imagine, he was quite the celebrity at Longview . . . the rest of us, less so. Therefore I have no desire to talk about that hellhole!' He decided to deflect the conversation onto Erin. 'Where did you grow up?'

'Hove, actually!' Erin said, referring to Brighton's affluent neighbour. Brighton was the nearest city to Telscombe Cliffs, and as soon as they'd been old enough to do so, they'd spent almost all their weekends there.

'Oh, very nice!' Ryan grinned.

'It was OK. So, you've all, like, known each other forever?'

Alisha answered. 'Except for Ben, we all went to primary school together, yeah.'

Erin waved a finger between Ben and Katie. 'And, let me guess, you two used to be an item?'

'Erin, can you stop interrogating my friends, please?' Greg frowned at her.

'I'm not.'

'No, it's OK,' Ben looked up at Erin through heavy lashes. 'Yeah, me and Katie were together for about three years.'

'I see. Sorry. I just wondered. I guess I have a sixth sense for stuff like that. I thought there was something there.'

Katie brushed sand out of her hair, feigning nonchalance. 'Not at all. It was a long time ago.'

Erin's shoulders seemed to drop. 'It's so funny. Ever since we got here, I knew there was something going on. Greg, you should have told me, so I didn't stick my foot in my mouth!'

Oh, clever girl, thought Ryan. She'd seen through the veneer of cheesy grins and poolside dance routines. Just under the surface they'd all been scarred by last summer, something Erin was evidently picking up on. They weren't fooling strangers, let alone themselves. Ryan took a deep breath. Now was the time. They were all here, they'd all had a drink, the fire was hypnotic. It was the perfect time to talk about Janey. In a murder mystery, it's called the 'drawing room scene', where the detective gathers all the suspects to reveal what he or she has learned.

'Oh, for crying out loud!' Ryan exploded. 'Why don't we just talk about it now and throw the massive sodding elephant in the room onto the fire?'

'Ryan . . .' Alisha warned.

'No.' He was determined. 'Erin should know. Greg, I can't believe you haven't told her.'

Greg muttered something under his breath that sounded like, 'He better shut his mouth before I shut it for him.'

Suddenly Erin was the outsider more than ever. Confusion creased her pretty face. 'Tell me what? I didn't mean to start an argument.'

'You haven't.' Katie threw Ryan a disapproving glance, motherly as ever.

'Oh, come on,' Ryan continued. 'Did we really think we could hang out for two whole weeks without the subject of Janey coming up? I say we get it out of the way now and enjoy the rest of the holiday.'

A pause. 'You know what? He may have a point,' Greg sighed, folding his arms.

'Thank you, Greg. You know I'm right.'

'God, what can there possibly be left to say?' Alisha's expression was one of mild disgust.

But the floodgate was open now and all that Ryan had longed to say came gushing out. 'Everything. After Janey died, I had about a million questions but everyone clammed up. I've had a year of bursting to know, but it's like someone passed a secret law – the "We Don't Bloody Talk About Janey" law.'

'Ryan, you're being a dick,' Alisha said.

'I'm not. Wanting to know what happened does not make me a dick.'

Erin spoke up. 'Guys, I'm really sorry. I didn't want to cause this.'

'You didn't,' Ben said. 'Can we all take it down a notch? Ryan, you've gone to the *bad place* again.' Ryan rolled his eyes, but said no more. Ben continued. 'It's fine to talk about it. It happened. Not talking about it doesn't change anything.' As he spoke he kept his gaze fixed on the fire. There was something robotic about his voice, like he was taking extra care to control it.

'OK, what is going on?' Erin's voice wobbled. 'You're all really freaking me out now.'

Ryan looked to Ben, who gave him the slightest of nods, but where to start, and how much to reveal? He wasn't sure it was right to air all his suspicions at once. 'We had a friend called Janey.' He selected his words precisely. 'This time last year she killed herself.'

'Oh, God, that's awful!' Erin's eyes widened.

Ben took a deep breath. 'I . . . I was dating her at the time.'

Those eyes widened further. 'Oh. Right. But I thought . . .'

Katie intervened, her coy eyes fixed on the sand, only flashing up for the briefest of moments. 'We'd broken up the Christmas beforehand.'

'Oh. OK. I'm so sorry, you guys. I mean . . . about *everything*.'

Ryan continued. 'It was on the day of the leavers' ball. Janey jumped off the top of Telscombe Cliffs. Or so goes the official version of events.'

A pause. Then Ben said, 'What's that supposed to mean?' The fire made Ben's skin glow like bronze, but his expression was inscrutable.

Ryan shrugged. 'Just that there was no note. Only a body.' More choice word selection.

'Jesus, Ryan, do we need the gory details?' snapped Alisha.

'I'm sorry.' He paused. He couldn't do it. He couldn't accuse his friends of murder. It was too dramatic, too high-concept, even for him. Frustration crawled under his skin. What did he really want to say? 'It's just so sad,' he finally blurted out. 'So pointless. There'd been . . . a big fight at the ball and she ran away. Janey was even more dramatic than me, if you can believe that. She was angry, but we never thought she'd do something so stupid. I mean . . . none of us went after her . . .'

Those last six words summed up the problem. She could so easily have been stopped. Any one of them could have talked her out of it. A tear pooled in the corner between his eye and nose. Alisha hooked her arm through his.

'It's not your fault,' Erin offered. 'I think once someone's decided to do something like that . . .'

'She put us all through hell. You know for *four weeks*, before they found the body, we thought she'd been abducted or something,' Greg cursed. 'She wasn't thinking straight. It was such a selfish, bullshit thing to do. We all get pissed off; we don't chuck ourselves off a cliff.'

'Greg. Don't,' Alisha said gravely.

He was only saying what they'd all thought, though. Everyone has an argument from time to time – but they don't kill themselves. *This* was what had haunted Ryan all year – it was so *stupid*. So *unlikely*. If it *had* been TV, it would have made far more sense for Alisha to die – with all her recklessness she would have made a perfect cautionary tale. So many things about that night didn't make any sense. Janey should have been here, with them, right now, on the beach.

Erin spoke again, her curiosity now bordering on nosy. 'What was the fight about?'

'It doesn't matter,' Ben said simply, clearly battling to maintain an even tone.

'It doesn't' Alisha agreed. 'What matters is that none of us did anything. Not one of us went to see if she was OK – we were all too wrapped up in our own stupid stuff. I sometimes think it was our fault she jumped.'

Although the fire crackled and spat, the beach was suddenly freezing cold. 'Do you think—' Ryan started.

'Do I think what?' Greg downed the last of his beer.

Ryan steeled himself. 'Do you really think Janey killed herself?'

Orange and amber and gold and white danced in all their eyes: Ben, Greg, Katie, Alisha and Erin. At first no one spoke, everyone waiting to hear what everyone else would say. The silence was deafening.

Katie broke it. 'Ryan, the only person who truly knows what happened that night is dead.'

SCENE 7 – ALISHA

Alisha stared at the fire for what felt like hours. Eventually, the roaring flames lost their will to fight, tiring to feeble tongues before dying to embers. They still glowed scarlet though, and they still gave heat. When she poked them with her stick, they flared up angrily in a shower of sparks. Alisha had no idea how much time she lost to this pursuit; it was hypnotic.

Most of the others had drifted back to the villa, blaming coldness or tiredness. Maybe it was all too much: the flight, the wine, the sun. Janey. Katie remained on the other side of the ashes, a pashmina around her shoulders. The pair sat in companionable silence. For years, Alisha had wished she could *be* Katie. Katie seemed perfect to her. Like, now, she was wearing a crisp white summer dress. Alisha was not the sort of girl who could wear white and not smear ketchup down herself.

It wasn't just Katie's dress sense, though, it was everything about her. She was an only child, she lived in a gorgeous house, she had Ben, her grades were flawless. That was before you even got started on her do. The girl basically had *Little Mermaid* hair. It was a mystery to Alisha, therefore, why Katie had a sadness in her eyes these days. She smiled and chatted but there was a pain there; Alisha could see it.

Perhaps Katie blamed herself for what had happened.

The mood had lightened a little after the talk about Janey, but the elephant, although acknowledged, hadn't gone anywhere.

'Hey, Miss Katie. You OK?' Alisha asked.

Katie nodded and gave her a kind smile. 'Of course. How are you?'

'I'm peachy. You looked a million miles away.'

'I'm fine, I promise – just sleeping with my eyes open,' Katie said, sweeping her hair off her face. 'Today's been a long day.'

As if on cue, the unmistakeable, tall silhouette of Ben ambled over the sand towards them. As much as she'd love to be a fly on the wall of whatever was about to happen, Alisha had no desire to play the gooseberry.

'Hey,' she said. 'I'm gonna get ready for bed.'

Katie took a deep breath, clocking Ben at the same time. 'I'll be in in a minute.'

Alisha walked over and kissed her on the head, noticing that Katie still used the same shampoo – it smelled like toffee. It was a reminder of how close they'd been once upon a time. Alisha wasn't sure they were any more. The gesture felt awkward. It was as though Janey had been the stitching holding them together. After she jumped, everyone fell to pieces, tumbling miles apart in different directions.

Alisha turned and left Katie alone with the tide and the embers – and Ben. As she passed Ben, she gave him a smile of encouragement but continued towards the villa. Her flip-flops clacked on the stone tiles as she climbed the stairs, allowing her fingers to brush the hedgerow that grew along the perimeter.

Out of the corner of her eye she saw a sleek green lizard dart under the cover of a flat stone, quicker than lightning, and she made a mental note to try to photograph the little fella tomorrow if she could find him. She was getting accustomed to doing things alone – it was starting to feel like that was her lot in life.

When she arrived at the top terrace, she paused before the sliding doors and looked back at the bonfire. Ben was nestled beside Katie, his arm around her shoulders. Obviously, Alisha couldn't hear what they were saying, but they were deep in sombre conversation, both shaking their heads with down-turned mouths and furrowed brows.

Then Katie rested her weary head on Ben's shoulder and, with his free hand, he stroked her hair.

Alisha sighed. She felt happy for her friend and, at the same time, utterly, utterly lonely.

SCENE 8 – RYAN

Perhaps it was the wine or maybe it was the whir of the air-conditioner, but Ryan couldn't sleep. Gritty black-and-white flashbacks filled his head – fast edits to confuse yet tantalise the audience. Hundreds of disturbing, violent scenarios played out in his mind's eye however much he tried to block them. He pictured Janey's last minutes at the top of the cliff. Did she fight? Had she been dead already when she'd got there? He imagined a lone car parked in the hotel car park with the boot open. He saw a figure, shrouded in black, take Janey's body out of the trunk and drag her to the edge of the cliff.

He rolled over, making a 'hmph' noise. Who was he kidding? It had been suicide. His overactive brain was making up stories. Stupid and illogical Janey's death may have been, but it had been the final episode so someone had had to die. Those were just the rules of television – the big finish.

He rolled over, the thin, sweaty sheet becoming tangled in his bare legs. He was hot and bothered. With a sigh he rolled off the bed and opened his bedroom door. Not turning any lights on, he crept past the other bedrooms. The air smelled of night-breath and he could hear Greg gently snoring alongside Erin, the lucky cow.

He tiptoed into the lounge where Ben was sprawled face-down on the sofa-bed. Like Ryan, he wore only his boxers and moonlight filtered through the gossamer drapes onto the smooth canyon in the centre of his back. It looked hot – even though Ryan didn't fancy Ben in the slightest. He could understand why girls fell for his puppy-dog eyes and dimples, but Ryan preferred a bad boy. Always had.

He snuck through to the kitchen. Believing horror stories about what would happen if you drank local water (maggots would hatch in your stomach), he opened the fridge and took a bottle of mineral water. Pausing in the dining area, he looked out into the night. They were so alone here. Their nearest neighbour was a cruise ship that skirted along the very edge of the horizon.

God, it was so humid. The water was already too warm.

He didn't see Ben's rucksack until he kicked it, sending its contents spilling over the tiles. Biting his lip to keep from cursing, Ryan rubbed his stubbed big toe. Ben didn't stir, his head facing the wall. 'Ben?' he breathed. There was no response. Ben was in a deep, deep sleep. Ryan stooped to tidy the mess.

This was only hand luggage. Ryan scooped up a phone charger and an iPad, a copy of *New Scientist* magazine (Ben was such a geek), some contact lens solution, half a warm Dr Pepper and his wallet. He was shoving everything back in the bag, when something else caught his eye. At the bottom of the rucksack was something oddly familiar. He reached for it, his fingers closing on the rough sack material and pulling it out into the moonlight.

It was a mask. One of *the* masks from the night of the ball – which to the students of Longview High was also known as 'Prank Night'. It was a *ghastly* thing. Ben and Greg had cut eyeholes in the sacks, drawn on deranged grins in marker pen and worn them over their heads. Ryan smiled as he remembered. With everything *else* that had happened that night he'd totally forgotten about the Scarecrow Prank. It had been his idea – based on a story he'd written – and it had worked brilliantly. That night would have been one of the best nights of his life . . . had Janey not died.

He slipped the mask over his head and tiptoed to the mirror on the wall near the stairs. In the gloom his head look malformed, truly something from a child's worst nightmare. He remembered the voice . . .

'What are you doing?'

Ryan cried out and whipped round, almost knocking the mirror off the wall. He had to steady it to prevent it falling. Ben sat up on the sofa, took one look at the mask and recoiled, almost tumbling off his bed.

Ryan yanked the mask off. 'Ben, it's just me,' he whispered.

'Ryan, what the bloody hell are you doing? You scared the crap out of me!' Ben exclaimed.

Ryan couldn't suppress a giggle – the look on Ben's face was priceless. 'Well, now you know what it feels like. Do you remember this?'

'Of course.' Ben rubbed his eyes. 'Why did you bring it?'

'I didn't. I thought it was yours.'

Ben shook his head. 'I lost mine. Must be Greg's. What time is it?'

'But it was . . .' Ryan stopped. He couldn't be bothered to argue. Perhaps it was Greg's bag, not Ben's. 'It's still early. I just came to get water.'

'OK.' Ben rose off the sofa with his long legs. Looking at the defined muscular ridges that ran over his hips, Ryan thought maybe he did fancy Ben a bit. Then again, if he had to think about it, he probably didn't.

'Just gonna use the loo,' Ben mumbled. The poor thing was half asleep as he sloped across the lounge. Ryan threw the hideous mask onto the dining-room table, from where the hollow eye sockets watched him return to bed.

SCENE 9 – ALISHA

Alisha stretched out in the empty bed, purring like a cat as she extended her limbs as far as they'd go. She had no idea where Katie had gone, but it was cool to have the bed to herself for a while.

With brilliant sunlight pouring through the blinds, making zebra stripes across her bare legs, the morose pity-party mood from last night evaporated immediately and she felt silly for being so mopey. She sat up and ran a hand through her 'fro which, at this time of the day, looked either really *Vogue* editorial or like a particularly scrappy bird's nest depending on your point of view.

Muffled voices carried through the air vents. She heard laughter and at once felt like she was missing out. This was why she rarely slept late any more – it seemed like a waste of a day. Alisha bounded out of bed, pausing only to pull a baggy Metallica T-shirt over her head. She didn't want to miss the action.

When she got to the kitchen, it was buzzing.

'Morning!' Erin greeted her with cabin-crew cheer. 'Coffee or tea?'

'Ooh, tea, please.'

'And we've got all sorts of *continental* goodies,' Ryan added in a weird American version of the British accent. 'We totes have our own branch of *Patisserie Valerie* out on the terrace.'

Alisha wandered out onto the top terrace. It was quite the spread: croissants, pastries, cake. 'Oh, my God, death by carbohydrate!' She sat down next to her brother.

'That's the general idea,' Greg said, wiping icing sugar off his chops. 'My trainer is like four hundred miles away, so I'm not having chicken for breakfast!'

From her position on the other side of the table, Katie laughed and selected an apricot Danish. 'Seriously? You have chicken for breakfast?'

'He has chicken for every meal.' Erin grimaced. 'We basically live in Nando's. We might as well pay rent there.'

With the neon-blue sky and dazzling, cleansing sunshine, the awful shroud of the 'bonfire confessions' was washed away. This was a new day, a fresh start. As awful as last night had been, Ryan's words were spot on – things were out in the open now and the group seemed altogether more relaxed. Perhaps they could just enjoy the rest of the holiday. Alisha mentally planned her day – maybe she'd have a go at surfing or something.

Ryan sat down with a glass of orange juice. 'I'm so glad we talked last night.' It was like he had read her mind. 'You know what, this fortnight could even be like a tribute to Janey.'

Behind her, inside the villa, Alisha heard a door slam shut. The wind again.

'I think you're right,' Ben agreed. 'It's time we moved on. We're all still alive and Janey was never a fan of moping.' Alisha didn't say a word, but that wasn't strictly true; Janey had loved a good sulk.

Alisha wondered what had happened after she'd left Katie and Ben alone on the beach. Katie had come to bed about half an hour later – plenty of time for her and Ben to have

. . . Alisha pushed the idea from her head; for some reason it made her queasy. Instead she raised a glass of pineapple juice. 'OK, here's to Janey Bradshaw, then. She was the best.'

Everyone scrabbled for something to toast with. Coffees, teas and juices were raised. 'To Janey.'

'Don't start without me,' a new voice interrupted.

Six heads turned. Six faces fell.

Framed by the sliding doors stood a beautiful new arrival. A pastel headscarf held flowing, dirty-blonde waves off her face. The skin on her long, bare legs was the deepest gold tan. A stone gleamed in the hollow of her belly button. She smiled, but there was not a trace of kindness in it. 'To Janey.'

It was Roxanne Dent.

SCENE 10 – RYAN

Ryan could only gawp, mouth hanging open. If this were the summer special, it was suddenly must-see TV. This was *priceless*. They'd renegotiated contracts, they'd signed on the dotted line and they'd brought back Roxanne. Of course they had.

The timing was *perfect*. Would this require a flashback? Roxanne Dent – high-school Lolita, boyfriend stealer and best friend turned arch-nemesis of Alisha Cole was in the building.

There was a moment of stillness, in which Ryan and, he assumed, the others, processed whether or not this apparition was real. She could be a mirage, a figment of a sun-frazzled mind.

But then Alisha spoke, breaking the spell, and it seemed all too real. Colour had drained from her face. 'What's going on?'

'Hey, Alisha,' Roxanne said with added sugar. 'I know things were weird between us but—'

Alisha cut her off. 'What the hell is she doing here? Is this a wind-up?' Ryan could almost taste her anger. On the rage-o-meter she was flashing orange.

'Oh, wow. Alisha, try not to—' Katie began.

'OK, I'm not kidding. Will someone please tell me what's going on?' Alisha's face contorted and, through sheer frustration, it looked like she might cry. Roxanne, on the other hand, was as cool and serene as an iceberg. Man, she was good. Ryan memorised her poise for future stage use. She held her hands up peacefully.

Alisha pushed back her chair. The iron legs caught in a groove between the paving slabs and the chair toppled backwards.

Greg was quicker than his sister. In a single fluid move, he rose from the breakfast table and placed himself between the two girls. 'Alisha, maybe we should take a walk on the beach or something . . .'

Roxanne remained tranquil, looking almost bored at how predictable Alisha's reaction was. 'Good to see you too, Alisha. Are you finished?'

Alisha took a deep breath. 'Oh, my God, you have got some nerve coming here . . .'

'Alisha, I really don't want any trouble. I just came to chill for a few days.'

'What? You're kidding, right?' Alisha's voice was sounding more and more strained.

Next to Ryan, Ben stood and steered Roxanne into the lounge. A subtle move, but it put distance between her and the oncoming storm that was Alisha in full flow. Greg stayed with his sister, while Ryan and the others followed Ben. There was no way Ryan wanted to miss this. It was probably the most exciting thing that had happened all year.

Of course Roxanne Dent needed to be here. What would any story be without a villain? Ryan could tell Ben was trying to remain as polite as possible, but his friend had never been keen on her.

'Roxanne, it's great to see you, obviously, but what are you doing here?' Ben asked.

Roxanne smiled. Ryan had forgotten just how gorgeous she was. The mass of blonde hair, the upward curve of her perpetually parted lips, the button nose – it was all *delicious* somehow. 'What do you mean?' she replied. 'Katie invited me.'

Cue sitcom-style head-swivel. All eyes turned to the redhead.

Katie seemed about to deny it when her face went milk-bottle-white followed by pillar-box-red. 'I did,' Katie said, her wide eyes unblinking.

'What?' Ryan couldn't keep the shrill horror out of his voice. Was she mad? Did she harbour some secret desire to see Alisha tear flesh from another human?

'On Facebook.' Katie could only manage random words. She looked like she was about to cry.

'Again ... what?' he asked more gently. Katie was the ultimate go-to person for peacekeeper. This was an epic screwup. Monumental. But also *fabulous*.

Roxanne raised an eyebrow – a mixture of genuine confusion and creeping annoyance. 'I was chatting to Katie on Facebook a few weeks back, and she said you were all coming out for the last couple of weeks of July. I was in Morocco, but I told her I'd be coming to Spain, so she said, "Why don't you drop by?" So I did!'

'So you did,' Ben repeated. He seemed to be in an even worse state of shock than Katie; his face was a sickly ashy grey.

'I ... I was being polite.' Katie couldn't even look at the others. Beyond the patio doors, Greg could clearly be heard telling Alisha to chill out.

Roxanne's face fell. 'Oh, God. Have I been the biggest remedial in the world? That wasn't actually an invite, was it? This is so embarrassing. Am I a homewrecker?'

'I think you mean party-crasher,' Ryan muttered under his breath, 'but, yes, that too.'

'No.' Katie snapped out of it, remembering her manners. 'No, it's fine.'

Ryan followed suit. More than wanting to reassure Roxanne, he felt bad for Katie. 'It's great to see you, Rox.' He gave her air kisses. 'You look fierce as ever.'

'You too, babe. Have you been working out?'

'Do you know, I have. Thank you for noticing.' Ryan grinned back, although he wasn't fooled by the compliments. Gay, straight, young, old – Roxanne thought she could wind any man around her finger, and he wasn't falling for it for a second.

'I'm really, sorry, Rox. It was my bad. I totally forgot about the Facebook chat. I only woke up ten minutes ago. You came as something of a shock! But, of course, you're more than welcome.' Katie gave her old friend a hug.

'Hmm, I dunno about that, hon. I don't want Alisha to have a fit,' Roxanne replied.

'She'll calm down,' Katie promised. 'I'll talk to her.'

Roxanne looked out to the terrace, where Alisha was angrily gesticulating at her brother. 'This is really awkward. Maybe I should just go.'

'No,' Ryan said. 'Don't be silly. You've come all the way from Morocco or wherever. You can't just leave straight away.' If nothing else, he thought, life was certainly more *colourful* with Rox around. Also, having a common enemy might help to glue the rest of them back together.

'Absolutely. We're just having breakfast. Come join us.' As Katie said it, Ryan observed Ben. Thinking no one was looking, he scowled into the shadows in the corner. Ben's face looked all wrong without a smile. It was unnerving. Ben said nothing, but prowled out of the lounge to join Greg and Alisha on the terrace.

'That'd be awesome,' Roxanne smiled. 'I could murder a coffee.'

Katie and Erin sprang into action, both falling over themselves to accommodate the newcomer.

Ryan brought Rox up to speed. 'Oh, Roxanne, this is Erin, Greg's girlfriend.' Erin stepped forward to greet her properly.

A flicker of amusement flashed across Roxanne's face. Just for the briefest of moments, but long enough for Ryan to register it. 'Oh, hi. How are you?' Roxanne gave her a lavish kiss. It was almost too lavish, like it was designed to make the smaller girl uncomfortable.

'I'm good, thanks. Nice to meet you.' Erin remained as sweet as ever. 'Did you say you'd been travelling?'

'I did. I started out in Bangkok, then went on to Goa, then flew up to Scandinavia to stay with my aunt. Since then I've been InterRailing around Europe, and been to Egypt and Morocco. It's been a pretty sweet year.'

Ryan knew Roxanne's enthusiasm was at least partly staged. Her year out was being funded by her father's life insurance. Both her parents had died before her eighteenth birthday – that was how Rox had ended up in Telscombe Cliffs in the first place. She'd had to live with her uncle and aunt because she hadn't yet turned eighteen when she was orphaned.

Taking a deep breath, Ryan opened the door to the terrace.

Alisha looked right at Roxanne, the fire in her eyes not fully extinguished. She sprung off the low wall she'd been perching on. 'Don't worry, Roxanne, I'm not gonna do anything. Enjoy your breakfast.' Alisha turned to Katie. 'I'm not staying here with *that*.' Alisha stomped past Roxanne, creating a wind as she went, and marched right for the bedrooms.

'OK. Well, this is going well.' Roxanne sucked air through her teeth and sat down at the head of the breakfast table, bold and steady. The others all now stood around the table like they'd been stupefied, watching her tuck into a pain au chocolat.

'What did you expect, Rox?' Greg looked angry. Reclaiming control of the situation, he sat down opposite Roxanne. If this was a game of chess, here were the king and queen.

'She can't still be mad about Callum,' Roxanne said through a mouthful of pastry. 'That was *years* ago.'

Ryan joined them. *I'm probably a knight*, he decided. 'Oh, come on, Rox, it was only last May.'

'And I feel really bad about it, I do,' Rox said, 'but it's all just high-school stuff. It was nothing then. It's even less now.'

The muscles in Greg's jaw tightened. They fought like cat and dog, but Ryan knew that under all the bravado and teasing he truly loved his sister. 'Alisha was heartbroken.'

'I've said I'm sorry about sixteen million times, Greg. P.S. you are looking hot.'

Greg was caught completely off guard and blushed rose pink. Ryan hid a smile at Roxanne's audacity. He snuck a glance at Erin and saw the first hint of negativity on her face. Her right eyebrow twitched.

'Well, thanks, but that's not the point, Rox,' Greg muttered.

Roxanne sighed, throwing her head back. 'Can we not do the big post-mortem? I'm here now. I left my hostel at, like, six. I thought you all knew I was coming or I would have never ever, ever come!'

Greg threw Katie a deathly look.

'I totally forgot. It's my fault,' she said, still looking flustered.

'Brilliant.' He shoved an entire croissant into his mouth.

'Oh, Greg,' Roxanne giggled. 'I'm meant to be meeting a

friend in Paris in a couple of days – I'll be out of your hair before you know it. Am I OK to crash for a night or two?'

'Of course,' said Katie, who seemed to be grovelling.

'I'll go in with Ryan,' Ben said quietly. 'Rox can take the sofa-bed.'

'I, for one, am fine with those sleeping arrangements.' Ryan gave a cheeky wink, knowing Ben would get the joke. He and Ben had gone top-and-tail since first school. Ben took up a lot of room, but at least he didn't snore. Ryan's joke went some way to lighten the mood.

Roxanne smiled. 'Do you think I should go talk to Alisha?'

'No!' Ryan, Katie and Greg all exclaimed, Greg almost choking on his breakfast.

'I'll go.' Katie held up her hand to stop Roxanne from leaving the table. 'You know Alisha – she needs to let off steam. It'll be fine.' Katie headed for the bedrooms and Erin followed.

Ryan stayed where he was, eager to hear about Roxanne's World Exploits Tour, but secretly wishing he could be a fly on that bedroom wall. Alisha had never claimed her revenge over Callum. Ryan suspected she was far from finished.

SCENE 11 – ALISHA

A lisha pulled her suitcase out from under the bed. She flung open the lid and started throwing clothes from the wardrobe into the case. Wire hangers pinged off the rail and clattered to the tiles.

And then she stopped.

This was insane. She was acting like a crazy soap-opera person.

She plonked onto the bed with a thud, bouncing up and down a couple of times. Her rage-filled mood swings were getting fewer and further between, but when they hit it was like a hurricane in her head. On the news you saw those swirling, vivid weather fronts sweep over an island. It felt like that but, as with any tropical storm, they always blew over eventually.

Roxanne, though. She was *such* a bitch. Normally that would be a terrible thing to say but, in this case, Alisha felt, it was merely stating legitimate fact.

There was a timid tap on the bedroom door.

'Who is it?'

'It's Katie and Erin,' Katie called.

Alisha paused. She didn't want them to see her looking demented, but a quick self-scan indicated the storm had passed. 'OK, come in.'

Katie entered the room looking a lot like a lion tamer entering a circus ring. 'Are you OK?'

'No.' Alisha flopped back on the bed.

'Alisha, I'm so sorry. When I spoke to Rox on Facebook I never thought for a second she'd actually turn up.'

'You invited her?' Ooh, the cyclone was circling again.

'She was in Morocco. I thought we were safe. I guess I felt guilty because I knew she'd find out about the trip somehow and feel left out.'

'Oh, my God, is that bitch for real?' Erin asked, checking they were out of earshot. Alisha couldn't stifle a laugh – she hadn't expected that from Erin at all.

Katie sighed. 'I understand this is a bit of a reach but, once you get to know her, she's really lovely.'

Alisha bit her tongue long enough to consider the fact that for a long time she and Roxanne had been as thick as thieves. Roxanne had this thing, this *spotlight*, and when she turned it on you, you felt like a star – invincible and special. But then Rox had worked her magic on Callum . . . God, when would she stop being angry about that?

Erin didn't seem convinced. 'I don't know, Katie. I mean, that was all a bit dramatic, wasn't it? The big entrance and all that.'

'That's pretty much her style. I guess she's a little . . . high maintenance.'

'You can say that again.' Alisha grimaced.

Katie sat on the edge of the bed, rubbing Alisha's calf in a comforting way. Erin perched on the chair, saying nothing more, but lending moral support.

'You really need to have a word with your guilt complex, Grant.' Alisha sat up, rubbing her eyes.

'I know, I'm an idiot!' Katie laughed. 'Do you really think I would have deliberately put you two in the same room?'

Alisha managed a half-smile. 'No. God, I could kill you, though. I'll kill her, *then* you!'

'What did she do?' Erin asked the inevitable question.

'She stole my boyfriend!' Alisha blurted out, well aware of how ridiculous that sounded.

'Alisha Cole . . .' Katie warned.

'OK, whatever. My boyfriend, Callum, dumped me and then, about twenty minutes later, he was with her.'

Erin nodded sagely. 'Oh, I see.'

'Yeah, pretty suspicious, right?'

Katie gave her a surprisingly good shoulder rub, massaging the Roxanne-shaped knot under her collar bone. 'We don't know if there was any overlap, Alisha. Rox swears there wasn't.'

'I don't care,' Alisha said. 'It's like there are rules – you don't wear red and purple together; eyes or lips; tits out or legs out; *you don't sleep with your mates' exes!*'

'They *are* very simple rules,' agreed Erin.

Katie moved on to her neck, massaging the space under her ears. It was bliss. 'Alisha, I am going to say something, and you have to promise not to punch me, OK?'

Alisha frowned. 'I'm not promising.'

'Callum is hardly blameless in all this. He knew you and Rox were friends. Let's have just a little female solidarity, please.'

Alisha sighed. She had read *How To Be a Woman* twice, but girls like Rox Dent made sisterhood hard. 'You know what it is? You know why I really wanna rip her eyes out?'

'I really didn't need that image, but go on,' Katie said.

'We were there for her, man. All that crap she went through and we were there for her.' Alisha turned to Erin. 'There was

71

this big sad story – her mum died of cancer and then her dad died, like, a year later.'

'In a freak scaffolding collapse,' Katie added with a grimace. 'It was awful, like something from *Final Destination*.'

'So, anyway,' Alisha went on, 'Rox came to live with her uncle in Telscombe Cliffs. She was an orphan, and even though she was this massive slut—'

'Alisha!'

'Sorry. Even though half the school hated her, we properly looked out for that girl. And this is what you get in return – one thieved boyfriend, no waiting.'

Katie sighed. 'What do you want me to do? She's just said she's only staying for a couple of days. Do you think you can cope? It's totally your call, my love. One word from you and I'll send her packing.'

Alisha thought for a second. 'You know what? I'm gonna be the bigger person. I mean Callum Granger is such a loser anyway, they actually deserve each other. I'll be mature and cool and sophisticated. Three things Roxanne Dent is not.'

'You show her who's boss,' Erin smiled.

'Thanks, you two, I feel less mental now.' Alisha rolled off the mattress and brushed herself down. 'Right. I'm gonna go find out if that shady bitch is still shagging my ex. Coming?'

SCENE 12 – RYAN

The sand was red hot under his feet. It was almost too intense to bear, burning like hot coals. Ryan had two choices – run forward to the cooler sand near the surf, or go back to the villa and get some flip-flops. As he was carrying one end of a pool lounger, he opted for option A and kept going.

'Christ, this sand is hot!' he yelped at Roxanne, who held the other end.

'Run for it!' Roxanne squealed with a giggle, and he was reminded that once upon a time it had all been fun and games. In TV terms, Roxanne had been introduced in the third season to spice up flagging ratings. She was a stunning blonde with a hedonistic streak to rival Alisha's. That was sort of the problem – perhaps the two girls had been too similar, trying to occupy the same niche like red and grey squirrels. And look how well that had worked out for the red squirrel.

Unlike Alisha though, Rox was, and always had been, selfish. A ride on the Rox Train was sure to be the night of your life, but it was always rolling in the direction she wanted to head.

Looking at her now, Ryan could only hope her travels abroad had matured her. 'Is this a good spot, do you reckon?' he asked.

'Yeah, it'll work. Ryan, you should have seen the beaches in Thailand. They are, like, seriously swoon-worthy.' For a moment her eyes misted over. 'I missed you this year.' She seemed genuine.

'Yeah. It's been a funny old year,' he replied, also honestly.

Just like that, the sentimentality left her, drifting away like the wisps of cotton-wool cloud overhead. Rox smiled. 'Oh, let's not get all "Camp Boo-Hoo"!'

There was the Rox Ryan remembered. He looked up to see Alisha marching down the stone steps with purpose, making a beeline for them. He lowered the lounger, wishing he had a dart gun like a safari ranger – he might need to use it on one or both of his friends. 'Rox, Alisha's coming . . .'

'Good. We should clear the air.'

Ryan fixed her in a steel-trap glare. 'Roxanne Dent, I want you to play nice.'

'I always do,' she said with mock innocence. She perched herself on the lounger and waited for her rival with bored nonchalance, as if she were freaking Cleopatra.

Alisha reached their position. Behind her, Greg and Ben carried another lounger, while Erin held a cooler. Katie trotted beside Alisha, struggling to keep up. Roxanne didn't stand to greet her foe. She reclined on the lounger. If she was scared of Alisha, her body language didn't give that impression.

Alisha stood over her, casting a shadow. 'I'm sorry about that. I lost it.' For once, Ryan was happy to stand back and be a passive viewer. This scene had been a long time coming: Alisha vs Rox – The Showdown.

Roxanne shielded her eyes with one hand. 'It's OK. I thought you knew I was coming.' Next to Alisha, Katie winced.

Alisha threw down her beach towel and sat on it. Katie

sat alongside, lending moral support. Ryan stood in the surf, cooling his feet.

Alisha finally spoke. 'I know. I'm not happy, though, Rox.'

'Look. I handled things really badly but it all feels like a hundred years ago. Can we move on, Lish?' Roxanne tossed her artfully tousled waves over her head. 'I missed you guys. If I've learned one thing on my travels, it's this: boys come and go, but friends are forever.'

Spoken like a true boyfriend-stealer, thought Ryan. There was something odd about Roxanne's delivery – it was oddly fake and stagey, even for her.

Alisha took a deep breath. 'What about Cal? Did he . . . come and go?'

Roxanne giggled. 'Ha! Yeah. Things fell apart as soon as we got to Thailand. We just didn't get on. I went off to Goa and left him there. I think he was planning on going to Sydney.'

Ben and Greg caught up, dropping the last of the loungers onto the sand.

'You OK, Lish?' Greg, protective as ever, cast a wary eye over the conversation.

'Yeah,' Alisha said. Even in the sweltering sun, her expression remained ice-cold. Far from impressed, she looked up at Roxanne with wide, hurt eyes. 'So it was all for nothing then? He left me for you and then you dumped him?'

Roxanne made an overly horrified face, the result grossly disingenuous. 'Oh, no! Not at *all*!'

Katie took Alisha's hand (possibly as a subtle form of restraint). 'Roxanne, I'm not taking sides, I'm really not, but that's what it sounds like,' she said.

'You know the real shame about the whole thing?' Roxanne said, lying on the lounger with her back perfectly arched to show off all her assets. Her flawless, toned body almost glowed under the sun. Her bikini was little more than dental floss. Even Ryan could appreciate how smoking hot she was. 'If there had been more of a gap between us, it wouldn't have been a big deal,' she finished.

Ryan bit his lip to prevent himself laughing aloud and heard Katie make a quiet huffing noise under her breath. He highly doubted Roxanne was right about that.

She went on. 'But the fact is, Lish, you *know* you and Callum were on the rocks before he even met me.'

That was true, but Alisha had been the last person to see it coming – as is often the way with break-ups.

'OK. Got ya,' Alisha said with icy calm.

'I think you're being really cool with this, Alisha. I so hope we can be friends again, don't you?'

Alisha stood up. 'Roxanne. I'd *love* for us to be friends again.' Then she leaned in and gave Roxanne a glorious OTT kiss on the mouth.

Roxanne's eyes widened in shock and Ryan stifled a giggle; his respect for Alisha Cole had just shot through the roof.

Alisha pulled back and grabbed a snorkel set from her beach bag. 'Right. If my new bestie will excuse me, I'm gonna go swimming. There aren't sharks out here, are there?'

'Not in the water,' Ryan said with a sly smile.

'Yes, there are,' Roxanne said, apparently failing to pick up on his jibe. 'This is the Atlantic coast and it's the height of summer. There are sharks everywhere.'

Ryan couldn't help but wonder whether *she* was referring to the ones in the sea.

With Alisha in the water, the atmosphere cleared. Frankly, it was too hot to be angry. The midday sun beat down and lethargy fell over them all. As Ryan sunned himself, Katie hid under a beach umbrella, shifting her lounger to follow the shade every fifteen minutes like a vampire with OCD.

'Dear Lord, this is so dull!' Katie exclaimed, throwing aside her course text. '*The Role of the Novel in Bourgeois Ideology*. Kill me now.'

Ryan grinned up at her from his towel. 'There's a copy of *Heat* in my bag upstairs.'

She rolled her eyes. 'That's going from one extreme to the other, isn't it?'

Ben had resolved to keep himself busy, or so it seemed. He was affable and polite to Roxanne, but wouldn't engage with her either. He'd wheeled the portable barbecue down and now fatty burger smoke billowed across the beach. He was quite the pyromaniac this week.

Greg and Erin, bless them, had taken on a time-honoured project – namely, Digging a Massive Hole. Ryan had to admit, it was pretty impressive – only the tops of their heads now poked out above ground level. The goal, as ever, was to see how far you could dig before hitting water. It kept them quiet.

Eventually, Alisha emerged from the sea, every inch the Bond girl in her bikini. Water ran off her enviable curves and Ryan wasn't the only one who noticed. Even through the spiral of smoke twirling from the barbecue, Ben couldn't take his eyes off her. Ooh, that was interesting. Instinctively, Ryan looked at Katie to see if *she'd* seen Ben gawping, but she was waving her phone around searching for a signal and didn't seem to have noticed.

'I thought I could smell food,' Alisha called from the surf.

'Grub's up!' Ben replied, blushing.

They helped themselves to burgers and salad, ketchup and

mustard and formed a picnic circle on a beach mat. Roxanne and Alisha kept their distance, but it was a relatively civilised lunch.

'So what's the plan, Rox?' Ryan asked through a mouthful of burger. 'What are you doing next year?'

'Oh, God knows. I missed all the UCAS deadlines. I'll probably go back to Telscombe Cliffs for a year.'

'Oh, brilliant,' Alisha muttered under her breath.

'My uncle's bought this massive new house. He says I can help him renovate it. I quite like the idea of that instead of uni – sort of property-developer-type stuff.'

'Sounds good,' Ryan replied.

'I don't wanna stop travelling really, but I'm running out of money.'

'Bummer,' said Greg. He opened his cool box, which was filled with stub bottles of beer. 'It's after lunch. That's beer o'clock, right?'

'Absolutely!' Ben grabbed a bottle. 'It's happy hour somewhere.'

'Do you know what we should do?' Roxanne squealed. 'We should play a drinking game!'

'No,' Katie groaned. 'I'm not even drinking.'

'Oh, go on! It'll be fun! You can just drink your Coke.'

'I'm in,' Alisha said. Ryan suspected there was no way Alisha was going to back down to Rox. Anything Rox could do, she could do better.

'Awesome. Does everyone know how to play I Have Never?' Another groan rippled around the circle. Only Erin shook her head. 'It's easy,' Roxanne told her. 'You take it in turns to say something you've never done. If someone else *has* done what you've said, they have to take a drink. It's hilarious!'

'OK,' Erin said. 'So, like, I have never been skiing?'

'Yes! Everyone who *has* been skiing takes a drink!' Roxanne said.

Ryan took a swig of ice-cool beer, condensation trickling over his fingers. Alisha, Greg and Ben all took a mouthful of whatever they were drinking, too.

'But it's much more fun if you go a little more hardcore than skiing,' Roxanne added.

Ryan sat forward. Roxanne Dent could try as hard as she liked, but *he* was head of entertainment this week. 'OK, I'll go first,' he said. 'I have never snogged a girl.'

Ben, Greg, Erin, Alisha and Roxanne all took a drink. Only Katie failed to drink. 'Oh, wow!' she exclaimed. 'How lame am I? And that's not even true, Ry; you and Janey kissed.'

Ryan laughed. He and Janey had 'dated' in the way that thirteen-year-olds 'date' – namely he'd bought her a McDonald's and taken her to see *Transformers*. They'd even had a snog in her bedroom; Janey had turned Radio One up to full volume to mask the sound of their lips smacking, lest her dad hear them and go on the warpath. Even then he'd known, on a fundamental level, that girls, for all their sweetness and softness, just didn't hit him where it counted. 'So sue me, I lied!'

'When did *you* snog a girl?' Greg turned to Erin.

'Wouldn't you like to know?' Erin winked.

'I snogged *her*.' Alisha jabbed a finger at Roxanne, unable to keep a smile off her face.

'Oh, God, that under-eighteens club in Brighton, I remember. Shameful!' Roxanne laughed.

'Nothing like a bit of faux lesbianism for the *lads*.' Ryan emphasised the last word as if it had a Z in it. 'So predictable.'

'In that case,' Ben said. 'I have never snogged a boy.'

Everyone but Ben and Greg drank.

'That was a little easy, don't you think?' Katie smiled.

'I just wanted to see you all drink,' Ben replied with a grin.

'You should give it a whirl, you might like it.' Ryan waggled his tongue in Ben's direction. Ben flicked him on the forehead. 'Ow!'

Roxanne leaned forward, an odd expression on her face. Ryan couldn't quite read it, but, if pushed, he'd have to say she looked *self-satisfied*. What was her game? Katie and Alisha weren't even drinking alcohol, so the game seemed a bit pointless – unless she wanted to find out something. 'OK. I have a juicy one,' she said. 'I have never made a kinky little video.'

Oh, the clever little witch. Ryan didn't say anything and certainly didn't take a drink; he was admitting nothing. He looked around the circle. That had been a little more risqué than anyone had been expecting. There were a few nervous giggles but no one drank.

'Really?' Roxanne said.

Deny everything. While there was still a possibility that this was just a wacky party game, he wasn't confirming a thing. It *could* be a coincidence that Roxanne had mentioned vids. 'I've texted some pretty choice photos – does that count?' Ryan asked, testing the water.

'You know,' Roxanne began in a sing-song voice, ignoring Ryan, 'this game only works if everyone tells the truth.'

The gang shared confused glances. Ryan put his acting skills to the test, playing the part of *confused innocent*.

'What do you mean?' Ben asked.

'Well, I know for a fact that at least one of you is lying,' Roxanne said flatly.

'And *how* do you know this *for a fact*?' Greg did a pretty good Rox impression.

'Because I've seen it.' Roxanne had a wicked glint in her eye. *This* was the relish on her burger.

'No way!' Ryan exclaimed, almost blowing his cover. Was she really going to expose him? In front of everyone? She wouldn't dare . . . would she? He fought to keep his cool.

'I have!'

'So who was it then?' Greg asked.

'I don't think it's my place to say. Apparently, the subject doesn't want anyone to know about it. Shame. It was pretty hot.'

Ryan knew full well how hot it had been, but that wasn't the point. *If* Roxanne *had* seen it . . . oh, God, it didn't bear thinking about. Maybe it wasn't even *that* video she was referring to. Call him an insane optimist but maybe Katie and Ben had had a video moment back in the day. Yeah, fat chance.

'Are you sure?' Ben demanded. 'Are you sure it wasn't just a porn look-a-like?'

Roxanne laughed. 'No. It was the Real McCoy.'

Alisha looked sceptical. 'And how have you seen it? Were you in it, too? That wouldn't be a massive surprise.'

Roxanne brushed off the dig. 'Well, that's the thing with committing stuff to a camera phone: these things tend to get about. Personally, I'd never be dumb enough to leave evidence lying around.'

There was a moment's silence. 'OK, this is a bit weird,' Ben said, visibly cringing. 'I don't need to think about my mates in the buff. It's a bit creepy, Rox. How about, I have never wet myself in public?'

Thank God for Ben Murdoch. Ryan could have hugged him for changing the subject.

Greg took a big drink. 'Cheers mate!' Nervous laughter ran

round the group, everyone relieved at the reminder of Greg's primary-school incident.

Ryan was still preoccupied with the video. He could only pray he hadn't flushed beetroot-red. *How? How had Rox seen it? When? Where? HOW?* He had gone to great lengths to make sure that video didn't exist.

The game carried on, as did the satisfied look on Roxanne's face. She *was* the cat among the pigeons, never mind the person who put the cat there.

Ryan sat on his hands to stop them from shaking. He dare not even look in Roxanne's direction; if she caught his eye it was all over. He'd never been on the receiving end of her stirring until this point, but now he knew exactly how Alisha felt: burning, white-hot hatred.

SCENE 13 – RYAN

It was so weird. Ryan had searched high and low, but he couldn't find the scarecrow mask anywhere. Greg had denied bringing it, which didn't make any sense. If it weren't for the fact that Ben had seen it as well, Ryan would have assumed he'd dreamed the whole encounter. He didn't know why it was bothering him so much, but why wouldn't anyone admit to bringing it? And where was the bloody thing, now? He'd left it on the table, but it was no longer there. In a TV drama, this would *definitely* be relevant somehow.

Ryan had come in from the sun to find the horrid thing gone from the dining table and, even worse, he was unable to recall if it had been there over breakfast. The missing mask bugged him and he couldn't resist raising it with the group. No one had seen it and, once again, Ben denied bringing it, even though it had been in his bag.

Ryan spent the rest of the afternoon looking under plates and magazines with no success. Now, at sunset, Ryan gazed out of his bedroom window as the sea reflected the purple and tangerine stripes of the sky. It was beautiful. You didn't get views like that in Manchester.

When Erin called them all for dinner, he gave up looking with a sigh and joined the others. After the second day of uninterrupted sunshine, Greg and Alisha were more tanned than ever, Ben's forehead looked a little red while Katie, of course, was still pale and interesting. Ryan was quietly satisfied with his bronze glow. It suited him – he could easily audition for an Australian soap, now, with his gold skin and surfer's curls. They noisily settled themselves at the table, Ryan choosing to sit next to Katie.

Roxanne made a late entrance. Ryan swallowed his anger and battled to maintain a poker face. Tonight she wore a distressed grey dress that, on anyone else, would have looked like it had come out of the bin, but on Roxanne looked rock and roll. She'd managed to pull off the same look with her hair too: effortless pillow-damaged waves.

That was the thing with Rox. Ryan had never known someone to be so self-consciously sexy, including himself (and he thought he was mighty fine). Boys ate it up with a spoon. She knew full well she was sexy, but always followed it with a chaser of *Who, little ol' me?* It was impressive. If *he* tried that with guys, he'd get a black eye for his efforts. Ryan decided if straight boys were dumb enough to fall for it, it was their problem.

Roxanne's wrist caught Ryan's eye. She was wearing a charm bracelet he recognised at once. It was Katie's – the one Ben had got her on their first anniversary. Ryan had helped Ben design it, although, he had to hand it to his friend, he had great taste. Ben Murdoch made a devastatingly thoughtful boyfriend. The charms were a K, A, T, I and E (obviously); a tiny silver copy of *Jane Eyre*; a pair of sneakers to reflect their first date at Foot Locker; a heart made out of her birthstone and a spaniel (apparently he was like the puppy she'd never had).

Katie had noticed, too. She looked embarrassed, but said nothing. Ryan wondered how bold you'd have to be to wear someone else's charm bracelet. Why had Rox *really* come here? To humiliate him? Why bother – he hadn't crossed Roxanne as far as he knew. No. He sensed there was something bigger brewing just out of sight and, not for the first time, he felt entirely at the whim of the great executive producers in the sky.

Roxanne picked up on Katie's awkwardness. 'Oh, you don't mind, do you? I saw it on your dresser.'

'No, of course not,' Katie replied, but it looked very much as though she did mind.

'Thanks. I thought it went well with my ensemble!'

Ryan looked at Alisha, certain a 'you're used to taking things that aren't yours' comment was about to be forthcoming, but, although she glowered, Alisha kept her mouth shut. Her self-control had improved.

Dinner was less successful under Greg and Erin's watch. Perhaps they really did eat at Nando's every night. If the fish was a little soggy, the vegetables were sponge-like. Still, they were all ravenous and plates were cleared.

Small talk ping-ponged across the table. Tonight was cooler, so they ate inside but kept the patio doors wide open. Thankfully, Roxanne mostly looked on in silence, allowing Ryan to take centre stage. He was determined to show her that her spiteful little game on the beach hadn't scared him. Tonight's topic of conversation was how crazy actors are, and the lengths they go to for roles.

'It's insane!' Ryan concluded. 'I mean, this one girl, Freya, she eats one cracker a day. And don't even get me started on my roommate. He has chicken and cabbage every single night of the week. I mean, he looks great . . . but the smell . . .'

'Nothing tastes as good as skinny feels!' Erin giggled.

'That's utter rubbish,' Alisha said. 'Only some cotton-wool-eating psychopath could think that.'

'I know a ballet dancer who actually does eat cotton wool,' Ryan said, nodding like the oracle of gossip.

'You can't live like that.' Greg played with the rim of his beer bottle. 'You gotta put the fuel in if you want the machine to go.'

Ben chuckled next to him. 'Dude, the fact you just called your body a machine is as depressing as eating cotton wool.'

The table laughed. Ryan was finally feeling relaxed.

A knife tapped on the side of a wine glass. It was Roxanne. She was making a snatch for his microphone. What an attention whore! The table went quiet.

'I'd like to say something . . .'

'There's a surprise,' Alisha muttered.

Roxanne pretended not to hear. She smiled a saccharine smile. 'I just want to say, thank you for having me. Thank you, Katie, for inviting me.'

Katie tucked her hair behind her ear and smiled demurely. 'That's OK.'

The penny dropped in Ryan's head. Roxanne hadn't been sitting quietly. She'd been *waiting for her moment*. His heart started to pound.

'You all obviously hate my guts,' Roxanne continued, 'but they say your school friends are the ones you keep for the rest of your life, and I just think you guys are the *best*. It's so lovely to see you all laughing and joking like nothing happened.' Her voice was drenched in sarcasm.

'Rox, is this going somewhere?' Greg asked as politely as he could.

'I just thought it would be nice to raise a toast to Janey Bradshaw.'

A groan ran around the table.

'You're too late, Rox.' Ryan shot her a dirty look. 'We did the big Janey talk last night.'

Roxanne laughed. A proper, she-found-all-this-hysterical laugh. 'Yeah, right.'

'Yes,' Katie said with some conviction. 'Everything's out in the open.'

'Oh, really? So you admitted it then?'

'Admitted what?' Alisha spat. 'There's nothing to admit.'

'Oh, Alisha, honey, don't tell me you believed that whole "suicide" story? I thought even you had more common sense than that.'

The table became a merry-go-round, spinning around Ryan. He couldn't believe what he was hearing. Roxanne was airing his innermost thoughts. At once he felt validated that he wasn't alone in his suspicions, and gutted that Roxanne was ruining the party just as he had been starting to enjoy himself.

This was the last straw for Ben. 'You know, I've bitten my tongue all day, but I've had enough of your sh—'

But Roxanne cut him off mid-sentence. 'Didn't they tell you, Erin? One of them killed Janey.'

SCENE 13 (CONT.)

You'd have to have a break there, Ryan thought. If it was TV, that'd be the end of the episode, or, at the very least, a commercial break. He didn't know whether to kill Roxanne or shake her hand. This was kind of what he'd been planning to say at the beginning of the week, so she'd saved him the embarrassment, but she'd also stolen his limelight. Again.

There was a chorus of disapproval but, before that, almost undetectable to an outsider but noticeable to Ryan, was a split second of horror. It flashed across every one of their faces. That, thought Ryan, could be interpreted in two ways: most of them were probably simply appalled at what Rox had said, but maybe one of them was terrified that they'd just been outed as a killer. What if Ryan's suspicions had been right all along? What if one of them had . . .

'You know what, Rox,' Greg laughed it off, interrupting Ryan's thoughts. 'You're such an attention seeker!'

'It's all shock tactics with you,' Ben agreed, glaring up at her from under his heavy brows.

'It is a bit mental, Rox,' Ryan said almost pityingly. Her speech, while nicely dramatic, did verge on cringeworthy. His confrontation would have had much more finesse.

'Like, seriously? Do people not look at you enough, Roxanne? Do you want your own reality show or something?'

Alisha asked. She seemed to be finding this quite funny.

Roxanne didn't even flinch. She repelled the comments like oil on water. 'Did I want to shock? Absolutely. I wanted an honest reaction. I wanted to see your guilty little faces.'

Katie closed her eyes for a moment like she was counting to five to temper her thoughts. 'Rox,' she said, ever the voice of reason. 'This is insane. We didn't kill Janey. We didn't.'

'Actually, one of you did,' Rox told her emphatically.

'Give it a rest!' Ben slammed his knife onto the table. Plates jumped. Ryan had never seen Ben like this. It unnerved him – but it was kinda sexy. Ben did brooding well.

Roxanne tucked her hair behind her ear. 'Let's talk about that night, shall we?'

'I'm not listening to this.' Greg pushed his chair away from the table.

'You'll sit down, Greg.' Roxanne's tone didn't give the option of refusal. 'I've got a few more *I Have Nevers* that you don't wanna miss.'

Greg shot her a venomous glance but did as instructed. Ryan had forgotten how fiery Greg's temper could be; now he noticed how he balled his fists until the knuckles were white before lowering himself back into his chair.

Roxanne reclined in her seat, making sure her audience was ready for the show. Ryan hadn't seen her like this before, and he had to admit he was impressed. This took some guts. 'Don't any of you think it's a little odd that there was no suicide note?' Rox asked.

It was super odd, no doubt about it. The question hung over the table. Ben finally answered as he peeled the label off his bottle of beer, trying to look uninterested. 'Rox, we *know* why there wasn't a note. Janey went to the cliff angry and drunk. I don't think she was thinking straight, do you?'

Roxanne paused, making the most of her *coup de théâtre*. 'Yes, she was drunk. Yes, she was angry. But this is *Janey Bradshaw* we're talking about. Let's say for a second that she did want to kill herself . . . it would have been to make you feel guilty and she would have had the last word. She'd have wanted *you* to suffer that for eternity.' Rox pointed an elegant finger at Ben. 'But, more than that, what about her poor mum and dad? What about her place at Warwick? What about her little brother? Janey had a lot to live for. In fact, I don't think Janey would have jumped at all. I think she'd have totally bottled it.'

'Well, obviously, she didn't.' Alisha rolled her eyes.

'It's not obvious to me,' said Rox. 'I think she was pushed.'

'What?' Ben tried to laugh it off, but didn't quite convince. 'Roxanne, this is a new kind of crazy. Are you on meth or something?'

'I have proof.'

That shut everyone up. In fact, it felt as though everything was on pause. It was so quiet, Ryan could hear the clock ticking out the seconds on the upstairs landing. It ticked in time with the cogs in his brain. He'd been right. He'd been right this whole year. Someone *had* killed Janey. *One of them.*

'Well, who did it then?' It was Erin. It was the first time she'd volunteered to speak since Rox had started her little announcement. Her face was grim, her eyes determined. 'You know, I don't even know you but, where I come from, you don't turn up at other people's homes and start accusing people of murder.'

Roxanne rolled her eyes. 'Lighten up, honey. You wanna hear the way they talk about me. That's what always pissed me off.' She glared round at them all. 'When I first moved to Telscombe Cliffs, I wondered how I was ever going to be as good as you lot. You were like these perfect, gorgeous *Abercrombie & Fitch* people. Then I realised you were as bad as everyone else – just with bigger, faker smiles.'

'Tell us, then, if you know. Who did it?' Erin demanded.

Roxanne grinned. 'That's the thing, *Erin*.' She said the name as if it were a punchline. 'You think you know this lot? You don't. There are some pretty big secrets flying around. You're only seeing what they want you to see, and here's a bombshell – Janey wasn't by herself on the cliffs. One of them was with her.'

'For God's sake, Rox, who was it?' Katie snapped, her voice high-pitched and strangled.

'What's wrong, Katie? Guilty conscience?' Roxanne asked.

'Leave her out of this,' Ben warned.

'She's full of crap,' Ryan observed. There was a key problem with her claim to have evidence. He sat back, a triumphant look on his face. 'If you really had proof that one of us had pushed Janey off a cliff, you'd have gone to the police last year.'

'Oh, very good, detective, you found me out. Actually, Ryan, I've been doing my own digging this year. At first I thought Janey had jumped, but there was this little niggle at the back of my head that wouldn't go away, so I did some research. I discovered a few things and I wasn't so sure any more.'

Ryan knew all about that little niggle. 'What things?' he prompted.

'Well, that's the problem – if I tell you, you won't pay me.'

The table exploded. There were some expletives, but mostly laughter. In that moment, Ryan realised that this was all scripted. Roxanne must have been working on it for months. He was almost in awe, it was so audacious. Every subtle pout and raised eyebrow had been practised in front of the mirror. He wasn't the only one living life in a TV show. Alongside *Ryan: Acting Up*, Rox had her own spin-off: *Roxanne's Revenge*. Tragically, hers probably got higher ratings.

'I must be dreaming,' Katie muttered, downing her wine.

'You are out of your tree!' Greg laughed.

'Are you actually going to try to blackmail *students*?' Erin shook her head. 'We're skint!'

'Nice try.' Roxanne smiled. 'You might think I'm an idiot, but I've planned this very carefully. I was going to wait until we were all back in Telscombe Cliffs, but then Katie told me about this little holiday. It's perfect! We're away from everyone and I get you all to myself. Basically, travelling's not cheap. I ran out of money about a month ago, and working in bars is not my idea of fun. So here's the deal – you pay up or I take everything I've got to the police and the press.'

Cue more screaming and shouting around the table. The words rattled inside Ryan's skull. The rug had been yanked out from under him. This was a new low. Roxanne didn't even care about the *truth* or *justice* for Janey. She just wanted another year out. The girl really was Satan in an All Saints dress.

'Stop!' Katie cried, pleading with the table to calm down. 'Just stop! Roxanne, we don't have any money.'

'Yeah, right. This one plays Championship football,' Rox said, gesturing towards Greg. 'And, don't forget, I know your parents as well. None of you exactly *need* the student loans you took out, so you can start by sending them in my direction. Frankly, I think that's pretty generous; I could have asked for a lot more. I just want enough to get by.'

'Lucky us,' Alisha said.

'She's bluffing,' Ben put in. 'She hasn't got anything on us.'

That produced an even more dazzling smile from Roxanne. 'Oh, really, Benji, you know I have. With all the skeletons in the closet, I'm surprised any of you bitches has room for clothes! The police will have to reopen the case. And think of the press! Janey was a very pretty girl. She looked great on those front pages. Won't it sell even more papers if the beautiful girl turns out to have been *murdered* instead of killing herself? And your names will be all over it.'

A grim, grave silence followed. No one looked up from their empty plates. Ryan and, he guessed, the others, knew Roxanne was right. The police wouldn't be able to ignore new evidence and the papers would *love* it. Tilda Honey's prize-winning marrows had been getting too many column inches again.

'Think about the person sitting next to you. Do you know where they were when Janey went over that cliff?' Roxanne asked.

Ryan pondered that. They'd all told the police where they'd been that evening, but all of them had chunks of time where they'd been alone. Ryan remembered every detail of that night – the most minute details – but he didn't know what had happened to Janey. That was why his heart was now thundering in his ears – because he'd already lost countless hours of sleep over every single word Roxanne was saying.

'So that's it,' Roxanne concluded. 'You guys all hate me anyway, so I might as well make a bit of money out of what I know. I figure you can't hate me any *more*.'

'Oh, I don't know,' Alisha murmured. Her skin had turned a horrible shade of puce.

'You can't do this,' said Katie. 'It's blackmail. It's a crime.'

Roxanne properly laughed at that, her first unrehearsed

action in a while. 'Oh, I'm literally *begging* you to call the police. I can't wait to hear what they'll have to say when I show them what I've got.'

Greg seemed defeated; his head fell into his hands. 'I haven't got bundles of cash upstairs in a metal briefcase, Rox.' Ryan wondered whether, if he did, Greg would happily pay right now to make the problem go away.

'That's OK,' Rox said airily. 'There's a bank in Cádiz, I checked. I'll wait until you empty your accounts and then I'll go. You'll never see me again, and I'll give you back all your dirty laundry. Some of it's pretty juicy, actually.'

'Greg, what is she talking about?' Erin stroked his arm. 'What did you do?'

'Nothing! I didn't do anything!' he snapped, pulling his arm back. 'You better pray I don't see you again, Rox, or you are dead, I swear.'

'All I want is the money, honey.'

'You're not getting any money!' Ben shouted. He pushed away from the table and prowled the length of the terrace doors the way a tiger stalks his perimeter in a zoo.

'Well, then, let's see what happens when the shit hits the fan, Ben. Some of it's gonna stick!'

The room devolved into bright red chaos. Erin started to cry as Greg continued to ignore her. Ben and Roxanne hurled insults at each other over the table, with Ryan giving Ben a helping hand. Greg punched a fist into the wall, leaving a dent and bits of knuckle-flesh in the plaster. He cursed in pain, kissing his skinned hand.

Ryan couldn't have predicted what would happen next.

Katie sprang to her feet. With a cry, she flung her arm back and hurled her empty wine glass about an inch over Roxanne's head. The blonde screamed and ducked. The glass careered into the far wall, where it shattered, exploding into shards no bigger than dust.

'Everybody, *shut the* _____ *up!*' Katie didn't miss the word out, but Ryan knew it wouldn't be allowed on TV. He looked on in stunned silence with his mouth hanging open like a goldfish. Katie Grant so wasn't the swearing, glass-throwing type. 'Roxanne, I can't believe you've done this. We were friends.'

'Were we? You're lovely, Katie, don't get me wrong, but you were *assigned* to look after me on my first day. You only ever *tolerated* me.'

'That's not true. I defended you to people time and time again.'

'In that case, I'm sorry. I've always been terrible at making friends,' Rox told her. 'For some reason, girls just don't warm to me.'

Regret. Ryan saw it – there was a flicker of regret in Roxanne's eyes. She'd done well in her role as villainous bitch, but it wasn't real, it wasn't truly her. How could it be? Being one-dimensional is really hard because you have to shut off all the other parts of yourself. Ryan, at various times, had tried being cool, funny, sexy – and it never worked for long because, eventually, you get angry or morose or camp and you can't help it. As much as Roxanne wanted to be calculated and detached, she was still a human being and Ryan could only imagine how hard this whole scene was to pull off.

It didn't matter, though. She'd done it now.

Katie continued, 'Roxanne, we are *not* paying you. I've never heard anything so ridiculous in my life.'

'Then I'll go to the police.'

'Roxanne, please.'

'Sorry, Katie. Come too far, haven't I? Can't back out now.

95

It's way too late for that.' Roxanne swiped the last remaining bottle of wine from the centre of the table. 'I imagine you guys have a lot to discuss – namely, who's gonna drive to the bank – so I'm gonna take a walk on the beach.'

Six faces looked at her in gormless disbelief.

'I'll see myself out.' Roxanne sauntered through the double doors and onto the terrace.

No one said anything. There weren't words in the English language to describe what Ryan was feeling, so he could only imagine what the others were thinking.

Greg fell back onto the sofa. Erin hugged her arms to her body. Alisha stared at her wine glass.

'I suppose I should clear up the glass,' Katie said eventually, looking exhausted.

'I'll do it,' Erin offered and went to fetch the dustpan and brush.

Ryan looked at each of them in turn. The Jock. The Geek. The Good Girl. The Bad Girl. If Roxanne were to be believed, not only was one of them a killer, but now there was *proof*.

SCENE 14 – ALISHA

As Erin swept up the broken glass, a suffocating silence filled the room. It was unbearable – exactly like the four weeks during which Janey had been lost. Back then, it had felt like no one was allowed to speak, because *anything*, even the faintest whiff of mirth, might sound disrespectful to their missing friend.

Alisha couldn't stand it. She wanted to scream. She wanted to grab Katie by the shoulders, shake her and say, 'TOLD YOU SO' – she'd known right from the start that Roxanne was psychotic and no one had listened.

Well, Roxanne Dent could go to hell.

It was Ryan who broke the silence. 'So. One of us killed Janey. Bit of a shocker.'

Ben swore loudly. 'None of us killed Janey! She's making it up!'

Alisha flinched. She hated to see him so mad. It wasn't like Ben at all. 'How do you know? Were you there?' she asked.

'No!' he said at once. 'But . . . but . . .'

'She said she has proof.' Katie's face was paler than ever – pure chalk-white like the cliffs back home. 'One of us . . .'

'No way!' Greg barked. 'As if.'

'But what if it's true?' Ryan paced the lounge, hands on hips. 'Oh, come on – don't act like it hasn't crossed your minds before. The Janey situation was fishy long before she washed up in the marina.'

'Ryan!' Katie snapped. 'Don't. It's not funny.'

Greg now rose from the sofa, trying to wrest control from Ryan. 'Then who was it? We might as well get everything out in the open.'

Everyone started talking at once and Alisha covered her ears with her hands. She needed a drink the size of Belgium; she couldn't handle this.

'Well, of course you're all going to deny it,' Ryan said vehemently.

'Why would any of us want to kill Janey?' Katie protested.

It went on and on.

Alisha closed her eyes and imagined Roxanne right now, sitting on the beach sipping wine, laughing at the trail of road-kill she'd left in her wake. It didn't seem fair.

Her brother cursed loudly and threw his hands in the air. 'She's not getting a penny outta me. I'm not paying for something I didn't do.' With that he stormed out of the lounge, Erin hot on his heels.

'Oh, I guess that's the end of the discussion then.' Ryan helped himself to another beer.

'It is,' Ben agreed. 'No one's going to give Roxanne the money. It'd be basically admitting they were guilty.'

Alisha peeked out from behind her curls. 'Maybe . . . maybe in the morning we can talk her out of it.'

Ryan and Ben seemed to consider that.

'Maybe,' Ben muttered.

Katie was sitting hunched on the floor tiles, her back against the wall. 'This is all too much to take in. It was just meant to be a holiday, you know? It's turning into a total nightmare.' She pushed herself up. 'I'm going to bed.'

Head hanging, Katie shuffled out of the lounge.

'Will you make sure she's OK?' Ben asked Alisha, obviously worried about his ex or girlfriend or whatever she was these days.

'Sure.' Alisha followed Katie. That was her role – the supportive best friend – and she knew how to do her job well.

'This is unbelievable.' Alisha closed the door behind herself. Katie was already stretched out on the bed, her arm over her face. 'I mean, this is seriously like something off TV, right?' She crawled onto the foot of the bed and sat alongside her friend. 'Katie, are you OK?'

'No, Lish, I'm so far away from OK, it's not even in sight. Did that actually just happen?'

Katie looked in desperate need of cheering up. Alisha said, 'I think so, but we *could* all be hallucinating. I mean, Greg's fish was pretty rank.'

Katie sat up, now panda-eyed from smudged make-up. 'Go ahead. Say it.'

'Say what?'

'*Told you so* – about Roxanne.'

'The thought hadn't even crossed my mind,' Alisha lied. There was a knock at the door. 'Who is it?' Alisha called.

Ryan slipped in through the door. 'Don't think for a second that you two are leaving me out of the gossip. What's going on?'

Katie reached out to him. 'Can I have a Ryan-hug?'

'You may.' He obliged.

Alisha smiled. Ryan-hugs were the best: strong and muscular but without even a whiff of sexual chemistry.

'Better?' he asked.

'A million times better,' Katie said as Ryan joined them on the bed. 'Where's Ben?'

'He's doing the dishes. I don't think he wants to talk about it.'

'Well,' said Alisha, 'no prizes for guessing what we're talking about.'

'The crisis in Gaza? The political situation leading to the First World War?'

'Almost . . .' A half-smile crept back to Katie's face.

'Roxanne!' Alisha exclaimed. 'And the fact that she's totally effing lost the plot.'

They said nothing for a moment. Alisha looked between her two friends, wondering whether Roxanne had really been telling the truth. But the thought of either of her two closest friends pushing Janey Bradshaw off a cliff was plain stupid.

'What do you think she knows?' Ryan whispered.

Alisha sighed. 'Oh, come on. You don't buy what she said, do you?'

'I don't know.' Katie hugged her legs to her chest.

'I know there are things that . . . look *bad*,' Ryan said. 'Perhaps Janey didn't jump . . .'

Alisha tutted. 'For God's sake! No one thinks that.'

'Don't they?' Katie fiddled with a lock of hair, her fingers nervous. 'There were rumours, Alisha.'

'That was all just gossip. Katie, she jumped off a cliff! How many times are we going to have the same conversation? It was suicide. The police said so; the coroner said so; her parents said so.'

Katie slipped out of her dress and pulled her dad's old shirt over her head as pyjamas. 'But Roxanne has a point. I mean, I know *I* wasn't there, but what about Ben?'

Ryan laughed. 'Ben? Ben Murdoch? Are you crazy? He

wouldn't hurt a fly. In fact, if he saw two flies fighting, he'd break it up.'

'Well, I know it wasn't me, so that only leaves Greg,' Alisha said. 'And why would he kill Janey? I'm not sure he really knew she existed. You know what Greg's like – if it's not playing football or having sex with him, he's not interested!' The others chuckled agreement. Alisha shifted position on the bed, unable to get comfortable. She was tired, sticky, hot and bothered. The air vents were carrying voices all around the house and Erin's high-pitched interrogation of Greg was particularly audible.

'Roxanne's right about one thing, though,' Katie said. 'I mean, you knew Janey, do you really think she'd have killed herself?'

'I don't.' Ryan inspected a nail.

Alisha chewed her lip before shaking her curls. 'Not on a normal day, no. But she was so freaking mad, Katie. You didn't see her at the ball.' Alisha vividly remembered that night and she'd never seen Janey, actually, scratch that, she'd never seen *anyone*, so angry.

'What happened that night?' Katie asked.

'You *know* what happened,' Alisha told her. Although Katie had been too ill to go to the prom, Alisha had given her the highlights many times before she'd left for Norwich.

'No,' Katie said indignantly. 'I've heard about fifty different remixes, half of which were from people who weren't even there. I need the definitive version.'

Alisha snuggled in alongside Ryan. 'I don't know what I can say that hasn't already been said.'

'From the top, I want to know *everything*. And Ryan, I don't need the TV-movie version, just the facts. The last time I saw Janey was before I got sick. We both bought shoes. I remember, because I started feeling crappy while we were trying them on.'

Alisha took a deep breath before beginning. 'OK, from the top. It was the day of the prom. You were already ill. I met Janey in town; we got our hair done together . . .'

FLASHBACK – LAST YEAR (ALISHA)

It was almost seven o' clock when Alisha stumbled over her front lawn, narrowly avoiding falling into the water feature. Time had slipped away somehow. Alisha had lost about two hours – like one of those alien-abductee people. She thought it was probably best to creep in through the back door; there was a slim possibility that if she could get to her room, her parents might think she'd been there the whole time. Of course, that optimism was the drink talking. She was dead meat.

She didn't know where the time had gone. All afternoon she'd been in the salon with Janey. It was ironic – Janey had spent hours getting her hair curled, and Alisha had spent the afternoon getting hers straightened. It had all been going swimmingly until she'd got a text from Rich and Cleo, some guys from her art class, suggesting she come and meet them for a few warm-up drinks in the park. It was so sunny, she hadn't been able to say no.

And that was where she'd lost two hours. And now the floor felt like it had turned to treacle, or perhaps it was her legs. She knew she had to pull herself together and fast. It was almost time for the ball. You can't *arrive* at the ball wasted. What would Prince Charming make of that? Alisha stifled a hysterical giggle at the thought. She had to be sensible now or she'd be in BIG TROUBLE.

Alisha slipped through the back door, closing it as gently as she could. She cringed as it gave a mean-spirited creak. Thankfully, the washing machine was on, disguising some of her noise. There must be an equation for it – Ben would be able to work it out – like the more you try to be quiet when you're drunk, the noisier you are.

Some raucous game show was on in the lounge, indicating that at least one of her parents was home. It was Thursday night – was that one of Mum's Pilates nights? Alisha couldn't remember. Either way, she was down to her last warning about coming home drunk. But, the way she saw it, she was only going to be young once so she might as well make the most of it.

She made it past the door to the living room and started up the stairs. Years of coming in past curfew had taught her which stairs groaned when you stepped on them – the fourth and seventh – and she skipped these steps.

The staircase was lined with pictures of Greg: Greg and Dad playing football, Greg at the academy, Greg on the youth team, Greg in his Brighton kit. Alisha often thought that her mum and dad had somehow engineered having twins just in case Greg needed a kidney.

She managed to get all the way to the top step before tripping over her own feet. Balls. She froze. Nobody came rushing out to tell her off, so she darted for the cover of her room. She flicked the lights on and looked at her reflection in the mirror on her dressing table. All that time in the salon chair, and her hair was already curling in at the ends. She looked rough before the night had even started. Below the mirror was the photo that she couldn't bring herself to put away. You're supposed to burn photos of your ex ceremonially – watch the corners singe and curl before you let them drop into a convenient metal bin. She wasn't strong enough, though. Alisha sat on the edge of the bed and picked it up, repeating her strange new ritual.

She must be a masochist. Staring at a constant reminder of something she couldn't have. The picture showed her and Callum on the music trip to Berlin last September. His hair had been longer than ever back then, falling over his eyes like a sheepdog's. Both of them wore matching, beaming smiles. His arm was thrown casually around her shoulders while she rested her head against him. They looked so happy. *He* looked so happy. So how could he leave her for that bargain-bin Barbie?

Alisha didn't notice the shadow fall over the foot of her bed. 'What are you doing?'

She gasped, almost dropping the photo. 'God, Greg, can't you knock?'

'I said what are you doing? The limo's gonna be here in twenty minutes.'

'Well, then, piss off and let me get ready.'

Greg looked immaculate in his tux with the single diamante stud in his ear. She looked like something that a cat had coughed up. Good twin and bad twin.

'Are you drunk?' Greg demanded.

'Nooo!' she exclaimed in such a ludicrous manner, she could only be drunk.

'You're a mess.'

'Thanks for that.'

He caught sight of the photograph in her hands. 'Christ, you're a loser.'

From nowhere, a sob burst out of her mouth. It must have been waiting for the right moment to escape, and now it was free.

Greg huffed. 'Oh, don't start booing, woman.'

'I don't wanna go, Greg. *They'll* be there.'

'Of course they will. It's their leavers' ball too.'

Now the tears were out, they came readily, pouring down Alisha's cheeks. 'It's not fair.'

Her brother had run out of sympathy weeks back. He grabbed her wrists and yanked her off the bed.

'Ow!' she cried. He didn't let go. He dragged her out of her room and towards the bathroom. 'Let go, Greg. You're hurting me!'

'Good!' he tossed her into the bathroom, where she almost tumbled into the bath. This was the *real* Greg Cole – the one only she saw. 'You need to a get a grip so bad, Lish.'

'Shut up.'

'Oh, grow up. Callum didn't dump you for Roxanne. He dumped you because you're a frigging mental case. You're a pissed-up clown, Alisha. No one wants to shag a clown.'

She scrabbled around in her mind for any sort of a comeback, but all she could do was cry. It wasn't her fault. It *wasn't*. It was all Roxanne. If she hadn't arrived . . .

'Get your arse in the shower. If you're not ready, we're going without you.'

She hurled a bottle of shampoo at his head, but it only succeeded in splattering against the door as he slammed it behind him.

Alisha ran late, but Greg did wait. Teetering on skyscraper heels, Alisha trotted to the midnight-blue limo that waited at the end of their drive. She'd just about managed to rescue herself. She wore a structured, short bronze dress that made her skin almost glow. She'd thrown on as much make-up as she could and she'd hastily re-ironed her hair. She'd pass. If

Callum and Roxanne were there, she could at least show her face.

Alisha had never been in a limo before, but it turned out they were pretty tacky. The seats were arranged in a doughnut shape along the sides of the stretched section and were covered with pink Playboy Bunny cushions. A blue striplight flashed around the ceiling of the car as if it were a squat, low-brow nightclub on wheels. It was only missing a mirror ball.

Not hugely mobile in the dress, she sort of slotted herself into the back of the car. All the others were already there – except one. 'Where's Katie?'

'She's ill!' Janey pulled a sad face. 'I got a text saying she's been feeling worse and worse all day. Like proper flu or something.'

'She going to miss the ball?'

'Yep. She must be really sick, bless her.' Janey looked regal in her custom-made red gown. Alisha had seen it on a hanger, but that hadn't done it justice. The material flowed around Janey's body in crimson waves. It put Alisha's own high-street dress to shame.

'Ah, well,' Ryan said, handing Alisha a glass of fizzy wine. 'All the more for us. A toast to poorly Katie!'

They toasted. Greg threw her a sideways glance as she gulped back the wine. He wouldn't say anything in front of the others, though; that wasn't his style at all.

Ben grinned at her. 'Great dress, Lish. You look beautiful.'

A butterfly bomb exploded in her stomach. 'Aw, thanks, mate.' In a parallel universe she'd marry Ben Murdoch. She remembered the first time she'd met him at Ryan's bouncy-castle party, aged eight. If she'd had any sense she'd have put a ring on it then and there. But all those years he'd been her brother's best friend and Greg would have killed her if she'd made a move on Ben. Of course, when things are forbidden, it just makes them ten times sexier.

Fate had had other plans for them, anyway. Ben had got together with, first, Katie and then Janey (which, to be perfectly honest, Alisha had never really 'got' – they were such a mismatch), while she'd fallen for Callum. Look how far that had got her.

Alisha noticed a plastic bag by Ben's feet. 'What's in there?'

Ben and Greg shared a sly grin.

'What?' she repeated.

'We're gonna make a couple of stops before we get to school,' Greg told her.

'What are you up to?' Janey smiled, holding Ben's hand.

Greg pulled a box of eggs out of the bag for all to see. 'As it's our last day at Longview, well, except for results day, I thought it was time to settle some old scores.'

'It's prank week. It's traditional,' Ryan reminded her.

Janey snapped her hand out of Ben's. 'Oh, what are you doing? Why would we want to get into trouble now?'

'Relax! What are they gonna do? Expel us? We've graduated!'

'Benjamin!' She meant business. 'No!'

Greg laughed. 'Yeah, *Benjamin*, do as you're told.'

'We're on Ravel Drive,' Ryan announced.

'Driver,' Ben tapped the black glass partition behind him, 'can you slow down as we pass number twenty-four?'

The partition slid down. The driver was the brother of a guy on Greg's team. 'Remember,' he said, 'I don't know anything about this, yeah?'

'Dude, that's fine,' Ben replied. He grinned and slipped the driver a twenty.

'Whose house is it?' Alisha asked, excited now.

'Mr Wallis's.'

'Oh, he's such a pervert!' Alisha cried. 'He's always leching at Year Eleven girls.'

'*And* he failed my coursework because I was five minutes late handing it in,' Ben said. 'Payback time.'

The limo slowed to a crawl. 'Are you ready?' Greg opened the sunroof. He rested the egg box on the seat and took two eggs out. Ben also grabbed a couple. The pair squeezed through the sunroof, wobbling as the car continued to move.

Ryan pushed the button to lower the window. 'I gotta see this.'

Mr Wallis's house was an unassuming bungalow not far from where Alisha and Greg lived.

'Ready?' Greg shouted. 'Go!'

The missiles flew at the house. One cracked against the wall, another fell short on the garden path. The next hit the front door, but Ben's second egg really found its target with the lounge window. The egg shattered, but made a clang against the pane of glass. The noise seemed to echo down the entire street.

Both boys threw themselves to the floor of the limo. 'Drive, man, drive!'

Tyres screeched as the limo sped away and everyone fell about laughing. All except Janey, who wore an unimpressed pout. Alisha could hardly breathe. The eggs were pretty funny, but the look of terror on Ben's face was even better.

'Did he see us?' Ben wiped a tear from his eye.

'I don't think so,' said Ryan. 'He didn't even come out.'

'Amazing!' laughed Alisha. 'Genius.'

'Oh, baby girl, that was only the warm-up,' said Ryan, and Alisha noticed a cruel glint in his eye.

*

Their second stop was at the home of Kyle Norton, a weasel who had given Ryan grief since day one of Year Nine. Norton had called Ryan every homophobic name under the sun. Alisha wasn't sure, and didn't care, if Ryan were gay. Although he and Janey had dated for a while, Alisha did get a certain vibe. Either way, Kyle had just got a dog turd through his letterbox by way of a parting shot.

After they sped away from Kyle's house, they left Telscombe Cliffs altogether, driving away from the coast. The guys wouldn't tell Alisha where they were heading this time.

The limo eventually stopped about a mile and a half past the school. It was darker out here, no streetlights and no milky moon shining off the sea. The tyres crunched on gravel as the limo made its way down a dirt track off the main road. Alisha leaned past Ryan to get a better look out of the window. A crudely painted sign hung on a wooden gate: CROWE FARM – NO TRESPASSERS. Beyond the gate stood a blocky, run-down-looking house. Alisha could just about make out a tired weather vane creaking on the roof and a scarecrow slumped on a pole, his head hanging on by a thread.

'Guess who lives here,' Ryan said.

'Satan?' Alisha quipped. Her head felt light from the cava she'd downed on top of the alcohol she'd consumed earlier. 'Where are we?'

Greg chuckled. 'This is Mrs Finching's place.'

'Oh, well, that figures,' Janey sighed. 'I knew that woman was a witch.'

'I know, check out the haunted house,' Ben put in. 'Finding it took some serious espionage. I had to nick a letter out of her handbag to get the address.'

'Ben!' Janey slapped his arm. 'Are you deranged? Why are

you hell-bent on spoiling prom night? We only get one in our whole lives! One!'

'This woman has made our lives miserable since Year Seven,' Ben protested.

'I'm not denying she's an überbitch, but, seriously! Stealing her mail?'

'I put it back after I'd looked.'

'Can you remember what she said to us in that detention?' Greg asked Alisha.

She gasped. 'Oh, my God, yes! I'd forgotten that.'

'What happened?' Ryan asked.

'OK, well, a whole load of us got detention for messing around in English. You know what she was like, always keeping half the class in for no reason,' Greg explained with a scowl. 'Anyway, we were in over break and, after ten minutes, she let everyone go except me and Lish.'

'OK . . .'

'She told us that before we could go we had to clean the carpet – get all the bits out. And then she said, and this is the best bit, "It's what you darkies are good at."'

'No way!' Ben exploded.

'It's true,' Alisha confirmed.

'That racist bitch!' Ben's face had actually turned red with anger.

'Oh, my God, did you tell someone?' Janey, conversely, had turned pale with disgust. 'Mr Cunningham would have fired her arse for sure.'

'We never did,' Greg admitted. 'We were, what, thirteen? At first I thought I'd heard her wrong – like, how could someone say that to our faces? It was only when Lish and I talked about it later that we realised we'd both heard the same thing.'

'We thought people might think we were making it up,' Alisha sighed. Sadly, as she'd got older, she'd encountered racism again – most of it casual, from ignorant people who didn't even realise that what they'd said was wrong. None of it had been as savage as the English teacher's comment all those years ago.

'So what?' Janey said. 'Have we got eggs for Finching, too?'

'Oh, God, no.' Ryan shook his head. 'We've got something much better lined up for that hag. When I was in Year Nine, I entered a Halloween writing competition and, I'm pleased to say, came third. So I submitted the same story as English coursework and Mrs Finching gave it a D. She said it wouldn't scare a child.'

'OK . . . and?' Janey's interested was piqued.

'Time to bring the story to life!' Ben declared. From the carrier bag, he pulled out what looked like two old potato sacks. He handed one to Greg and kept one for himself. With a wink, he pulled the sack over his head.

It was horrible. They'd cut crude eyeholes into the sacks and drawn on leering grins in rough black marker pen. They looked like something from a nightmare.

'Oh, my God, they're horrible.' Alisha grimaced. 'Puppets, clowns and scarecrows are the *worst*.'

'Thank you,' Ryan said. 'See? Scarecrows *are* scary, whatever Mrs Finching said.'

'It gets better.' Greg's muffled voice came from inside his sack.

Ben slipped his iPhone out of his pocket and fiddled with it for a second. Then he slipped it under the hood and spoke. But the voice that emerged wasn't his. It echoed around the back of the limo, distorted and deep, each word sounding like it was being dragged from the beyond. 'Hello, Janey. What are you wearing?'

Ryan cackled with glee. 'Awesome!'

'What *is* that?' Janey asked in awe.

Ben held the phone away from his mouth. 'Voice changer app.'

Greg rocked back in his seat. 'Man, she is gonna properly freak out.'

'You're gonna ring her?' Alisha asked. 'How did you get her number?'

'You know Mel Sheridan in Year Twelve? Her dad is Mr Sheridan – I gave her ten quid to get the number from his phone,' Ben said.

'This is really mean.' Alisha finished her cava and poured herself another flute full. 'Finching must be, like, a hundred years old!'

'She has it coming,' said Ben. 'It's only a prank call. She'll get over it.'

'Ben, you can't ring her.' Janey, uptight at best, strung-out at worst, put her foot down. 'She'll one-four-seven-one your arse and call the police.'

Greg pulled his hood off. 'We're not completely stupid, Janey. We're going to use my phone and I've turned off caller ID.'

'Oh, whatever!' Janey knew she was outnumbered. 'If we get caught, I'm saying it was all your idea. My dad would ground me for a month.'

'Come on, let's do it,' Ben said.

The limo driver had already turned the engine and lights off. Greg and Ben pulled their masks back on and slipped out of the car, crouching low like commandos.

'Are you coming to watch?' Ryan asked, getting out of the other side.

Alisha sighed. 'Why not? Shame we won't be able to see the look on her face.' She swung one leg out and then the other, trying to dismount the limo like Kate Middleton might. It wasn't successful; Ryan had to pull her upright. She staggered on the uneven track.

Behind her, Janey hoisted up the folds of her dress and climbed out of the car. 'Well, I'm not sitting in there by myself,' she said huffily.

'You guys hide back here where she won't see you, or we're screwed,' Greg said.

'You ready?' Ben asked Ryan.

'I sure am,' Ryan replied.

Ben handed him both his and Greg's phones. 'Make it scary.'

'Bitch, please. I was born to do this.' Ryan crouched in the shadows, Alisha and Janey alongside.

'Hurry up, it's chilly,' moaned Janey.

Greg and Ben took up their positions on the vast lawn in front of the house. An outside light glowed inside a dirty glass porch and a TV flickered from one of the downstairs rooms. Other than that, the farmhouse was quiet as a crypt.

Ben and Greg stood like scarecrows in the middle of the grass, arms hanging at disjointed angles. In the light from the house, they cast long, awful shadows across the lawn.

'Here we go,' Ryan muttered. He scrolled through Greg's phone until he found Finching's number. While it was ringing he held Ben's phone – the one with the app – in front of his face. 'This is going to be so— Hello? Margaret Finching?'

'Yes. This is she.' Alisha could hear the old cow's demented bark from where she crouched by Ryan's shoulder. 'Who is this?'

'I have so many names . . .' With the app, Ryan sounded demonic.

'What? Who's there?'

'You've been a bad, bad girl, Margaret—' Ryan stopped abruptly and looked at the phone. 'Uh, she hung up on me.'

'Are you surprised? It sounded like a dirty phone call!' Janey giggled.

'Call her back.' Alisha poked Ryan in the ribs.

Ryan did so and waited. 'If you hang up on me again, Margaret, you'll be sorry!'

'Whoever this is, stop it, right now! I won't hesitate to call the police.'

'The police can't catch me, Margaret. Look out of the window.'

'I will do no such thing.'

'We're coming for you . . . We're coming to take you away.'

Alisha had to clamp her hand over her mouth to stop herself from giggling. Ryan was so into the role, his sinister tone never faltering.

'Go to the window,' he said. 'NOW!'

A net curtain twitched. A sour-lemon face and a cloud of white hair appeared in the window. On cue, Greg and Ben staggered forwards using jerky, zombie-style movements.

Finching immediately pulled away from the window. 'What are you doing?' she shrieked.

'It's time for you to pay, Margaret. All those children you've been so cruel to . . .'

'I'm calling the police!'

'It'll be the last thing you do.'

Ben and Greg had reached the downstairs window. They clawed at the glass, groaning.

Ryan looked at Greg's phone. 'She's gone. Quick.' He

stood up, hitting his head on a branch. 'Ow! She's calling the police,' he hissed loudly at Ben and Greg.

The masked scarecrow zombies didn't need telling twice. They turned from the window and sprinted over the lawn.

'We gotta get out of here!' Greg yelled.

Alisha took Janey's hand and they helped each other up.

Greg stood next to the limo and pulled his mask off. 'Will you two get a move on?'

'Do you wanna try running in five-inch heels?' Alisha demanded.

'I can barely walk,' Janey groaned. She almost fell into the back of the limo and Greg shoved her in the rest of the way. Alisha scrambled onto the back seat, Greg right behind her and Ben climbing in last.

'Mate, just drive!' Ben said.

'Go!' Ryan added, banging on the partition.

The limo, as glamorous as it was, wasn't the ideal getaway car. The three-point-turn out of the drive was agonising. It occurred to Alisha that the lads' master-plan might not be exactly airtight.

'Hurry it up!' Ben fidgeted in his seat.

Alisha looked back at the house. A shadow moved in the farmhouse window. 'Oh, God,' she said. 'How fast can the police get here?'

'Not fast enough,' Greg said, laughing. 'Man, you should have seen her face!'

'Quick, she's coming out!' Alisha cried as the front door opened.

The limo swung back into the country road with a jerk. Greg and Alisha were thrown back into the seats, while Janey and Ben toppled forwards onto the floor.

They'd done it, though. The limo tore down the lane and

back onto the main road. Ben whooped and high-fived Greg, and then Ryan. 'Job well done.'

'Dude, that was too close,' Ryan breathed, holding his chest.

'That was awesome!' Ben kissed Janey fleetingly on the lips. 'Now to the ball! See? Best night ever!'

Alisha's heart was still racing so she helped herself to more cava, despite a frown from Greg. She sipped it, and threw him a *what are you gonna do about it?* look.

Ryan handed back the phones. 'Here you go.'

'Thanks,' said Ben. 'J, can you put this in your handbag?'

'Sure.' Janey took the phone and slipped it into her purse.

'So that was Ben's big mistake,' Alisha said, stroking Katie's hair. Her friend lay sleepily across her lap. 'If he'd just held onto his bloody phone, it never would have happened.'

'It was an epic fail,' Ryan added. 'If Ben—'

'If Ben what?' Ben asked, sticking his head round the door.

'Nothing,' Alisha said, perhaps too quickly. 'We were just talking about Rox.'

'Where *is* Miss Dent?' Ryan asked. 'Selling drugs or trafficking kids or something?'

Ben smiled, although Alisha could tell his heart wasn't in it. 'I think she's by the pool.'

There was no way Alisha could tell the next part of the story with Ben present. She faked a yawn. 'I might get an early night.'

Ryan looked disappointed, but he must know they couldn't talk about this in front of Ben. 'Me, too. Come on, Benjamin, let's tell ghost stories like in the olden days.'

'Sure thing,' Ben sighed. 'You girls OK?'

Katie could only manage a sleepy nod.

'We'll be fine,' Alisha said. She wondered if she should leave Ben and Katie to it, but Ben was already out the door.

Ryan turned back and hissed, 'Don't you dare carry on without me.'

Alisha smiled. 'To be continued.'

SCENE 15 – ROXANNE

Roxanne sat by the swimming pool, dragging deep on a cigarette. She thought it was fitting. *Bad girls always smoke – it's one of the ways you can tell they're bad.* Her hands shook. It seemed no amount of nicotine would calm her nerves tonight.

What have I done? Her heart was still pounding. The walk on the beach had done nothing to help. She was a ball of crackling tension, her knuckles white and her fists balled. There was no going back now. She'd done it. She'd actually done it. Before arriving at the villa, she hadn't been sure she'd have the strength to see it through. As it had turned out, stage fright was no match for her.

So what was this coldness in the back of her skull? It felt like doubt was drilling into her head. It was possible she'd just made the biggest mistake of her life – and she'd made a few. What she had just done was criminal. She was now a criminal. This wasn't like when she'd used Google in the French exam; blackmail comes with a jail sentence. She stubbed out the cigarette on the tiles and held the smoke in her chest for as long as she could before exhaling.

That was the end of her friends, anyway. Maybe *that* was why she felt so lousy. She had just screwed them over royally. It served them right. They'd had it coming – did they really think she hadn't heard all their bitchy comments about her? Roxanne's a fake. Roxanne's a bitch. Roxanne's a slut. That hadn't bothered her so much – everyone loves a good bitch behind their friends' backs. No, what had really annoyed her was how they'd all pretended to be so lily-white, when not one of them was anything like innocent.

There was something in her, though, that had just wanted them to like her. Everyone wants to be liked and there was something mightily appealing about that group – their love for one another seemed so unconditional; with all their little in-jokes it was like they were speaking a foreign language half the time. She pulled back her hair. So weak – no one ever got anywhere through being nice. She had to learn to be ruthless. She was a shark, not a dolphin. What good was it having friends that had never liked you in the first place? Make some money and get the hell out of this villa – that was what she needed to do. Frankly, she could buy some new friends. These were worthless. She was going to be so much bigger than them. One day, they'd look back and regret the way they'd treated her, she knew it.

Without warning, the pool lights went out. The water – aqua-blue one second, black the next – was now a pond of rippling ink. Roxanne sprang off the lounger and looked back towards the villa. There was no one in sight. The terrace doors stood open. There was a dark six-inch gap.

The lamps along the terrace stairs snapped off next. Roxanne flinched. There was now only the moon and the pale ghost of the moon on the sea.

Roxanne heard the terrace doors slide further open, followed by light, cat-like footsteps. 'Hello?' she called, and felt slightly ridiculous. 'I was just having a fag.'

A black shape descended the stairs. Nothing more than

a shadow – a shadow which seemed to pour down the steps towards her.

Roxanne swallowed hard. She'd seen this coming. You can't blackmail people and not expect a backlash. 'Is this about earlier? I'm not going to change my mind. You can threaten me if you want, but it won't change anything.'

The figure advanced. She still couldn't see who it was; they stayed in the darkness of the palms and shrubs.

'You can't do anything to me. *Everyone* knows I'm here. If you hurt me the police will know in minutes.' This wasn't strictly true. In fact, there was only a girl from a bar in Rome who even knew she'd been planning to come to Spain.

The figure stepped onto the poolside tiles and finally emerged from the shadows. Roxanne gasped. She couldn't help it. She couldn't even pretend not to be scared.

It was wearing a hideous scarecrow mask.

SCENE 16 – ALISHA

Today, Alisha was the first up, not the last. She breathed in the tranquillity, the stillness of the villa, savouring it before it filled with rowing friends. It was like waiting for a hangover to kick in. She hoped that after everyone had slept, they'd be able to handle things with a minimum of drama.

She used the bathroom and then went downstairs to make a cup (or vat) of coffee before the onslaught. Alisha tiptoed through the lounge, not wanting to wake Rox, only to find the sofa-bed already folded away neatly – the bedding piled on top. Confused, Alisha went to the French windows.

Roxanne was down in the pool, taking an early-morning swim from the look of things. Alisha left her to it and walked through to the kitchen. It was way too early to deal with Rox. She could wait until after a cup of coffee. Sometimes you need a cup of coffee (or three) to be able to face the day, and Alisha wasn't a morning person at the best of times.

Katie padded into the lounge, running her hand through her tangle of auburn waves. 'Morning, camper.'

'Oh, hey, did I wake you?'

'Not at all. I've been dozing for ages.' Katie nodded at the empty sofa-bed. 'Where's Rox?'

'She's in the pool. Tea?'

Katie looked out of the terrace doors. 'Yes, please. I know

I shouldn't, but I'll have two sugars. It feels like a two sugars sort of day. God, last night actually happened, didn't it?'

'Yep. Roxanne *is* trying to blackmail us,' Alisha confirmed. She glanced up to see her friend standing in the middle of the sliding doors, a puzzled expression on her face. 'Katie?'

'Lish, come here.'

There was a serious edge to Katie's tone, so Alisha did as she was told, abandoning tea-making duties. 'What is it?'

'What *is* she doing?' Katie pointed down at Roxanne, who looked like she was floating on her back. 'She's in her dress from last night.'

'Rox?' Alisha called down. There was no response. 'Oi! Roxanne!'

'Alisha . . . is she OK?' They looked at each other. Neither said anything. The colour seeped from Katie's lips and Alisha felt her skin prickle like there were pins all over her body.

'Roxanne?' Alisha's voice was shrill now. Panic clutched her throat like a fist. She was no fan of Roxanne Dent, but . . . She started towards the stairs. *I will remain calm*, she thought, but that lasted about a second as Alisha broke into a run and took the steps two at a time, almost tripping and tumbling. Katie followed right behind her.

By the time she was halfway down, Alisha could see that Roxanne was *not* OK. She was absolutely still, her arms floating away from her torso, caught in her net of blonde hair. Her eyes were wide open but seeing nothing.

SCENE 17 – RYAN

Ryan stood in front of the bedroom mirror, applying moisturiser with SPF to his face (because, as everyone knows, regular sun cream is too oily for your face). 'Benjamin! Wakey, wakey!' He had no qualms about waking up Ben. That giant had hogged the covers all night – it was just what he deserved. 'Will you rub sun cream on my back?'

'No. Go away. I hate you,' Ben replied.

Ryan chuckled – right up until he heard the scream. It was ear-splitting. That's the thing with screams. He'd been in plays where actors had been required to scream and you could always, *always* tell they were faking. A real scream is unmistakeable.

This one was real.

He took one look at Ben and they both darted out of the bedroom. It was Alisha and it was coming from downstairs.

'Greg!' she yelled, her voice shrill, raw and red. 'Greg!'

Ryan reached her first. She was framed by the sliding doors onto the terrace. 'What's up?'

'Roxanne's in the pool!' Alisha spat the words in his face.

'So?'

'Look!'

He looked down and saw what she meant. Roxanne wasn't *swimming*, she was *floating*. 'Oh, my God.' Ryan ran towards the steps with Ben hot on his heels as Greg arrived to investigate the commotion.

'What's the problem? Seriously, I could hear you from . . .' Ryan heard Greg saying as he raced down the steps. He arrived at the pool. Katie stood at the edge of the water, her hands over her mouth. Behind him he heard Greg call for Erin.

Ryan pushed past Katie and dove into the pool. As he did so, Roxanne was sucked under. No longer a piece of floating art, she rolled in the water like a dead thing. A carcass. His stomach turned, but he ignored it. The morning water was bitter and any remaining cobwebs were expelled. He had to get her out.

Ryan felt Ben plunge into the water alongside him as he reached out and touched Roxanne. She was cold. Now that he was here, he didn't know what to do.

'Rox?' Ben spluttered. 'Roxanne? Can you hear me?'

'What happened to her?' Ryan spat pool water out of his mouth.

'I don't know.' Katie cupped her face in her hands.

Ryan spotted a wine bottle lying on its side underneath one of the loungers. 'Oh, God. Maybe she got drunk and slipped . . .' Ryan murmured. With both of them grabbing hold of her, they pulled Roxanne under, rather than keeping her afloat.

'Ryan, let go,' Ben said. He wrapped his arm under her armpits and started swimming towards the edge. Roxanne continued to look past the sky. 'Katie, help me!' Ben yelled. 'Katie!'

Katie seemed to snap out of her shock. She came to the side of the pool and reached down.

It was going to be fine, Ryan thought, just fine. CPR. They'd do CPR and it would be fine.

Katie hooked her hands under Roxanne's arms, but they slipped away. Rox was heavy. A dead weight. 'Alisha, help me!' Katie sobbed.

Alisha, borderline hysterical, hurried over to help; her hands shook and her cheeks were wet with tears.

'Pull her out!' Ben told the girls as he and Ryan held Roxanne's body steady at the edge of the pool.

Katie and Alisha took one arm each. Ryan felt Roxanne's spine grind against the rim of the pool as the girls heaved the body out of the water. He pushed on Rox's thighs and, with a soggy splatter, Roxanne landed on the tiles. Katie and Alisha fell back from the momentum.

Ryan hoisted himself out of the pool. Light bounced off the surface of the water like a mirror ball. It was dizzying. It was noisy. Ryan couldn't focus. The ground whirled around him like a carousel. *This was really happening.* Funny, but when drama happens in *real life*, it doesn't feel like a TV show at all. He felt he should be ready for this, should know what to do. He flipped through his inner rolodex of scenarios, desperately searching for the episode where the characters had found a friend floating unconscious in the pool. He drew a big fat blank. He could only look on in impotent horror.

Ben was at Roxanne's side. Ryan hadn't even seen him get out of the pool. 'Roxanne?' Ben put his face next to hers. 'She's not breathing.'

Ryan leaned in close. She *had* to be.

'Is she dead?' Katie closed her eyes.

'No!' Ben replied. Katie's eyes snapped open and she rushed to Rox's side to aid the revival. Ben looked at her. 'What do you do? Do you do the mouth or the chest first?'

'You don't do the mouth any more,' cried Ryan. 'It was in that advert.'

'But she's not breathing,' Ben replied.

'What happened?' It was Erin. She ran down the stairs wearing a dressing gown, her hair dripping wet. She must have been in the shower.

'We found Roxanne in the pool. I don't know – maybe she was drunk . . .' Ryan said, pointing at the discarded bottle. He stood and stepped over Rox's legs to roll out the bottle. It was empty. She'd finished the whole thing. She must have been wasted.

'Stand back,' Erin commanded, suddenly a different person. 'Give me space. Has someone called an ambulance?' No one answered. 'For God's sake! Do it!'

Alisha picked herself up off the floor and ran for the villa. Erin felt for a pulse in Roxanne's neck. She leaned in closer and listened for breathing.

'What are you doing?' Ryan demanded.

'I'm a medical student.'

'You never said—'

'You never asked!' Erin snapped. 'How long has she been like this?'

'I don't know.' Ben held his head in his hands.

'Well,' Erin ran her fingers over Roxanne's arm, 'rigor mortis hasn't set in, but if she's been in cold water the whole time it will have delayed the onset. Oh, God! Who found her?'

'Alisha did.' Ryan coughed up some pool water.

'I was with her,' Katie put in. 'I . . . we thought she was swimming.'

'How long ago was this?'

'Just a minute ago.'

It was just a minute ago, Ryan thought, but it had been the longest minute ever. Time had stopped. It felt as though this was all there had ever been.

'At a guess, she's been dead for at least four hours,' Erin said, 'although I can't be certain. There's a head injury, too.'

'What? No!' Ryan gasped. 'Save her! Do mouth-to-mouth!'

Erin adopted the patronising tone that all TV doctors use to break bad news to patients' families. Ryan figured they must teach it in med school 101. 'Ryan, she's *cold*. She must have fallen or dived in and hit her—'

'Ry?' Ben interrupted, staring at Ryan with horror in his eyes.

'What?' Ryan snapped.

Ben's lips moved but it took a moment for the sound to come out. 'Your hands . . .'

The bottle was sticky. Only now did Ryan look down and see that it wasn't red wine all over his fingers. It was redder than any red wine. It was blood. He cursed at the top of his lungs and let the bottle slip through his fingers. It landed on the thick bottom rim and rolled across the tiles, leaving a red trail as it went.

'Oh, my God!' Katie screamed, springing back as it rolled her way.

'What the f—?' Ryan gasped.

'Is that blood?' Erin demanded, cutting him off.

Ryan looked up again to see Greg standing at the foot of the stairs, not blinking. His eyes were almost as dead as Roxanne's. They didn't move, his gaze never leaving Roxanne's body.

Ryan felt his stomach heave. He would *not* vomit. None of the dramatic scenarios he'd ever played out in his head involved him throwing up over himself. 'I don't get it.' He held his blood-caked hands away from his body like they were radioactive. Slowly it dawned on him. This was no accident. 'I mean, who did this? Why? I . . .' Words and sentences were tangled like spaghetti in his head.

Roxanne was dead.

In the middle of the chaos, she was the only one who had the decency to keep still. Erin reached over and pulled her eyelids down. That was better. Now she was beautiful again. Not dead, sleeping. Ryan had to get the blood off his hands. He plunged them in the pool and scrubbed as hard as he could.

'Someone hit her,' Erin said gravely. 'I can't tell if she was dead before she hit the water, though. The head wound doesn't look *too* bad . . . She *probably* drowned.'

'She was out here by herself,' Katie sobbed. 'Someone must have attacked her.'

Ryan imagined some inbred mutant crawling out of the hillside. Something from a horror film – a missing link or genetic experiment gone awry.

'Which one of you did it?' Greg demanded.

The accusation jolted Ryan back into reality. Time ticked by normally again. The ground stopped spinning and the cacophony ceased. Only a songbird chirruped gaily, darting from tree to tree. It seemed really inappropriate.

'What?' Ryan said eventually. Not a mountain mutant. Greg was referring to *them*.

Alisha burst onto the top terrace, the cordless phone pressed to her ear. 'I can't understand what you're saying,' she wept. 'Do you speak English?'

Greg looked at the body and then looked at his sister. 'Alisha, hang up!'

'Slow down . . . I don't speak Spanish!' she cried.

'Hang up!' Greg repeated.

Alisha ran down the stairs. 'Does anybody speak any Span—'

Greg roared. 'ALISHA, I SAID HANG UP!' He grabbed the phone out of her hands and ended the call.

'What are you doing? We need an ambulance!' Alisha screamed.

'Are you insane? She's *dead*!' Greg prowled over to look at Roxanne's body. He considered her face for a moment, before saying, 'She's dead,' again.

Erin grabbed his arm. 'Greg, we still have to—'

'We can't!' he snarled in her face. Erin recoiled. 'Don't you get it?' Greg asked, his eyes burning. 'One of *us* killed her.'

SCENE 18 – RYAN

Ryan's thought process went like this . . . Roxanne is dead. This is *bad*. One of us killed her. That is *worse*. People might think I did it. That is *worst*. His mind-set changed channels. He stopped worrying about Rox and started worrying about himself.

'No way,' Ben argued. 'No way. She . . . she must have fallen in . . . she'd been drinking . . . maybe she banged her head.'

'Dream on.' Greg's face was contorted with anger and frustration. 'She's been murdered. Someone bottled her and left her to drown.'

The problem was, Greg was right. The cogs of Ryan's brain were at once turning too quickly and too slowly. But he was absolutely sure that Greg was right. One of them *had* killed Roxanne.

Ryan had spent his whole life living a TV drama and, suddenly, he was in one for real. The fantasy was definitely better than the reality. This was way too close to home.

'What?' Alisha asked, trying to snatch the phone back from Greg.

'Well, what did you think, Alisha? Some random person came off the beach and murdered her?' Greg asked.

'Maybe. Or perhaps someone broke in . . .'

Greg raised an eyebrow like he was struggling to communicate with simpletons. 'One of you lot obviously killed her.'

Ryan laughed. 'Well, of course! It wasn't you, was it, Greg?'

'No, it bloody wasn't!'

The hysteria wouldn't stop. It gripped Ryan's body like a vice until he was shaking uncontrollably with shallow, horrid laughter. 'OK, then,' he said. 'Who did it?'

Everyone started speaking at the same time. Ryan couldn't make out the individual excuses, but they were all emphatically negative. 'So I suppose it was the Beach Monster, then.'

'Can we all just stop?' Ben cried. 'This is insane. It can't be happening. I know some prat always says this, but there *has to be an explanation*.'

'Oh, wake up!' Greg barked, getting up in Ben's space, throwing his weight around. 'Roxanne said that one of us killed Janey – and now Rox is dead. That's a pretty big coincidence.'

Ryan considered who could have killed Rox . . .

1. Random local murderer. God, he hoped it was a random local murderer. The fact that this would be the best possible scenario was an indication of just how bleak their situation was.
2. Greg, Alisha, Ben, Katie or Erin killed Roxanne while sleepwalking or possessed by a demon. He could only dream.
3. Greg, Alisha, Ben, Katie or Erin killed Roxanne deliberately.

Janey *and* Roxanne. Ryan dimly recalled reading about the differences between serial killers, spree killers and mass murderers. One more body and one of his school friends would officially qualify as a serial killer.

Erin pushed Greg away from Ben, trying to lift the phone from his hands. 'Greg, we *have* to call the police,' she said.

'We'll be arrested.'

'We won't. We'll tell them what happened,' she pleaded.

'What happened is that one of us killed her. Are you blind?' Greg snapped.

'He's right.' Ryan sat next to Roxanne's head, combing his fingers through her matted hair. She was so still, so serene. She'd spent so much time *trying* to be beautiful. All she'd ever had to do was stop. Ryan had never seen her so lovely. 'Greg's one hundred per cent right. We will *all* be arrested. This wasn't an accident. I don't think her head slipped onto that bottle, do you?'

'Who did it?' Alisha sobbed. 'Who did it?'

Everyone noisily denied it and started pointing fingers.

'She said she knew something about you.' Greg jabbed a finger in Ben's direction. 'Something to do with Janey.'

'Oh, piss off!' Ben responded. He gestured at Roxanne, his face red. 'As if I'd do this!'

'Well, one of us did,' Greg spat.

'No,' Katie said from behind her hands. 'No way. We wouldn't . . .'

Greg glowered. 'After last night, I'm not surprised. Whether one of us killed Janey or not, Rox was gonna blackmail us *all*.'

'Greg!' Erin snapped.

'OK. Enough is enough.' Katie stood up, some colour returning to her face. 'Greg, please give me the phone. I really, really think we should call the police.'

'Are you all crazy? One of us has murdered Rox, and you

want to call the *police?*' Greg was not handing over the phone. 'We'll all go down. Life sentences.'

Ryan really, *really* didn't want to go to jail. Jails were not for boys like him. Jails were for scary, heroin-addled psychopaths with tattooed faces.

Erin continued fluttering around Greg like a hummingbird, trying to soothe her boyfriend. 'Greg,' she purred, 'this is a crime. It has to be reported to the police.'

He rolled his eyes. 'I'm not a total frigging idiot. I know it's a crime, I just don't wanna get arrested. I don't want my *sister* getting arrested. I don't want *any* of you getting arrested.'

A brief silence followed this. It was still so early in the morning, but Ryan felt exhausted. He'd known these people for years. How well did he really know any of them, though? Everyone has secrets. We're all acting, all the time – Ryan knew this better than anyone. Everyone has the face they show people and the face for when they're alone in bed with only their thoughts.

Ryan continued to play with Rox's hair. He looked at his friends the way they were looking at him – with suspicion. His chaotic thoughts ordered themselves. The dominoes were falling faster for him than for the others and he could predict exactly where the trail was leading.

There was no way he was getting caught up in a murder investigation. That was so *not* his story arc. The funny thing was, he was ready for this. Now that his mind was calm, all that TV was about to pay off. A lifetime of films had left a file ready-made in his mind called 'What to do with a body'.

'Of course one of us killed her.' Ryan didn't mean to shout, but that's how it came out. 'Did you miss the episode last night where she blackmailed us? It's not just Janey – she said she had dirt on *all of us*. Obviously someone didn't want their secret getting out.'

'So it wasn't you either, then, Ryan?' Alisha wiped her nose.

'No. *I'm* pretty much secret free.'

'Yeah,' Ben argued. 'But you wanna be an actor. Maybe she had something embarrassing.'

'That's right, Ben. She got hold of my Year Nine audition for *Little Shop of Horrors* so I killed her.'

'Stop it!' Katie gulped back more tears. 'Just stop it! Roxanne's dead. We are *not* going to stand around making stupid jokes. We *have* to call the police.'

'No.' This time Ryan controlled his voice. 'I'm with Greg. We have to talk about this.'

'There's nothing to talk about.' Erin tugged her wet hair off her face.

Ryan stopped playing with Roxanne's hair. Her head lolled to the side. 'Yes, there is. I am *not* going to jail over Roxanne Dent.'

'Amen to that.' Greg seemed to breathe a sigh of relief now that he had an ally.

'We wouldn't go to jail,' Katie protested.

'Oh, for God's sake!' Ryan pointed to the body on the floor. 'We are screwed. They are gonna throw the book at us so hard, it'll hurt. Somewhere in this villa is incriminating evidence about *all* of us. We don't know what Rox was hiding.' Except, of course, that he knew only too well. That video – if it went viral, it didn't bear thinking about.

'Well . . . well that doesn't mean anything,' Katie said, although now she sounded far less certain.

'Don't you people watch TV? We all had a motive. We all had the opportunity. There were no witnesses,' Ryan pointed out.

Erin shook her head. 'That's not true. We were all sharing rooms.'

'Ben, did you leave the bedroom in the night?' Ryan turned to his roommate.

'Yeah, I went to get some water, but so what? That doesn't mean—'

'I know. The point is, I never heard him go. Any one of us could have snuck out of our rooms. The police will crucify all of us – for Rox *and* Janey. I don't know about you, but I *really* don't wanna be the pretty nineteen-year-old in a man's prison.'

That mental image read on everyone's face for a moment and there was grim silence. Alisha started to cry again, fresh tears making streams down her cheeks. Greg put his arm around her and she leant against him. Silently, Alisha had sided with her brother. Ryan steeled himself. He knew this was awful. The *right* thing to do was to call the police. But sometimes the right thing isn't the *clever* thing.

'Damn it, you're right.' Ryan wasn't sure if Ben was talking to the group or himself.

Katie rushed to his side. 'No, Ben. No.'

'Katie, they're right. Any of us *could* have done it and none of us is going to admit to it.'

'I didn't even know her!' Erin exclaimed.

'Yeah, but who even are you?' Ryan demanded, surprised at the venom in his voice. 'We know jack about you. You could be an escaped lunatic serial killer, for all we know.'

'Back off, Ryan,' Greg snapped.

Ben's body went limp and he flopped onto a sun lounger. 'Oh, God. They'll reopen Janey's case, won't they?'

Ryan nodded, sensing he was grinding Ben down. 'Roxanne had evidence about Janey. I guess it's here at the villa – unless whoever did this,' he gestured at the body, 'got rid of it.'

Ben buried his head in his hands. 'What will my dad say? And my mum? Oh, God.'

'This is insane!' Katie made another grab for the phone. Greg tossed it into the swimming pool. 'Greg!'

'It's the end of the discussion,' Greg told her flatly.

'There's another phone in the master bedroom,' Katie said. 'Look, if we *don't* call the police, things will just be a million times worse.'

Greg charged towards her, suddenly bull-like. Ben stopped him before he could reach her. 'Worse than what, Katie? Worse than jail? I'll never play football again if this gets out. We'll be all over the TV; is that what you want?'

Ryan laughed again. So true. But that was not how he intended to break into TV – on the evening news, accused of murder. Oh, God, "The Telscombe Cliffs Six" – that's what the press would call them.

Katie did her best not to flinch as Greg's rage burned like a forest fire. 'Greg, did you . . . do this?'

'I swear I did not.'

'Then please—'

'No.'

Another penny dropped for Alisha. 'Oh, God, we have to get out of here. One of you is properly mental – like, dangerous.'

'We can't leave,' Ryan told her. 'They'll find the body and then come after us. Anyway, Lish, unless you plan on blackmailing us, I'd say you're probably safe. The only reason Rox died is because she was going to expose one of us.' Ryan pointed at the body. It wasn't even Roxanne any more, it was just a thing. A terrible thing. He wanted it out of sight. 'We need to get rid of *it*.'

'Agreed,' Greg stated.

'You and Erin dug a pretty big hole on the beach,' Ryan remarked under his breath. He wanted to laugh; the hysteria was bubbling up again. He suppressed the urge.

'No.' Ben left the lounger, his eyes red. 'We can't bury her in sand. It'll get washed away by the tide.'

'I was kidding!' Ryan said.

'I wasn't.' Greg paced the swimming pool, hands on hips. Ryan could tell he was struggling to form a plan. 'We'll dump her at sea. There's the boat, right? We'll wait until it's dark, go out into the middle of the ocean and throw her over the side.'

Katie stepped forwards. 'I can't believe we're having this conversation. Ben, please, tell him we can't do this.'

Ben looked as though his heart had just broken on the spot. 'I'm sorry, Katie, I can't go to prison. Have you ever seen inside a jail? You wouldn't last a day. I wouldn't. None of us would.' He pushed his hair out of his eyes. 'When I went to Cambridge, my dad was so proud. I . . . I can't . . .'

Ryan decided it was time to wheel out the big guns. 'Alisha, do you want Greg to go to prison?'

'No!'

'Excellent. Katie, do you want Ben to go to prison?'

'Of course not!'

'So we need to get rid of Roxanne's body, then. It's the only way,' he said firmly.

Katie sighed and turned away. Ryan was oddly fascinated by the whole scenario. No play in which he'd ever performed had been this macabre. These were his friends. Overnight they'd gone from being schoolmates to murderers and ghouls. He was no better. It was funny – he'd assumed Janey's death was the finale. Turned out, it was only the beginning – the pre-credit sequence.

'We can get rid of her stuff. Did anyone even know she was here?' Greg asked.

'I don't think so,' Ryan replied. 'She said coming here was a last-minute decision. She was travelling alone.'

Greg strode back to Katie. 'Did you arrange it on Facebook?' She ignored him. He seized her arms. 'Was it on Facebook? Tell me!'

Alisha pushed her brother off. 'Greg, leave her alone.'

'Yes,' Katie admitted.

'Good. You'll delete the messages, OK?' Greg meant it. His anger was hotter than the sun. Ryan swore he could *feel* it.

'Greg, I'm not doing—'

'Delete. The. Messages.'

'It won't do any good,' Katie protested. 'It'll only delete the messages at my end.'

Greg thought about this. He stalked away like some wounded lion.

'Wait, though,' Ryan said. 'Do we even have to? We could just say she went for a swim last night and drowned. We could even call the police ourselves.'

'No,' Erin replied with authority. 'The head injury would be way too suspicious.'

'Crap. Well, anyway . . . Rox never confirmed her trip. Katie, you weren't expecting her yesterday. We'll just say she never came,' Ryan decided.

'Ryan, why are you doing this?' Katie asked. She crossed to his location and took his hands. 'Please . . . if this were a film, we'd be screaming at the screen, right now. We'd all be saying "Don't do it, you idiots! You're out of your minds!"'

Ryan shook his head. 'No, we wouldn't.'

'What?' Alisha said.

'We wouldn't. We'd be saying "Dump the bitch in the sea."'

'No, Ryan, that is *not*—' Katie started, but he cut her off.

'Yes, it is. If this were a film, you'd have been waiting for Roxanne to die. You'd have been expecting it.' He pointed at each of them. 'Nerd, Jock, New Girl, Bad Girl, Good Girl *and* The Bitch. The bitch always dies. We've all seen the bloody films. We know exactly what to do.'

'We dump the body,' Ben whispered.

'They never get away with it,' Katie said, grasping at straws. 'In the films, they always get caught.'

'Well, it's a bloody good job we're not in a film then, isn't it?' Greg gave her a cold look.

'So we might just get away with it,' Ryan finished. 'Katie, I know this is awful. We are all clearly going to hell, but we don't have to go to prison. There are six of us still alive, and Rox is dead. If we call the police, we might as well *all* be dead. It'd be *over* for us. There is nothing we can do to bring Rox back to life now, and I want to know what happened to Janey, but I'm not risking my life to find out.'

'He's right,' Greg said. 'We'll wait until it's dark.'

'Wait!' Ben snapped. 'We need to vote on this.'

'We vote?' Katie was aghast. 'This isn't an election for Head Boy, Ben.'

'We vote. We all agree to go with the majority. It's the only fair way.'

Ryan could see that Ben was squirming. This row must be torture for him. He'd known Ben since they'd been babies and all Ben ever wanted to do was keep the peace, keep everyone happy. But drama did seem to have a knack for finding him.

'I . . . I wish there was another way,' Ben mumbled.

'But there isn't.' Ryan pulled his old friend into a hug. He looked like he needed it.

'Thanks, mate. OK. Here we go. Who votes for us to bury Roxanne at sea?' Ben asked.

'You can't make this sound better than it is, Ben.' Katie looked at her ex with a mixture of disgust and sheer disbelief. 'We won't be burying her, we'll be *dumping* her. *Dumping* her body at sea.'

Greg ignored Katie and turned to Erin. 'Baby, listen, I am so sorry you had to see all this. You know I love you.'

Ryan knew a lie when he heard one, and he knew Greg didn't love Erin. She seemed to buy it, though.

She started to cry. 'Greg, I'll get kicked off my course. I have worked so hard . . .'

'Only if we call the police,' Greg insisted. 'If we don't, we can go on as normal. All we have to do is hide Roxanne. She's *already dead*. Erin, please. There's no way I'll be able to play if I get arrested. My career will be over. So will yours.' Hard, heavy sobs wracked Erin's thin frame. 'Please, baby. For me,' Greg finished.

'OK,' was all Erin said.

Greg kissed her hard on the lips. 'Thank you. I promise it's gonna be OK.' He hugged her tight.

'So,' Ben said. 'Raise your hand if you agree we hide the body.'

Ryan couldn't back down now; he raised his arm. Greg and Ben did, too, followed by a reluctant Erin. Katie abstained. Alisha said nothing, but had already made her feelings clear enough.

'OK, then. It's decided,' Ben said.

'We'll wait until it's dark,' Greg added.

Ryan realised he was holding his breath. He exhaled shakily, fighting a new wave of nausea. Although glorious sun beat down on them from a cloudless sky, they were in a dark, dark place.

SCENE 19 – ALISHA

Not for the first time, Alisha wondered whether this could all be a particularly vivid dream. Rox was dead. Ryan and Greg wanted to dump the body. A minute ago, she had just agreed to it. It was wrong and she knew it was wrong, but she'd agreed nonetheless. She was most surprised at Ben – she'd always had him down as someone with an iron-clad moral compass, but he'd gone along with Greg pretty quickly. But then, so had she. As awful as it seemed, it felt *easier* to let Ryan and Greg take control, to be the bad guys.

Alisha pushed her hair off her face. 'This is so, so messed up,' she said, incredulous.

'If we all stick together,' Ryan said, 'it'll be fine.'

Alisha knew it was over. There were no arguments left. 'How? How, Ryan? How will this ever be fine?' Sooner or later, someone would miss Roxanne. She was – had been – vile, but someone out there cared about her, surely? The thought that no one would even notice she'd gone was too sad to contemplate. No – eventually Rox's uncle would report her missing and then they'd have to lie. Forever.

'Well, obviously, it's not exactly ideal.' Ryan threw his hands up. 'We're meant to be eating ice-cream and getting drunk, but that's impossible! After what happened to Janey it was never going to be fine! We were screwed before we got on the plane. One of us is playing an astoundingly clever game – making sure we're all implicated in Rox's death. I'm almost impressed.'

Alisha looked down the beach. The sun was climbing higher in the sky with each passing minute. The sand was golden, the sea was tropical blue, the villa was dazzling white, the dead girl was ghost grey. Spot the odd one out. Alisha couldn't think of anything else to say. Next to her, Katie slipped her hand into Alisha's. It was good to know one of them sympathised.

Erin spoke, cool and professional again. 'We need to move the body. We can't leave her by the pool all day. Someone might walk down the beach and see her.'

The boys sprang into action, suddenly united by a practical task. They took up position around Rox's body. Katie hid her face in Alisha's shoulder.

'Nobody but us has walked down the beach in forty-eight hours,' Ryan pointed out.

Greg nodded. 'Yeah, but we can't risk it. *If* someone sees, we're dead. We'll have to take her inside.'

Ryan slapped Greg's arm. 'No! Are you mad? Don't you watch CSI? We'll get her hair and DNA all over the villa.'

'You're right. We'll have to wrap her in something . . .'

Alisha pulled on Katie's hand. 'This is sick. Let's go inside.'

Katie nodded. The pair started for the stairs.

'Hey! Where do you think you're going?' Greg didn't miss a trick.

'Inside,' Alisha said. 'I'm not touching a dead body. This was your idea; you deal with it.'

'Fine,' Greg caved. 'Lish, are you OK?'

Alisha thought about that. The irony that she would give anything, literally, anything in the world that she possessed, to have *Roxanne Dent* with them, right now, was not lost on her. 'I'll be fine,' she said eventually.

'This is for the best, Lish.' Her brother turned his attention to the dead body, ready to move it.

Alisha led Katie up the stairs to the villa. 'What about you, Katie? Are you OK, hon?'

'No.'

'I'll get you some water.' Alisha pushed open the sliding doors and steered Katie straight to the sofa. Katie flopped down onto it, resting her head on her knees. Alisha's mouth was bone-dry. This was happening. No going back. Events had taken on a demented momentum; the runaway train was careering downhill.

Alisha decided to focus on looking after Katie. She hurried to the kitchen and grabbed two glasses from the side of the sink. She took some mineral water from the fridge, and, with shaking hands, managed to fill both glasses without spilling. She carried them through to the lounge, ice rattling against the sides. 'Here – drink this.'

'Thank you.'

Alisha sipped the water, her lips like parchment. 'I'm sorry,' Alisha whispered, confessing her sins. 'In a choice between my brother and my best friends in the world on one side, and Roxanne Dent on the other . . . Well, it's no contest.'

'It's not your fault.' Katie closed her eyes and held the ice-cold glass to her temple.

'Janey and now Roxanne. Who could do something so . . .' Alisha mused.

Her train of thought was interrupted by Ben, who stepped through the sliding doors. 'Can we talk?' he asked.

Alisha nodded and perched next to Katie on the sofa, suddenly awkward.

Ben knelt before them. He reached for Katie's hand, but she recoiled. 'Katie, I'm sorry.'

'Who are you?' she whispered.

He looked at her like it might be a trick question. 'It's me.'

'No, it's not. The Ben I knew would never agree to this.'

'The Ben you knew changed when his girlfriend killed herself,' Ben replied flatly.

Even Alisha flinched at that. Perhaps none of them knew how hard Janey's death had hit Ben. He'd seemed so strong, so resilient, but perhaps it was all a front. 'I'm just, *just* getting my life back on track and then this . . . Roxanne was going to blackmail us all, Katie. I'm not going to feel sorry for her.'

Katie blinked back tears. 'Answer me one question.'

Ben guessed the question. 'Did I kill her? No. I swear to you.' Katie nodded. Ben went on, 'But we have to do this. I know it's awful, but we've been friends forever and we have to protect each other.'

Alisha saw Katie's eyes narrow. For a split second, she really thought Katie might slap him, but then all the fight ebbed away, her shoulders sank and she simply said, 'OK.'

'You'll do it?'

Katie batted a tear from her cheek. 'Ben, how can you ask that? You know I'd do anything for you.'

Alisha shot off the sofa like it had bitten her. Sorry, but this was all a bit much. It was too intense, too intimate, and she couldn't sit there and listen. There was something curled up at the bottom of her stomach – a hard knot that felt a little like jealousy. It didn't make sense, and the timing was mightily inappropriate, but it would be nice if there was someone in her life who cared for her the way Ben cared for Katie. 'I . . . I'm gonna see if Greg needs me.'

She swept out of the lounge and onto the top terrace.

A hand over her eyes to shield them from the sun's fierce glare, Alisha looked on in morbid fascination as Ryan and Greg carried Roxanne up the stone stairs onto the terrace. It was every inch the car crash you slow down to peer at. Greg held her arms, Ryan her legs, and she swung like a hammock between them – butchers carrying meat. They laid her down on the patio.

Ryan stepped over the body. 'Where's Roxanne's bedding? We need to wrap her up or we'll leave evidence everywhere.'

'I'll get it.' Alisha turned away, dumbstruck. It seemed that wherever she went, she walked into a surreal melodrama. She pulled the door open and cannoned straight into Ben's broad chest. She couldn't look him in the eye. God, she might never be able to look anyone in the eye ever again. What was it gonna be like after they'd dumped Rox? Every time she walked past a policeman she'd get cold sweats and palpitations. This feeling was going to get worse and worse, she just knew it.

The lounge was now empty. 'Where's Katie?'

'She went up to her room,' Ben replied.

She glowered at him. 'I'll go see if she's OK.'

'Lish!' Greg called from outside. 'Where are the sheets?'

With a sigh, she took the neatly folded pile of sheets, which, of course, Roxanne had never used, and flung them in Greg's direction. Just because she had agreed to this didn't mean she was happy about it. Not by a long stretch.

'Hey, Lish.' Ben took hold of her arm. 'Greg's right. This *is* for the best.'

Oh, who was he trying to convince? 'Is it? You really think so?'

He nodded, but there was so much pain in his eyes it made Alisha's chest ache. He had such a beautiful mouth. How had that never occurred to her until now? Why was it occurring to her *at all* when the corpse of her nemesis festered just behind them? 'I'm gonna check on Katie,' she said again and broke away from him, unable to deal with a feeling that she didn't fully understand. Not looking back, she hurried across the lounge, leaving Ben to deal with the extreme twistedness on the terrace.

When she entered the bedroom, Katie was just sitting on the end of the bed, a hollow, unblinking stare on her face.

'Hey, hon,' Alisha said gently.

'I told Ben I'd go along with whatever Greg and Ryan are cooking up. Right now, I just want to go home,' Katie told her.

Alisha nodded. In a weird way she was glad Katie wasn't trying to stop them. She wanted all this over with as fast as possible. It was like a living, breathing nightmare. 'Who do you think . . .'

'Don't.' Katie blinked back tears. 'It's too awful to think about. Why would anyone want to kill Roxanne?'

That drew a wry laugh from Alisha. 'Who *wouldn't* want to kill Roxanne?' Then she took Katie's hand and gave it a squeeze. 'Too soon?'

Katie managed a little laugh in response. 'Too soon.' She went on to answer her own question. 'She knew something about Janey . . . and it got her killed. One of us killed Janey *and* Rox.'

'It *might* be someone else – like someone prowling the beach,' Alisha pointed out. 'And maybe Janey *did* jump . . .' Alisha was often accused of being naive, but she didn't care; it was better than being jaded and cynical.

'Fat chance!' Katie laughed. 'Greg's right. This is all because of Janey. It's all connected. God, what happened that night? There's something in there, Alisha. Something we're missing.'

It's probably really obvious and we're just not seeing it. What happened at the ball?'

'I don't know. I was drunk, Katie. Really drunk,' Alisha admitted, feeling ashamed.

'Please, Lish. What do you remember?'

Alisha took a deep breath and folded her legs. 'OK. We can do the extended disco remix if you want. It's not like we're going anywhere, is it? Remember where we'd got to? We pranked Mrs Finching and then headed for the ball?'

Katie tensed up. 'Yes. Go on . . .'

FLASHBACK – LAST YEAR (ALISHA)

They were kind of late for the ball; it was already well underway by the time they arrived. Other students were spilling out of the gymnasium, one girl already tossing her dinner onto the netball court while a friend held her hair back. Without Katie there, Alisha couldn't help wondering who would hold *her* hair back later. A group of guys from the rugby team had chosen to dress identically in kilts and were busy flashing each other for a group photo.

The friends didn't care that they were late. They were buzzing. After the pranks, they felt oddly invincible. Maybe it was the cheap, fizzy wine but, as they sauntered into the gym, Alisha felt like she was walking on air. Nothing could touch her tonight.

'OK! Where's the bar?' she demanded.

'Beyond the line of defence,' Ryan joked, pointing to the row of teacher chaperones who were sitting in front of the bar, looking thrilled at losing their evening.

Alisha made a beeline for the bar.

Greg's hand suddenly wrapped around her arm. 'Don't you do anything to embarrass me,' he hissed in her ear so that only she would hear.

'Isn't your date waiting?' Alisha asked and pointed at the bleached blonde blow-up doll her brother was currently dating.

Alisha proceeded to the drinks area, which was manned by the ball committee. Once there, she allowed herself to have a sly look around. No sign of her skanky-boyfriend-stealing-nemesis, Roxanne, yet.

Ben sidled up alongside her. 'You OK, Lish?'

Busted! 'Yeah. I was just seeing if *she* was here yet.'

'Oh, I see,' he said. He put a big arm around her shoulders and gave her a squeeze. It was harmless and brotherly, but her skin hummed at his touch. 'You know what, Cole? You are worth a hundred Roxanne Dents. It's official. I did a very scientific study.'

She rested her head on his broad shoulder. 'You're very sweet, Ben. A massive liar, but very sweet.'

'I mean it. You have something she doesn't.'

'And what's that? Big boobs?'

He chortled. 'I was gonna say "a soul", but them, too!'

Alisha felt her face flush. She could either say something rude and witty, or simply take the compliment. 'Thank you.'

'Any time.' He took two drinks. One for him and one for Janey – his girlfriend. God, she envied them. All these Noah's Ark couples going two-by-two and she was here alone. Where was *her* Ben Murdoch?

'Oi, Cole!' It was Ryan. He came up from behind and poked her in the ribs. 'Can you dance in those shoes?'

'What do you think?' She took his hand in her left and a drink in her right and led him to the floor.

They danced. They danced a lot. Alisha's feet felt like they were on fire and sweat ran down her back. The metallic dress could well see her roasted by the end of the night, but it was a perfect evening. Janey had cheered up, thank God, and had hoisted her dress up to dance. Even Ben joined in, although his dancing left a lot to be desired. Greg just stood at the edge of the dance floor, a protective arm around his vapid date.

That was when she saw them. Alisha froze, although no one seemed to notice. It was the music crowd – Callum's friends – she spotted first. Black eyeliner and skinny jeans with skinnier ties. That was just the guys. The girls were all in black – ripped fishnets and lank hair. Bringing up the rear of their group was Callum, hand in hand with Roxanne. She wore a clingy, flesh-coloured dress. She might as well be nude. Blonde hair fell in carefully messed-up waves down her back. Around their wrists they had matching purple ribbon bands. They must have done a festival together.

Alisha felt it like a kick to her stomach. It was pain. It was hate. She could almost see the darkness blurring the edges of her vision. Someone squeezed her hand. It was Janey.

'Take a deep breath. She *wants* a reaction, remember. Don't give her the satisfaction.'

Alisha exhaled. Janey's voice guided her down off the ceiling.

'Oh, crap, I have to be on stage.' Ben broke away from the group and Alisha realised it must be time for the speeches. He pushed through the crowd to join an annoyed-looking Rosalyn Chung, the Head Girl, on stage. Alisha could almost see her lips mouth the words *Where the eff have you been all night?*

'Good evening, Longview!' Rosalyn began. 'Welcome to the Leavers' Ball!'

A girl from Alisha's photography group came up next to her. 'Psst, Lish, do you want a vodka jelly? We snuck them in.'

'Sure.' She took the shot and knocked it back, chasing it with beer. Wow, that was cider, wine, beer and vodka all in one evening. The room spun a little, but she needed the drink. How else would she cope with the Callum and Roxanne show?

One of the techie geek crew fiddled with Ben's collar, attaching a mic to the lapel of his tux. Ben took his place behind the lectern with Rosalyn. 'Can you hear me OK?' he said. The crowd roared agreement. 'This is a momentous night. We've been in this gym on many occasions, but this is the very last time we'll set foot in this school.'

'Except for Results Day,' Rosalyn put in.

'Exactly. This is our last chance to have some fun before we all go our separate ways. A chance to say goodbye.' There was a chorus of *awww*s from the audience. 'But we can't go without sharing a drink, a dance and our Longview memories.'

'With that in mind,' said Rosalyn, 'the Ball Committee, led by Roxanne Dent, have put together a video montage. Can we have a round of applause, please?'

As the hall clapped, Roxanne made a cute curtsey. Alisha mimed gagging onto Ryan's tux. A projector screen behind Ben and Rosalyn lit up, revealing a banner heading, LONGVIEW HIGH SCHOOL – FRIENDS TO THE END, along with the school insignia of a seagull flying over the cliffs. There followed a pretty standard array of photos from the last seven years: school shows, sports days, Science and Literature awards. Alisha briefly glimpsed herself in a photo of a sculpture day they'd hosted with a visiting artist a few years back. Ryan and Janey cheered as an image of them as Sally Bowles and Emcee in last year's *Cabaret* flashed up.

The film changed pace with an animation of a yearbook opening up.

'Urgh, how *American*!' laughed Ryan.

The Ball Committee had kindly assigned roles to people. Ben and Janey were awarded the honour of 'Prom King and Queen' – and a couply photo appeared on the display.

'Oh, that's so sweet!' Janey grinned. Her face soon fell. The first photo (Janey and Ben on the pier) changed to a second (Janey and Ben sitting on the grass verge outside the science block) but then it changed a third time. The new picture showed Ben in a tight embrace on the clifftop, but the girl he had his arms around wasn't Janey. It was Katie.

A gasp and a giggle ran around the room. It was tradition – the yearly photo montage *had* to be a little risqué – it was just one of those things. Janey looked far from impressed. From the stage, Ben mouthed 'sorry'. Alisha whirled to glare at Rox, who stifled a giggle with the rest of the Ball Committee.

'Is that an *old* picture?' Janey demanded, her jaw clenched.

'Of course it is,' Ryan assured her. 'It must be.'

Alisha wasn't sure, but the offending image had vanished now, replaced by the next part of the montage, so she couldn't scrutinise the clothes or hairstyles.

Janey reached into her purse and took out her phone. 'What are you doing?' Alisha shouted as the crowd laughed at whatever was on the screen.

'Nothing.' Janey frantically tapped away on the touchscreen.

Alisha turned back to the montage. Next up was 'Class Clown'. An image of Kyle Norton flashed up – his pants around his ankles. That was the thing – the montage was meant to be a piss-take. Janey didn't seem to appreciate the joke. Kyle, however, made a wild wolf-call at his new title.

'Let's see how funny he is when he gets home and steps in shit,' Ryan whispered.

Some more classmates were honoured. 'Brainiac of the Year' (Olivia Hewitt) was first, then 'Sickeningly Cute Couple' (Tori Holmes and Lucie Slade) and finally 'The Matt Fisher Award for Supreme Cool' was awarded to Matt Fisher. Next up was 'Superstar' – who else could it be but Greg? A montage of his early days with the Brighton Youth Team appeared on screen. The auditorium rewarded him with a mighty cheer. He was their golden boy – a claim to fame for everyone. The people in this room would forever be able to say they went to school with footballer Greg Cole.

Alisha rolled her eyes. She had enough of this at home. She took another vodka jelly.

'Longview's Got Talent' was up next. It was Ryan. He made a giddy bleating noise. There was a selection of pictures of his lead roles, along with a note to say that he'd been accepted into performing arts college. The room applauded and Ryan took a bow.

And that's when the picture changed. Alisha's mouth fell open. She clutched Ryan's arm. It was her. She was crawling out of a bush, her skirt up around her waist. One shoe had fallen off and there was make-up smudged down her cheeks. The caption read, 'Most Likely to Need Rehab'.

Year Thirteen burst into rapturous claps and cheers – by far the biggest of the night. They laughed so hard tears ran down their faces. *Look at Alisha Cole – such a hot mess! Thank God we're not like her.* At least, that's how Alisha interpreted the mirth. To her, this was definitely a laughing *at*, not *with*, moment.

She saw Roxanne laughing and her stomach clenched. Taking Callum from her wasn't enough for Rox, was it? She wanted to *ruin* Alisha. The room turned red. Reason and logic burned to nothing, leaving only rage. Her feet moved like they were possessed and Alisha careered across the dance floor, shoving aside anyone who stood in her way.

Roxanne didn't see her coming until it was too late. 'Alisha, can't you take a jo—' she began.

Alisha grasped her blonde hair and swung her, head first, into the fire-escape door. With a satisfying rip, she felt the hair come away in her hands. Roxanne screamed and slumped to the floor. Alisha couldn't stop now, though. She delivered a precise toe to Roxanne's stomach and Rox choked.

'Get up, you bitch!' Alisha yelled.

Hands wrapped themselves around her. Many hands. She didn't know whose. She was dragged away from the sobbing blonde wreck on the floor.

A strong hand yanked at her wrist. 'Alisha! What are you doing?' It was Mr Kemp, the physics teacher. Alisha looked around, realising that the auditorium was now silent. All eyes were on her. Greg had never looked more angry.

'She's dead! Dead!' Alisha screeched.

Callum helped his girlfriend off the floor.

Mr Kemp pulled Alisha towards the main exit. 'Alisha, how much have you had to drink? You need to go home and sober up.'

'Let go of me!' she wailed. The fight poured out of her body and she felt herself go limp: a deflated balloon girl.

'YOU AND KATIE?' The voice boomed around the auditorium like the voice of God, freezing everyone in their tracks. Alisha recognised that voice. It wasn't God, it was Janey. She scanned the room, looking for a glimpse of the crimson dress. Janey was nowhere to be seen, and neither, for that matter, was Ben. He'd gone from the stage and Rosalyn now stood there alone, fuming at her ruined moment.

'You went through my phone?' Ben's disembodied voice echoed. He sounded outraged, although Alisha knew that that was the piss-poor defence used in only one type of argument. But where were they? Every single word they said was loud and clear but they were nowhere to be seen. Then it dawned on her – their conversation was being picked up by Ben's microphone.

'How long has it been going on? Tell me!' Janey cried.

As realisation set in, there were gasps and giggles from the audience. Alisha's head was spinning – and not just from the drink *or* the fight. Ben and Katie? When? Now? But that would mean . . . Oh God. Ben had cheated on Janey with his ex.

'Janey, it's not what you think . . .' Ben's words rang out, amplified.

The room erupted: more gasps, but mostly laughter. Half the crowd covered their mouths in shock, half couldn't conceal their glee at the unexpected interval show. Even Ryan couldn't keep his delight at the scandal out of his eyes.

'Don't lie! How could you?' Janey screamed. The door to the boys' changing room at the left of the stage burst open and Janey tumbled back into the hall with Ben close behind. As they entered applause greeted them.

'Nice one, Ben!' Kyle Norton whooped. 'Take the mic off next time, you dick!'

The colour seeped from both of their faces. Alisha tried to rush to her friend's side, but a new hand held her back – Greg's.

'Don't you dare. You've done enough for one night,' he said in her ear.

'But Janey . . .' Alisha saw a thick tear roll down Janey's face. This would kill her. Janey was the proudest person she knew. The humiliation – she'd be broken by it.

Thank God for the DJ having the common sense to turn the music back on at that moment. Any further words were drowned out by *House of Pain*.

The walls felt like they were crumbling down. Alisha didn't even notice Greg drag her away. All she could see was Janey swing for Ben. It seemed to happen in slow motion. Ben's head snapped back as her hand made contact with his cheek. Miss Hoffman tried to pull them apart, but Janey spat in his face, turned and stalked away.

Janey's scarlet dress was the only colour in the washed-out, grey room. As Greg practically carried Alisha out of the main exit, Janey pushed through the fire escape and fled into the night.

It was the last time anyone saw her.

Unless one of them *had* seen her again – and killed to keep it a secret.

SCENE 20 – ALISHA

'When did it happen? You and Ben, I mean,' Alisha asked Katie as they sat there together on the bed.

Katie just managed to blink back the tear before it left her eye. She took a pause to compose herself before replying. 'It was a totally normal day. I think it was a Wednesday. Yep, definitely a Wednesday because we'd had "Enrichment".' Enrichment activities were those that were designed to strengthen their personal statements for university. 'Ben and I had both chosen pottery. How lame is that? We were carrying our crappy little clay jugs home after school and it was a really gorgeous sunny day. We walked along the cliff path. We sat down in the grass and watched the sea, talked about everything we wanted to do this year. We were so excited. I don't even know how or why, but we started reminiscing about stuff. He said I was still the best kisser he knew. I said I'd remind him sometime. And so I did.'

Alisha frowned. 'It was just a kiss?'

'There's no such thing as *just* a kiss.'

'I guess you're right.'

Katie ran a hand through her auburn hair, looking thoroughly exhausted. 'It was all those clichés, Lish. It was opening the floodgates, Pandora's Box, forbidden fruit. It was ridiculous. He was with Janey, we were *both* leaving in a few months, but we started texting. It was mostly harmless but Janey must have read *dozens* of messages. It was along the lines of "maybe we made a mistake", "maybe we should have never split up" – that sort of stuff. God, sometimes I can't even remember why we did break up.'

Alisha smiled kindly and said, 'Because you were fourteen when you got together. What? You were gonna marry your first boyfriend? Be his child bride?'

Katie laughed. Alisha remembered telling Katie at the time that there were plenty more fish in the sea. As it turned out, all the other fish were cheap fish fingers and Ben was finest caviar.

Katie continued. 'Poor Janey. I can't imagine how she must have felt. She must have thought we were all laughing behind her back.'

'The ball was brutal – everyone laughing in her face,' Alisha agreed.

Katie gasped suddenly. 'Oh, God! What if Ben followed her out and . . . '

Alisha frowned, still unable to imagine Ben hurting anyone. Ben, who had always made her feel so safe. When he was around she'd always felt like nothing bad could happen. So many times she'd been wasted, unable to put one foot in front of the other, but he'd been the one who'd made sure she'd got home or got in the taxi. Until she *saw* Rox's evidence with her own eyes, she wouldn't believe that Ben had done anything to hurt Janey. 'Try not to think about it,' she told Katie.

'How can I not? You can't remember anything else about that night? Nothing?"

'After Greg dragged me out, I didn't even see which way Janey went. He stuck me in a taxi by myself and sent me home. I doubt they'd have let me back into the ball, to be honest.'

'So that means Greg, Ryan and Ben are all unaccounted for.'

Alisha shrugged. 'You're the only one who *is* accounted for that night. No one saw me get home.'

Katie gave her hand a squeeze. 'No one's accusing you of anything, Lish.'

There was a tap on the door and both girls jumped. Ben appeared. 'Hey, are you OK?'

Neither girl replied, letting their faces say it all. On memory lane, Alisha had momentarily forgotten about Roxanne. Now the thought of Rox was back like a migraine. *What were they about to do?*

'Yeah, that was a stupid question, sorry,' Ben said sheepishly. 'Katie, we need to know where you keep the cleaning stuff – mops, buckets and so on.'

'Why?' Alisha asked, and then immediately cottoned on. They had to clean away the evidence. 'Oh. Right.' It was time to go and face the reality of what she'd signed up for.

SCENE 21 – RYAN

I n America, four times a year, TV channels do something
called 'sweeps' where they take ratings for all the big
shows. Accordingly, the shows in question go all out to ensure
that people will stay home and watch. They'll write some
momentous event like a wedding or natural disaster into the
script. In this case, Ryan reflected, the 'writers' had opted to
kill a villainous character and have the rest of the cast dump
her body at sea.

Thinking about it like that was the only way Ryan could
handle it. It was all a ratings-winner. Roxanne was a villain.
What she had tried to do was criminal. She had this coming.
Don't think about what *really* happened. Don't dwell on the
fact that one of them was a killer, and that *all* of them were
now accessories. Don't acknowledge the truth.

As darkness fell over the villa, Ryan changed into a plain
black T-shirt and jean shorts before tucking his distinctive
curls under a baseball cap. He'd worked too bloody hard to
end up in jail and if they didn't carefully dispose of Roxanne's
body he didn't see how they could avoid it. If no one was
going to admit to her murder – and why would they? – they'd
all be put under lock and key.

Plus this made for a much better story.

The rest of the afternoon had been a macabre affair. While

Roxanne lay on the dining-room table, wrapped up like a mummy, they'd cleaned the villa from top to bottom. You could literally eat your dinner off the floor tiles now. They'd all diligently chipped in – all except Katie and Alisha. He sensed they were on thin ice with those two. It was hot, hard, sweaty work. The sun was no longer a friend but an enemy, making every small movement a major undertaking. It beat down on them like an oppressive physical force. Ryan had spent all afternoon on his knees by the pool, scrubbing every inch of the floor. If they were going to do this, they had to do it right. By the time they'd finished there were only three jobs remaining. They'd have to drain the pool. It looked clear blue as ever, but it *must* be full of Roxanne's blood. They couldn't work out how to use the pump, so they decided to leave it until the following day. They needed to burn all Roxanne's stuff so that no trace of her presence remained. The last job was disposing of Rox herself.

All day he'd waited for sadness to kick in. It hadn't. When people die you're meant to feel sad, but fear of his own incarceration was all Ryan could feel – it was all-consuming. He couldn't lie to himself, but he had to pretend sadness to fool the others or they'd think he was a monster. That's the thing with death – he'd noticed it when Janey was finally found – everyone knows how you're *supposed* to react; you're meant to drop to your knees and howl at the sky with clenched fists, but what if it doesn't come? What if you don't cry? What if you just feel cold?

Ryan left the safety of his bedroom. He'd avoided the others for most of the day. What conversation was there to be had beyond 'did you get all the blood off the tiles?'? He entered the lounge to find them all sitting around in terse, jagged silence as the sky beyond the windows deepened to the colour of a bruise. The villa seemed smaller, more claustrophobic. 'Is it time?'

'Yeah,' said Greg. Erin hovered at his side, staring blankly at the wall. It was like she'd checked out of reality. God, hadn't they all? Ryan's relationship with reality was tenuous at the best of times.

'Please,' Katie begged, eyes wide and honest. 'Is there anything I can say to change your minds?' Next to her, Ryan felt cold, hard and more than a little evil.

Alisha sat next to Katie on the kitchen counter. 'Whoever did this, you know you're taking all of us down with you.'

Ryan raised an eyebrow. If Alisha was hoping to guilt the murderer into a confession, she was going to be sadly disappointed. He suspected that this was exactly what the killer wanted – to diffuse the guilt among the crowd. When no one responded, Ryan said, 'Big shock. No takers on the jail sentence.'

Greg rose to his feet. 'Come on. We can talk about this forever, but she'll just start to smell.'

Katie looked like she might throw up.

'Once we do this, there's no going back.' Alisha hopped off the counter. 'You know that, right? We can't fish her out and say it was a mistake.'

'Everything's done.' Greg slid open the patio doors. 'Once this is over, all we have to do is burn all her stuff and drain the pool.'

'Wait,' Ryan said. 'What about the evidence she said she had?' He hadn't forgotten that, somewhere, tucked away in the villa, there was the proof that one of them was wearing a very convincing mask.

'We can search when we get back,' Greg told him. 'But this comes first. No body. No crime.'

That sentiment hung in the air for a moment. 'Come on,' Katie sighed. 'If we have to do this, let's get it over and done with.'

'She's right.' Greg clapped a hand on Katie's shoulder. 'Katie, it'll be fine. We do this and we can carry on as normal.'

Katie didn't look at all convinced, but went along with it with a nod of her head. 'I'll go start the boat up.'

'Are all the outside lights off?' Ben asked.

Ryan hurried to the kitchen and depressed the switches. The terrace and pool lights flashed off. 'They are now.'

The five of them hovered around the dining-room table and its gruesome centrepiece. 'How do we do this?' Ryan finally asked.

'Same way we got her up,' Greg sighed. 'Ben, which end do you want?'

'Dude, I feel sick.'

'Just don't think about it, mate.'

'For God's sake, I'll do it.' Ryan took the leg end. The quicker they started, the sooner they'd finish. Greg slotted his hands under what-used-to-be-Roxanne's shoulders but, now that she was wrapped up, he couldn't hook his hands into her armpits and she was harder to hold.

'It might be easier for me to do it alone,' Greg suggested.

'Are you sure?' Ryan asked.

Greg nodded. In life, Roxanne had been actress-thin. With little effort, Greg hoisted the mummy off the table. The body seemed stiffer than before, the corpse refusing to slump over Greg's shoulder. Of course – now that she was out of the water, rigor mortis had set in. Ryan winced; it didn't bear thinking about.

Greg moved quickly. He swept out of the doors and onto

the terrace. Ryan exchanged a guilty glance with Ben before following.

The jetty was about two hundred metres down the beach from the villa. In the diminishing light, it was just a dark, crooked shape jutting into the sea. A worn stone walkway at the end of the pool terrace led straight to the wooden structure. The jetty itself had seen better days; the wooden slats were uneven and stood on worn skeleton legs which reached down into the water.

Katie was already climbing into the boat. Ryan's nautical knowledge was non-existent but he could see that the vessel was white with no sail, so it had to be some sort of motorboat. It was bigger than a speedboat, but smaller than a yacht.

Greg paused to heave the body back onto his shoulder. The sheets were coming undone and a foot now stuck out at the bottom of the wrap. Ryan scanned the beach, terrified someone would be out with a dog or something. They hadn't seen another soul in three days, so it figured that *now* would be the time when someone would show up. Thankfully, it was still deserted.

The boat started with a stutter, coughing water out of the exhaust vent.

'Hurry up,' Katie shouted. 'Before someone sees.'

Once at the jetty, Greg lowered the body onto the slats. Alisha turned her nose up at her brother, walking straight past him towards the boat.

'Let me help,' Ben offered. The two of them carried Rox the rest of the way over the creaking catwalk.

'Do you think anyone saw?' Erin asked Ryan.

'I don't think so.' Ryan looked back over the silver sand. The interval street lights stretched all the way down the coast, and Zahara de los Atunes twinkled on the horizon, but only the villa windows watched them like eyes. 'Did you lock up as you left?'

'I just shut the terrace door.'

'It'll be fine.' Ryan hurried down the jetty towards the boat. Greg was already aboard, and Ben lowered Roxanne into his arms. There was a ladder into the back of the boat, but it was unsteady. Ryan was reminded of his fear of the sea. Once you've seen *Jaws* . . . Ben grabbed his arm and helped him on deck. He, in turn, offered Erin a hand.

'Are we all aboard?' Katie asked. 'Take off the rope.'

Ryan unhooked the blue rope that tethered them to the jetty.

'I can't believe we're actually doing this,' muttered Alisha.

'Just drive, or sail, or whatever the word is.' Greg loomed over Katie at the helm. 'No lights.'

'Greg, I have to. It's the law.'

'You're kidding, right? No lights.'

Katie turned off the lights and they sailed out onto the endless black sea.

The bow of the boat cut through the water like a fin. Ryan cursed the noise the propeller made – wasn't there a silent mode? Waves sloshed up against the sides and he felt either seasick or simply sick.

Now that they were here, it didn't seem like TV any more. It wasn't a jolly romp. It wasn't a teen thriller. It was real. The night air was somehow both humid and cold, clinging to his skin like grease. He didn't even know what type of crime they were about to commit. Manslaughter? Perverting the course of justice? Murderer-helping? One of them, in all likelihood, was a killer. A chill twisted the base of his spine.

The beach was still in sight, the villa a dot of light in the distance because they'd left the lights on inside. Ryan kept his eyes fixed on that. He figured they couldn't let it out of their sight or they'd never find their way back. That thought scared him most of all. But on the other side of tonight, there would be a new day: a new start.

Why is this taking so long?

'Is this far enough?' It was like Greg had read Ryan's thoughts.

Katie stopped the engine. The boat lurched with the waves, the sea making gulping-glugging noises against the side of the vessel.

Ryan's head felt full of fluid, swishing with the water. 'Far enough for what?' he asked.

Ben spoke up. 'We need to make sure she won't wash up on the beach.'

'She won't.' Greg pointed to a pile of rocks near the door to the boat's cabin. 'I put them on earlier. We can weigh her down.'

'But how is that going to work?' Alisha pointed out. 'What if the rocks come off ? She's already coming undone.'

Alisha had a point. The last thing they needed was the body bobbing to the surface in a couple of hours' time. Ryan started to look around the floor of the boat. 'Katie, have you got any rope on this thing? We need to secure her better.'

'I don't know,' Katie sighed with a distant look in her eyes. Ryan got the impression she had switched off. She was refusing to engage with the whole thing. He knew she felt that he'd abandoned her. And, in that moment, he also knew that he'd never get Katie Grant back. She was lost to him. No more Ryan-hugs. It was a price he guessed he'd have to pay for his freedom.

Ben lifted one of the seats. 'There's rope in here. We can use that.'

Katie peered out from under her fringe, dark shadows circling her usually sweet eyes. Through gritted teeth she muttered, 'You don't have to use rope and rocks. In the cabin there's all my dad's diving stuff. You can use his belts and weights.'

'What belts and weights?' Alisha asked.

'For deep sea diving.' Greg's eyes lit up. 'They stop you floating back to the surface. That's awesome. Thanks, Katie.'

She said nothing, but turned away from them and laid her weary head on the steering wheel.

Greg was already rummaging around in the cabin. He emerged a second later carrying a bag overflowing with diving tackle. 'This weighs a ton.' He threw it onto the boat floor. Ryan got stuck in. There were three or four belts tangled together. He pulled at one until it fell away from the others. At the bottom of the bag were square yellow weights of different values.

'Won't it be a bit suspect if the police find Rox's body with a diving belt attached?' Ryan suggested.

'They won't find her,' Greg said confidently. 'Sharks will be able to smell the blood from miles away. In a few days there'll be nothing left to find.'

'Oh, my days!' Alisha threw her hands up. 'Could you at least try not to sound so excited about this?'

'I guess we should unwrap her then,' Erin said, changing the subject and getting to work with no complaints – as efficient as any surgeon and without a trace of squeamishness. Ryan assumed this wasn't the first corpse she'd ever seen if she was studying medicine.

'This is sick.' Alisha twisted her body away, refusing to look.

In the moonlight, now unwrapped, Roxanne glowed. She was otherworldly, ethereal. Her skin and lips were bleached white, and only her eyelids looked dark. Her face already appeared sunken, her cheekbones more prominent. She belonged to the dead now.

The first pangs of guilt struck Ryan like lightning bolts. Suddenly, he didn't want to do it. This was too much. He thought of Rox's uncle and aunt in Telscombe Cliffs. There *were* people who'd miss her. He steeled himself, gripping the rim of the seat behind his back.

Get it together! a harsh voice in his head told him. It was too late to save Roxanne. Guilt wasn't going to achieve anything. Nothing he did was going to bring Rox back from the dead. It was over for her. It didn't have to be over for him. He tried to draw strength from Greg, who seemed so cool, so strong.

Greg clipped the belt around Roxanne's waist and pulled it as tight as it'd go. There was no further need for cumbersome ropes and bed sheets; the sleek belt would be sufficient to weigh the body down. 'There.'

There was a moment of silence. Everyone knew what came next.

'What do you want to do?' Ben looked to Greg.

'I don't bloody know. It's not like I do this shit every week, you know. I guess we just tip her over the side.'

'Wait,' Ryan said. 'Don't you think we should all make a pact or something? Like swear that we'll *take it to the grave?*'

'You watch way too much TV,' Alisha said bitterly. 'As if any of us are *ever* going to bring this up.'

Katie was still in the drivers' seat, quietly resigned. 'You know, it's still not too late. The police don't ever have to know we brought her out on the boat. We could put her back in the pool.'

169

'No,' Erin said matter-of-factly. 'They'll know now. They'll be able to tell how long she's been dead, and then they'll know we're lying.'

'So we're stuck,' Ryan concluded. 'We've gone too far to back out now.'

'Exactly. We need to finish the job.' Greg loaded the rocks he'd placed on the boat earlier onto the sheet that had been wrapped around Rox. Then he tied the corners together to create a sack and threw it over the side of the boat. 'That takes care of the sheet,' he said. 'Now, come on!' He manoeuvred himself to Roxanne's head and once more slipped his hands under her arms. 'God, she's heavy, now!'

'That's the idea,' Ryan said as he and Ben helped to haul her to the left side of the boat. Ryan had no idea if that was starboard or port, but it was the side furthest away from the villa and the shore.

'Do you think we should say something?' Katie wondered. 'Like a prayer, maybe?'

'Was she religious?' Erin asked.

'I don't know.' Katie shrugged.

Ryan looked at Roxanne. There was so much they didn't know about her and never would. They all paused because a pause was required. The three men looked at each other. There wasn't a word for what Ryan was feeling. It was dark, it was *awful*, but it was as exciting as any taboo ever is. There's always a thrill in going too far.

'Just do it,' Greg breathed.

And, between them, they lifted Roxanne's body over the edge of the boat and let her fall.

The sea was hungry. Blackness swallowed her. It all happened so fast and Ryan couldn't help feeling that something so huge shouldn't be over so quickly. The speed made it seem inconsequential. The weights at Roxanne's waist tugged her down at once so that, within a second, her body had vanished, followed by her lovely face. Her hair trailed above and, finally, her ice-white hands sunk out of sight.

The sea claimed Roxanne Dent, but the last thing Ryan saw going under was Katie Grant's charm bracelet.

SCENE 22 – RYAN

He was so entranced by the weird beauty of Roxanne sinking, that Katie's scream almost tipped him over the edge.

'She's wearing my bracelet!' Katie leaped to her feet, rocking the boat.

It took a moment for the information to sink in, longer than it had taken the dead girl to sink in, anyway.

Greg shrugged. 'It's only a bracelet.'

Ryan jolted to his feet. 'No! It's got Katie's name on it. If someone finds it . . .'

'Shit!' Greg exploded.

After what they'd just done, there was no way Ryan was letting a bloody bracelet ruin everything. Without a word, he pulled his hat off, climbed up onto the edge of the boat and dived in.

He held his breath and waited for the cold to hit him. Hit him it did.

To say the water was cold didn't do it justice. He had to resurface. The ice water hurt his bones and his jaw shook with a violent judder. 'Oh, my God, that's cold!' he cried before diving back under. How quickly would she sink? The weight belt had been heavy. He kicked down with all the force his legs could muster. He could just make out Roxanne's white-blonde hair below him. She was going down fast.

But she could no longer swim and Ryan could. As he kicked further, deeper, the water became blacker and more claustrophobic. It was like swimming into a vacuum. In the darkness, Roxanne was a beacon.

Ryan's chest felt swollen. His cheeks puffed out and he started to release precious air one tiny bubble at a time. He was *not* letting her get away. As stiff as she was, her arms floated at her sides, the gleaming bracelet almost mocking him. *Can't catch me* . . . His leg muscles burned and his eyes stung. Salt water caught at the back of his throat.

Fingers outstretched, he grazed her hand, but then it slipped away again, like gas. Another kick and he caught hold of her hair. Harsh, but helpful. He almost climbed down her body, taking hold of the bracelet. There was only one way it was coming off. *Sorry Katie* . . . Ryan yanked on the chain as hard as he could, but it didn't budge. The first whispers of panic fluttered in his head. He needed to breathe. He needed to get back to the surface.

That was when it brushed against his bare legs – something smooth, slick and muscular. Something moving. Something swimming.

Air tore from his lungs in horror. Not caring whether he ripped the girl's hand off, Ryan wrenched his arm back. The bracelet broke and links scattered. He palmed what was left and flailed around, looking for whatever had grazed him. He saw only black water.

But Ryan was certain that there *was* something in the water with him. He kicked for the surface with frantic vigour, hoping to scare whatever it was away. The white rectangle of the boat was right overhead. He would have to swim out to avoid coming up directly underneath. He steered himself diagonally, the water thinning with moonlight as he neared the surface.

He broke into the air with a scream. 'Get me out! Shark!'

That did the trick. About ten arms shot over the edge of the boat. He seized whichever were nearest and allowed them to drag him out of the water. He fell into the boat and panted, waiting for his vision to stop whirling. He couldn't move. He was spent.

Questions came thick and fast, but he couldn't focus.

'Ryan?' It was Katie. 'Ryan?'

He coughed, the taste of salt all the way to his stomach. 'I got it.'

'Where is it?' Katie's eyes were full of hope. Ryan realised they'd wanted the bracelet back for very different reasons.

'I'm sorry, I had to break it to get it off.' He handed her the remains. Katie nodded, but couldn't completely hide her disappointment.

'There was a shark?' Alisha asked, helping him upright.

'I don't know. There was something. It felt big.'

'That's good,' Greg said. 'Sharks are good.'

Ben ignored them all, gazing out over the sea. Who knew what he was looking for? 'We did it. We actually did it,' he muttered.

An awful silence followed. Somewhere in the distance a buoy clanged, reminiscent of church bells. Ryan couldn't bear it. It wasn't that he was scared of awkward silences— Oh, who was he kidding? He was *terrified* of awkward silences. 'So!' he said brightly. 'Who's for sangria?' The others ignored him. 'Just me, then?'

'Come on,' Greg shouted. 'Let's get the hell out of here before the coastguard sees us.'

Katie didn't move for a second, fixated on the sad remains

174

of the bracelet in her hands. Then, coming back to life, she returned to the pilot's seat and started the motor.

'Wait.' Erin unfolded her legs. 'What about the bottle?'

'Oh, yeah. Chuck it over the edge.' Greg looked at Ryan.

'Well, I haven't got it,' Ryan replied, sopping wet and clutching his body for warmth. He should really get the wet clothes off before he caught hypothermia and they had another body to deal with.

'Mate, I told you to bring it.'

'No, you didn't.'

'Yes, I did.'

'You didn't.'

Katie spun the wheel as hard as it would go, making the boat swing round so violently that both boys staggered, close to going overboard. 'For God's sake! It doesn't matter!' Katie snapped. 'The sodding bottle doesn't matter! And will someone please give Ryan some dry clothes before he freezes to death?' The tone of her voice silenced them.

'I support that notion.'

Greg picked himself up off the floor of the boat and threw Ryan his hoodie. 'We'll get rid of the bottle with her stuff.'

'How are we going to do that?' Erin asked. She looked so different. Without her make-up, she had tiny little eyes, puffy from crying.

'We'll have another bonfire. Tomorrow night,' Greg replied.

Nothing more was said. They'd all said way too much already. Greg wrapped an arm around Erin. Katie drove in silence, her hair blowing behind her. Ryan sat next to Alisha, but she looked out over the ocean, unwilling to engage with the rest of them.

The boat chugged back towards the jetty, the coastline coming back into focus. Ryan worried that someone *must* have seen them. A lone boat in the empty bay must stick out a mile, even without lights. The clean, white vessel probably shone against the inky sea. Ryan hoped any onlookers would just think they were a load of drunk kids having a party-boat night. If they'd been really clever, they'd have brought some beers out with them. The coastguard would have frowned upon it, but probably a lot less than they frowned on dumping corpses.

Because that was what they'd just done.

Suddenly, Alisha sprang up like an excited puppy. She leaned over the side of the boat, looking towards the villa. A mane of curls blew around her head. 'Oh, my God! Look!'

'What?' Everyone seemed grateful for the distraction.

Alisha pointed to the shore. 'There's someone outside the villa.'

Ryan felt his heart drop through the bottom of his stomach. 'Katie, stop the boat.'

She twisted the key in the ignition and the boat choked to a halt.

'There can't be!' Ben exclaimed.

But there was. The outside lights were all off, but the interior lights had been left on, and now a silhouette could be clearly seen, making its way around the outskirts of the property. The shadow moved from window to window. Dark hands traced the glass, trying to get in.

'We're screwed,' Greg breathed.

'It's fine,' Ryan said. 'It's fine. We cleaned everything up.'

'Everybody get down.' Ben ducked beneath the side of the boat. 'They might just go away.'

They were too far from the beach to see properly. The figure was nothing more than a stick-man prowling around the house. The ghost-like figure peered inside, like Cathy looking for Heathcliff – only it was looking for them.

'Can they see us?' Erin whispered.

'No way. We're too far out, right?' Ben replied, his forehead creased with worry.

The silhouette slunk down the side of the house, moving closer to the beach with every step. 'Katie, were you expecting anyone?' Ryan asked.

'No. I have no idea who it is.' In the pale moonlight, Katie's fraught face took on an almost blueish tinge. It was quite beautiful.

'Did you call the police?' There was a hint of a threat in Greg's voice.

'I swear I didn't.'

As the figure neared the sand, moonlight lit her. It was a woman. A breeze blew dark hair around her face – long, chestnut hair. The wind chime played a tuneless, haunting song as she stood in front of the patio doors, looking out to the sea. The mystery girl held a hand to her eyes and scanned the horizon.

There was something familiar about the way she moved, the way she stood. An overwhelming wave of déjà vu hit Ryan as he stared at her across the water. 'No way!'

Katie gasped. 'Is that . . .'

Forgetting that he was supposed to be hiding, Ryan leaned as far as he could over the edge of the boat, his eyes straining. It wasn't possible.

A sliver of ghostly moonlight hit the contours of the woman's face and Ryan almost tumbled overboard.

It was Janey.

SCENE 23 – RYAN

I t *was* Janey: the hair, the body, the stance. The way she
stood, resting on her hip so that it jutted to the left, as if
the world were wasting her time. Ryan's brain malfunctioned.
One part of him was thrilled to see his old friend – he wanted
to wave and call her name – but another part knew he must
be seeing a ghost, something impossible, something *dead*.

He reviewed the possibilities . . .

1. Janey had a long-lost twin. Maybe she'd been trying to
   tell them something with the Shana/Lana thing.
2. It was a ghost. No. Even Ryan wasn't messed up enough
   to think that a supernatural element was about to creep
   in. It wasn't that kind of show.
3. Somehow Janey had survived – or never fallen in the
   first place – and now here she was! (If that was the case,
   what had they buried?)

The figure stared out to sea but, if she did see the boat,
her eyes didn't linger on it. Her hand fell to her side and,
resigned, she moved up the other side of the house, heading
back towards the front entrance. A moment later, Janey
melted back into the shadows and Ryan allowed himself to
breathe again.

'That's impossible.' Ben's lips were the same ghastly white as his face.

Greg ran forwards, tripping over his own feet in his rush to reach the driver's seat. 'Katie, go!'

'What? Where?'

'Go! Drive! Sail! We need to catch her. We don't know how long she's been there. She might have seen us.' Beads of sweat shone on Greg's forehead.

Katie's jaw dropped. 'Greg, that was Janey. Janey's alive!'

'It can't have been.'

'It was!' Alisha cried. 'You saw her. It looked *exactly* like her.'

'But . . . but . . . she's dead,' Ben murmured, staring at the villa, unblinking.

Greg screwed his eyes shut. 'I don't bloody care whether it's Janey or not. We just need to get back to the villa NOW!'

Katie twisted the key in the ignition and they were off.

'Oh, my God!' Ryan exclaimed suddenly. A magnificent epiphany had just come to him and something about it felt *right*. 'What if *she* did it?'

No one had to ask what action he was referring to.

'You think Janey killed Roxanne?' Alisha asked.

'Well, why not? Janey is meant to be dead, but for some reason she's creeping around outside the villa. What if she was creeping around outside the villa last night, too?'

'But why?' Katie said, sounding exasperated. Her hair hung in damp ropes around her face, the sea mist clinging to it. 'Why would she?'

'Because we left her.' It all made sense to Ryan now. 'What if she never fell? Or what if she fell but didn't die? We all abandoned her at the prom and this is her revenge . . . Or something.' Ryan tailed off. It sounded a little far-fetched now that he came to say it aloud.

Ben actually laughed. 'OK, you've finally lost the plot. That was *not* Janey.'

'It was,' Alisha put in.

Greg clenched his fists. 'Who cares?' he barked. 'Whoever it was might have just seen us throw a dead body into the sea. We have got to stop her before she calls the cops. Katie, speed this thing up.'

Ryan thought it best not to ask *how* Greg intended to stop her from calling the cops.

Katie was no expert and the boat very nearly ploughed all the way through the jetty. If there weren't dead girls *everywhere* tonight, it might have been quite funny, mused Ryan as they clung to the rails for dear life.

As soon as they were close enough, Greg jumped off the vessel and sprinted towards the villa with Alisha and Erin close behind, leaving Ryan and Katie to deal with the boat.

Ben was dumbstruck – staring out at the sea, but not seeing it. He was doing a chillingly realistic impression of a zombie right now.

'Ben? Benj, are you OK?' Ryan asked.

'I'll be fine,' he said but, privately, Ryan thought he was in a whole different postcode from 'fine'.

Katie killed the engine, left her seat and held out a hand for Ben. If she couldn't get through to him, no one could. 'Come on,' she said, her voice as soft as cotton wool. He took her hand but said nothing. 'Let's not . . . let's not assume anything, OK? Just because Janey's back doesn't mean she . . .'

'We don't know what she wants,' Ryan added, 'so let's go find out. It's *Janey*! She's *back*.'

Ben nodded and helped Katie off the boat. From the jetty, Ryan could see that Greg, Erin and Alisha had almost reached the villa. He hurriedly tied up the boat.

'Let's go,' he said and, together, the three of them raced down the jetty, the boards groaning under their weight. They reached the stone path, flip-flops clacking over the paving slabs. There was a patch of skin where the rubber strap chafed Ryan's still-wet toe, but he couldn't worry about the sting now.

Greg was already charging around the perimeter of the house by the time they reached the bottom terrace. Ryan pounded up the stairs to the top terrace and opened the patio doors, noting that they weren't locked. That meant Janey could be inside – how very 'horror film'. Once in, Ryan switched on the outside lights. The lamps on the terraces and around the pool came alive.

His shoulders tensed as he peered outside, his mind half-expecting to see a vengeful dead girl, but Janey, if that's who it had been, was nowhere in sight.

'Janey!' Alisha yelled from the right-hand path at the side of the house. 'Janey, where are you? It's us.' Ryan left the kitchen and followed the sound of Alisha's voice.

Katie joined him while Ben went the other way in search of Greg.

'Did you see her? Was she here?' Ryan asked as he and Katie caught up with Alisha.

Alisha turned to them. 'No, nothing.' The three of them ran onto the front drive where the cars were parked. The end of the drive opened out onto the long coast road, but even that was deserted. Night bugs sang and whistled in the palms and bushes, but the front of the villa was as quiet as the back. On land, there was stillness, not even a hint of a breeze.

'Where did she go? She was here like five minutes ago. She

can't have vanished.' Katie kicked at the gravel on the drive.

Ryan paused to let his frenetic heart rate slow. Janey Bradshaw. His world shifted to accommodate the possibility that she was alive. If she was, then the last twelve months were completely rewritten. It changed *everything*.

It seemed insane to think Janey had waited this long, waited until they were all together again, before revealing herself. But of course, in a way, it all made perfect sense. Revenge is a very powerful thing. It can change people. Ryan quite liked this interesting new twist. He certainly hadn't seen it coming and, if he was honest, if one of them had to be a psycho killer then better Janey than the others. He'd already mourned her loss.

Greg and Ben appeared from the bushes at the other side of the house.

'Anything?' Ryan asked.

'No,' Ben said. 'If she was here, she's long gone.'

'Or hiding.' Alisha paced up and down the drive. 'What if Ryan's right? What if she's come back for us? What if she saw and called the cops?'

'We all need to . . .' Ryan mimed simmering down with a graceful descent of his arms. 'We don't know what she did or didn't do, what she did or didn't see. All we do know is that she sure as hell can't get mobile phone reception out here.'

Greg cursed and slammed his way back into the villa through the front door. 'This is bullshit!' His cry shook the walls.

Ryan rolled his eyes at Alisha. Oh good, another Greg tantrum. That would help exponentially. They followed him inside. Greg smashed the bedroom doors open, turning on all the lights. He went from room to room, kicking aside anything that blocked his path. He was in hurricane mode.

'You don't think she's in here, do you?' Alisha said.

The bedrooms empty, Greg stormed down the stairs into the lounge to greet a wide-eyed Erin, where she waited, a knitted blanket around her shoulders. 'Baby, what's—'

'We're dead!' he barked.

Ryan helped himself to a glass of wine and poured one for Greg, too – the poor guy seemed to be spiralling out of control.

'If Ja— whoever that was, saw us, and God knows how long she was there – then she might have seen the whole thing for all we know. The body, the boat, everything!' he repeated, eyes wide, nostrils flared, like a bull entering the ring.

'We don't know that,' Alisha said, trying to soothe her brother's temper.

'If that was Janey,' Ryan drained his glass and refilled, 'then she's come back from the grave, mate. I don't think she's calling anyone, let alone the cops, do you? She's waited this long for a reason.' He offered Greg the wine, but Greg batted it away.

The veins in Greg's temple seemed to pulse. 'We need to find her. We need to find her NOW before she can get to anyone else.'

Ryan frowned. If Greg was seriously suggesting what he *thought* he was . . . Ryan saw Katie's mouth fall open and guessed that his friend had reached the same conclusion.

'Oh, my God!' Katie gasped. 'Are you saying that we should kill her, too?'

'What? No . . . that's not what I . . . shut up!' Greg snapped.

'Greg, chill, man.' Ben held a hand to Greg's chest, which only seemed to anger him further.

'Get your _____ hands off me!' Ryan again censored for the more delicate viewer. Greg shoved Ben back, the way footballers do referees.

Katie immediately went to Ben's defence. That was one of the things Ryan most admired about her: she had always, *always* stood up to bullies. 'Then what did you mean, Greg? What are you going to do if you find her?'

Greg looked confused. 'I said shut up!' he snarled.

'No! You *have* to listen to me, Greg.' Katie took hold of his shoulders. 'I mean, is that the plan now, to go around killing everyone who might tell on us? Are we next, Greg? We all saw. When does it stop?'

It happened so fast. Greg's hands were suddenly clamped around Katie's throat. Greg was so much bigger. He dwarfed Katie, making her seem frail. With all his weight, he thrust her backwards and she hit the wall, her head making contact with the rim of the mirror.

His hands tightened around her neck. He was going to kill her.

SCENE 24 – RYAN

Cliffhanger ending, or what? Evil Greg throttles virtuous Katie. Cut to credits, with no 'next time' trailer to reveal poor Katie's fate. It was all so unexpected that Ryan failed to react for a second, then his brain finally worked out that this wasn't all for his entertainment.

He was nearest. He leapt forwards, knocking his glass of wine to the tiles, where it shattered into vicious-looking shards. He grabbed Greg's arm, but Greg was *strong*. It was like his whole body was locked onto Katie. Her eyes were wide with terror, her cheeks flushed.

Ben was right behind Ryan. Although less ripped than Greg, Ben was taller. He hoisted Greg's chin up so that, in reflex, Greg fell backwards, releasing Katie. She slid down the wall as Alisha and Erin rushed over to her. Greg and Ben both staggered back and toppled over the coffee table.

Ben howled as he struggled to his feet again, stepping on the broken glass and slicing his heel open. It didn't deter him for a second, though. He wriggled free and lunged at Greg, grasping his vest and lifting him off the tiles. With more strength than Ryan would have given him credit for, Ben shook Greg as if he were a ragdoll. 'Come on, then!' spat Ben. 'If you wanna fight, fight me!'

Ryan took a step back, assessing the chaos. It was carnage;

there was a crimson filter over everything. 'What are you doing? Ben, stop!' he yelled over the din.

Ben snorted down his nostrils and shoved Greg back onto the tiles. Greg lay still, his legs hanging over the coffee table and his hands covering his face. Shame. That was pure shame and he deserved to feel it. Ryan turned to Katie.

Erin was already checking her out. 'Are you OK? Let me get a look at your neck.'

Katie nodded, rubbing her throat. There were handprints on her skin and tears ran down her face. She *wasn't* OK.

Greg picked himself up out of the rubble. He and Katie looked at each other from their opposite corners. 'Katie . . . I'm so sorry.' His face fell. Whatever demon had possessed him had now left his body. 'I . . . I'm so sorry. I don't know what happened. I'm sorry.'

'It's OK,' Katie croaked.

'It is *not* OK!' Alisha shoved her brother in the chest and he went down again. 'When did you start hitting girls, Greg? Erin, does he hit you?'

Erin look on in sheer disbelief. 'No. God, no! What kind of idiot do you think I am?'

'I'm sorry,' Greg repeated, his flushed face a horrid clay colour. 'I'm gonna . . .' Greg rose to his feet and powered up the stairs, taking them two at a time.

The lounge decompressed. Ben helped Katie up and tried to embrace her, but Ryan saw her resist.

'I'm fine,' she said, pulling away. 'Please don't make a fuss.'

'I'm sorry, Katie, but he's not getting away with that.' Alisha's eyes were wild and unblinking. She headed towards the stairs.

'Lish! Please,' Katie said. 'Let him cool off. I think I've hit my drama limit for the day. For *any* day. Ever.'

Behind them, Erin flopped back onto the sofa, sobbing behind her fingers. Ryan went to her side.

'Aw . . . don't cry,' he said – more for his sake than hers; Ryan found crying people very hard to deal with.

'I want to go home,' she wept.

Ryan rubbed her back, unsure of what to say. What *does* one say after someone's boyfriend has just tried to strangle someone else? This was uncharted conversation territory for all of them. 'It's gonna be fine,' was the best he could do.

'I've never seen him like that. I . . . I was so scared,' Erin sobbed.

'We all were,' Katie murmured. Typical Katie, allowing Erin to steal her spotlight. Ryan would never stand for that.

'I want to go home,' Erin repeated. 'I hardly know any of you . . . I just want to go back to halls and see my friends and ring my mum.'

Poor thing, thought Ryan. Whoever Erin was, she was now bonded to them for life. This secret would hold them together forever. That was pretty cool, actually. *A dark secret.* They could all meet up in ten years' time for a Murder Club reunion. One of them would die then, too, naturally, leading neatly into a sequel.

Ryan shivered, remembering that it was all really happening.

'It will all seem different in the morning,' Katie said soothingly. She looked to Ryan for support but he drew a blank. What was this poor girl to think? She'd only known most of them for a few days and now she was an accessory to murder – or something like that. Greg should never have brought her. What kind of monster brings a girlfriend on a mates' holiday, anyway?

'I'm not staying with Greg tonight,' Erin said firmly, shaking

187

her dainty head. 'No way. Not after what he did, total effing psycho.'

'I don't think he's—' Ryan started, but he'd just seen something he'd never thought possible so he broke off.

'It's OK,' Ben said as he tended to his bleeding foot. 'Rox won't be using the sofa-bed, will she?'

Erin nodded and wiped her nose. 'Fine. I'm leaving first thing in the morning.'

'You can't!' Ryan said, perhaps a little more forcefully than he'd intended. 'If we go home early, people will know there's something wrong. They'll ask questions. You know I'm right.'

Katie rubbed her eyes. 'He does have a point . . .'

The silence that followed suggested Alisha and Ben also agreed, albeit reluctantly.

'And what about Janey? Shouldn't we find her?' Alisha said finally.

Oh, God, *Janey*. 'Do you *really* think it was her?' Ryan felt his brain jump tracks back to that worry. There were so many in his head, he was struggling to keep up.

'You saw her,' Alisha told him.

'We all saw *someone*.' Ben winced as he held a dish cloth to his heel.

Alisha pouted. 'Are you saying she *didn't* look like Janey? Ben, it *was* her.'

'So where is she?' Ryan snapped. Another silence followed. 'Let's get real for a second which, I know, coming from me is pretty rich. But are we *really* saying that Janey Bradshaw, who wouldn't go into town by herself because a tramp once touched her leg, has staged her own death and then returned on the one-year anniversary to wreak revenge?'

'No!' Ben said firmly. 'We were at her funeral. She's dead.'

'Wouldn't it be better if it was Janey, though?' Alisha

demanded. 'Isn't it better if *Janey* killed Rox than if it was one of us?'

'Janey *is* one of us,' Katie said sadly.

Ben inspected his wound. 'Maybe the girl we saw was someone else.'

'What? A clone? An evil twin?' Ryan asked. 'And people say I live in fantasy land!'

'I'm just thinking of all the possibilities. We all assumed one of us killed Roxanne because of the blackmail thing, but what if there is someone else – someone who's been watching the villa. Watching us.'

'Oh, that's a comforting thought.' Ryan rolled his eyes. 'We're miles from anywhere at the mercy of a beautiful psycho girl. At least it's original.' He walked to the patio doors and gazed out. The sea rolled onto the beach, insects buzzed around the lanterns, the filter whirred in the pool. But, beyond that, in the hills, there was only darkness and what the darkness contained. Anyone could be waiting for them, watching.

Katie suddenly jumped off the sofa and darted into the kitchen.

'What's wrong?' Alisha asked.

'I just had an awful thought,' Katie shouted back at them. 'We didn't lock the doors. She could be inside the villa.'

'Greg checked the bedrooms,' Ryan reminded her, shrugging it off.

'But he didn't check everywhere.' Katie's voice was full of apprehension. 'Nobody looked in the cellar . . .'

SCENE 25 – ALISHA

Alisha gulped. It felt like there was a lump of apple lodged in her throat, Snow-White style. The door to the cellar was next to the fridge-freezer in the kitchen. It opened with a fingers-on-blackboard screech and a wave of stale, damp, earthy air hit them as if they'd opened a sealed tomb. Alisha stared down into the void. The others were right beside her but it brought scant comfort. The kitchen light only illuminated the first three or four stone steps; the rest dissolved into shadows.

'The lights don't work down there,' Katie admitted.

'Of course they don't,' Ryan deadpanned. 'It wouldn't be nearly as scary with the lights on, would it?'

'I'll get a torch,' said Katie, turning away to rummage around in the cupboard under the sink.

'Hello?' Ben called down into the gloom. 'Anyone there?'

Predictably there was no response.

'You didn't actually think that was going to work, did you?' Alisha laughed. It was pretty scary, but she figured that as long as they all stuck together they'd be fine.

'It was worth a try.' Ben took the torch from Katie. 'Come on, Ryan.'

Ryan took a great stride backwards. 'Are you mad? Why do I have to go?'

'Cos we're the guys.'

'Ben Murdoch, that is pure sexism.'

Alisha chuckled. 'On this occasion, I fully support the sexism.'

Ryan scowled at her. 'Women died for equal rights, Alisha.'

'They died for the right to vote, not for *this*.' She waved a hand at the obvious gateway to hell that stood before her.

Ben sighed. 'Ryan, don't be a wuss. There's probably nothing down there, anyway.' He shone the torch down the stairs, which seemed to go on forever.

'Probably?' Alisha didn't care for those odds. Still, they couldn't stand here all night and here was a chance to prove, for once, that she wasn't totally useless. 'Sod it. Let's get it over with. I'll go.'

'We'll *all* go,' Katie said. 'Safety in numbers.'

'No!' Erin gripped Katie's arm. 'Wait here with me. I'm not going down there. You all think I'm stupid, but I'm not *that* stupid.' She glared at them with red, sore eyes. 'I've had enough of this crap. I just wanted a week in the sun with my boyfriend and I ended up trapped with a load of freaks and murderers.'

Alisha couldn't face another argument. 'Fine.'

'I'll wait with Katie, too,' Ryan said. 'Just in case.'

Ben glared at him. 'Ryan, you are such a p—'

'Er – swam with a shark to save your arses!' Ryan pointed out.

Ben backed down. 'Whatever. Come on, Lish.'

'After you,' she said with an optimistic smile. For the first time since they'd found Roxanne, it felt like it was OK to smile again. Hell, if the tables had been turned, Rox would have had them all doing commemorative tequila slammers and playing strip poker by now. She might have been a total cow, but she knew how to party. Ben returned the smile and took the lead.

As soon as Alisha stepped onto the stairs, the air changed. It was cooler, for one thing, and the walls glistened with moisture. The fusty air caught in the back of her nostrils and she was acutely reminded of her fear of cellars. The odour was so familiar, unlocking some childhood terror she must have repressed.

Without thinking, she grabbed Ben's free hand in both of hers. She hated being so feeble, but this was almost worse than the boat trip. Ben's torch was weak, casting only a thin puddle of light.

'All right?' he asked.

She nodded, but wasn't. They were hunting for a dead girl. What if Janey really was down here? What then? And Janey was probably the best-case scenario. Anyone else, a stranger, wouldn't hesitate to hurt them.

Janey's funeral drifted back into her mind as it had done several times that evening. She recalled sitting outside the chapel, behind the hut where they ran Sunday School for kids. She'd crouched behind a wheelie bin drinking peach schnapps, the sugary concoction all she'd been able to get her hands on.

The undertakers had been having a cigarette outside the fire escape. The shroud of drizzle had abated for five minutes, but the sky was still a menacing mercury grey. They'd been entirely unaware of Alisha's presence.

'Poor cow,' a spotty young undertaker with a face like a stoat had said. 'Four weeks she was in the sea, you know.'

'Aye,' his elderly colleague had agreed. 'By the time she washed up in the marina, there was nothing left of her. Fish food.'

At the time Alisha had been so drunk she'd hardly processed their words beyond mild disgust, but now she wondered. What had been dragged out of the sea was a blob, by all accounts. Between the fall onto the rocks and the weeks of decay, it was a wonder they'd identified Janey at all. So wondrous, in fact, that perhaps they hadn't. Who had they buried? What if it wasn't Janey?

Janey Bradshaw, back from the grave and out for revenge. Alisha imagined her crawling out of the sea at Telscombe Cliffs, clawing her way over the shingle, that red dress in tatters. Maybe she'd come out of the sea *wrong* – damaged, somehow. Not Janey, but something else. Something evil enough to kill.

Alisha clung tighter to Ben's hand and kicked her vivid imagination into touch. She'd been spending too much time around Ryan.

The stone stairs were worn smooth. The light from the kitchen faded as they neared the bottom and the cracked, off-white walls gleamed like bone. The narrow passage opened out into the cellar. It was more spacious than Alisha would have liked, with far too many hiding places. It was cave-like down here; somewhere water dripped from the ceiling, each drop echoing like they were at the bottom of a well.

Ben swept the torch around, scanning the room. Light glinted over dozens of bottles of wine stacked neatly in a wooden lattice rack. Junk was piled all around the room: bought-with-best-intentions gym apparatus, forgotten patio furniture, old tins of paint and a couple of boxes of rat poison. A generator buzzed and Alisha wondered if the pool machinery were down here, too.

'What do we do?' she whispered.

'I guess we have a look in all the nooks and crannies,' Ben replied, sounding none too keen.

Alisha gulped. It was pitch black and the torch light seemed to be fading as though the batteries were dying. 'OK. Let's definitely not split up.'

Ben gave her hand a squeeze. 'Best plan of the day.'

They checked behind the first wine rack and found nothing. Cobwebs were strewn over everything and each bottle of wine was caked in a thick white dust.

'Janey?' Ben called, the word catching in his throat as if he couldn't bring himself to say her name. There was no reply.

'Ben, I'm scared,' Alisha confessed.

'You?' Another hand squeeze. 'No way. You're dead hard.'

Alisha snorted but appreciated his attempt to distract her.

'It's true. You've been pretty cool all day,' Ben told her.

'Oh, yeah. Today was our finest hour, I reckon.' There was a scurry of tiny feet. Alisha hoped it was a mouse.

'I mean it. I was proud of you, today. You kept your head together the whole time. I didn't.'

The thought of Ben being proud of her made something light and warm ripple through Alisha's body. She pushed the sensation away, reminding herself that Murdoch was off limits. There was no way she could ever compete with Katie for his affections, and nor would she. That was exactly what Roxanne had done to her, so she knew how damaging it was to a friendship.

Ben shook his head, checking under a dust sheet but finding only spare patio chairs. 'God, today was a nightmare. A total effing nightmare. I wish I'd never come.'

The opposite of the good feeling passed through Alisha. She was disappointed to hear those words. The whole 'Roxanne' situation was awful, but she was pleased to be back with her friends. She'd been alone in Telscombe Cliffs for a year. In some ways, Alisha wondered if she'd always been alone; in her family, Greg had always been the golden child. It felt good to be a part of something, even if it was a murderous pact. 'I'm glad you're here,' she said quietly. Her voice could not have sounded more pathetic and simpering if she'd tried. *You are such a tool*, she told herself.

Ben made a noise somewhere between a laugh and a sigh. 'Come here, you nutter.' He held his arms wide for a hug and she embraced him, drawing strength from his friendship. 'You know, you've really changed, Lish.' He released her, and they moved further away from the safety of the staircase.

'Thanks!'

'No, I mean in a good way. You're so chilled out now – like a whole different person.'

'Ha! I think we've all changed, don't you?'

Ben agreed. 'Yeah. In Cambridge, I dorm with this guy called Rupert.'

'Rupert? Figures.'

'Right. He says there are three stages of human disappointment: the first when you realise your friends are dicks, the second when you realise your parents are dicks and the last when you finally realise that you're a dick, too.'

Alisha laughed. 'I hear that.' She pointed at a sturdy wooden door towards the back corner of the cellar. 'What's in there?'

Ben led the way over and examined the door. 'I think this brings you out round the side of the house by the pool.'

Alisha nodded, remembering that they were now on the same level as the swimming pool.

'Anyway,' Ben added. 'No one got out this way.' He grasped

a heavy, rusted padlock that hung from a bolt-lock as if testing its strength. Alisha saw there was a key hanging from a nail in the doorframe. If someone had come down this way, they could have easily got out, but the padlock was firmly shut.

Ben swung the torch in an arc, casting the light over an old armoire that had been left to decay against the back wall. It was plenty big enough for . . .

Alisha took his arm once more. 'You don't think?'

'I dunno.' With an unsteady hand, Ben reached for the wardrobe door, took a deep breath and tore it open.

Alisha shrank back, but it contained only mouldy children's books and enough candles to last through a nuclear winter. *Embarrassing overreaction, much?*

Ben exhaled. 'So, yeah, I agree,' he said, continuing their earlier conversation. 'We're all totally different – except Katie maybe. I hope she never changes. When Janey died, I think it just put everything into perspective, you know? It changed us. All that Longview drama feels like a hundred years ago now. It was all so trivial – who fancies whom and all that. We're not the people we were at school.'

'Don't. Remember, I haven't officially left yet. I'm still there.'

'Maybe what happened to Janey was the kick up the arse we needed.' Ben pulled a dust sheet off an exercise bike and then covered it again, satisfied it wasn't Janey's zombie.

Alisha sighed. 'You're right. Janey's death was the biggest wake-up call ever. You know how you think you've got forever to get it right, like you have unlimited goes on the ride or something? Well, you just don't. One day Janey was there, with all the potential in the world, and the next she was gone. I didn't wanna end up like that. To be honest, out of all of us, I was the one who most needed to change, right?' Alisha looked into Ben's eyes. There wasn't even a hint of judgement there. It wasn't Ben's style.

He shrugged.

'Oh, come on. You were there. You know what I was like – 'Most Likely to Need Rehab'. God, I just want out of that crappy town.'

'Sorry I abandoned you.' Ben placed a warm hand on her shoulder, squeezing the muscle in just the right spot to release about five years of tension.

Alisha smiled, suddenly feeling tipsy – but not the kind of tipsy that comes from drink. 'Not your fault, is it?'

'Whatever happens, we should stay in touch,' Ben said. 'Properly this time. And not just say it, but actually do it.'

'We should.' For some reason the air seemed thicker and Alisha felt breathless. Her heartbeats-per-minute switched up like a club remix and she dared herself to look up at Ben. He was gazing down at her and, if she didn't know better, she'd have sworn it was *the* look, not *a* look. Funny how time seemed to slow down, like the universe was giving them extra time to make it happen.

In that moment, Alisha was scared – scared that she was imagining it and that Ben wasn't in the same moment. But his hand was still on her shoulder . . .

What about Ben and Katie? a little voice in her head said. She chose to ignore it, swept along by the golden feeling inside her. Oh, God, it had been a while; she wasn't sure she remembered what to do.

This was the moment. Do or die. Now or never.

Never. Ben broke the connection, twisting to look over his shoulder. 'Can you hear that?'

The candyfloss feeling in Alisha's tummy was replaced with sudden dread. 'What?'

'I thought I heard something.' Ben shone the torch over the very back of the cellar. In the wall there was an arched alcove. This time, Ben took *her* hand. They edged closer and Alisha realised she was chewing a hole inside her cheek. The weak buttery torchlight traced the edges of boxes of junk piled into the space, but the alcove went deep into the wall.

'What's behind the boxes?' Alisha whispered. Janey, or the massive spider from *Harry Potter* – she didn't know which she was more afraid of.

Ben let go of her hand and took a step inside the cubbyhole. He shifted the boxes to one side. A foul smell drifted out and Alisha covered her mouth and nose with her hand. 'There are some shelves and stuff back here, but I swear I heard something . . .'

'Ben, maybe we should do the clever person thing and get out of here.'

'Can you smell that?' he asked, by way of reply.

'God, yes.'

Inside the alcove, Ben shone the torch over the shelves, revealing tinned food mostly. It was a free-standing unit, and Alisha could see that there was space behind. It was the perfect hiding place.

'Alisha, hold the torch for me,' Ben said. 'I think there's something back here.' He passed the torch to her and she shone it onto the shelves as he took hold of both sides of the unit and shuffled it from side to side, trying to get round it.

As he rocked the unit, something slid off the top shelf. Alisha screamed – a proper, full-throated, damsel-in-distress scream. A matted, hairy thing fell directly on top of Ben. He reacted just as it hit him, flinging himself back and crashing into Alisha, sending them both toppling into the nearest wine rack. Bottles clanged to the cellar floor and Alisha clung to the rack to stop it from tumbling over entirely.

'Shit!' Ben cried, scrambling away from whatever had fallen on him. It now lay on the floor by his feet.

'Oh, God!' Alisha exclaimed. It was disgusting. It had once been a cat (probably) or a fox or a dog (less likely), but it was now so decayed it was hard to tell. Pearl white maggots wriggled through the rotting flesh, making a moist squelch as they did so. Alisha gagged and swallowed – she would *not* vomit in front of Ben.

Ben brushed at his hair like a mad person, shaking maggots off his head. 'Gross!'

Alisha looked away from the sad thing. 'It must have come down here to die,' she said.

Footsteps pounded down the stairs and Ryan appeared in the pool of light at the cellar entrance. 'Are you OK? We heard you scream,' he panted.

'It's fine,' Alisha said. 'We're fine.' They weren't in a cave any more, just a cellar, and the close, intimate atmosphere had dissipated in Ryan's presence. There was no Janey down here. Just them and a decaying, passion-killing corpse. Alisha dismissed the almost-kiss immediately. Her imagination had obviously been firing on all cylinders. Thank God she hadn't tried to kiss Ben – maximum embarrassment averted, not to mention an ocean of boyfriend-stealing drama with Katie.

'It's just a dead cat.' Ben picked himself off the floor.

'Ah! The scary cat.' Ryan said, nodding sagely. 'A standard horror-film classic.'

SCENE 26 – RYAN

'What do we do now?' Alisha asked. They were gathered in the lounge. Erin was curled up on the sofa under a throw, looking very much like she wanted the whole world to curl up and die like the cat in the cellar.

'Well, I need to shower, for one thing,' Ben sighed, having disposed of the dead lodger in a bin liner. 'I suppose it's over for now. Rox is . . . gone, and we're safe in the house. Janey, or whoever the hell we saw, isn't in here with us.'

'Why isn't that more comforting?' Ryan sat on the arm of the armchair. He'd never felt so awake – alert and ready for whatever the next episode would bring. He had a feeling the night was far from over.

'I'll tell you what,' Katie said, standing up. The weals on her neck were less livid now. 'When I was little and my mum and dad were working away, I used to stay at my Gran's. If I had nightmares, or couldn't sleep, we always had a tea party in the kitchen – with a teapot and scones, the lot. Nothing is scary at a tea party, so we'll have a tea party.'

'Girl, we're gonna need something stronger than tea,' Ryan muttered.

'Darling, please, I was about to suggest sangria.'

Ryan smiled at Katie. Some of the colour had returned to her cheeks. Maybe their friendship would survive this, after all. 'Now you're talking,' he told her. 'You save me a glass. I'm gonna see how Greg is.'

'Leave him.' Disgust filled Alisha's voice. 'I can't believe what he did.'

'Oh, come on. You know that wasn't Greg. He must have gone to the dark side or something.' Although it was inexcusable, Ryan had never seen Greg like that before. Today they'd all been living inside a pressure cooker. Greg had been the leader all day, and just because Greg Cole wasn't the type to ask for help, didn't mean he didn't need it. 'I'll be back in a minute.' Ryan stuck to the wall, worried about any leftover shards of glass even though Katie had swept it up while Ben and Alisha were exploring the cellar.

He climbed the stairs and crossed the landing. Placing an ear to Greg's door, he listened for signs of life from within. Then he knocked. 'Greg? It's Ryan.'

There was a moment of silence. 'What?' came the gruff reply.

'Is that Jekyll or Hyde?' Ryan asked with a smirk. Hopefully humour would diffuse the situation, not exacerbate it.

More silence. The door opened suddenly and Ryan collapsed onto the other side, his face colliding with Greg's chest.

'What do you want, Ryan?' Greg asked, stepping aside to let Ryan into the room.

'Charming. I just came to see if you were OK after your Hulk moment.'

Greg closed the door and threw himself onto the bed. He folded his arms behind his head and closed his eyes. 'Piss off, Ryan. I don't wanna talk about it.'

It occurred to Ryan that this was the first time they'd been alone together all week. 'That's a shame, because we're gonna.'

Greg scowled and sat up straight. He shot him a filthy look. 'OK, then. If we're gonna talk,' he said in a harsh whisper, 'let's start with how Roxanne Dent ended up with a video of you and me getting it on.'

SCENE 26 (CONT.)

'Oh, I wondered when that little twist would surface,' Ryan said, trying to feign boredom.

'Keep your voice down!' Greg hissed.

A plot twist, as Ryan understood it, is when previously hidden information comes to light, putting a whole new spin on the story. He should know; this was *his* very own twist – his secret tryst with pro-footballer Greg Cole. A secret so potent, he'd never told anyone. Not a soul. The risk to Greg wasn't even worth the attention Ryan so craved. More than that, it was his very own little drama. The only *real* drama he'd ever had (before this week) and he didn't want to jinx it.

'I don't think anyone can hear us, Greg, do you? They're all downstairs hunting for the ghost of Janey, or whatever.'

'I don't care. Keep it down. And answer my question.'

'What question?' Ryan hovered in the doorway, hands on hips.

'How did Roxanne see that video?'

Ryan shrugged. 'I have no idea. We don't even know that she *did* see it. You know what Rox is – *was* – like. She might just have been stirring.'

Greg rolled off the bed and pulled Ryan away from the door. He even went so far as to stick his head out into the hall to see if anyone was within earshot. The last twelve months had done nothing to dampen his paranoia at being 'outed', then. It really was a passion killer.

Ryan sat on the edge of the bed, trying to be sexy without looking like he was trying – trickier than it sounds. The second you start *trying* to be sexy, you look like a pound-shop porn star. As weird as the circumstances were, he couldn't deny that he was more than a little happy to be alone with Greg again after all these months. If he was honest, he'd assumed he'd never see Greg again. The more successful Greg was, the more paranoid he became.

'Are you kidding?' Greg came back to the bed but sat at a safe distance. 'She must have seen it. Remember the I Have Never game? She knew about the video.'

Ryan sighed. He'd been running through the possibilities ever since that game on the beach. Deep down, he knew Greg was right. Somehow, Roxanne had seen *that* video – a video that wasn't meant to be seen by anyone but him and Greg. It was so monumentally stupid. He of all people should have known that anything committed to camera in the internet age was destined for the whole wide world to see. 'I can only think of one way for Rox to have seen it.'

'And what's that?'

'Can you remember when Janey dropped her phone down the toilet at school?'

'No. Ryan, just get on with it.' Greg clearly wasn't in the mood to reminisce.

'Well, long story short, I gave her my old handset – which was the one we used to make our . . . home movie. I guess Janey could have found it on the phone and shown Rox.'

Greg's rage threatened to return. His eyes almost fell out of their sockets. 'Are you *kidding* me?'

'I thought I'd deleted it. I wiped the SIM. It must have been saved to the handset.'

Greg swore so loudly the walls shook. Ryan gritted his teeth.

'I'm sorry. That's all I can think of. But if Janey did see it, she never said.'

Greg didn't look up. 'How stupid are you? I'm screwed. If people see that video, I'm gonna have to kill myself!'

And people said *Ryan* was melodramatic. 'Oh, come on, Greggle. It's a pretty hot video,' he quipped. 'You might gain a few fans – a huge gay following at least.'

Greg charged at him. That comment had obviously been a red rag too far. With sweating hands he took hold of Ryan's face. 'It's not a joke, Ryan. Do you have any idea what my life will be like if this gets out?'

He didn't flinch. Instead he stood and gave Greg a hard shove. Their liaisons had been as routine as clockwork. Stolen, or drunken, moments followed by the same performance from Greg: big, angry, guilty tantrums about how, if Ryan ever told anyone, Greg would kill him. Ryan, still alive, wasn't convinced.

'I don't exactly want that video to be my first feature film either, Greg! I didn't tell anyone about it, so sit your arse down and chill out.' Ryan stood firm. Greg didn't scare him. In this battle of egos he wasn't going to be the bitch.

The air between them shimmered like the scorched beach. The attraction was still there. Ryan remembered how he'd become addicted in the first place. As they stood nose to nose, squaring off, Ryan swore he could feel the magnetism drawing their bodies ever closer. As angry as he was, he wanted Greg. And Greg wanted him, too. It was something powerful, chemical, and they were both dwarfed by it.

Ryan was quite certain that sometimes love looks like it does in the films – cherry blossom and holding hands and swoon at first sight. But in his experience, sometimes love comes from somewhere else – somewhere dark and angry and sweaty and red. That was Ryan's love for Greg, and the only love he had ever known. One day, Ryan hoped, he would know the first kind – the pure kind that everyone longs for – but, until that day, he would take what he could get.

'Are you gonna strangle me, too?' he asked, a hint of a mean smile creeping onto his lips. 'Are we gonna get all *Fifty Shades of Gay*?' He could feel Greg's hot breath on his face. It would be so easy to lean in for his lips.

Greg crumpled to the bed. Ryan had won that round. Or lost – depending on what the outcome could have been.

'That video can't come out,' Greg moaned.

'The video can't or *you* can't?'

'I'm not gay.'

'I never said you were. Are you still seeing guys?'

Greg looked horrified. 'No!'

Ryan laughed bitterly. 'Oh, don't act so shocked. I was there, remember; you seemed to quite enjoy it.' He sat opposite Greg on the bed, feeling it was wise to leave a couple of metres between them.

Greg altered his position on the bed to face Ryan properly. His face softened, the anger that drove him loosening its grip. 'There was only ever you, you know that. It was our *thing*.'

That was the correct answer. A little firefly buzzed in Ryan's heart. 'I suppose I should feel honoured.'

Greg half-smiled back. 'You should.'

It had been 'messing around' for Greg and, although Ryan had known this, it had never been 'messing around' for him. It wasn't until he'd felt a jealous, burning desire for

Greg Cole that Ryan had even realised he preferred boys to girls. Every time he'd witnessed Greg with one of his 'beard' girlfriends, he'd plotted their violent downfall. He hadn't done anything though – he'd just stood back and watched Greg parade each insipid stick insect around, waiting and aching for the intervals when the rising football star would seek his company. Greg had no idea how he felt, and Ryan was just pathetically grateful he'd got the secret scraps Greg had thrown him.

It had started after football one ordinary day in Year Eleven. The shower in the changing room. Greg had initiated it that time and every other time. Ryan was powerless to resist and never said no. This sad dance had persisted throughout the rest of their time at Longview – Ryan had been at Greg's beck and call.

'Seriously?' Ryan asked now. 'No other guys?'

'It's not that I didn't want to, but I can't trust anyone else. Can't risk it,' Greg told him.

Ryan didn't pretend to understand Greg's situation, but he felt something like sympathy. 'Lots of sporty people are out now,' he said reassuringly. He knew that wasn't true, but it was worth a go.

'I'm not gay!' Greg said too loudly. '. . . Do you think they heard?'

'No,' said Ryan. 'I'm not saying you're gay, but it's OK for you to fancy dudes *and* girls. I know, big revelation!'

Greg rolled his eyes. 'I don't know *any* gay footballers, or even any *bi* footballers. They don't exist. Ryan, you have no idea what it's like – the pressure. When I first joined the team, do you know what one player said to me?'

'What?'

'We were in the changing room—'

Ryan grinned. 'Remember the changing room? Good times . . .'

Greg returned the smile. 'Behave, you! So this player, an older guy, comes up to me and says "black or white?".'

Ryan was confused. 'Eh?'

'He said I had to decide whether I was one of the black players or one of the white players. Apparently, in football, it matters. I had to pick a team.'

'That's awful. He was just a racist dick, right?'

'Ryan, that was one of the black guys. Can you imagine if I threw some dude-on-dude action into the mix? My life wouldn't be worth living. I already get monkey chants at away games.'

'If that's what it's like, why do you do it?'

'What is it you said before? "Don't hate the player, hate the game"? It's the game, Ryan. It's football. And football is me. It's just how it is. I am never, ever going to say I like guys.'

The crushing wave of disappointment that crashed inside Ryan surprised even him. He'd thought a year away would cure him of this futile love sickness but, somewhere tucked away inside, he had clearly still been carrying a candle of hope that Greg would come out and skip across a field to greet him with open arms. That flame had just flickered. What had he thought? That one day he'd be the first-ever male footballer's wife? Not likely. But he had dreamed of that future many, many times. He and Greg playing Mr and Mr in a fancy LA mansion: kids and dogs and servants by the pool. 'I think that's very sad,' he said simply.

'Oh, yeah, boo-hoo. My life as a minted professional footballer is really tough.'

Ryan shot him down with another glare. 'You know that's not what I meant. You may be a massive tool, but I still want you to be happy. Even if it's not with me.' He looked away, embarrassed at showing his cards even a little. Greg ran a hand up his arm and onto his shoulder. Ryan pulled back.

'Hey,' Greg said. 'We can't worry about that now. I think we have enough on, don't you? I'm proper freaking out. You saw what happened – I flipped out on Katie. We need to get it together or we're screwed.'

'Exactly,' Ryan agreed. 'No offence, but that video isn't our biggest worry. We just dumped a body in the sea.'

'But if the video turns up we have more motive than anyone.'

Ryan wanted to say '*YOU* have more motive than anyone,' but held his tongue. A gay actor was hardly a headline any more, however a gay (or bi-bloody-curious-or-whatever) footballer was news. Greg had pretty much just spelled out his reasons for killing Roxanne – if he had done.

It might have been ego, but Ryan liked to think he knew Greg Cole better than anyone. He'd certainly seen things most teenage fan girls could only dream of. Beyond the obvious, there was one thing the two of them had in common: ambition. Two years ago, Greg would have stepped over anyone to go pro. He would have killed for it.

It suddenly became clear to Ryan: he'd helped Greg dispose of Roxanne because he loved him. If he was being *really* honest, he'd sort of just assumed that Greg had killed Rox and everything Ryan had done since then had been to protect Greg. That blew. 'Look. The video has to be on Rox's phone, or at least her laptop. If we're burning all her stuff tomorrow, the proof'll go up in smoke, won't it?'

Greg's eyes clouded over. 'But what if she made loads of copies or emailed it to people?'

Ryan slid his fingers along the bed sheets until they wove

into Greg's. Their skin coming together created a power in him. With power like that, you could rule the world, he thought. It was rich and wild and bright. 'We'll sort it.'

He'd expected Greg to recoil, but Greg released his hand and ran his fingers up the smooth, extra-sensitive skin of Ryan's forearm. The air was so charged, so heated, lightning seemed inevitable. Ryan felt his eyes close, already anticipating what the kiss would feel like . . .

It didn't happen. Instead, Greg yanked him into a bear hug, complete with manly back slapping. 'Thanks, mate. I couldn't have got through today without you.'

Bromance. Whoever invented that term should be shot at dawn, Ryan thought, but he just said, 'No worries. It's over now. We just need to get rid of her stuff – and work out if Janey's back from the dead!'

Greg released him. 'It's over,' he repeated, clearly trying to convince himself.

Ryan stood, ready to leave. He'd sacrificed enough dignity for one evening. His days of begging Greg for anything were behind him. 'I think Erin is crashing on the sofa tonight.' Well, OK, *almost* behind him. 'Do you want me to stay with you?'

Greg reacted immediately. 'No. Not here. God, no.'

'Cool.' Ryan said it with as much insouciant breeziness as he could and swept out of the room. 'Insouciant' was a word he'd learned recently; it meant blithe unconcern. Tonight he was playing the role of someone who didn't care one way or the other. No one wants to see a broken heart.

SCENE 27 – RYAN

Ryan slipped out of Greg's room, almost colliding with Katie as she emerged from the bathroom. She wore a towel dress with matching towel turban. She blushed modestly and he did everything he could to make his exit from the master bedroom look casual. He'd hidden his 'affair' for years; he was pretty good at it now.

'Greg is Greg again,' Ryan said. 'For what it's worth, he seems pretty sorry.'

Katie didn't look up from the floor. 'OK. I suppose I'll talk to him in the morning.' She shuffled towards her room, not once looking him in the eye. He couldn't stand it.

'Katie, please. Don't be angry.'

This time she did look at him. 'Ryan, he could have . . .'

'I don't mean Greg – by all means be mad at him. I meant me.' An awkward pause. 'I'm not.'

'Girl, please. You've barely spoken to me since we . . .'

She gave a sad sigh. She seemed so resigned, as though all her spirit had been leached away by the events of the day. 'What do you expect, Ryan?'

He leaned against the wall, too tired to support his head. 'It's all over now. Can't we just be normal again? I hate you being angry with me; it feels like crap. What can I do to make you laugh again?'

Katie's blue eyes widened and there was so much pain in them, Ryan could almost feel it. He could see that she, too, longed for a rewind – some divine intervention that would have seen their planes grounded so that none of them had ever arrived in this accursed place. 'I don't know, Ry. You went too far this time,' Katie said softly.

He smiled in the hope she would too. 'When did I ever go less than "too far"?'

That elicited a half-smile, but it came and went like a summer cloud. 'This isn't like when we bleached your hair, Ryan. We can't *fix* it. What you – *we* – did was terrible. I'm not sure it's something we can ever brush under the carpet.'

Ryan rubbed her arm. She looked cold. 'We were just looking out for each other, *protecting* each other.'

'I know you, Ryan. I know you think this is all a movie, but in real life—'

'Believe me, this feels pretty bloody real!' Ryan interrupted.

'There are bound to be consequences. There always are.' She shrugged. 'At least there should be.'

'Yeah.' He agreed wholeheartedly. 'And the consequence is that we have to live with it. But I can't lose you, Katie. I just can't.'

Katie swallowed and closed her eyes. Ryan thought for a moment that she might cry, but she held the emotion back. 'You won't lose me.' Another faint smile. 'Lord knows, I've been trying to shake you for years.'

A broad smile broke out on Ryan's face and he pulled her into an embrace. He buried his face in the warm, damp towel on her head. He felt better. His friends were his family.

SCENE 28 – ALISHA

Somewhere halfway between sleep and waking, Alisha dreamt of sharks. In her dream, she, like Ryan last night, was lost in a thick, black soup of a sea. Scarlet folds billowed around her and she couldn't help but think of red roses, velvet petals unfurling around her body. She was wearing Janey's dress.

Alisha couldn't breathe, but didn't need to. She was looking for Ben. She had to find Ben but he was somewhere out of reach and she couldn't see him. She was suddenly angry – where was he? She knew, too, that somewhere, Roxanne and Janey were down here with their dead eyes and cold skin.

The sharks circled, keeping her in one place. They cut through the water silently; only a silver smile or a flash of pristine white underbelly reminded her they were there. They were elegant but deadly, teasing her with a nudge as they passed by.

Underwater someone was screaming.

No. Wait.

Someone really *was* screaming. It was Katie.

Alisha's eyes popped open and the dream was instantly forgotten. She pushed herself up onto her elbows and saw the empty space alongside her in the bed. 'Katie?' She cleared her throat. 'Katie!'

'I'm in the lounge! Quick!' She could tell her friend wasn't playing. Alisha swung her legs off the bed and hurtled onto the landing, colliding with Ben and Ryan. Ben's shoulder made contact with her lip and she cried out. *One day this week*, she thought, *it'd be nice to wake up to a cup of coffee.*

'Sorry,' he said.

She ignored the sting and carried on down the stairs, taking the lead. As soon as she turned the corner, the cause of Katie's distress was clear. The three of them stopped dead in their tracks, their bleary eyes trying to make sense of the scene.

They'd been left a message. It took up most of the right-hand lounge wall.

THINK ON THY SINS

The ugly words had been scrawled in huge letters by someone using manic, frenzied brushstrokes. It was the the handwriting of a madman in what could only be blood: a dirty reddish-brown shade. On the coffee table lay the dagger from the galleon, daubed in the same sticky fluid.

'Oh, my God!' Ryan exclaimed. 'Who did that?'

Ben's face registered disbelief. 'This can't be happening.'

Alisha rushed over to hug Katie, who was shaking.

'I just found it,' Katie gasped. 'I came down to put the kettle on and it was *there*!' She reached out towards the letters, her fingers hovering in front of the writing. 'What does it mean?'

Greg appeared at the foot of the stairs, red-eyed. He stared at the wall in shock. 'No way. You are having a laugh. Who did this?'

'Janey!' Alisha cried, feeling suddenly sure. 'It *was* her last night. She must have seen what we were doing. She knows everything. *Think on thy sins* . . . like the sin of dumping someone's dead body at sea!'

Greg looked doubtful. He glowered at Katie. 'Did you do this? Is this to get me back cos we didn't call the police?'

'Oh, of course, I'm full of tricks like that. Would you care to strangle me again, just in case, Greg?'

Alisha hid a smirk, thinking, *You go, girl!*

Greg drew a measured breath, trying to regain his poise. 'I'm sorry, Katie. I'm properly sorry.'

Katie backed down too. They had bigger things to worry about. 'It's OK. Well, it's not OK at all, but, right now, we need to work out who did this.'

'Someone must have broken in last night.' Ryan poked at the letters with a finger. He sniffed experimentally.

'Wait.' Greg had frozen in the centre of the room, his face draining from its usual brown to grey to green. 'Where the bloody hell is Erin?'

SCENE 28 (CONT.)

The sofa-bed was empty, with the sheets crumpled in a heap at its centre.

'Wasn't she with you?' Alisha's eyes widened.

'No. She never came up. Ryan said she was sleeping in here, so I left her to it. I figured everyone would have calmed down if I waited until morning. But where is she?' His voice became shrill at the end of the sentence. 'Who saw her last?'

Alisha's stomach churned. She'd been awake for five minutes and it felt like she was being bombarded. The message on the wall, Erin missing . . . she couldn't take anything else. At least not until she'd had a coffee. A BIG one. 'Erin?' she screamed up the stairs. There was no response.

Ben was lost in thought. 'I don't know, man. I *think* she was there when I got a glass of water at about one a.m.'

'You think?'

'I didn't turn the lights on . . .'

'Erin!' Greg ran upstairs. 'ERIN!'

'I'll check the cellar.' Katie hurried off to search.

Panic flapped in Alisha's chest. If someone had broken into the villa last night, Erin would have been right there on the sofa – and the message was written in blood. Whose? Dizzy, she staggered to the patio doors and flung them open.

'Erin!' she called. 'Erin, are you out here?' The pool was empty and the beach was a pure white page, entirely unwritten on. 'I can't see her. The blood . . . .' Alisha grimaced. 'What if it's . . .'

'Don't even say it!' Ben snapped.

Greg tramped back down the stairs. 'She's not up there and her mobile went straight to voicemail. Is she outside?'

'I . . . I don't think so.' Alisha gripped the back of a chair at the dining table. Time was moving too fast again, just as it had when they'd found Rox. That had only been yesterday, but it felt like a hundred years ago.

Katie's footsteps slapped up the cellar steps and she burst back into the kitchen. 'Nothing down there.'

'Erin was upset,' Ben said, trying for a soothing tone. It soothed no one. 'Maybe she went for a walk, or into town or something.'

'The cars are both still outside. I checked.' Greg fell onto the sofa before springing straight up again. Nervous energy crackled around him. 'We have to call the police.' He strode towards the stairs, aiming for the phone in the upstairs bedroom.

'Oh, *now* you wanna call the police!' Katie couldn't hold that one in.

It was Ryan, however, who stepped into his path. With a hand to Greg's chest, he said firmly, 'No way, man. You're kidding, right? Are you forgetting last night's entertainment?'

Ben blocked his way, too. 'He's right, Greg. Think about it. We can't call the cops. This doesn't change anything. We haven't even got rid of Rox's stuff.'

'I don't care. We'll tell them it's ours. Get out of my way!' Greg snapped.

'No.' There was a cool determination to Ryan that Alisha

hadn't seen before. This was a coup. He was taking over from Greg as alpha male. 'You're not thinking *straight*.' The final word was emphasised. 'Everything you said yesterday is still true. We are never, ever telling anyone about what we did. If we bring the police here, we might as well show them where we dropped Rox.'

Greg's eyes glazed over. 'But . . . Erin . . .'

'Roxanne was left for us to find. But there's no sign of Erin. If she was dead, I think we'd know about it. I'm pretty sure this isn't even blood.' Ryan gestured at the writing on the wall. 'I mean, smell it. It smells like paint. Someone is messing with us and we have to find out why. We'll search for Erin, but, believe me, we are *not* calling the police. Not after everything I did for you,' he paused, 'yesterday.'

This was spiralling out of control. All this testosterone in the room was making Alisha gag. She stepped between them. 'Cool off, both of you. Ryan's right. We need to look for Erin. Last night she kept saying that she wanted to leave—'

'All her stuff's still up in our bedroom, Lish.' Greg rubbed his temples. 'We start searching now. And we don't stop until we find—'

The doorbell rang. At least, Alisha assumed it was the doorbell – it hadn't rung once in the time they'd been at the villa so she wasn't entirely sure.

'What is that?' Ryan asked.

'The front door,' Katie replied, looking as baffled as the rest of them.

The bell rang again.

'Who is it?' Alisha couldn't keep the panic out of her voice, but wondered, wildly optimistically, if Erin had somehow locked herself out.

'I'm not psychic!' Katie breathed. She pointed at the huge

red words on the wall. 'We can't let them in. Whoever it is. They'll see all this.'

The chime sounded a third time, followed by a sharp knock.

'Is there such a thing as Spanish Jehovah's Witnesses?' Ryan asked.

'Just ignore them,' whispered Greg. 'They'll give up and go away.'

The group fell silent. Alisha didn't even breathe in case it made a noise. About ten seconds passed, maybe more – her muddled head kept forgetting the numbers. She was just beginning to think that their ruse had worked and whoever it was had gone . . .

No such luck. There was another, louder knock. And then a woman shouted through the letterbox in a strong Spanish accent, 'Hello? Is anyone home? It's the police.'

SCENE 29 – RYAN

Boom! The room seemed to shift under his feet. For a second, Ryan thought he might pass out. Silver stars swam in his field of vision as though he had kaleidoscope eyes.

The police officer shouted again, 'Hello?'

Ryan panicked; they were all going to prison. Maybe if he was lucky he could charm some half-decent daddy-type into protecting him in the showers. 'What do we do?' Ryan hissed.

'We can't let her in!' Ben was aghast. 'She'll see . . . the writing. And Rox's stuff is everywhere. And the dagger—'

'Shut up!' commanded Greg. 'She'll go away.'

Katie shook her head with vigour. 'No. What if she comes around the back?' She pointed at the bloody message. 'If she comes to the patio doors she'll see the writing.'

Greg curled his hands into fists. 'Then just get rid of her. We need to find Erin.'

'*I'm* not doing it!' Katie protested.

'It's your house!'

Ryan took her hand. 'Come on, we'll both go.' He threw Greg an evil look. He'd wondered whether, after opening up last night, Greg might be different this morning, but no. Leopards and spots, et cetera, et cetera.

He led Katie upstairs. 'Coming!' he called towards the front door.

'Ryan, I'm a terrible liar,' Katie whispered. 'Remember when we went shopping during double maths . . . I got us both detention.'

'Just let me do the talking.' Ryan was in his boxer shorts. Katie was in her dad's old shirt. This was going to look really, really dodgy. Undeterred, he opened the door.

Ryan gasped. A genuine, mouth-falling-open gasp. Katie's hand flew to her collarbone, like she, too, was trying to prevent her heart from leaping out of her chest.

Janey stood on the doorstep.

Except that it wasn't Janey. The woman in front of them was so like their old friend that it was uncanny. Anyone would do a double-take. She was a fraction older than the friends, in her early twenties, but with Janey's chestnut hair falling over her shoulders and the same ocean-blue eyes. On closer scrutiny, the differences become more apparent. This woman's lips were fuller than Janey's had been, her eyebrows and tan a little darker.

The police officer took a step back, reacting to *their* reaction. 'Hello,' she said, looking confused. 'Is this your house?' At least Ryan thought that was what she'd said. Her accent was almost impenetrable.

Ryan couldn't speak – so much for him doing all the talking! But it was so *weird*. She was a true doppelgänger. The penny dropped. *This* was the girl who had been outside the villa last night. Her police uniform was little more than an aertex T-shirt and shorts. No wonder she hadn't stood out as a cop.

'You were here last night,' Katie muttered.

'Yes.' The 's' sounded like a 'th'. 'My name is called Luisa

Batada. I am responding to an emergency call made yesterday morning at eight-fifty.'

Ryan's brain finally kicked into gear. Alisha had made the call in the middle of the madness. 'Oh! But we hung up. We didn't need an ambulance, after all.'

'Yes. Even a joke call is investigated.'

'You took your time,' Ryan mumbled under his breath.

'Sorry?'

'Nothing.' He smiled brightly. 'We're OK.' If this woman *hadn't* seen anything last night some neat lying might get them off the hook. Ryan could lie for England. 'My friend . . . stepped on some glass. We thought we needed an ambulance, but we didn't.'

Luisa was even more beautiful than Janey had been. She brushed her thick hair back over her shoulder and frowned. 'You know, it is very serious to call one, one, two.'

'We know. We're *really* sorry.' *Ooh, that was a bit much*, Ryan thought. Perhaps he was laying it on a bit thick with the sweetness and light. He caught himself doing that awful thing British people do, talking slowly and loudly for the benefit of foreigners.

'May I come in, please? It is normal to check.' Luisa didn't give anything away. Her face was impassive, her tone polite but firm.

'No!' Katie squeaked and bit her tongue.

Ryan gave her a look that could easily kill.

'Is there a problem?' The first trace of suspicion flickered across Luisa's face.

'Not at all,' Ryan said, buying time while his brain cooked up some more lies. 'It's just that you can't come in the lounge, right now.'

'The lounge?'

'You know, like . . . the living room.' His mind was drawing a blank. He needed a *really* good reason not to let her into the lounge and he needed one *now*.

'Ah, OK. Why?' The police officer fixed him in a vice-like stare. Ryan got the distinct impression this woman didn't stand for any crap.

Ryan panicked and an idea came to him. It seemed plausible so he went with it. 'Well, it's just that there are people having sex in there.'

Katie's mouth fell open.

'They are having sex?' repeated Luisa.

'Yeah!' Ryan laughed. He was stuck with it now. 'Us kids! What are we like?'

Luisa was unimpressed. 'Listen. I check and then I go.'

Ryan stepped out of the door, dragging Katie with him, and closed it behind them. 'Why don't we go sit on the terrace—'

'No!' Katie squeaked.

Oh, yeah, you'd see the writing from the terrace! Ryan realised. 'It's such a nice morning,' he said instead. 'Why don't you go sit by the pool and I'll make sure everyone . . . has . . . finished so you can look around.'

'Finished the sex?' said Luisa.

'Yes.'

'It's just this way.' Katie led the policewoman down the steps at the side of the villa. Ryan fell into step alongside his friend. 'Everyone's having *sex*?' she breathed.

'I'm sorry, I panicked.'

'Is this your house?' the officer asked.

'It's my dad's,' Katie replied. 'We're just on holiday.'

'OK. How many people?'

'Six,' Katie said.

'Five!' Ryan almost screamed. 'Just five!'

Katie had apparently forgotten about Erin. 'Oh, yeah, five! I can't count! *Cinco!*'

Luisa was becoming more suspicious by the second. Hopefully, she thought they were just stoned or something; the truth was so much worse. Ryan and Katie formed a human shield blocking her from the top terrace and sending her down another flight of stairs to the pool level. She seemed put out at having to take a sun lounger over a proper chair.

Above them, the terrace door slid open and Ben emerged.

'Who is he?' Luisa asked.

'That's Ben and I'm Ryan and this is Katie.' Ryan handled the introductions.

The police officer narrowed her eyes. 'He isn't having sex.'

'No. He doesn't like sex.' Ryan threw Ben an apologetic glance.

Ben's eyes widened. Katie gave him an *I know* look as he joined them at the poolside and offered Luisa his hand. 'Hi, I'm Ben.'

'Luisa Batada from the Civil Guard.'

'She's come to investigate why we called an ambulance yesterday.' Ryan hoped Ben could pick up the threads of the lie quickly.

'Yes!' Katie might as well have punched the air. 'Show her your foot!'

'My foot?'

'Yes!' Ryan urged. 'You know – where you stepped on the glass, which is why we called the ambulance but then realised we didn't need it.' He was well aware that this scene was tipping into farce territory. But who doesn't love a little farce every now and then?

'Oh, right.' Ben sat on a lounger and held up his foot. There was a now-dirty plaster half-attached to his heel. 'It looked worse than it was with all the blood.'

Luisa took a cursory glance. 'OK. I came last night and there was nobody home.'

How were they going to answer this one? 'We were out on the boat,' Katie admitted. 'It was, like, a boat party.'

Luisa didn't like the sound of that. 'You should not take the boat out at night. Was there drinking?'

'I sailed the boat and didn't drink,' Katie replied. That much was true.

'You are lucky the coastguard did not find you.' That was also true.

Alisha and Greg burst through the patio doors at the same time. Ryan saw them a second before Luisa turned. Greg gave a subtle thumbs up. The villa was safe. At least Ryan hoped it was.

When Luisa saw the twins she stood up. 'Is it OK for me to look now?'

'Yes. They were the ones having sex,' Ryan said.

Alisha's and Greg's faces began to twist in sheer horror, but Ryan's unblinking stare must have sent the telepathic message it was meant to. Greg cottoned on before Alisha could protest. 'Yeah. This is my girl.' He slung an arm around his twin.

'Oh, my God.' Alisha screwed her eyes tight shut and went along with the ruse.

'Sorry about that,' Greg said. 'We didn't realise the police were here.'

'It's OK.' Luisa now looked more bored than suspicious, which Ryan took to be a good sign. 'Is this everyone?'

Ryan ran the numbers in his head. 'Yes.'

'OK,' said Luisa. 'I will check the house and go.'

'Please . . .' Katie motioned for Luisa to follow her back up the terrace stairs. Ryan followed them into the villa, light-headed from holding his breath.

At first glance, Alisha, Ben and Greg had merely tidied the lounge and kitchen. A quick glance confirmed that the 'blood'-covered dagger was no longer on the coffee table. The sofa-bed had been tucked away and the bedding folded into a neat pile. Roxanne's luggage was nowhere to be seen.

It took Ryan a moment to work out what was different: the wall. Rather than try to wash off the gruesome lettering, Alisha, Greg and Ben had nailed the sofa throw onto the wall as if it were a tapestry instead of a blanket. It was a traditional Spanish pattern so it didn't look out of place. The only problem was that they'd done a slapdash job of hanging the throw and it bulged and draped unevenly. Furthermore, the nails jutted out of the plaster. The throw didn't look at all secure. If it fell . . .

Luisa seemed satisfied though. She proceeded out of the lounge and up the stairs. Ryan threw a look over his shoulder to Alisha, who gave a reassuring nod. On the top landing, the policewoman gave only the most basic of checks to each of the bedrooms. Ryan saw Roxanne's backpack resting alongside his case at the foot of his bed. It blended perfectly.

'Is everything OK?' Katie asked.

'Yes. Sorry to come so early,' said Luisa, heading for the front door.

'No problem.' Katie smiled. 'Sorry about the emergency call. It won't happen again.' She opened the door.

Ryan felt his shoulders drop. Next to him, Alisha also seemed to relax.

'Be safe,' Luisa said. Then she paused on the threshold and looked back into the house, as if having second thoughts. That moment seemed to last for an eternity. Eventually, she reached into her pocket and handed Katie a crisp, white business card. 'Next time, if there is any problem, call my phone, OK?' Luisa scanned their faces, trying to find the missing puzzle piece she could evidently sense. She was no fool. She could feel their unease, Ryan could tell.

'OK, thank you.' Katie murmured.

Finally Luisa nodded and stepped outside. 'Goodbye,' she called. 'No more sailing at night. And . . . wear a condom.'

'We promise!' Ryan smiled, waving like one of the bloody Railway Children. As soon as Luisa reached her patrol car, he slammed the door shut. 'Right. We need to talk.'

'Erin,' Katie stated simply.

Ryan shook his head. 'Nope! Not that. This – if that was our Janey, then that means one of *us* is the killer.'

SCENE 30 – RYAN

They piled down the stairs back into the lounge.

'At least we don't have to worry about the resurrected corpse of Janey hunting us down and killing us,' Ryan said. 'I didn't think it was *that* kind of story, somehow.' Although it would've been *cool* if it had been. Zombies make any story at least forty-five per cent better.

Alisha shook her head. 'But that means one of us killed Rox.'

'Not necessarily.' Ben shrugged. 'There could be someone else watching us. Someone we haven't even thought of.'

'Unlikely.' Ryan wondered if it was too early for a drink, or a Valium, or three. '*Think on thy sins*. This isn't a random thing. This is someone who *knows* us.'

There was a profound silence. Each of them kept a safe distance from one another, the air ripe with almost tangible mistrust. A glaring spotlight was firmly back on them all. Luisa had been a diversion, nothing more than a red herring.

'What does that message even mean?' Alisha demanded, scowling at the throw which hid the letters on the wall.

'Isn't it obvious?' Greg snapped at his sister. 'Think about what we did.'

Ryan wasn't so sure it *was* obvious, but Katie spoke next. She was sitting on the edge of the sofa, hugging her knees like she was in the brace position for a crash landing.

And, oh, how we've crashed! Ryan mused.

'It's from *Othello*,' Katie said.

Greg eyed her warily. 'How do you know?'

Katie babbled, panicking. 'Everyone knows! I didn't write it, if that's what you're suggesting. I . . . if I had, why would I admit knowing it?'

Ryan had heard the phrase before – he thought it had been in a Bond film. The others all looked baffled but, of course, whoever wrote it would be going all out to appear clueless.

'What does it mean?' Alisha asked. 'In the play.'

'It's from the scene where Othello tries to get Desdemona to confess to an affair she didn't have,' Katie explained. 'Desdemona had been set up, but Othello asks her to try to remember what she's done – to "think on her sins".'

Ben sighed, looking pasty. 'Someone wants us to confess.'

Ryan squeezed the bridge of his nose. The embryonic headache in his skull was only going to grow as the day progressed, he feared. 'Confess to what? None of this makes sense.' The others waited for him to continue. He took centre stage, Poirot-style. 'Not being funny, but if the killer is one of us then they've got away with it! Rox tried to blackmail us, but the killer stopped her and we've *all* been getting rid of the evidence. All the killer had to do was sit tight for another week and then get the hell out of here. So why would he – or she – mess with us? It was all over.'

'Well, obviously bloody not,' Greg hissed through his teeth. '*Where's Erin?*'

'Exactly!' Ryan agreed. 'Where *is* Erin? Why write on the wall? Why did someone bring that scarecrow mask from the night Janey died? And where is it now?'

Greg sprang off the dining chair he was sitting on and

kicked it across the room. 'It doesn't matter! Erin is missing. If she's dead it's my fault. I . . . I should have looked after her better.'

Greg's pain hurt Ryan. For one, he'd never seen Greg feeling such grief. For another, he knew Greg would never feel that way for him. If he died, Greg wouldn't even shed a tear. If it was a match day, he wouldn't even come to the funeral. 'It *does* matter, Greg. We need to figure out what's going on.'

'No.' Katie wiped a tear from the corner of her eye. 'Greg's right. We can't sit here theorising about Shakespeare while Erin's missing. She might need our help.'

Her words cooled Greg. 'Thank you. Please, can you all help me?'

Ryan took a deep breath. The questions would have to go on ice. 'Let's get looking, then,' he said.

Katie took control in the warm manner of a *Miss Honey* primary-school teacher. 'OK, so, where could she be? She was very upset last night; she may have just left to go home. But if not, then where else? The beach? Or maybe she walked to Zahara de los Atunes.'

'What about that B&B we drove past just down the coast?' Ben suggested. 'Perhaps she went there.'

'I can't see her handbag anywhere,' Alisha offered. 'It was that huge pink Mulberry one. It's gone. Maybe she took it with her.'

'It's worth a try.' Greg closed his eyes. Every molecule of Ryan's body wanted to go and comfort him. The conversation last night had released the kraken inside him. All his good work at forgetting Greg Cole had come undone. He was jealous of Greg's feelings for Erin. Pure and simple. Acknowledging the sensation didn't make it any less searing hot. Who was

Erin? Some pretty med student. There was no way that she and Greg had the heat they'd had. No way. She was nothing more than a 'beard', so why was Greg in such pain?

A new thought occurred to Ryan. Erin had been alone in the lounge all night. Could she have left the message on the wall? That raised the same question again: *who was Erin?* She was a contradiction – a cutesy medical student, sweet as apple pie but with a sharp aftertaste. Ryan wondered if Erin was as good at pretending as her 'bifriend' was.

Katie ran for the stairs. 'I need to get dressed. Give me two minutes.'

'Me, too.' Alisha followed close behind.

Ben also headed upstairs to throw on some clothes but Greg held Ryan back. Ryan was gratified to see that his friend had to drag his eyes away from Ryan's naked torso to make eye contact.

'Hey,' Greg said.

'Hey what?'

Greg leaned in to whisper. Ryan, instead, leaned in to kiss him because fortune favours the brave. Their lips brushed.

'No. Don't.' Greg's protest was empty, half-hearted. Ryan persisted. This time Greg returned the kiss, albeit hesitantly. Ryan swore he could feel Greg melting into the embrace, but then Greg pulled back, his expression pained, torn. 'Ryan, please. I can't do this. I need to find Erin.'

Ryan drew himself up. 'Fine.'

Greg sighed. 'Listen,' he whispered. He brushed the back of Ryan's hand with a finger. 'I need you to stay here.'

'What?'

'While we're out, looking for Erin, I need you to stay here and turn this place over. Find Roxanne's phone, her laptop, anything. Just get rid of it. OK?'

Ryan realised he was a dirty little secret that needed to be destroyed. 'I see. Burn the evidence.'

'You understand, yeah? I need to make things right. There's a chance that Erin . . . we might find her.'

Ryan wasn't prepared to surrender any more of his dignity. 'I hope you do. Erin is very sweet. She deserves better than you,' he told Greg.

'I know.' Greg looked embarrassed. Maybe that was what he saw in Erin. She was something 'good' to elevate him out of all the 'bad' in his life. Ryan was left to wallow in the mud alone.

Katie galloped down the stairs, now wearing short shorts and a simple tennis T-shirt. 'Right, I'm ready.'

'Cool,' Greg said. 'Ryan's gonna stay here in case she comes back to the villa while we're gone.'

'OK, good call.'

Alisha and Ben also returned to the lounge, ready for the search.

'OK . . .' Greg tried to take charge, but it was clear his attention was unfocused. There was only Erin on his mind. 'OK . . . I'll drive into town, I guess.'

Katie took his hands. 'Greg, you're shaking. You can't drive like this. I'll take you in my hire car.'

'OK.' Greg looked grateful for the support and Ryan realised why he loved Katie so much. Even after last night, she had forgiven Greg entirely, never holding a grudge.

'Lish – stick with Ben, yeah?' Greg said. 'I don't want anything to happen to you.'

Alisha nodded. 'Sure.' And Ryan could swear she was *blushing*, but there was no time to think about that now.

'*No one* calls the police – even when you get a signal,' Ryan warned.

Greg sighed impatiently. 'I won't! Can we not have this debate now? We need to find Erin.'

They agreed to search all morning and meet back at the villa by two. If there was no sign of Erin by then . . . well, there was no plan B. They'd cross that bridge when they came to it. They worked so well together, Ryan had to remind himself that one of them was, in all likelihood, a cold-blooded killer.

Ben and Alisha set off down the beach, while Katie and Greg drove down the road to check out the B&B and then go on to Zahara de los Atunes. The second they were all out of sight, Ryan got to work. First he made himself a strong black coffee. The night before he'd barely slept a wink – Ben had been up and down like a jack-in-the-box and every time he closed his eyes all he saw was Roxanne's dead face. He had a horrible feeling it would be a while before any of them slept like regular people again.

He took Roxanne's rucksack out onto the top terrace. It was a brand-new morning in paradise. The sky, sea and sand dazzled him but he could no longer appreciate their beauty. Everything was tainted; the pristine white walls of the villa looked grimy up close, the sand was strewn with driftwood and the sea was full of corpses.

Ryan tried to focus on the task in hand. He realised that the hardy built-in barbecue on the top terrace would be the ideal place to burn Rox's stuff. He tipped the bag upside down and shook the contents onto the paving slabs. Roxanne had been travelling pretty light: one pair of jeans, two pairs of jean shorts, sandals, a light cotton dress and some very skimpy underwear. On a positive note, it was a surprise she'd bothered with underwear at all. A heavy toiletry bag hit the ground with a thud and that was it.

Ryan rifled through the numerous pockets. He found

headphones, a purse, a collection of weird and wonderful-looking currency and then he hit the jackpot: his old mobile handset. Clearly it had travelled from him to Janey and then on to Roxanne. He guessed Janey must have been feeling charitable when she upgraded; Roxanne had always had less money than the rest of them. That explained one mystery.

Ryan wondered if Janey had ever gone through the videos on the phone. He allowed himself to smile. As bad as it was for Greg, he wished he could have been a fly on the wall when Rox had first seen him and Greg on tape in the Cole family caravan.

He could almost hear Roxanne's screech of horror, followed by her cackle of delight. It made him sad. He was never going to hear that filthy laugh ever again. And there it was! The sadness had finally found him.

Wait a second. Little Tetris pieces fell into place to form a grim picture. Janey and Roxanne. The thing they had in common was this phone. One phone with one incriminating video. Had Greg known about it the whole time? A whole flock of *what ifs* screeched around like ravens. *What if* Greg had killed Janey to get at the phone? *What if* he'd come away empty handed and then killed Rox to finish the job? Ryan closed his eyes. *I'm in love with a serial killer.* He had to forget the idea. *Remember it's all a plotline. None of it's real,* he told himself. Because if that were the case, there was only one person left in the whole world who knew about the affair: Ryan himself. That put him on the endangered list, to say the least.

A message on the wall from Shakespeare, though? That so wasn't Greg's style. Ryan would be amazed if Greg could even spell 'Shakespeare' correctly. That didn't mean he hadn't hurt the girls, though. He'd hurt Katie last night.

He banished the thoughts. Greg had never hurt him and never would. With a sigh, Ryan switched the handset on. The battery was almost gone, but there was enough juice to discover it was password locked. He tried Rox's year of birth with no luck. He tried her birthday with similar lack of success. In a last-ditch attempt he even tried four zeros, one, two, three, four and his old password, but it was no use.

The only record of the good times he'd shared with Greg Cole had died with Roxanne Dent.

SCENE 31 – ALISHA

A sumptuous wind rolled in off the sea, kissing Alisha's face. Good thing, too. In the moments when the breeze died, it was too hot to bear, like being under a grill. She allowed herself only minute sips of water, knowing she and Ben had an immense trek ahead.

They walked away from the jetty. Katie and Greg were headed south towards Zahara de los Atunes, so they chose to head north towards Barbate. The sand was too hot to walk on, so she and Ben stuck to the cool, hard-packed wet sand, allowing the fizzing surf to run over their toes.

In other circumstances a walk through the surf with Ben Murdoch would be desirable, even romantic. You see it all the time on the TV adverts for travel companies – a gorgeous couple walking hand in hand through the white foam while some cheesy love song plays. But Alisha didn't dare appreciate it for a second; it would seem totally wrong. Still, she was secretly thrilled she'd been paired with Ben.

It was weird to think this was the same sea that now concealed Roxanne's body. In the light of day it looked so innocent, so safe.

'Do you think we'll find her?' Ben spoke first and Alisha was glad. For some reason, after their search of the cellar, she felt awkward around him. It was as though, now she'd noticed how hot Ben was, she couldn't *stop* noticing it.

'I hope so,' she replied, realising she was so tense her throat hurt a little. 'I really hope so. I mean, why Erin? She wouldn't say boo to a goose.'

'Exactly. She had nothing to do with anything,' Ben said. 'At least, I don't think she did.'

'Maybe she just got in someone's way,' Alisha suggested. Man, that was a bleak thought. 'Or maybe she just did a runner. She was having a full-scale meltdown last night. After what my darling brother did, I can't say I blame her really.'

'There's no one up ahead for miles, Lish.'

Alisha used her hand as a visor. 'I know, but we have to look. Maybe she went for a swim.'

'Do you really believe that?'

'No,' Alisha admitted sadly.

'I think she's dead.' He wasn't trying to be sensational, he was just being real. That was Ben Murdoch. Alisha stopped and looked up at him. There was nothing she could say so she took his hand instead and said nothing. She didn't need to. He understood and pulled her in tight, sealing her inside his arms. He rested his chin on the top of her head and she felt at peace for the first time in a year.

All of a sudden, things didn't seem very fair. She hadn't asked for any of this and she certainly hadn't killed anyone. After a year of purgatory in Telscombe Cliffs, all she'd wanted was a bit of fun in the sun with her old school friends. 'Come with me.' She dragged Ben diagonally across the sand.

'What are you doing?' Ben trotted to keep up.

'Wait and see!' They ran the way children run – all arms and legs. Alisha led him to the top of the hill at the end of the beach. Then she threw her arms out as if presenting the view. The other side of the slope opened out into sand dunes like craters on the moon. She and Ryan had discovered them on the first day while hunting for a location for their photoshoot. 'Come on!' Alisha cried. 'It's fun.'

She charged down the first hill, the momentum propelling her straight up the next incline. Wind rushed around her, transporting her back in time. She was twelve again – on a family holiday to Tunisia, playing hide and seek with Greg in the dunes.

'We're meant to be looking for Erin!' Ben called after her.

'Bet you can't catch me!' was Alisha's response. She felt alive. In fact, she couldn't remember the last time she'd felt so lightweight and free. Not since she was about twelve – before all the high-school drama had kicked in, before Callum, before she'd first tasted whisky or vodka. She'd spent so much time trying to prove to the world how grown-up she was, she'd forgotten how much fun it was to be young.

Roxanne, Janey, Erin. For the next hour, she wanted nothing more to do with any of them.

A smile broke out on Ben's face and it was like the sun coming out from behind a cloud. 'Bet I can.' He set off after her. Alisha screamed and followed the curve of the next dune. Behind her, Ben's feet skidded in the sand and he slid all the way down the slope on his bottom. Alisha doubled up with laughter. The look on his face was priceless.

'Oh, now you're in trouble,' he yelled. He landed back on his feet and pursued her.

With a whoop, Alisha powered up the next hill and looked for a hiding place. Marram grass swayed with the wind and would make for good cover. The brow of the next dune was particularly grassy so she sprinted for that. She almost didn't notice Ben reach out and grab for her back. Squealing, she ducked out of the way and rolled down the dune, the sand talcum-powder-soft and warm on her bare arms and legs. She had just about made it to her feet again when Ben slid right alongside her, seemingly riding the sand.

He barrelled into her and wrestled her off her feet. Alisha could hardly breathe for laughing. His arms were around her waist and he snuck in a tickle to the ribs for good measure.

'Get off me!' she laughed, tears running down her face.

'No! Got ya!' He grinned. He pushed the hair off her face and she felt the weight of his body on top of hers. It felt *right* somehow.

Their lips were so close together it seemed inevitable. Like magnets pulling each other together. He leaned in to kiss her and she felt nervous. It had been a while. What if she couldn't remember how to do it? What if there was some cool new way of doing it that no one had told her about? For the first time in a really long time, *this* kiss mattered.

She needn't have worried. Ben's lips were soft, warm and perfect against hers and suddenly she knew just what to do. She hooked her hands around the back of his head, pulling him in closer. Hip to hip. He kissed her harder and something dormant awoke inside her. *Desire.* She'd almost forgotten how it felt. It was like a carnival running through her veins.

Alisha felt intensely aware of every inch of her skin, of Ben's hands on her sides, of the fact that she was wearing only a bikini top and shorts. Instead of feeling vulnerable and exposed, though, she felt safe and calm in Ben's arms and, when his fingers traced the soft skin of her waist, she shivered, and in a totally good way.

The sun beat down on her and it was so, so easy to imagine that this was heaven.

Only then the voices started to bleed into her head, reminding her of everything she'd been trying to forget and draining the electricity from Ben's fingers. 'Ben, stop,' she whispered.

'Are you OK?' He stopped at once, rearing back to look down at her. His legs were entwined with hers in the powdery sand.

'I'm fine.' She brushed sand from his cheek. 'But this is really bad . . . I mean, we're meant to be looking for Erin, and what about Katie? She would kill me if she knew . . .' She pushed him back and Ben rolled off her, sitting upright in the sand.

He nodded, ruffling his hair. 'God, Lish, I'm sorry. I got carried away.'

'No.' She sat close alongside him. 'Don't apologise. *That* was perfect. It felt like I'd been waiting a really long time for that.'

'Worth the wait?'

'Oh, yes!' Alisha announced way too loudly. She blushed. So uncool.

'I knew you'd be a good kisser. It's all about the lips.'

She raised an eyebrow. 'You've been thinking about my lips?'

Ben beamed. 'I'm a guy with eyes. Of *course* I've been thinking about you. You must know you're insanely hot, Alisha.'

The sun got about a hundred degrees hotter and her face blazed. 'Shut up.'

'It's true.'

Alisha rubbed her eyes, making vivid mauve clouds swim under her eyelids. 'But what about Katie? And Janey?' She looked him in the eye. 'Are you just the biggest manwhore ever?'

He laughed. 'Oh, God, how do I answer that? I guess I

didn't really *see* you until it was too late. By the time Katie and I broke up, you were with Callum. And I didn't think you . . . saw *me* like that. I had a hunch you thought I was just Greg's massively nerdy mate.'

'Well, I did!' Alisha giggled. 'It took me a while to realise there was more to you than that.'

A moment of silence followed. Gulls squawked and the waves sighed beyond the dunes. 'Katie and I are over,' Ben said at last. 'We were over a long time ago. It's why we broke up. We realised we were best friends and nothing more.'

'But the other night . . . on the beach?'

'Oh, what, that? We needed to talk. We had a lot to catch up on and she needed a friend. I will always love Katie; she was my first girlfriend, but I'm not in love with her.'

'Childhood sweethearts . . .' Alisha mused.

'. . . don't always wind up together,' Ben finished for her. 'Real life isn't like TV.'

Alisha's head spun. She had just kissed Ben Murdoch. She didn't keep a diary, but if she did, tonight's entry would be a bumper edition, featuring a lengthy and highly florid account of every minute detail, from the feel of his lips against hers to the ecstasy of his touch. 'OK, but why did you get with Janey?' she asked.

And the temperature dropped as quickly as it had risen. Ben's gaze fell and he looked awkwardly into the sand. 'You were *still* with Callum,' he said quietly.

Alisha was confused. Did he really like her, or was she just the last one of the gang left? Her gut told her that Ben Murdoch was about as far away from being a 'player' as you could get. Maybe it really had been just a case of bad timing.

Either way, this was more bad timing. Alisha clambered to her feet. 'Come on. We need to look for Erin.'

Ben rose. 'Are you sure we're cool, Alisha? I don't wanna give you the wrong idea. I really do—'

Alisha cut him off. 'Ben, it's fine. We were both caught in the moment. It doesn't mean anything.' She always had been a bull in a china shop, and saying those lies smashed her heart to smithereens, but she couldn't and *wouldn't* do to Katie what Rox had done to her.

From the look on Ben's face, she'd just drop-kicked his heart all the way down the beach. She led the way out of the crater. This was for the best.

SCENE 32 – RYAN

A black, toxic column of smoke curled away from the villa into the sky. Ryan coughed back the noxious fumes and hurled Roxanne's towel onto the fire. The idea to barbecue the dead girl's belongings had seemed like a good one at first, but he was starting to suspect he could well be sending a smoke signal to the police.

He couldn't bring himself to burn the phone. He didn't want to let go of the video even if he couldn't watch it.

Tyres crunched down the drive at the top of the villa. Ryan frowned – he hadn't been expecting anyone back so soon. He heard voices drift around the side of the building, but couldn't tell if there were two or three people. He hoped for three. The front door slammed shut as he headed through the terrace doors. A few moments later, Greg plodded down the stairs, shoulders hunched, with Katie close behind. Erin's absence spoke for itself.

'No luck?' Ryan asked anyway.

'She texted me,' Greg said. 'We'd only been driving for about five minutes when I got a signal, and then her text came through from last night.'

Ryan felt as though a ten-ton weight had been lifted from his back. Erin was alive. 'Oh, thank God!'

'I know, right?' Katie dropped her beach bag onto the

kitchen counter. 'We thought about going to the airport to see if we could find her, but she texted at, like, four a.m. so she'll probably be home by now.'

A new, arguably worse thought than Erin being dead occurred to Ryan. 'What if she tells the police?'

Greg wouldn't look him in the eye. 'She says she won't.'

'Oh, well, if she *says* she won't then I guess we're all fine.' Ryan rolled his eyes.

'Ry, back off,' Katie said. 'He's upset. And, anyway, Erin can't say anything, just like we can't.' Katie looked out at the inferno on the terrace. 'Is that Rox's stuff?'

'Yep. I got rid of everything.'

'Did you burn her phone?' Greg asked, eyes burning into Ryan.

'Yeah,' Ryan lied.

'What about her so-called "evidence"?' Katie asked.

He shook his head. 'If she did have anything it wasn't in her luggage. You know, she might have made the whole thing up. Perhaps it was just a way of getting money out of us.' Ryan didn't really believe it, but it was an avenue worth considering. If he hadn't had such massive doubts of his own about Janey topping herself, it would have been fairly plausible.

Both Greg and Katie looked disappointed by this news. Resigned, Katie headed for the stairs.

'I guess we'll have to carry on looking,' she said. 'I'm going to take a shower. Greg, are you gonna be OK?'

'Yeah. Yeah, thanks Katie. Thanks for driving and everything.'

'No worries.' She disappeared upstairs.

Ryan waited until he heard the bathroom door shut. 'Greg, what's going on?'

Greg steered him out of the villa. 'She heard us.'

'What?'

'Are you deaf? I said *she heard us*. What we said last night. Erin was in the shower while we were talking – she heard the whole effing conversation through the air vents.'

Holy mother of little baby Jesus. Ryan exhaled deeply. 'Shit.'

'Er, YEAH!'

'What did she say?' The bonfire was still crackling and Ryan wafted the smoke away from his face.

Greg folded his arms. 'She wasn't happy, put it that way. I think . . . what with everything else, it was the last straw.'

'Do you think she'll tell people . . . about us?'

Greg exploded. 'How the hell should I know? I'm not a bloody psychic, Ryan!' His reaction suggested he was far more worried that their sordid fling would come out, than about Erin spilling the beans about Roxanne – which struck Ryan as mixed-up priorities.

Ryan was about to reach for Greg's hand when a familiar pair came into view at the edge of the pool. It was Ben and Alisha, back from their trek on the beach. Both looked tired and tousled, like they'd survived something. Everyone was wilting in the relentless sun.

'Hey,' called Ben as he and Alisha made their way up the terrace stairs to join Ryan and Greg. 'How did you get on? We didn't even find a footprint in the sand, I'm afraid.'

Greg backed away from Ryan as if he had leprosy. 'No worries,' Greg muttered, blushing. 'Erin went home. She's fine.'

'Oh, my God!' Alisha threw her arms around her brother in relief. 'I was so worried.'

'It's cool. She's OK.' Greg, however, didn't look OK. He looked fraught.

Ryan noted that Ben looked a little embarrassed, too. He hovered at Alisha's side like he wasn't sure what to do with his hands. For a moment, Ryan wondered if something might have happened between him and Alisha on the beach, but then he laughed it off. The viewers would never buy those two together – everyone knew it was all about Ben and Katie.

'That's really good news, mate,' Ben said. 'You must be so relieved.'

'Yeah.' Greg did a poor job of looking relieved. 'I reckon my arse is dumped, though.'

Ben gave a wry laugh. 'Plenty more fish in the . . .' He pointed in the direction of where they'd dumped Rox's body and the smile fell from his face. 'Well, you know.'

Alisha tugged on his arm. 'This is a good thing,' she said gleefully.

'What is?' Katie joined them on the patio, towelling her wet hair.

Alisha sparkled. 'Erin's fine. We're safe!'

Oh, if only it were that simple, Ryan thought.

'I hate to be a harbinger of doom,' Katie said, 'but someone still killed Roxanne.'

'And unless Erin wrote that message on the wall, there's something bigger at play,' Ryan said, fully aware the statement was on the histrionic side.

The five of them stood in a loose circle on the top terrace. They'd come a long way from playing tag and kiss-chase at Telscombe Cliffs Primary School. For the first time, Ryan felt the prick of tears. One of these people wasn't his friend any more. This wasn't just about Janey and Roxanne; there was something else going on, but he had no idea what. Who had written the message on the wall – and why? *Think on thy sins.*

Lust, ambition, greed, anger, envy, deception, murder.

Between them they had so many sins, thinking on them might take a while. 'I think we should go home,' he announced.

'But you said—' Alisha started to argue.

Ryan cut her off. 'I know what I said – that it will look suspicious. But if we all stick to the same lie we might just get away with it. Hell, we don't even have to leave Spain, but I would feel a whole lot safer in a highly populated tourist area with five bars of phone reception.'

'I second that,' Ben said with a sigh.

'I dunno.' Greg massaged his temples, looking drained. 'People are already going to be asking questions about why Erin left.'

'It does look a little shady,' Katie agreed. 'Sooner or later someone's going to notice Roxanne is missing. And then what? People might start to put two and two together. *This* is why we should have gone to the police yesterday, guys. It's going to follow us around forever. With all these lies, one of us is bound to slip up sooner or later.'

Ryan knew she was right. He might have to start writing them somewhere secret to keep everything straight in his head.

'Maybe we're safe here,' Alisha said, ever the optimist. 'Rox only died because she blackmailed us.'

'This isn't just about Rox.' Ryan was on a roll. 'What about Janey? We still don't know why *she* died.'

It was all too much for Greg. 'I can't do this.' He squatted down, face in hands as if his spine could no longer support him. He swore at the top of his voice. 'I need a break.' He stormed through the sliding doors and headed for the stairs.

That left four of them. 'I think we should leave,' Ryan repeated, 'like now.'

Ben chewed his thumbnail. 'Ry, no one wants to get out

of here more than me, but we haven't even drained the pool yet.'

Ryan sighed. He'd forgotten about that little task. Doing it in broad daylight felt a little risky – all it would take was one stray surfer and they'd have a witness to testify they'd changed the pool water. Highly suspect. 'OK. I guess we drain the pool after dark and get the hell out of here tomorrow. Right?'

This time, no one argued.

Greg was crying in the shower. Ryan sat on the bed in Greg's room listening to the patter of the water and how it failed to cover the shaking breaths and low sobs. The air vents carried the noise with clarity. No wonder Erin had heard. The sound of Greg crying was more disturbing than any other part of this week. Ryan wondered if he was the only one even vaguely holding it together.

Ryan was an actor, the star. He'd never envisaged himself as the director/producer. He didn't want to call the shots. But if everyone else was going to crumble, he'd have to. Somehow, he wasn't exactly sure where, the black and white had bled into one another to form a mucky grey. He wasn't sure who the heroes were any more. He couldn't even say with certainty that he wasn't a villain.

The pipes groaned as Greg turned off the shower. The bathroom was quiet now, except for a few sniffs as Greg dried his eyes. The door to the en suite opened and Greg entered the bedroom, a towel around his waist.

Ryan expected more anger, a command to get out and stay out. Instead, Greg's face was puffy and red, his posture hunched. Greg was broken. He dragged his feet across the tiles, saying nothing. He leaned over Ryan and took his face in his hands, tilting it towards him.

The kiss that followed was the Hollywood kiss Ryan had always wanted. It was fireworks, sweeping violins, the final frame in the pouring rain. It was the kiss that said Greg *needed* him.

Ryan wrapped his hands around the back of Greg's head and pulled him closer. Greg climbed onto the bed and tipped him onto his back. The kiss intensified, Greg's mouth pressing hard against Ryan's. There was a desperation to him, a frenzy. Ryan could so easily allow himself to be swept away, but he found himself anchored to reality.

Questions. This was what he had always wanted, so why was his head full of questions? Was this weird angry-hate snogging? The fact that Greg had pinned Ryan's hand above his head suggested so. Did that matter? Was this Greg finally accepting the way he felt? Or was this more about Erin than Ryan?

There were too many questions to enjoy the moment.

'Stop!' Ryan said between kisses. He'd probably regret it later, but Greg wasn't in control any more. He was.

Greg didn't stop though. He tugged back on Ryan's hair and started on his neck, his tongue working its way up to his earlobe. Ryan shivered, but clung to this side of ecstasy. 'Greg, stop.'

'What's up?' He looked up. 'Am I doing it wrong?'

Ryan laughed. 'No! No that, as ever, was very good! But what are you doing?'

'What does it look like I'm doing? Greg raised an eyebrow and rolled off Ryan, flopping next to him on the bed. 'I don't know, Ry. I don't know what I'm doing. I'm a mess. I'm a total effing mess.'

'No shit, Sherlock.'

He covered his face with his hands. 'It . . . it . . . Oh, God.'

'What?' Ryan prodded.

'It's like I'm constantly spinning plates. All the time. It's like if I stop for a second one'll come crashing down. Then another and another. It never stops, Ryan. It never bloody stops.'

Ryan pulled Greg's hands away and gave him a tender kiss. 'It's not easy being you, is it?' he said, his face millimetres from Greg's.

'I've told so many lies, I think I've started to believe them.'

Ryan wondered how many lies *he'd* told this week.

'I should have just got with you in the first place. You've been so good to me and I've been a total massive idiot.'

Ryan laughed. 'Well, yes. I'm not gonna argue with that. And we do get together in the end, Greg, don't worry. But not, like, till the end of series six.'

Greg propped himself up on his elbow and ran the tips of his fingers across Ryan's stomach. 'What?'

Smiling, Ryan said, 'It sounds mad, but I like to pretend we're all in a big TV show.'

'That does sound a *bit* mad . . .'

'Thanks! But it gets me through the day. You know, on TV, everything will all work out in the end. All the people who are meant to get together *will* get together. You can't get to happy-ever-after too fast, though. You have to overcome all the obstacles, all the twists and turns.'

Greg planted a kiss on Ryan's shoulder. 'But how do you know where the end *is*?'

'It's when I'm happy.'

'And then you'll stop?'

'Well, I won't need to pretend any more, will I?' Something told Ryan that the stopping point was a long way off. Here was Greg, half-naked, vulnerable, and entirely his. For now. But he knew from experience that if they were to fall asleep, when they awoke, the walls would be all the way up again. 'Come on. Get dressed. I suppose we should pack or something.'

'No, wait. Don't go.' Greg took hold of Ryan's waist. He looked so lost, so needy. Ryan could gloat about the power shift, about how far the mighty had fallen, but he mainly felt sad for his lover. 'Can't we . . . chill for a while?'

Ryan could only argue so far. He was human at the end of the day and Greg's warm, smooth skin begged to have his hands on it. 'OK.'

'Will you just hold me, yeah? Like you used to?'

A lump rose in Ryan's throat but he swallowed it back. 'Yeah. Am I being big spoon or little spoon?'

'Big.' Greg rolled over, his back to Ryan. Ryan wrapped his arms around him and let himself be content. For now, he closed his eyes, rested his head and allowed himself the notion that *this* could be the happy ending.

SCENE 33 – ALISHA

The heat wouldn't let up for a second. Even with the air-con on, she could feel sweat running down the arch of her back. Alisha squirmed uncomfortably, but it wasn't just the blistering temperature. She couldn't get the kiss out of her mind. She scrolled through endless Spanish TV stations – shopping channels, music videos, news – without seeing any of them. Instead, she played the kiss on constant loop, trying to recapture the soaring sensation that she'd felt. Ben and Katie were outside on the terrace, but neither was speaking. Even their comfortable silence made her a little jealous.

If she talked to Katie, perhaps she'd give them her blessing. But it seemed unlikely after what Katie had said about their secret clifftop kiss and subsequent text messages. Now that Alisha had had a chance to dwell (and dwell and dwell) on it, that's what she didn't understand. If Ben and Katie had been 'best friends and nothing more', then why did they start getting it on behind Janey's back? That made no sense whatsoever.

But she couldn't forget what Ben had said on the beach. Maybe he really *did* like her. Alisha's imagination started to run away with her, taking her far into the future. She always did this. She'd meet a guy a couple of times and then start thinking of loved-up scenarios: a weekend break to a cottage (does anyone *actually* do that?), meeting his parents, a cosy night on the sofa with a takeaway. All that before they'd even held hands.

Oh, this is a waste of time! Alisha thought. She badly needed to chill out. What did she think was going to happen? Their love would be the miracle glue to keep the group together? After a year of cabin fever in Telscombe Cliffs, she'd been so excited about the holiday and being back with her friends. But they weren't her friends any more. One of them was a killer and they had *all* done a terrible, awful thing. You don't get a 'happy ever after' after that.

If Janey wasn't already dead, Alisha would have killed her. She allowed herself a secret smile at the thought. A part of them had gone with Janey off the edge of those cliffs. Those endless, carefree summer holidays when they'd hung out in Ben's garage, walked back from Brighton because they'd spent their bus fare on clothes, practised dance routines in Ryan's living room. They were gone and recapturing them was like trying to get a butterfly back in a jar.

Alisha knew there was a bottle of vodka in the freezer. She was feeling far too lucid; maybe she'd do something about that. She clicked off the TV. No. She had to stay sharp. Who bloody knew what her brother and Ryan were plotting upstairs?

If only they'd listened to Katie yesterday, none of this would have happened. OK, maybe she really was a simpleton, but she believed the police would have sorted this out. There'd have been fingerprints on *something*, some shred of evidence linking one of them to Roxanne, and then at least the rest of them would have been off the hook.

In a weird way, Alisha had got her wish – the old gang was back together again. For eternity. They were all bound together now by their terrible secret, until the day they died. That was a terrifying thought. Alisha threw herself back on the sofa in despair. As she landed on the cushion there was a faint *thud* behind her as something fell to the floor. There must have been something resting between the back of the sofa and the wall.

Climbing to her knees, Alisha peered down the crack. It was a book. Her arm was just about skinny enough to retrieve it. She pulled it out and saw it was a battered paperback edition of *On the Road* by Jack Kerouac. She grimaced. Why couldn't people read normal books instead of trying to be clever? She'd seen the film version starring K-Stew and it had been super-dull. She figured it was one of Katie's course novels and wondered if the book were any more interesting than the film had been. She began to flick through.

Katie was using an envelope as a bookmark. It slipped out as Alisha turned the pages.

But the envelope was addressed to *Roxanne*. It carried the address of a hostel in Thailand and three stamps. The penny dropped: this book wasn't Katie's, it was Roxanne's.

A good person would not have looked in the envelope. A good person would have sealed it in a sandwich bag to prevent 'evidence' from being 'contaminated'. Alisha was under no illusion that she was one such saint. She tore the envelope in her haste to get inside – and glimpsed photos and letters.

'What's that?'

Alisha recoiled, snatching the stash to her chest. It was Katie coming in through the terrace doors. 'OMG, Katie!'

'What?'

'You know Roxanne said she had "evidence"? I think I just found it.'

SCENE 33 (CONT.)

Katie's eyes widened. 'What? *How?*'

Alisha held up the paperback. 'This was hers. Ryan must have missed it. I found an envelope inside.'

'Oh, my God! What's in it?'

'I don't know. Do you think we should look?'

'Er, yeah.' Katie looked out of the terrace doors.

'Where's Ben?' Alisha asked.

'He's throwing rocks into the sea.'

'Moody.'

'Quite!' Katie scurried to the bottom of the stairs. 'Let's go up to our room, just in case.'

Alisha jumped off the sofa and followed Katie upstairs. Once inside their bedroom, the girls sat opposite each other on the bed, legs crossed, leaving a space in the middle for whatever was in the envelope.

'You know what this means don't you?' Katie said.

'What?' Alisha replied. It felt like her heart was beating inside her skull.

'If Roxanne had evidence and we can work out who killed her, then this can all be over. I think we should go to the police, confess that we helped dump the body and just hope they go easy on us.'

Alisha felt a new hope break in her chest. They could

untangle themselves from this web and be *free*. And if they got into some trouble for helping to dispose of Rox's body, well, it was nothing they didn't deserve. No one had *forced* them to go along with the plan yesterday. Maybe there *should* be some comeuppance. 'Best have a look then.' She looked at the envelope in her hands. 'Katie, I'm nervous.'

Katie nodded. 'Me too. But it's better to know. Ignorance is never bliss.'

'One of the lads might have murdered Rox.'

'One of them *did*,' Katie said flatly.

Without another word, Alisha reached into the envelope and spread its contents over the blanket: a mixture of photos – some old-fashioned gloss six-by-fours and some printed on regular paper – and what looked like notes that Roxanne had scribbled. It seemed that Rox had spent her year out playing detective.

The first photo that caught Alisha's eye was one of Janey. Janey, happy and smiling at the ball – the night she'd died. She was posing with Roxanne, their arms around each other. It was typical of Janey to be so two-faced, Alisha thought. If memory served, Janey had spent most of the ball with her, pulling Rox to pieces.

'Woah!' Katie held a sheet up to the light for closer inspection. 'Look at this.' She passed it to Alisha.

It was a grainy printed photo, like a screen grab, of two people sharing a passionate kiss. The poor quality made their heads look a little like two alien blobs colliding in space, but when Katie turned it the right way up, the faces came into focus. The paler of the two was undeniably Ryan, his hair a lot shorter than it was now, suggesting that the picture was a couple of years old, at least. The second, although twisted slightly away from the camera and making an unattractive snogging face, looked like her brother.

Alisha's brain rebooted and she took another look. Her eyes had obviously suffered a glitch. Why would Ryan and Greg be *snogging*? Had it been a dare? When had it happened? Alisha looked at Katie, who had her hand over her mouth in shock like a scandalised Victorian debutante. Katie pushed another two similar pictures in her direction. The next was clearer – a topless Ryan straddling Greg. The final one made Alisha scream.

'Oh, my God! Is that my brother's *penis*?' She covered her eyes with her hand. 'Take it away! Take it away!'

Katie whipped the offending photo away. 'It's gone!'

Alisha half-stood, half-fell off the bed and walked to the window. She needed to let in some air. Oh, yeah, she'd forgotten – there was no air. Just humidity. 'Oh, my God,' she said again.

'I know.'

'No. But,' Alisha panted, 'Ryan and Greg! RYAN AND GREG!'

'Keep your voice down,' Katie whispered urgently. 'They're just next door.'

'Oh, my days!' Alisha cried. 'You don't think they're in there . . . you know?'

Katie's face fell. 'No. No, surely not. Well, maybe . . .'

'Katie, this is insane. I mean, did you know?'

'No! Did you?'

'No! Greg has always had *girl*friends. Always.'

Her friend shrugged. 'Elton John used to be married to a woman.'

Her twin brother was Elton John. Alisha was not ready for this. It was like she'd somehow crossed into a parallel universe or something.

Katie examined the more graphic pictures. Alisha couldn't bring herself to look again, but she was pretty certain they were screen-grabs from a home movie. Greg had made a sex-tape. Never again would she be the more stupid sibling.

'You know what?' Katie turned the pictures face down, for which Alisha was grateful. 'This is what Rox had on Greg and Ryan. This was her blackmail material.'

'Katie, I'm gonna need a minute to get my head round this.' Alisha couldn't care less if Greg was gay. Frankly, if it meant an end to the gold-digging glamour-model girlfriends, she totally supported the move. It was the fact that someone she'd shared a human body with had managed to keep something so huge so secret for so long. She'd thought she knew Greg inside out – but if he could hide that, he could hide *anything*.

For the first time, Alisha *truly* envisaged Greg killing Roxanne. *Please don't let it be him.* She tried to distract herself with the rest of the contents of the envelope, hoping there was something that might get her brother off the hook. Better Ben or Ryan than Greg. Yes, she'd always been the black sheep next to him, but if Greg was a murderer it would break her mum and dad apart – the whole world would crumble. 'What else is there?'

'Wait, that's me!' Katie squeaked, seizing an old photo from the pile.

'Let's see.'

Katie held out an ancient-looking photo. It showed a cute red-haired child with a freckled button nose.

Alisha recognised Katie's mum propping her up next to a farm gate, feeding some horses. 'You look well cute.'

'Gosh, I must have been about two in that picture.' Katie turned it over. There was nothing written on the back.

Alisha didn't get it. 'What's that all about?'

'I have absolutely no idea.'

'Where did Rox get it?'

'Ditto. It is quite, quite bizarre. Why does Roxanne Dent have my baby pictures?' Katie stroked her face in the picture. 'It's a bit creepy – like she was stalking us.'

Alisha nodded. 'Told you. We should have ditched that girl the day she arrived.'

'Ditched her in the sea?'

'Very funny. You know what I meant.' Alisha returned to the 'evidence' and found a photo of Roxanne and Callum. After all this time, her blood still boiled. She wondered if there would come a day when that wouldn't happen. Even Rox's death hadn't stopped the anger.

'What's in that one?' Katie asked.

'It's just some random lovey-dovey picture of her and Cal. Look.' She gave Katie the picture.

'Is it from the ball? Is that what she was wearing?'

Alisha took a fresh look. Rox was wearing her naked dress, and Callum's bow tie hung loose around his neck. 'Yeah. Yeah it is.' Alisha rifled through what was left on the bed. As well as the photo of Rox and Callum, there was a similar one of the whole Longview music crowd – taken at the same time and place. They looked like they'd all leapt into Roxanne and Callum's shot – the group laughing, drinks in their hands.

'How is this evidence?' Katie frowned.

Alisha studied the faces carefully. 'It must have something to do with Janey. It's the night she died.'

'You're right.' Katie studied the photo again. 'Lish, was this taken on Telscombe Cliffs?

The quality of the picture was shocking. Thanks to her somewhat expert eye, Alisha guessed it had been taken on a camera phone and later printed. The flash made pale ghosts of the subjects and the background was pure black. But, over Callum's left shoulder, there was a milky cloud and the suggestion of a grassy edge. Katie was right. The white shape was probably the moon on the sea. 'Yeah, it looks like it. I wonder if they went to the cliffs after we'd been kicked out of the sports hall, to carry on drinking or whatever.'

Suddenly, Katie gasped and peered more closely at the photo. She was always pretty pale, but what little colour she did have had drained from her face.

'What is it?' Alisha asked.

'Look.' Katie passed the group photo to her. Alisha scanned the faces. Millie and Damon were the pair jumping on Roxanne. In the background was Ferdie, and, beyond him there was someone else, almost lost in the fuzzy image. Tall, dark hair, broad shoulders, puppy-dog eyes – it wasn't a great picture, but it was definitely Ben Murdoch.

'Is that—' Alisha began.

'It's Ben,' Katie confirmed. 'He was at the cliffs the night that Janey died.'

SCENE 34 – ALISHA

There was a horrible acidic taste in Alisha's mouth. How stupid she'd been. How babyish. *Ben can't possibly be a killer because you LOVE him*, said a high-pitched, mocking voice in her head.

Where were you when Janey Bradshaw vanished? had been a popular question after her parents reported her missing. They'd been over that night so many times, both with the police and among themselves, and they'd *all* denied being anywhere near the cliffs. Except that *Ben had lied*.

And Roxanne had discovered the lie. This photo was the proof. Alisha unfolded a piece of paper, covered in Roxanne's scribbled notes in different-coloured pens. 'She worked out where we all were when Janey fell,' Alisha told Katie.

Katie rubbed her face with her hands. 'What does it say?'

Alisha handed the paper to her. 'Nothing new. You were at home all night, I got taken home drunk, Greg and Ryan went into Brighton to carry on partying . . . and Ben *said* he went home . . .'

'But he didn't. He was at Telscombe Cliffs.' Katie stared at the photo in Alisha's hand. 'God, I've been such an idiot. I never thought that Ben . . .' Her voice trailed off.

Alisha studied the photo, at the same time remembering *that kiss*. She prayed that Katie never found out about it.

'Hey, I never thought that Ben would do something like that, either, Katie. He's a good guy. At least, I thought he was.' She shook her curls.

'But why, Lish? Why would he *kill* Janey? If he'd wanted to be with me, he could have just dumped her.'

'Dumped her off a cliff?'

'*Touché.*'

Alisha gave her hand a squeeze. 'All we know is that he was there, that he lied.'

Katie threw her head back, looking to the ceiling for answers. 'Why would he lie?'

Alisha could think of only one reason. 'Because he was guilty.'

'OK. So why would *Roxanne* keep it a secret?' Katie chewed her lip, on the very edge of tears. 'Why didn't she tell the police he was there?'

A light bulb went off over Alisha's head. 'That shady bitch! She didn't tell the police because she was planning to blackmail him.' The idea made a lot of sense. 'This was all about Ben,' Alisha went on. 'Don't you get it? She knew that Greg was the richest, because of the football, but she must have worried that the photos of him and Ryan wouldn't be enough, although, girl, they would have been, believe me,' Alisha said without irony.

Katie smiled grimly. She was clearly heartbroken at the prospect of her ex being a double murderer. Alisha was starting to think that she'd had a lucky escape on the beach earlier – who knew what Ben was capable of?

'So,' Alisha went on, her thoughts picking up speed and size like a cartoon snowball rolling downhill, 'Roxanne knew it was Ben. She knew he was there the whole time. But this is the only evidence she had.'

Katie poked at the sad pile of papers. 'It's hardly evidence.'

'Exactly! That's what all that bloody cabaret was at the dinner table. Rox knew her evidence was – what do they call it on TV? – *circumstantial*, so she talked it up. It was her best way of getting the money. She wanted to make us *all* think we were somehow involved, but she banked on Ben knowing he was guilty even if she couldn't properly prove it.'

It was a very strange feeling. Triumph on the one hand – Alisha felt pretty smug for figuring it out – but her satisfaction at having solved a puzzle was clouded by thoughts of Ben. In her story, she'd unmasked a killer. But Ben? It seemed *ridiculous*.

Katie was catching up. 'But if he killed Janey, does that mean . . .'

'That he killed Roxanne?' Alisha expelled all the air from her lungs. 'I guess so. He needed to keep her quiet. Maybe he thought she had better proof that he pushed Janey than she actually did.' Alisha paced over to the window and peered through the blinds. The sun was starting to set behind the villa. 'I mean, my brother clearly has anger-management problems . . .'

'No kidding.' Katie motioned at her neck.

'. . . but I don't think he'd kill Roxanne over some boy-on-boy action.'

Katie nodded. 'According to Roxanne "Nancy Drew" Dent's notes, she reckoned Greg and Ryan were "together" when Janey fell.'

Another piece of the puzzle fell into place. 'That would make a lot of sense,' Alisha agreed. 'At the time they said they'd "walked home together". Greg's a sneaky little git. Why didn't he just tell the truth? Is he that scared of what people think about him?'

She had to hand it to Rox, she'd done a pretty good job of tying up the loose ends. When Janey Bradshaw fell to her death, Alisha had been throwing up at home, Katie had been ill in bed, Ryan and Greg had been doing God-knows-what, and Ben had been at the cliffs. With Janey.

Just hours earlier Alisha had been plotting an elaborate future with Ben Murdoch. Now he was a murderer. Even when a little dream dies, you have to mourn its passing. It left a black mark on her heart. Alisha embraced Katie; it was the best she could do to apologise for what she'd done on the beach. Ben wasn't hers to mourn, she told herself. He was Katie's.

'What's that for?' Katie asked.

'Because it's over and that's a relief. I couldn't see a way out, you know?'

Katie held her tight. 'It's not over.'

'It is. When we get home we can just call the police and show them the evidence.'

Katie let Alisha go, shaking her head. 'No. That won't work.' She seemed adamant. 'What would we do? Show them Roxanne's woeful evidence? There's a reason she didn't show it to us. We'd have laughed her all the way to Portugal.'

'But, still, it might be enough,' Alisha said, clutching at really crap straws. 'Ben will have to confess!'

'No, he'll just deny it and we're back to square one with all of us going down for killing Rox. He could just as easily say you killed her because you hated her, or Greg because of the gay thing.'

Alisha sighed. 'That still hasn't sunk in. Greg and Ryan. I mean, think of the children!'

Katie snorted. 'I know. If that's not natural selection, I don't know what is. But we need to keep focused.'

'Sorry.'

'If we stay the night here, maybe we can get Ben to confess ourselves and record it.'

Alisha rolled her eyes. 'Well, that should be easy. What are you gonna do? Drip water on his head or prod him with a red-hot poker? I still say we get out of here tonight and take all this stuff to the police when we get home.'

'No.' Katie looked to the ceiling like she was shuffling ideas in her head. 'I have a better plan. We do exactly what Roxanne did.'

'Act like skanky sluts?'

'No. We blackmail him.'

'Are you *serious?*' Alisha's eyes almost fell out of her head. Katie seemed genuine, though. The colour had returned to her cheeks as if she'd tapped into an emergency reserve of 'fight'.

'Yes! We'll tell him we found Roxanne's evidence and that we've called the police. Hell, we can even *call* the police – that Luisa Whatever-her-name-was gave me her card. If we act like we truly *know* it's him, he'll *have* to say something.'

Alisha finally found herself on the same page as her friend. 'And I could record it on my phone!'

'Precisely. Obviously we've been watching the same bad TV as Ryan.'

'Or,' Alisha said, 'he could just murder us all and do a runner.'

Katie's face fell. She reconsidered for a moment. 'No. No, not if he thinks there's really solid evidence linking him to Janey.'

Alisha nodded. 'And what happens after he confesses?'

'Hopefully the police won't be too far away.'

'I don't know, Katie. He might lose it.'

'I know. It *is* dangerous, but it's the only way we can get our lives back. Don't you see? If we pull this off, it'll all be over and done with for good. Janey, Roxanne, this week, *everything*. We can tell the police he *made* us help him get rid of the body. It will be finished tonight.'

Alisha didn't want to stay in this villa with a murderer for a second longer than she had to, but she could see that Katie's plan might just work. And she *really* wanted her life back. 'When are we gonna do it?'

Katie pursed her lips. 'Now.'

SCENE 35 – RYAN

Ryan was suspended in the richest, most restful sleep he'd ever had when he was rudely awakened by Alisha's wails reverberating through the villa. He hadn't slept a wink last night, but he'd found a new kind of peace in Greg's arms.

However, as soon as he heard Alisha shout, 'I can't take this any more,' he and Greg sprang to attention.

'Is that Lish?' Greg rubbed his eyes.

'What is she doing?' They rolled off the bed, Greg searching for the nearest pair of pants. He selected some Hollister sweat shorts and hoisted them on, almost collapsing to the floor in the process. Ryan was way ahead of him. As soon as he reached the top of the stairs, he saw Alisha hauling her suitcase across the lounge, collecting the things she'd left scattered down there. 'Alisha, what are you doing?'

She turned to face him, her nostrils flared. 'I don't know why I've listened to you, Ryan, but I'm not playing the sassy brown sidekick in your weird little soap opera any more. I'm going home and I'm calling the police. I'm confessing!'

He reached her position and tried to snatch the suitcase from her, but she yanked it back. Greg hovered behind him, while Ben looked on in shock from the kitchen. 'Alisha, you can't! Don't you understand? *We got away with it.* Whoever killed Rox isn't going to say anything – and neither are we.'

'But what about the writing on the wall, Ryan? We're never gonna be safe until we tell the truth. It's the only way.'

'Alisha, please. For me,' Greg appealed.

'Nice try, Greg. I'm not listening to you any more. This time you're wrong and I'm right. I'm calling the police and you can't stop me.'

There were footsteps behind them as Katie trotted down the stairs in her plimsolls. She wore a grave expression.

'What's up?' Ryan asked. 'You look awful.'

Alisha's babbling stopped in a heartbeat and Ryan realised it had been an act – a convincing one, at that. She was good.

Alisha, in her normal voice, said, 'Have you done it?'

Katie nodded. A very slight nod because her neck and jaw seemed to be deadlocked.

'What? What have you done?' demanded Greg.

'The police are on their way.' Katie walked right past them all and slid the patio doors shut before locking them.

Ryan realised that Alisha's performance had been nothing more than a diversion to get him and Greg out of the master bedroom, so that Katie could reach the phone. 'You're kidding, right?' His voice shot up about three octaves. She was locking them in and the police were on their way. They were screwed.

'No.' Alisha went to Katie's side. 'We know who did it.'

'We found Roxanne's evidence,' Katie added.

Ryan looked to his left, waiting for Greg to explode, steeling himself against the inevitable blast. But Greg failed to detonate. He started giggling instead; it was more than a little creepy.

'Brilliant. We're all going to jail,' Greg chuckled.

Ryan turned to his friends. If Greg wasn't gonna say something, he bloody well was. 'Have you lost your minds? What were you thinking? We had this under control!'

'We know everything,' Katie said calmly. 'Who killed Janey. Who killed Roxanne. When the police get here, we just need to give them the evidence.'

'When will they be here?' Ryan demanded. 'How long have we got?' The sky was falling. This was the end of the world as he knew it. For the first time, Ryan felt more than justified in his drama-queenery.

'I don't know. They said they'd be here as soon as possible. Before nightfall, I guess,' Katie replied.

Ben cleared his throat and Ryan looked up to see that his friend's skin had turned a sickly green. 'What did you find?' Ben asked.

'As if we're gonna tell you!' Alisha snapped, eyes wild.

Ryan clutched at his hair. 'Oh, my God. We're screwed. We're actually screwed.'

'Only one of us is guilty.' Katie looked almost apologetic. 'I've locked all the doors, so none of us is going anywhere until the police arrive.'

'So, what?' Ryan spat. 'We just sit and wait to get arrested?' His T-shirt was soaked with sweat but his mouth was bone-dry.

'Absolutely.' Katie held her head high. 'I don't know about you guys, but I could use a drink. Anyone care to join me?' She crossed the kitchen to the fridge and pulled out the jug of sangria.

Was she tripping? 'Oh, yeah! Why don't we all sit around and have cocktails? It's only the end of the world . . . Let's get nibbles, too!'

Katie pulled glasses out of the top cabinet. 'Ryan,' she said pointedly, 'you'll be fine. Relax.'

What was that supposed to mean? *He* knew he hadn't killed anyone, and now Katie apparently did, too. His mind whirred. What had been in Roxanne's possession, and, more importantly, how had he missed it in his search? 'What do you mean, *I'll be fine?*' Ryan asked.

Katie ignored Ryan's question and carried the jug through to the lounge. As she set it down on the coffee table, a wave of the red liquid sloshed over the rim and onto the wood. She wiped it away with a hand so it wouldn't stain. Even in their final hour, Katie Grant still wanted things to be perfect. Ryan didn't know whether to laugh or cry.

'Is everyone having some?' Katie offered.

'Last supper,' Greg muttered, staring into space. 'Why not? I could use a drink.'

Katie poured out five glasses. Ben waited by the patio doors, leaning up against them. He was a sad silhouette, drowning in satsuma-coloured light. 'I don't understand. Where did you find it?' He sounded like a man with nothing left. Ryan stared at him in disbelief – surely not Ben?

'It doesn't matter.' Katie handed out the drinks. As she gave one to Ben, she stroked his hand. 'What matters is that all of this will be over.'

Ryan practically snatched a glass from her and took a gulp of sangria.

Alisha sniffed hers experimentally. 'I'm sorry, Ryan,' she said, 'but you were dead wrong, mate. There was no way we'd have got away with this. Like, no chance in Hell. It would have been with us until the day we died. Graduation, weddings, babies, *their* graduations. It would always be there. There's no way I'm living like that. We *had* to call the police.'

It was so unbearably hot. The peachy evening light cooked them through the windows as if they were ants under a magnifying glass. Ryan swigged another mouthful of the sangria and held the glass to his face, allowing the condensation to trickle down his cheek.

Ben pushed away from the window and sat in the armchair. He sipped his drink and closed his eyes. He had given up. Surely not Ben . . .

'Wait.' Ryan gulped at his drink with a shaking hand. 'I bloody well know *I* didn't have anything to do with Janey's death *or* Roxanne's. You two wouldn't have called the police if it had been either of you, so that just leaves Greg and Ben.'

Katie remained silent, avoiding eye-contact. Alisha stared into her glass, also saying nothing.

'Why would I have killed Janey?' Greg couldn't muster the passion to rant and rave. He looked exhausted. Ryan *still* couldn't bring himself to 'out' him. He wanted to point out that Janey could well have seen the video of them, but that seemed like paranoia (and Ryan was pretty sure Janey would have said something to him had she seen it), so that only left . . .

'Ben?' The word only just managed to crawl out of Ryan's mouth.

Ben didn't open his eyes. He sat with his head back on the chair. A tear had run over his cheek and into the corner of his mouth.

Ryan fought back tears, too. He could handle Greg being a killer – he understood it in a way – but not his oldest friend. 'Ben, look at me. What did you do?'

Ben's eyes opened and another tear ran down his cheek. 'I,' Ben started. His voice broke. He sat forward and rested his glass on his knee. 'OK. You have to believe me. This is what happened . . .'

FLASHBACK – LAST YEAR (BEN)

Ben tugged at the bow tie around his neck. The bloody thing was choking him like a leash. He undid his top button and finished the last of his beer, pitching the bottle at the bin. It bounced off the rim and missed. Typical. Everything about this night had been an epic miss. He messed up his hair, trying to get rid of the itchy gel. Who was he kidding? Trying to be a good, clean Head Boy – Cambridge material, *boyfriend* material.

He was neither. Ben always felt like he was being stalked by failure. All the flukes and strokes of luck, all the popularity contests he had no idea how he won. It was like the devil was on his back sometimes, waiting for him to put a foot wrong, ready to claim his payment. Now, sitting alone on the bench outside Janey's house, it felt like his luck had finally run out. He'd cheated on his girlfriend. And he'd been caught.

He retrieved his phone. It had survived being flung at him. He'd texted Katie about an hour ago, as soon as Janey had stormed out of the gymnasium. The text he'd sent had read: *Janey knows about us. What do you want me to do?* He knew better than to send text-speak to Katie; it was her pet hate.

Still no reply. He knew she was sick. She was probably asleep by now, but he lived in hope she might wake and pick up the message. He couldn't do this by himself – he needed to know he had at least one friend left. His mum always said he was a people-pleaser and he was. He *hated* the idea of people being angry with him, but that hadn't stopped him from playing with fire. The last few weeks felt as if they'd been lived by someone else while he'd been on the outside looking in. How else could his casual, breezy existence have gone so wrong?

He'd hurt Janey *and* jeopardised his friendship with Katie. He *loathed* himself. He was worse than his cheating scumbag dad. The way he'd treated his mum was a disgrace, always had been, and even though Ben had spent all his life trying *not* to be his dad, here he was doing exactly the same thing. The sooner he got out of this dismal town, the better. He needed to escape from all of them: Mum, Dad, Janey, Katie. The college chapter of his life couldn't have come at a better time.

He dialled Janey's mobile. He needed to man-up and explain, try to unpick the jumble of knots in his head. After a moment of static, it went straight to voicemail. The house behind him was pitch-dark, but he rang her landline regardless. He could hear the shrill tone through the window, but no one came to answer. God only knew where the rest of the Bradshaws were.

He could think of only one other place to look for Janey: the beach. Her home was so near to the cliffs that she would often walk the dog there late at night to clear her head. That was how he knew there was more to Janey than people realised. Everyone thought they were a weird couple – he was so laid back he was practically horizontal, while Janey was pretty much the living definition of a Type A/control freak personality. Every once in a while, however, she'd say or do something – just a silly little thing – and he'd see the real her.

When she wasn't *trying* to be cool, Ben thought, Janey was pretty cool.

But it wasn't enough. It made him feel like shit, but when he was with Janey there was something missing: a hole. He knew, and had known all along, that the relationship wasn't going to last. If only he'd had the balls to tell her that in the first place. If only he hadn't kissed Katie. He'd made such a mess of everything, and now he had to clean it up. He would *not* be his father.

Ben jammed his phone back in the pocket of his rented tux and raced across the coast road to the cliff path. A speeding cabby honked his horn as Ben crossed, even though he was nowhere near the vehicle. Ben screamed a curse at the taxi driver, but it didn't make him feel any better.

Janey lived opposite the kiosk and children's play area that overlooked the sea. It was a beautiful summer night – so balmy it almost felt like being abroad – and he became more convinced of his beach theory. He ran across the middle of the play area and heard voices. 'Janey?' he called, before realising the voices were mainly male. One of them he recognised as belonging to Kyle Norton, who apparently hadn't found Ryan's doorstep deposit yet. God, those pranks felt like a million years ago.

Kyle was drinking on the clifftop benches with what looked like the arty music crowd. Roxanne and Callum were engaged in a noisy public display of affection on a picnic table, with Rox moaning and groaning like a bad porn star.

Ben looked around, but Janey wasn't with them. 'Hey,' he said. 'Has anyone seen Janey?'

'Ooh, look who's turned up.' Roxanne pulled out of the kiss, her red lips smudged. 'It's notorious love rat, Ben Murdoch.'

'Dude!' said Callum. 'You are a DOG!'

Ben sighed. 'Can we not do this right now, please? Also, Callum, you cheated on Alisha, you tool.' Alisha Cole deserved ten times better than this cocky, greasy-haired turd.

That knocked the smirk off Roxanne's face. 'Gotta say, I'm impressed,' she snarled. 'Didn't think you had it in you, Benji. Quite the player!'

'I'm not . . . I didn't. You don't know what you're talking about, Roxanne.'

'Are you looking for her so you can beg her to take you back?' Roxanne asked in a sing-song voice. 'I warned her about you. I said you were still in love with Katie, but, oh, no, Janey knows best!'

Ben counted to five. Dear God, the next time Alisha wanted to punch this girl he'd be buying front-row seats. 'Look. Have you seen her, or not?'

'I have not.' Roxanne smiled sweetly – the smile that, infuriatingly, seemed to convince teachers she wasn't the spawn of Satan. 'We only just got here from the ball.'

Damn. He looked over the edge of the cliff. All that waited at the bottom was the surf creeping over the shingle. 'Thanks for nothing.'

'PHOTO!' screamed Kyle, waving his camera phone. Roxanne and Callum struck a pose.

'Do I look sexy?' Roxanne pouted. Ben rolled his eyes.

'I'll do another, wait a sec . . . Say "cheese", bitches!' This time another couple leapt into frame and much cackling and screaming ensued.

Ben walked away. He aimed for the cliff stairs, the worn zigzag pathway that led all the way down to the beach. He held on to the rusty rail which felt tacky on his skin, like the sea salt was clinging to the iron. He was thinking about that when he saw her.

She was further down the coast, next to the Overlook Hotel – just a red speck in the darkness, at the very, very edge of the drop. Janey had been wearing red. He prayed it wasn't her. He prayed it was a plastic bag caught in the bushes . . . but he knew it wasn't.

He charged back up the cliff stairs, vaulting over the rails and onto the coastal walk which led all the way along the top of the cliffs. Some of the vintage deco lamps were broken, but they gave enough light for him to be able to make out a female form standing at the very edge of the rocks.

There's no way she'd be so stupid, he thought as he began to pant. *She wouldn't, would she?* Maybe she would. This was his fault. *He'd* done this. He ran faster, his feet pounding the tarmac. It was a long time since he'd played any sort of sport and his chest burned, desperate for air. Flashes of pain shot up his shins, his legs unused to the punishment.

Oh, God, she was going to jump. She swayed backwards and forwards, like she was being charmed over the edge by the lull of the wind. Her scarlet dress swished around her legs; her hair fluttered like a veil across her face. *No, no, no! Oh, God, no!* He'd never meant for this to happen. He just wanted everyone to get out of this town, this *situation*, unscathed. Ben wished he'd never kissed Katie, or that he'd never agreed to date Janey, or that he'd just never even been born.

He wasn't religious, but he suddenly got back in touch with God and pleaded. *I'll do anything*, he thought. *I'll go to church every single weekend. Just, please, stop her.*

Clutching the railing, he bent over, gasping for air. He couldn't go on. 'Janey . . .' he tried to cry out, but his chest was too tight. He leaned back, trying to haul as much air into his lungs as he could. He had to stop Janey. His calves and thighs were jelly, but he forced them on, ignoring the pain.

He was getting closer. He could see Janey's creamy-white skin behind her hair. He could see black tracks running down her cheeks where her make-up had been smudged by tears. He could see that she still wept, though her body was statue-still. At least she didn't seem to be in a hurry, weighing up the vast drop before her.

But she wasn't safe. Her feet were right on the very edge. 'Janey!' Ben called. She didn't seem to hear him. A sob shook his body. If she died, it would be all his fault.

He reached the hotel car park. He was almost there. Janey momentarily vanished from view, blocked by the building. 'Janey!' He stumbled onto the lawns, almost tripping over his own feet. His girlfriend was now crouching on the grass, her skirts spilling around her.

Janey finally heard him. She turned, the wind whipping her hair off her face. He'd never seen her so beautiful: the dress, the hair, her pale skin. She was so raw and wild. Her eyes burned with rage and hate.

'Who's there?' She wiped her nose on the back of her hand. Fumbling with her gown and unsteady on her heels, Janey rose to her feet. She scanned the plateau, worry creasing her brow.

Ben realised he was standing in the shadows and she couldn't see him. He stumbled forwards.

Janey squinted in his direction. 'I said, who's there?'

Ben staggered out of the shadows. He was sure it couldn't be healthy for his heart to be racing like this, but he'd got to her in time.

Janey's face fell. 'Oh, it's you. Don't come anywhere near me, I mean it. I don't want to talk to you.' That said, Ben saw a look of satisfaction in her eyes. She'd been waiting on his arrival, banking on him following her. This was his punishment. She took a step backwards, her heel only inches from the very edge of the cliff.

He reached out towards her, offering her a hand away from the fall.

'Stay away!' she snapped.

'Janey, please.' He coughed, clearing his throat. 'What are you doing?'

'What does it bloody look like?'

'You do *not* want to kill yourself.'

'How do you know? Do you know what this feels like? Has anyone ever ripped your heart out?' she shrieked over the howling wind.

Yes, Ben thought, *Katie ripped my heart out when she ended things last year*. It had hurt like hell, but he'd got over it and even saw, now, that it had been the right decision. He held his hands up in surrender.

'Just piss off, Ben! Don't come any nearer,' Janey snapped.

From nowhere, an angry gust of wind rolled in off the sea, making Janey sway. 'For crying out loud, look at yourself!' Ben screamed. 'You've proved your point. You've got my attention.'

'Do you think I won't jump?' she demanded.

'No, I don't, so come away from the bloody edge! *Please!*' He held out his hand again. Ben had never loved heights. He felt queasy even this close to where the land ended. Nevertheless he inched closer, moving gingerly, as though he were trying to charm a cobra.

'Why did you even come, Ben?' Janey sobbed.

'To make sure you were OK. I've been looking for you for hours. Isn't that what you wanted? Haven't you been *waiting* for me to show up?'

Janey glowered in defiance. She actually took a step *towards* thin air. Ben held his breath lest he accidentally blow her off the cliff. 'Do you love me?' she asked.

'Yes!' he yelped.

'Tell me the truth, Ben. Do. You. Love. Me?'

Ben paused. This was the time to *not* be his father. It was time to do something his dad had never done: man up and be honest. 'Not like that.'

'WHAT? Do you love *her*?' Janey said the last word like it was poisonous.

'Not like that,' Ben repeated.

'What?' Janey asked, eyes wild.

'I really don't know, Janey. My head is a mess. I shouldn't have—'

'You shouldn't have *what*?' Janey interrupted. 'Shagged your ex?'

'I didn't . . . we didn't. It was just a kiss. It was a mistake.'

That seemed to soften her slightly. Ben could swear he saw her feet move a fraction closer to him.

'I should never have said yes when you asked me out,' he confessed. 'You know I'm right. I was properly on the rebound. You knew that, too. You did. I thought I *needed* a girlfriend in my life, but I don't think I did. I needed *friends*.'

She didn't deny it. She looked out over the sea. It was in the quiet moments like this that Janey was truly beautiful. 'I don't know what to say,' she wiped a tear away. 'You made me look so stupid.'

'I am so sorry. I never wanted you to find out like this. I just wanted to go to Cambridge, make a new start. I need to be single, I think. I've been dating since I was fourteen years old. I need time to *think*.'

All the anger ebbed out of Janey. Ben was right and she

knew he was right. They had been an error. She nodded. 'I'm sorry, too,' she said.

And then she fell.

She just went down. It was like she dissolved into the earth. She didn't jump, or even stumble. There wasn't a gust of wind to sweep her over the edge. The ground beneath her just crumbled.

Her eyes widened.

She was too stunned to speak.

But true terror was written all over her face. She knew what was happening about a split second before he did.

'Janey!' Ben dived forward. His arms made clumsy contact with her body. His first hand grabbed for her dress, but the bodice was sheer corseting and there was nothing for his hand to gain purchase on. His other hand found her shoulder as her arms reached for his. One hand found her wrist, but the other failed to properly connect with her fingers, and they slipped through his like sand.

It was only then that Ben realised he had hit the ground and was now sliding across the cool, damp grass. They were both going over the edge and there was nothing he could do to save Janey. It was all happening so fast . . .

He had to stop himself careering after her. He *could* save himself.

He let go.

He clutched a handful of long grass and clawed at the chalk cliff, just in time to stop his waist from tipping over the cliff.

Janey was falling – silently and so, so fast. It wasn't dramatic, or graceful. She just *plummeted*. She was already almost at the bottom.

Oh, God. Ben closed his eyes and heard only the faintest of sounds, like someone skimming pebbles. He opened his eyes.

Black stains covered the pale boulders at the foot of the cliff. A limp ragdoll in a red dress rolled in the ocean.

Ben didn't know how long he watched Janey, but he was transfixed. The tide was coming in, hungrier by the second, and, with each wave, it carried her further away from the shore. Soon those waves would pound the cliffs but, by then, Janey would have been swallowed whole.

Ben scrambled away from the sheer drop, backing up until his back smacked into a wooden fence post. Threads of ideas and sentences tangled in his head. Nothing made sense.

Janey was dead. Ben blacked out.

'I didn't kill her. I didn't,' he repeated for about the sixth time. Tears poured down his face. 'She fell. I don't even know how. She just went off the edge.'

His friends regarded him with a cocktail of horror, disgust and pity. He deserved worse. Alisha perched on the coffee table; Katie was cross-legged on the floor; Ryan sat next to Greg on the sofa.

'Janey didn't kill herself. It was an accident,' Alisha said, almost as though she were talking to herself. She thought for a moment. 'Ben, why didn't you tell the police?'

He hunched forward in the armchair, already feeling unburdened. It was like he'd purged his veins of something toxic. 'Why do you think? At first, I guess I must have been in shock. I don't remember anything until it started getting light. I must have been there all night. When I came round, I thought that, after what had happened at the ball, everyone would think that I'd pushed her. But I didn't. I swear.'

Alisha emphatically shook her curls. 'You should have said!'

'I know! Jesus Christ, I know that! It's *all* I've thought about, all year. I made a mistake. I panicked. And I kept my mouth shut. By the time my brain kicked in it was too late. Everyone was already saying she'd killed herself. Honestly, Alisha, if I could go back . . . God, I'd do everything differently.' He wiped his nose on the back of his hand. His unsteady breathing righted itself. With wobbly hands he took another sip of sangria. 'When the police get here, I'll tell them what happened. It's not going to go away unless I do, is it? I need to set things right.'

Alisha nodded, a tear of her own glittering in the corner of her eye.

Ben stood and pointed at the floor as if he were jabbing the villa itself. 'But you have *got* to believe me. I guessed that Roxanne somehow knew I was there that night, and I figured she'd try to pin Janey's death on me, but I did *not* kill Janey and I did *not* kill Roxanne. I would never, *ever* do that.'

Katie sprung up, flung her arms around him and pressed her face to his chest. 'I know,' she said.

He should have known that Katie wouldn't lose faith in him. He clung to her. God, he actually felt lighter, now. His secret was out. Only one final mystery remained. 'I didn't kill Roxanne,' he repeated.

Katie took a step back and smoothed Ben's hair out of his eyes, looking up into his face. 'I know,' she said again, calmly. 'Because I did.'

SCENE 36 – KATIE

At first, Katie wondered if they'd heard her. Her heart was pounding in her ears. Time seemed to have stopped. The truth was out and she couldn't put the genie back in the bottle. She allowed herself a moment to bask in pride. The hatred she felt for these people was a thick, squirming serpent in her gut, but she'd kept it expertly hidden for four long days.

She considered repeating herself, but Ben took a cautious step away from her, which suggested he was processing the information. 'What did you say?'

Katie met his gaze, ready now and never more certain of anything. Odd, how easy it was. After so much planning and preparation, she'd assumed it would be more momentous, somehow. *The Big Reveal.* 'I said, I killed Roxanne. I had to. She was about to ruin everything.'

Ryan laughed a nervous, tense laugh. 'Are you kidding? I don't get it.'

She'd expected something a bit more dramatic than idiotic confused faces. God, was she going to have to make a Powerpoint presentation or something? She really must have played her part flawlessly – even after she'd told the truth they *still* didn't believe it of sweet little Katie. She thought back over her performance. *I'd do anything for you,* flailing at the edge of the pool, weeping and wailing like a total effing victim all week. God, how stupid did they think she was?

'Do you want me to spell it out?' she tried again. 'I killed Roxanne. I'm going to kill you. It's all part of a complicated revenge scheme.' She shrugged wearily. The constant lying – having to pretend to be nice to a group of people she detested – it had been such a marathon. And there was still a lot of work to do before bed tonight.

Reality dawned in their eyes. Alisha welled up *again*. Poor Alisha – but just because she was the most clueless that didn't make her any the less guilty. Alisha was going to be the one Katie regretted killing the most, though. Ben, on the other hand, he'd be the easiest. All the love hadn't quite left her system, but she'd discovered that, when love is tainted, it leaves nothing but a thick, black tar in the heart.

'What? But *why?*' Alisha could only produce a whisper.

Katie rolled her eyes. She dearly wanted to avoid a *Scooby Doo* moment where she ran through her motives while they all somehow escaped. It wasn't *that* type of finale. 'That's the thing. The fact that you don't even know what you've done is why I'm doing all this,' she told them.

'I don't get it.' Ben backed away from her. How *dare* he look so innocent after everything he'd done? She'd really hoped she wouldn't have to do the chat. She had planned for it to be quick and silent. She wanted them dead, no blood or guts necessary. It wasn't about pain, it was just about settling the score. But now, seeing Ben's pious face, maybe she did want him to know how much suffering he'd caused. In fact, she wanted to rip that mask of innocence right off his face.

'Katie, what are you doing?' he cooed. 'This isn't you.'

'You don't *know* me.' She held back the red-hot, spitting fury that swelled inside her. 'Once upon a time, maybe you did, but that sweet little doormat died a year ago. And it's *your fault!*'

'I don't understand. What did I do?'

The volcano erupted. Katie slammed her untouched glass of sangria onto the kitchen counter, the red liquid spilling over the surface. 'That's the bloody point, isn't it? You don't even *know.* You're getting away with it all the time. You're like Teflon! Nothing ever sticks to you lot, does it? It's never your fault. Nothing you do has *consequences.*'

Ryan sprang off the sofa. 'You've lost your mind.' He ran to the patio doors and tugged on the handle.

'You can't get out,' Katie said smugly. 'I've hidden the key.'

'Katie, let us go!' he cried.

'What's the matter, Ryan? Is it all a bit real? What happens in this episode? How do the characters escape?'

'She's off her head.' Greg joined Ryan by the doors. 'We'll smash the glass, yeah? She can't stop us. It's only Katie, for God's sake.'

Katie laughed. He was such an arrogant prick. 'You might as well sit down, Greg. You won't get very far.'

'Oh, yeah? Why? What you gonna do?'

This wasn't a conversation Katie wanted to have. 'It's not what I'm *going* to do, it's what I already *did.*'

Their faces fell.

'What?' Ben asked, his voice unsteady.

Katie raised her untouched glass of sangria and said, 'Cheers.' She felt no further explanation was needed.

'Oh, my God.' Alisha was shivering; maybe it had already started. 'What have you done?'

Did it really need further explanation? 'Vodka isn't the only secret ingredient, put it that way,' Katie said nonchalantly. 'And if you must know, the other one is rat poison, so sit your arse down. It'll be just like falling asleep.'

SCENE 36 (CONT.)

Greg ran for her, or at least tried. He caught his foot on a chair leg and almost fell.

Ben sat back down, his eyes not focused on anything. Perhaps he'd already accepted his fate.

'You can't do this!' Greg cried.

'I already did. Don't make it worse,' Katie told him.

Greg teetered slightly, using the back of the armchair to support himself. The poison was finally working. *Phew!* For a second there, Katie had been worried she'd given them the safe sangria, the ordinary batch she'd been serving all week. The last thing she needed was them putting up a fight. Thankfully, though, they were all starting to look like they'd been well and truly poisoned, now. Greg sank back onto the sofa. Everything was going exactly according to plan. And so it should be. She'd spent the best part of a year getting it right.

Ryan staggered towards her, gripping the kitchen counter. 'You won't—'

'If you're about to say "you won't get away with this", so help me God, Ryan, I'll kill you twice!' Katie jabbed a finger in his direction.

'But the police . . .' Ryan's voice tailed off as he realised the police *obviously* hadn't been called. Katie had made a show of it for Alisha, but that was all.

'Will it hurt?' Ben asked, still staring into the distance.

'I don't know,' Katie replied honestly. 'But if it does, it's nothing you don't deserve,' she added, although she didn't quite mean it. She wanted payback, not suffering. It was weird. She'd been waiting for some sort of remorse to kick in ever since she'd clubbed Roxanne. Right after she'd done it, she'd lain down next to Alisha and waited to feel *something*: guilt, disgust, the overwhelming godlike power of knowing she'd taken a human life. But nothing. All she'd felt was the splinter of fury that had been under her skin all year. It numbed every other feeling in her body.

'What did we do?' Alisha sniffled.

'If you don't know—'

'Tell us!' Ben shouted.

'Oh, all right!' She couldn't do anything while they were still alive, anyway. Katie figured she might as well tell the story to pass the time. 'Ryan, come away from the knife block. I can see what you're doing.'

Ryan stopped edging towards the kitchen and came back to the sofa. Like Greg, he was unsteady on his feet, almost drunken. He wouldn't give her much trouble.

'First of all,' Katie said, brushing her hair out of her eyes, 'I want to make it very clear that I'm not mental, or psycho, or evil. I'm doing this because it's the *right thing to do*. You all got away with murder, so don't for one second think you're innocent.'

Ben looked at her, and the weight of the disappointment and hate in his expression almost knocked her over. Was he judging her? Oh, that was rich!

'What happened?' he asked.

Katie strolled into the kitchen and opened the bread bin. With a vaudevillian flourish, she produced the scarecrow mask like a rabbit from a hat. 'Does this ring any bells?'

'The mask!' Alisha's gormless expression was starting to grate. 'From prom night.'

Katie dragged a chair out from the dining-room table and set it down in the spotlight created by the last shards of sunshine breaking over the ocean. 'Are you sitting comfortably? Then I'll begin . . .'

FLASHBACK – LAST YEAR (KATIE)

I t had been the flu, proper flu, the type where your bones ache and freezing sweat soaks the bed sheets. It had come on fast and strong like some sort of Biblical plague. One second Katie had been shopping for shoes for the ball, and the next she'd been shivering uncontrollably.

She rolled over in bed. Not *her* bed as such, but her bed at the farm. Her mum was away 'on business', yet again. Katie knew she was seeing someone in London, but so far her mother wouldn't be drawn on the subject. A 'vital presentation', she'd called it. 'Go stay at your gran's house until you're better.'

It suited Katie fine; Gran had always looked after her when she was sick. The feel of the patchwork quilt, the smell of chicken soup drifting up from the kitchen, the sound of Radio Four through the walls – as weak as she felt, she knew she was in safe hands.

The door opened with a creak and Gran entered, a bowl of steaming soup on a tray with some fresh paracetamol. 'Have you slept?' she asked.

'A little bit. What time is it?'

'It's about eight, my love. Time to eat, if you can.'

'I'm not hungry.'

'Oh, come on, you can eat a little for your old gran. It's only soup and a bit of bread.' She set the tray down on Katie's lap and propped her upright with a pillow. Then she held the back of her hand to Katie's forehead. 'Your fever's coming down.'

'I feel awful.'

'Katie Grant! Finching girls are tougher than that! Don't make me tell you the polio story again.' Katie managed a dry laugh, although her throat felt like it was filled with broken glass. 'Go on, just have half a bowl and I'll see about some jelly and ice-cream,' her gran urged.

'I'm not five.'

'You don't want the jelly and ice-cream?'

'I didn't say that.' Katie smiled and her grandmother tweaked her chin.

The phone rang downstairs, the sharp trilling reverberating through the walls.

'I bet that's your mum ringing to see how you are,' Gran said.

'I sincerely doubt that.' Katie picked up the spoon and looked at the soup. For the first time in twenty-four hours she did feel her stomach rumble a little.

Her gran was already at the door. 'See if you can finish by the time I get back.'

Katie scooped up a spoonful and blew on it. Her head felt full of mucus and her eyes were watery. She sipped the soup. Predictably, she could hardly taste it but the warmth felt good on her sore throat. After a few mouthfuls, though, she was exhausted. The effort of lifting a spoon to her lips had spent what little energy she had. She couldn't even face moving the tray. She closed her eyes and rested her head back against the wall.

Suddenly, she heard a clatter. At first, Katie thought she'd kicked the soup off her legs somehow, but then she realised it was plates smashing and cutlery chiming against the kitchen floor. Her eyes flew open. 'Gran?' she called shakily.

She heard her name in response, but her gran's voice was weak and breathless. What was going on? Her muscles aching, Katie moved the tray to one side and swung her legs out from under the covers. As she rose to her feet, her vision swam and the room zoomed in and out of focus. 'Gran?' she repeated.

Using the walls for support, Katie ventured onto the landing and over to the top of the stairs. More crashing noises came from the kitchen. 'Gran, are you OK?' she called, slowly making her way downstairs. Every step felt like it was lurching up at her; she clung to the bannister with both hands.

'Oh, Katie.' Her gran was sitting on the kitchen floor, her right arm clutching her left. 'There are people in the garden. Call the police.'

'What?' The walls slid in and out like a shrinking room in a funhouse. 'What's happening?'

'In the garden.' Gran's lips were white. 'Katie, I need my tablets. They're in my handbag.'

Unsure which way to turn, Katie first ran to the kitchen window. Figures darted across the lawn. They wore something on their heads, like bags or masks. Whoever they were, they were making a getaway.

Katie charged towards the front door. What had they done to Gran? Fury burned off the effects of her fever.

'Katie, don't, it's not safe! Katie, I need my tablets.'

But Katie wasn't listening. There was no way they were getting away with this. It was bound to be some morons from school. She threw open the front door. Beyond the gate was a limousine – just like the one she was meant to be riding in tonight. She spied a red dress slipping into the back seat . . . Janey. This didn't make sense. Had her friends come to pick her up? Hadn't they heard she was sick?

But then she saw the mask. Horrible. Nightmarish. Worn by Ben. He pulled it off his head and clambered after Janey into the back of the car, the mask somehow falling to the ground and landing in a puddle on the uneven drive.

Katie stumbled out of the door, but by the time she had reached the gate, the car was already speeding away, kicking up gravel and dirt. She staggered back to the house, her addled brain struggling to make sense of the events – her friends . . . her grandmother . . .

'Katie!' Her gran's voice was weaker now. Katie slammed the door and sprinted back to the kitchen. Gran was slumped over, her eyes half-closed and her mouth hanging open as if all the strength had left her body.

'Gran!' Katie cried, as her grandmother's eyes fluttered shut. 'Gran, don't leave me . . .'

'So there you go,' Katie concluded. 'You killed my gran. You literally scared her to death.'

A moment's silence followed this revelation.

'Your grandma was Mrs Finching?' Alisha was agog. She cowered against the far wall, arms hugging her legs. 'You never said.'

Katie looked at Alisha like she was the scum of the earth. It was refreshing to give up the good-girl act. Being Saint Katie had been bloody hard work. 'Does that make a difference? Would you have let her off if you'd known? Do you only kill old ladies if they're strangers? Not that she *was* a stranger. You all knew her.'

'But . . . we didn't know,' Ryan said in a pathetic voice.

'I don't care!' Katie snapped. 'When I started school she told me not to tell people I was her granddaughter because she knew I'd get all kinds of grief for it. She knew what people thought of her. But that isn't what matters. What matters is that *you* gave her a heart attack.'

'It was just a joke,' Greg breathed. He wasn't looking too healthy. Gems of sweat shone on his forehead.

'Oh, yeah, bloody hysterical. I especially liked the bit where the police wouldn't investigate because she died of "natural causes". Between that – and Janey's vanishing act being so much more important than a sick old woman – you all got away with murder.'

'I . . . I'm sorry,' Greg said – only about a year too late. 'We didn't know she had heart trouble.'

'You knew she was an old woman. What did you think was gonna happen?'

'B-but . . .' Alisha chipped in, looking terrified, 'I heard about Mrs Finching's death. It happened *months* later – like, in the autumn, after you'd all left. There was an assembly at school.'

That was the wrong thing to say. That was exactly what the police had said. Katie kicked the coffee table halfway across the lounge. 'I DON'T CARE!' she screamed, the noise tearing at her throat. 'She never left the hospital after that night. She never got better. IT WAS YOU.'

'She was ill . . .' Ryan started.

'It was you.' Katie composed herself, pushing the burning hate as far down as she could.

'We never meant to hurt anyone.' Ben gripped the arms of the chair, his knuckles white.

Katie tilted her head, unsure whether to pity his ignorance or scratch his eyes out for being so blind. 'Well, that's the whole problem, isn't it? You *don't* think. Any of you. For ten years I've watched you play out these self-important little soap operas. You're each at the centre of a personal galaxy and, if something doesn't affect you directly, then you don't even notice it exists.' Ben was about to protest, but Katie ploughed on. '"Ooh, I'm secretly gay", "Boohoo, my mum and dad prefer my brother", "Wah, my dad's cheating on my mum". The world revolves around you. Everyone else is just a bit part. You left Janey to fall off a cliff. Roxanne died and all you could think about was what would happen to you. You killed my grandma and you didn't even stop to realise what you'd done. You were all too busy with your own precious lives.'

'That's not true.' Ben blinked, like he couldn't see straight.

'Isn't it? At least Ryan *knows* TV's messed up his head. You're all such sodding stereotypes – screwed-up rich kids with too much time on their hands. You'd think from your constant moaning that you knew *real* pain, *real* suffering. You've never known anything about it! Not until now, anyway.'

'What about you? You're no different. People die all the time, Katie – what makes you so effing special?' Ryan hissed through gritted teeth.

Katie laughed. 'Oh, I'm the biggest stereotype of all,' she said. '*Good girl gone bad.*'

'What are you going to do with us?' Ben asked, resting his heavy head on the back of the armchair.

Katie sighed; all this talk was giving her a sore throat. 'Why aren't you people dead yet? I knew I should have mixed it stronger.'

'Tell us!' Greg demanded. 'We have a right to know.'

The anger flared up, blinding white and noisy. Katie flew across the room and seized Greg's face in her hands, squeezing his skull. 'You killed my gran. You don't have rights, you self-centred bastard!' That wasn't going to help. She immediately cooled herself mentally and smoothed down her T-shirt. 'We're gonna have one last barbecue tonight.'

Ryan's face fell. 'What?'

'It's kind of clever, actually. I get to piss off my stepmum by torching her beloved villa *and* you lot get fried. As I understand it, it's pretty hard to detect traces of poison in crispy ashes.' Now they all looked *really* scared. Good. 'Luckily, I'll somehow escape to tell the tale.' Katie turned to see Ben, not sobbing like the others, but instead coolly regarding her through heavy eyelids. 'What?' she snapped.

'This isn't you. I know you. You're sick. Grief can totally mess with your head. We can get you help, Katie.'

'That'd be convenient, wouldn't it? If I'd lost my mind or gone mad or something. Well, sorry, you're shit out of luck. This is about justice – except for poor Roxanne. I wasn't actually *planning* on killing her when I did. I was going to poison you all together but, given her amazing blackmail plot, I had to speed things up.' She looked at Alisha. 'You know that photo Rox had of me and my mum? That was from my gran's house. Her bloody uncle only bought the farm after Gran died. Roxanne was all up on Facebook telling me how she knew who I really was – Mrs Finching's granddaughter.'

'That's why you invited her.' Ryan's face was now the same sticky, sweaty grey as Greg's.

'She was the only one who knew. It's a shame – she had nothing to do with killing Gran, but I had to make sure no one could figure out what I'd done. Anyway, she was another one who thought she could do what she liked and get away with it. It wasn't ideal, but I had to leave her body in the pool because Ben came down to the kitchen and I was worried he'd see me.' She'd so nearly been spotted; the whole plan almost derailed in a split second. It had taken the best part of two days for her to get everything back on track. 'The funny thing is,' she went on, 'I knew, I *knew* you'd never call the cops. I just stood back and watched – hell, I even *begged* you to call them. I knew you'd do anything to save your own skins . . . but Ben, you were the biggest disappointment.'

'Why?'

She rolled her eyes. 'Why do you think?'

'Because I'm not the guy you thought I was?'

'You can say that again. I mean, Ben, what are you supposed to think when you see your first ever boyfriend, someone you truly, truly loved, running away after he's killed your grandma? Do you have any idea what that felt like? How much it hurt?'

He held out a hand to her, which she took. His palm was cold and clammy. He stood to face her. 'I'm so, so sorry. I loved you, too. Maybe we could still give it a go?'

'Nice try, but it's not James Bond; there isn't an antidote.' Katie could scream, she really could. Scream at herself for ever being suckered in by his dreamy eyes and welcoming arms. She had allowed herself to love him, but she saw love now for what it was – brain rot. She'd let him into her system and she'd lost a part of herself. 'I thought you were pretty pathetic *before* you just confessed all about Janey, but, God, you didn't even have the balls to save her!'

'I'm sorry I couldn't be what you wanted me to be. I'm not a hero.'

The sadness of it made Katie feel awkward. She hadn't wanted any chat and yet it had become quite the dénouement. 'Whatever,' she said. 'No need to cry about it.'

Ben leaned in and touched her face. 'You know, you can say what you like, but I really did love you.'

She wanted to hate him, but those words cut right through her. No matter how much she tried to rid herself of him, he was still inside her heart. Flickering Instagram moments of the kiss on the cliffs played through her brain. She pushed them away, but they were surprisingly stubborn, refusing to leave her mind's eye. 'It's too late, Ben.'

He looked deep into her eyes, stroking her hair. 'What about one more kiss for old times' sake?'

His breath brushed against her lips. She was so close she could almost taste him. What harm would a goodbye kiss do? It was the final curtain for Katie and Ben . . .

His lips touched hers, and every other kiss they'd ever had replayed itself in her head. He was so gentle. It was white feathers in slow-motion.

He kissed her harder, hungrily, but she caught his wrist. This didn't make sense. He was dying and she was the one killing him. That only makes really specific people horny.

'What are you doing?' she whispered. Ben gulped, guilt all over his face. 'I said, *what are you doing?*' she repeated fiercely.

He held onto her, but she batted him away. He was barely strong enough to even hold himself up any more and he flopped back into the armchair. She turned her head and saw that Greg and Ryan had finally lost consciousness. They were slumped side by side on the sofa. She twisted the other way.

'Shit!' she hissed.

Alisha had vanished.

SCENE 37 – ALISHA

Alisha was under the bed in the master bedroom. She clamped her hand over her mouth to muffle her breathing. The faintest whistle down a nostril could get her killed. This was not a good hiding place. This was bound to be the first place Katie would look. Alisha had raced to the bedroom for the phone, but quickly discovered it had been ripped out of the wall.

Katie has gone mad. I don't want to die. Is Greg dead? I can't get out. I want to go home. Panicky half-formed ideas and images ran through Alisha's head. She wanted the world to go away, but it wouldn't let up for a second. She was being deluged.

She knew she didn't have much time until Katie noticed she had gone. Ben's delaying tactics would only work for so long. The front door and windows were all locked shut. The front windows, in typical bloody Spanish style, were covered with ornate iron bars. Katie had seen to it that they were trapped.

Katie. Jesus Christ. Something in her head must have snapped. If the brain's a machine, then a cog had definitely come loose. Katie had made a point of telling them all how sane she felt, but Alisha begged to differ. It was also too soon to let thoughts about Greg enter her head. She was going to feel so, so guilty. But not now. And Ben ... oh God, she'd been so wrong about Ben.

She'd never been so grateful for giving up drinking. Going tee-total had been a lot easier than she'd thought it would be. All those people who'd called her 'alcoholic' could stick that where the sun don't shine.

The role of 'hot mess' had been brilliant when Alisha was fifteen. She'd loved the notoriety. She'd been a freaking rockstar at Longview High. But when all her friends had gone to university and Greg had moved to Brighton, everything changed. It wasn't cool being drunk when there was no one to laugh with. More to the point, she couldn't spend another year at home. She had to get out, so she had to be sober.

Although there wouldn't *be* another year *anywhere* if she didn't get out of this nightmare.

All week she'd been ditching drinks into the sand, pot plants, bushes, whatever was nearest. She had kept it a secret for two reasons. The first was the summer she'd decided to be a vegetarian. As soon as she'd declared it, people had started wafting bacon sandwiches under her nose – people are tools like that. The second was, if she was honest, she hadn't trusted herself not to have a bad day (she'd come *so* close to drinking yesterday), and she'd figured that if she didn't make grand statements about being sober, then she couldn't possibly fail.

Later on she might think about destiny or fate but, right now, Alisha had to survive. *Katie wants me dead. I don't want to die. I have to get out.*

Feet thundered up the stairs. Alisha's time was up. Her hips and chest were pressed against cold, dusty tiles and, from where she lay, she could see only a section of the landing beyond the bedroom door. Night was falling fast, too. Only murky grey evening light filtered through the blinds.

A door slammed into a wall – it must have been the bathroom door as Alisha could see the corners of the entrances to both other bedrooms. She heard the telltale shriek of the shower curtain scraping back along its rail. Another slam and a pair of Converse-clad feet padded from the bathroom into the room Alisha had shared with Katie. Thankfully, Katie seemed to be taking the rooms in order of proximity, not logic.

How could Katie do this to them? They'd been friends forever. How can you kill people? It's not like swatting flies! There must be things inside Katie that weren't joined up right, otherwise she just wouldn't be able to. Alisha knew she'd never be able to. That's when it hit her: she might have to kill Katie. Her tears pooled on the tiles.

There was more banging and crashing as Katie turned over their room. Wardrobe doors clattered and Alisha heard the mattress being yanked off the bedframe. Katie was like a bulldozer. Alisha slid further under the bed, her heart galloping. If Katie chose this room next, there was nowhere for her to go. She considered changing position – moving into the wardrobe or en suite – but both options felt like she'd be backing herself into an even smaller corner.

Katie's feet moved back onto the landing. She paused at the open door to the master bedroom. Alisha held her breath.

Katie chose the closed door to Ryan and Ben's room. This was it. Alisha had to move *now*. She rolled onto her back and found herself staring up at a knife. She had to blink to check she wasn't hallucinating, but between the bed slats and the mattress was the dagger from the old shipwreck. Greg must have hidden it under the bed when the detective had visited that morning.

Oh, this changes everything, Alisha thought. *Game on.*

SCENE 38 – RYAN

Ryan's eyes opened. He must have drifted off. He remembered Alisha creeping for the stairs, but then he'd faded out. From upstairs, he heard the bang and clatter of furniture being overturned and wardrobe doors slamming: Katie searching for Alisha, he guessed.

Of course the killer had been Katie. Ryan cursed himself for failing to see it coming. It's always the second-least-likely person. If *he* was the least likely (as the main character) then Katie would have been the obvious choice. No one could be as sweet and innocent as she seemed. Even pretending it was telly didn't make it better, and, anyway, Ryan couldn't pretend any more. He loved Katie Grant and she was killing him. This was really happening. Katie's vengeance was a real, raw red.

Ryan slid off the sofa. Ben was lying on the floor. His long legs stuck out from behind the armchair. He must have tried to make a run for it, too. He'd not made it very far.

Ryan's head spun. It felt like being eighteenth-birthday drunk, or having a really bad fever, or maybe like going under anaesthetic at the hospital. It was all of those at the same time and all he wanted to do was sleep – but it wasn't sleep, it was death. That's what death is, Ryan realised: it comes to you disguised as sleep, it fools you. He fought to keep his eyes open.

This wasn't the ending, Ryan was sure. *This* was how it was going to go . . . He was going to crawl to the knife block on the kitchen counter. If Alisha didn't stop Katie, he would. He would ram that thing through her skull if he had to. Then he'd call an ambulance. They'd take him to hospital and pump his stomach or find an antidote or whatever they do. He'd be in hospital for a few days and then he'd go home to a hero's welcome. He'd be all over the TV, the guy who faced a crazed psychopath and lived to tell the tale.

'Ryan.' He turned around. It was Greg. He was in a bad way, but was clinging on to life. He could barely keep his eyes open but he reached out for Ryan. 'Don't go.'

Ryan rested himself against the now vacant armchair. 'I gotta get a knife. I need to help Lish.'

'Please wait with me.' Greg's head lolled to one side as if it were too heavy for his neck.

'Greg, stay awake. Open your eyes!' Ryan snapped. He crawled back to his friend (oh, he was far too weak to worry about defining their relationship now) and clutched his face, just stopping short of prising his eyes open. Greg's heavy lids opened just a fraction, just enough for Ryan to see the ice-blue of the iris.

'I can't. I can't stop falling . . .' Greg murmured.

'Greg, please. I need . . .' A fresh wave of tiredness hit Ryan. He tried again. 'I need to get help.'

'Stay with me.' Greg's eyes fell closed again. Ryan felt fingers intertwine with his. 'Just for another minute.'

Ryan kissed him, half because he couldn't resist and half as a tactic to wake him up. It didn't work. Greg was now sprawled on his side, legs hanging off the edge of the sofa. He was dying. Ryan realised that he was dying, too. There was nothing he could do to help Alisha; he could barely lift his own hands any more. Perhaps that was right. It's how it always is – the hero faces the villain alone. Ryan just hadn't expected Alisha to be the hero.

Ryan stroked Greg's beautiful face and, in that moment, he was oddly proud to have had that face in his life, however chaotic their love had been. Seeing Greg peaceful and serene only made him lovelier.

'Don't leave me alone,' Greg muttered again.

'I won't.' A tear found its way out. Katie could kill him, but she wasn't having this moment. Ryan rested his forehead against Greg's. 'I'm here. I won't leave you.' He nudged Greg's legs and Greg shifted them onto the couch. Somehow, Ryan dragged himself onto the sofa and lay next to Greg, the room spinning. It was like being in a centrifuge. 'I'll be the little spoon this time,' Ryan murmured.

Greg wrapped his arms over Ryan's chest and Ryan recognised belonging for the first time. They belonged to each other. It had come late in the day, but he was so glad it had come. There was a . . . *warmth* inside his chest. *This must be what proper, nice love feels like*, he thought. He allowed his eyes to close and it was bliss.

The only faith Ryan had ever had was in the religion of the happy ending – that everything worked out in the end and that everyone gets what they deserve. *Is this any less than I deserve?* (Insert flashback: Roxanne's head dipping under the black sea.) All those films and shows and books had lied. Not everyone gets a happy ending. But then, this was no fairy tale.

This was correct. There was no such thing as a 'Final Boy', only the 'Final Girl'. As painful as the truth was, the last survivor was never going to have been him. Ryan understood that now.

'I was meant to be the main character,' he whispered, not

sure who he was even talking to – himself, God, the sofa.

'You are,' Greg breathed the words into his ear. 'This is the last episode.'

They let the sleep of death take them together.

SCENE 39 – KATIE

Katie stood, hands on hips, in the centre of Ryan and Ben's room. This was *not* a part of the plan. Sweat ran down her back. How could this be happening? How could *Alisha* of all people be messing this up? Alisha might have been the hardest to kill from a moral standpoint, but she should have been the *easiest* to kill from a practical one. Why wasn't she dead? Liver damage should probably have finished her off years ago, as it was.

'Come out, come out wherever you are!' Katie cried. 'You know I'm not going to let you go, Alisha, so you're just wasting your time and mine.'

No reply.

Katie stormed back onto the landing. There was only one room left to search. Of course, the master bedroom. Alisha had probably gone in there searching for the phone. She should have thought of that. Her prey was now cornered. A smile crossed Katie's lips as she entered the bedroom, leaning forwards to peer under the bed.

She was so busy looking at the floor, she didn't see the door swinging for her face. It slammed into her, knocking her backwards. Her vision went black and then sort of glittery before she landed with a painful crash on her rear. There was a terrible pain in her face. Her hands flew to her nose, which now felt crumbly and wet and warm with blood. Katie howled in pain.

'I can't believe you fell for that!' Alisha lunged at her, from behind the door. There were still silver spots swimming across Katie's field of vision, but she saw that, in her hand, Alisha held her father's dagger. Where the bloody hell had she got that from?

'Stay where you are!' Alisha cried. Her face was black with dust but tears had made rivers in the dirt. Her eyes were as wild as the jungle of hair that fell over her face.

Katie pinched her nose. 'What are you gonna do? Stab me?' She tried to stand.

Alisha sliced at the air in front of Katie's face with the dagger. 'Stay there!' she squealed. 'Don't follow me.'

Katie smiled despite the copper taste filling her mouth. She could feel blood on her teeth. 'We both know you haven't got the guts to use that.'

Alisha wiped her face, inching backwards step by minute step. Katie realised this wasn't going to be easy. But perhaps it had all been going too well. That was the thing with best-laid plans.

Katie coiled and sprang. The shock tactic worked. Alisha's instinct was not to slash at her with the knife but to turn and run. Katie reached her at the top of the stairs and grabbed Alisha's wrist, holding the dagger as far away as possible. In response, Alisha pushed at Katie's face, blinding her. They wrestled for a moment and then Alisha slipped on the top stair. Katie was so entangled with her that she fell too.

They went down in an undignified knot of limbs. Alisha was now spread-eagled across the first few stairs. Trying to disarm her, Katie banged Alisha's wrist against the edge of the hardwood step, feeling the bone make contact. If she kept this up, she'd break Alisha's wrist. *Good luck stabbing me then, you bitch.*

Alisha clung to the dagger and wriggled around, using her knees to pin Katie to the wall. Then she seized Katie's hair.

'Ow!' Katie screeched in pain, relaxing her grip on Alisha's wrist for a split second. It was enough. Wrenching her arm free, Alisha blindly waved the blade around and nicked Katie's cheek – an inch higher and it would have been her eye. Katie fell back in shock. Maybe Alisha Cole did have some guts, after all.

Alisha slid away from Katie and down the remaining stairs, climbing to her feet once she reached the bottom.

Oh, no, you don't, thought Katie. She could not let Alisha get away. She sprang to her feet and leapt to the foot of the stairs. Paying no heed to the dead bodies on the sofa, she hurled herself at Alisha, kamikaze-style. Alisha went down like she was made of paper, folding onto the tiles. Katie scrambled upright and straddled her back, pinning her to the floor. Once more Katie seized her wrist and yanked her arm backwards. It gave a satisfying crack.

'That's for stabbing my face!' Katie spat. This was an adrenalin rush! *Way* better than killing Roxanne, who'd just looked at her with a sad 'I don't understand' expression. The thrill, so it transpired, really was in the chase.

With glee, Katie sank her teeth into the soft flesh of Alisha's hand. There was that metallic taste again. Alisha screamed and finally dropped the dagger. Katie snatched up the weapon. This was going to require a big clean-up effort but, what the hell, nearly done . . .

The ground moved. No, not the ground – Alisha. Somehow she'd managed to rise to her skinned knees and, all of a sudden, Katie was riding her like they were playing a game of horsey.

Caught off guard, Katie tried to regain her balance, but Alisha threw herself backwards, flipping them over.

With a cry, Katie toppled onto the coffee table, sending the jug of poisoned sangria crashing to the floor; little pink rivers surged along the grouting between the tiles. They ran towards Ben's dead face, pressed to the ground behind the armchair.

Alisha was already back on her feet. She hobbled to the patio doors. On the dining table was a sturdy wooden fruit bowl. Katie saw her reach for it to smash the glass. Katie still had the dagger, though, and, therefore, the upper hand.

She lunged towards Alisha, but her feet slid out from under her. Skidding in sangria, Katie tumbled over, giving Alisha the chance she needed.

Alisha half-jumped, half-rolled onto the kitchen worktop. Plates, bowls and glasses clattered and smashed out of her way.

'Where are you going?' Katie snarled, chest heaving. 'There's nowhere to run.' Alisha's reply was a mug flying towards Katie's face. It missed. 'Well, that's rude.' Katie raised the knife again and strode towards Alisha.

Alisha reached for the knife block, but Katie was quicker. With a swish of her arm it tumbled over the other side of the counter and out of Alisha's reach.

'Let's just get this over and done with,' Katie said.

But Alisha had other ideas. She took hold of the enormous pan they'd made the paella in.

Katie's face fell. 'A frying pan? You've got to be f—'

Like a seasoned baseball pro, Alisha swung it right at Katie's head. A black curtain fell.

SCENE 40 – ALISHA

Alisha couldn't quite believe that had worked. *A frying pan.* But it seemed to have done the trick. Hands shaking, Alisha stood over Katie's body. There was a glossy black-red puddle fanning out around her head and her eyes were closed. She looked dead. If Ryan were alive, he'd have told Alisha that the killer always comes back to life; even she'd seen enough crap horror films to know that. Alisha knew she should use the pan to properly bash Katie's head in – just to be on the safe side – but, even after everything, that seemed too *monstrous*.

Alisha's wrist was agony. She rested the paella pan on the counter and, stepping around Katie, hurried to the terrace doors. Locked. Of course. This close, she saw the windows were double-, if not triple-, glazed – the Grants had spared no expense. The glass was as thick as her arm. Breaking it on a good day would be hard; doing so with a broken wrist would be practically impossible.

She turned back to Katie's body. The key was probably in her pocket. If Katie was intending to get out once she'd killed them all, she'd have kept the keys on her person, surely. Everything was messy in Alisha's head, but she didn't remember Katie having much time to hide the key after she'd locked them in. It *must* be in her pocket.

Alisha tiptoed back into the kitchen, trying not to look at the couch where her brother and Ryan lay together. She would sit down and cry for a year or two once this was over, but first she had to get out of this God-awful place. She crouched over Katie's body. She was lying exactly as Alisha had left her, sprawled on the tiles. Alisha felt warm blood on her bare toes.

Through the gloom, Alisha scrutinised her for signs of life. Katie's chest didn't seem to be moving at all. Oh-so-gently, she felt a limp wrist for a pulse. There was nothing obvious, but she wasn't sure she was doing it right.

With shaking fingers, Alisha slipped a hand into Katie's left pocket. There was nothing there. *Damn.* In order to get into the right pocket, she would have to roll the body over. Grimacing, she took hold of Katie's shoulder and hip and coaxed her over, revealing the crack she'd made in her right temple. Alisha fought a wave of nausea and hooked her fingers into the right pocket. The key was there. She could feel the cool metal at the bottom of the pocket.

That was when Katie convulsed back into life. It was so sudden, Alisha felt sure she must have been only *playing* dead. The redhead grasped for her, but Alisha recoiled with a scream, falling back into the fridge door.

'Where do you think you're going?' Katie demanded.

Alisha didn't answer. Instead, she scrabbled to her feet, using the cellar door handle to pull herself up. The cellar!

The look on Katie's face suggested she'd figured out Alisha's plan almost as quickly as it had occurred to Alisha. She crawled over the tiles, blood streaming down her face, her mouth contorted in a red snarl.

But Alisha was quicker. She tugged open the wooden door and slipped through, slamming it shut just as Katie's hand inched round the doorway. Her fingers trapped, Katie shrieked before whipping her hand back. Alisha threw her weight behind the door, fumbling for the bolt. It was old and rusted, but it squeaked into place.

She was safe. For now. But the door wasn't strong and the bolt felt even less sturdy.

Katie knew it, too. 'Nice try, Alisha,' she said.

I should have hit her harder, Alisha thought, starting to descend the cellar stairs. The stone was ice-cold on her bare feet, but it revived her, brought her more keenly into the present. At the top of the stairs, Katie started to pound on the door, making it shake in its frame.

Alisha remembered that it wasn't the only way out of the cellar – there was also the door onto the pool terrace. There was even a key for it hanging on a hook. Tiny fingers of light filtered down from the kitchen onto the stairs. Beyond that there was only pitch darkness. Barely able to see an inch in front of her face, Alisha staggered into the shadows. She collided with the first wine rack, making the bottles jangle.

With Katie hammering on the kitchen door above, Alisha hurriedly felt her way through the cellar, trying to picture the layout from her previous visit. She could see *nothing*. A Year Five science lesson chose this precise moment to float back into her head: *we can only see if light enters the eye*. Down here, there was an almost total absence of light. Her eyes were out of action. Her breath shook and she reached out with trembling hands, trying to find a path through the void. Her fingers finally came into contact with something. She clung to the dustsheets and gym equipment, hoping her feet wouldn't land on anything sharp. Baby step by baby step she inched across the freezing floor towards where she *hoped* she'd find the exit.

She stumbled, crying out as she stubbed her toe, but staying upright. Sticking to the wall, Alisha's fingers finally found the rough wood of the door. She felt along the edges, recalling the key that had been hanging from a nail hammered close to the top of the doorframe.

'Give it up!' Katie screeched. Alisha heard wood splinter and a little more light filtered down into the cellar. Katie was almost through the kitchen door. In haste, Alisha slid her hands up the stone wall. Her fingertips made contact with something metal, but she was moving too fast and she knocked the key clean off the nail.

'No!' she gasped. A second later she heard a metallic clang as the key hit the floor, then a few quieter pings as it bounced and bounced again. Alisha dropped to her knees, patting the floor in a circle around her. The key could have rolled under anything. Alisha's hand came up against something hard and cold, wrapped in dust sheets – golf clubs or something. She tried to feel for the key underneath but she couldn't reach far and the golf clubs were heavy.

This was useless. *Useless.* Fresh tears ran down Alisha's face. She'd been so nearly free. She'd found Katie's error – the cellar door – and totally failed to exploit it. The kitchen door gave another sickening crack. Alisha was going to die, and all because she'd dropped a key.

Enough candles to survive a nuclear winter. Suddenly she remembered the armoire. The old wardrobe had been full of candles, and she was *pretty sure* there'd been a box of matches in there, too. Her candle of hope sputtered back to life. It wasn't over yet.

Up above, she could hear Katie screaming in rage. She'd be through and into the cellar any second now.

Alisha hurriedly patted her way around the walls until her fingers felt the smooth varnish of the armoire. Not wasting a second, she tugged the door open. Even in the pitch dark her hand could identify the cool wax of a candle. She grabbed it and felt for the matches. If she was right, they were jammed in at the end of the shelf. When her hand touched the cube-shape of the matchbox she wept with joy. Actually wept and didn't care.

Careful not to make the same mistake twice, Alisha controlled her nervous fingers as she felt for a match and struck it against the side of the box. She was acutely aware of every tiny detail. What is it they always say about being blind? The other senses compensate . . .

On the third attempt, the match sputtered to life and Alisha forced her trembling hand to light the candle. Now she could find the key and get the hell out of here.

She turned to start her hunt for the fallen key.

Alisha screamed. It tore the back of her throat and she almost dropped the candle in her horror. The heavy cold thing wasn't a bag of golf clubs.

It was Erin.

SCENE 40 (CONT.)

The candlelight danced wildly and threatened to go out altogether as Alisha fell to her knees. Shadows swung up the walls and over Erin's grey, stony face. Her eyes gaped up at Alisha, utterly lifeless. Alisha sobbed, choking on her tears.

'I guess you found Erin, then,' said a sing-song voice from the kitchen. The pounding on the door ceased for a moment. 'She was all packed and ready to go. I couldn't have that. I figured once you'd all died in "the accident" she'd come forward and tell the cops about Roxanne, so she had to go. No witnesses. Shame she ever came, really.'

Alisha shook her head. Erin hadn't done *anything* to deserve this. It wasn't fair. Although her body was mostly shrouded in a bedsheet, there were angry brown fingerprints around her neck. Greg had strangled Katie and, in return, it looked as though Katie had strangled Erin to death.

Next to the corpse was Erin's pink Mulberry handbag. Katie must have killed her and then jogged down the beach until she'd got a signal on Erin's phone so she could text Greg. Erin had been underneath their feet the whole time they'd been looking for her.

All the fight drained out of Alisha and, for a moment, she wondered if she should just sit here and wait for Katie to break in and finish the job. She could join the others: her brother,

315

Ben, Ryan. It would be *so* much easier, and she was *so* tired.

But then a silver glint caught her eye. She saw the key resting at the foot of the door and her despair vanished as fast as it had come, replaced by something much more vivid: the urge to survive. She really, really wanted to live. She crawled past Erin and prised the key out from the gap under the door.

'Alisha?' Katie yelled. 'Why have you gone quiet? I don't like it.'

Alisha ignored her, placing the squat candle on the floor and seizing the padlock in both hands. The key turned in the lock with a satisfying *click*. Alisha wrenched the padlock off, slid back the bolt and pushed the door open to be greeted by the combined scent of chlorine and sea air. It was the best thing she'd ever, ever smelled.

The door opened onto the side of the house, just tucked around the corner from the pool. Alisha staggered out, suddenly aware of her bleeding knees and damaged wrist – was it broken? She hobbled onto the pool terrace, making her way towards the beach. She was out in the open now; all she had to do was make her way to a public place like Zahara de los Atunes. Katie couldn't kill her there, right?

Aqua-blue light from the pool swirled around Alisha as if she were in a lagoon. She froze. An awful, awful thought occurred to her. Katie had *all* the keys.

Hardly daring to turn, Alisha looked up at the villa.

The terrace doors were ajar.

And then Katie was on her.

She burst through the air like a banshee, all hair and nails and blood. Alisha staggered backwards under the impact. Too late, she realised what was about to happen – they were going into the pool together.

The water felt steely and solid as it hit her back with a slap.

The chlorinated liquid rushed up her nostrils and the cold snatched her breath away. Alisha tried to roll out from under Katie's body.

Red blood clouded the neon-blue glow of the pool. Alisha surfaced, choking and gasping for air. Katie wasn't far behind. Her hands broke the surface and instantly grabbed at Alisha, dragging her under. Alisha sucked as much air as she could into her lungs before Katie's hands thrust her shoulders down.

But Katie was so strong. Alisha felt her hands clamping the sides of her head, holding her under. Kicking, and flailing her arms, Alisha tried to surface, but Katie held fast. Alisha's chest burned; her ribs felt like they were about to explode.

She suddenly remembered something she used to do when she was little. She'd blow all the air out of her lungs so that she'd sink to the bottom. It was worth a try. She exhaled, the bubbles rippling against her face. At the same time, she stopped splashing and, instead, wrapped her arms and legs around Katie.

Alisha sank and Katie sank with her. Katie kicked and kicked, but Alisha acted as an anchor. Once Katie was fully under, Alisha climbed up her body, keeping the other girl under the surface. For the first time she felt like perhaps she was going to get the upper hand. Hate twisted Katie's face into something ugly. She reached up and gouged at Alisha's eyes with her thumbs. Alisha had to let go or she'd lose an eye.

Her lungs were on fire as she surfaced and started to swim for the pool ladder. The steel poles jutted out of the water, just out of reach. Katie clawed at her legs – she wasn't going to give up – but Alisha kept swimming, ignoring the agony in her wrist.

Just as Alisha was about to reach the ladder and haul herself out of the pool, Katie suddenly rose up out of the water like a killer whale, grabbing Alisha again and pushing her under the surface. Alisha went down, rolled over and lunged for Katie's hair, clutching as many red tendrils as she could and yanking Katie's head under. Katie screamed, the water mangling the noise into something demonic.

Alisha braced herself. Both her hands were tangled in Katie's hair. She looked her old friend right in the eye. *One girl gets out of this alive*, she thought. *And it's going to be me.*

With everything she had, Alisha drove Katie's head into the edge of the pool ladder. There was a terrible *crack* and a crimson cloud billowed into the water. This time Katie's eyes remained wide open. She looked shocked at this ending.

Alisha let go, the hair drifting away through her fingers. Through bubbles and blood, she watched Katie float away. She had to keep watching. She wasn't taking any chances this time. To her photographer's eye, Katie looked beautiful, doll-like: her drifting auburn hair and china-white skin radiant in the underwater light.

Unable to stay underwater a second longer, Alisha kicked her way to the surface. She gulped in air, coughing and spluttering. With her good hand, she gripped the ladder and pulled herself out of the pool. Water ran out of her vest and shorts in great rivers. She sat on the tiles, but well away from the edge, just in case.

Keeping one eye on the pool, Alisha checked herself over. Her knees and elbows were bleeding. Her wrist was definitely broken. It seemed likely there were other broken bits too. In a minute, she'd set off in search of help but, right now, she needed to rest. *My name is Alisha*, she reminded herself. *I am alive. I live in Telscombe Cliffs. I want to go home.* The last thought lifted her. She clung to that fact like it was a rubber ring. She was going home.

Then she thought about Greg and her heart sank all over again. For better or worse, he had been the most constant thing in her life. For some reason, an old photograph flashed into her head: she and Greg as toddlers, in complementary boy/girl versions of the same dungaree outfit, sitting on the back step at home and looking utterly miserable. They'd hated those outfits so much, but now both of them loved that photo more than anything.

Her brother was gone. And Alisha finally understood the rage he'd felt and where it had come from. He'd been weighed down by the secrets, hiding half of who he really was. Sitting on the edge of the pool, Alisha made a vow. She wouldn't tell anyone. Greg's secret was now *her* secret. The real Greg would always be hers and the rest of the world could have the guy in the posters. She badly wanted to say goodbye, but she *couldn't* bring herself to go back inside that house.

It was time to go. Alisha struggled to her feet, gritting her teeth. She'd twisted her ankle going into the pool. She limped towards the water's edge. She had to be certain. That vivid red hair still drifted like pondweed. The water was now a faint rose-pink. Katie's hands swayed with the motion of the water.

'Alisha.'

She almost fell back in. She gripped the ladder to stop herself slipping. It was Ben. Ben Murdoch was lumbering down the stone steps, clutching his stomach. His skin was clammy and almost minty white. He looked really bad.

'Jesus, Ben! How . . . how did you?'

He reached the bottom step. 'I didn't drink that much. When she ran off after you I made myself sick. I saw it on TV . . .' He let the last part hang. 'I sorta passed out, though. Sorry . . . sorry I couldn't help you. I . . . I was too weak.'

Alisha couldn't hold back. She fell into his arms. She wasn't the last person on earth any more. He held her tight and she let it all go. She cried. She cried because Greg was dead. She cried because Katie, the version of Katie that had been her best friend, had died a long time ago. She cried because she was still alive.

'It's OK,' Ben whispered into her wet hair. 'You saved us, Alisha. You saved us.'

'I'm so sorry.' She felt his breath on her skin, and it was like a kiss.

'What for?'

'I really thought you were the killer. I'm so sorry.'

'It's OK, it's OK. It's all over,' he cooed.

She looked up at him, a tiny vestige of hope still alive. Maybe if *Ben* had survived . . . 'What about my brother? And Ryan?'

He shook his head. 'I— it was too late. I'm sorry.'

Alisha held him again, pressing her face into his chest. She hoped Ben wouldn't mind the fact that she was never going to let him go.

'There was nothing you could do.' He stroked her hair.

'Are you OK?' She cupped his sickly face in her hands. 'Are you sure?'

'I don't know. It hurts. I need to get to a doctor.' He assessed her body. 'So do you.'

Alisha nodded.

'I have my phone. We'll walk until we get a signal. Can you walk?'

Alisha nodded and limped towards the sand. Ben hooked his arm under hers, taking most of her weight. She smiled, and even that hurt her cheekbone. 'I bet we look bloody brilliant!'

'Pair of invalids, limping down the beach. We rule.'

This was gonna take a while, Alisha thought, as she saw the endless sand stretching out before them. It could be worse. There was the breeze, the tide, the moon and Ben Murdoch on her arm. They had all night. Who knew what tomorrow would bring? Alisha knew, as definitely as she'd ever known anything, that they'd have to tell the truth. It was the only way.

She looked out over the rippling silk of the sea and, in her head, apologised to Roxanne Dent. It was high time she let go of grudges, let go of never feeling good enough, let go of the past. Those things had kept her stuck in Telscombe Cliffs. Alisha breathed it all out. After tonight, all of those high-school dramas seemed stupidly small and insignificant.

'You were amazing, Alisha,' Ben said.

Alisha didn't say anything because she knew she'd only burst into tears. Instead, she slipped her hand into his and squeezed it tight. Ryan would have rubbed his hands with glee at this plot twist – two characters unexpectedly getting together in the series finale. *Oh, God, poor Ryan.* Alisha banished such thoughts. Who knew what would happen between her and Ben? There wasn't a master plan, this wasn't TV, and it was all for later. It was enough that they were both alive. The future didn't matter; they had now.

FADE OUT

Acknowledgements

They call it the 'Difficult Second Album' for a reason, so there's lots of people to thank for all the work and support that's gone into *Cruel Summer*. It's been a true team effort.

You'll note a lot of these people were thanked the first time round, but it bears repeating. SO! A *big* thank you to my agent, Jo, and also Ant, for their continuing support, and everyone at Orion (especially the tireless Amber, Jenny, Nina and Louise). Thank you, as always, to my mum, dad and sister – when things weren't going so well, you listened to some quality moans.

Kerry, Sam and Kat – thank you so much for reading *Cruel Summer* and for all your feedback. You're the best good cop/ bad cop team any writer could have.

To Catrin, Nic, Steve and Niall, thank you for making my first year in London so special. To the Brighton Crew – thank you for letting me escape to the seaside whenever I like!

Some things *are* different this time around, however. In London, I've made some precious new friendships with fellow authors and I can't stress enough how valuable these are to me. So to Tom Pollock, Cat Clarke, Tanya Byrne, Den Patrick, Sarwat Chadda, Will Hill, Kim Curran, James Smythe, Laure Eve, Amy McCulloch and *all* the UKYA Massiv, a heartfelt THANKYOUILOVEYOU. Finally,

Patrick, thank you for all the sage advice over burgers.

Hollow Pike had the best christening EVER thanks to the army of YA book bloggers, booksellers, teachers and librarians who supported me every step of the way. Over book tours and panel events I've gotten to know some of you as friends and I look forward to getting to know those I haven't. I can't say thank you enough and I hope you love *Cruel Summer*! See you on Twitter, lovelies.

To the First Story group at Lambeth Academy – you're so sickeningly talented, you make *me* raise my game. Keep writing and believe you have something to say.

Last, but by no means least, a thank you to Agatha Christie, RL Stine and Christopher Pike for the inspiration.

Find James on Twitter @_jamesdawson and at
facebook.com/jamesdawsonbooks

www.jamesdawsonbooks.com

She thought she'd be safe in the country, but you can't escape your own nightmares, and Lis London dreams repeatedly that someone is trying to kill her.

Lis thinks she's being paranoid – after all who would want to murder her? She doesn't believe in the local legends of witchcraft. She doesn't believe that anything bad will *really* happen to her.

You never do, do you?

Not until you're alone in the woods, after dark – and a twig snaps . . .

Hollow Pike – where witchcraft never sleeps.